Amish Romance
AT CHRISTMASTIME
Three Novels in One Volume

LINDA BYLER

Good Books

New York, New York

Copyright © 2020 by Linda Byler
All rights reserved. No part of this book may be reproduced in any manner without the express written consent of the publisher, except in the case of brief excerpts in critical reviews or articles. All inquiries should be addressed to Good Books, 307 West 36th Street, 11th Floor, New York, NY 10018.

Good Books books may be purchased in bulk at special discounts for sales promotion, corporate gifts, fund-raising, or educational purposes. Special editions can also be created to specifications. For details, contact the Special Sales Department, Good Books, 307 West 36th Street, 11th Floor, New York, NY 10018 or info@skyhorsepublishing.com.

Good Books is an imprint of Skyhorse Publishing, Inc.®, a Delaware corporation.

Visit our website at www.goodbooks.com.

10 9 8 7 6 5 4 3 2

Library of Congress Cataloging-in-Publication Data is available on file.

Print ISBN: 978-1-68099-626-5
eBook ISBN: 978-1-68099-679-1

Cover design by Mona Lin

Printed in the United States of America

Contents

Contents

A Dog for
CHRISTMAS

Chapter One

HENRY AND HARVEY WERE BORN ON A COLD January night, just before the blizzard of 1929.

Their mother laid them next to her, side by side in the double bed, wondering how they would manage to feed nine children when times were lean.

By the time the twins were six years old, she had borne four more babies, bringing the total to thirteen children. They managed from year to year until 1936, when the lean times became leaner still. Oatmeal gave way to cornmeal mush, ground from the leftover field corn and roasted in the oven of the Pioneer Maid wood range.

Rueben Esh, the children's father, worked the farm from morning till evening. Tall, thin, and just a bit weary, his brown eyes questioned why milk prices were so low. With thirteen children to feed, his mortgage payment was increasingly hard to meet.

Savilla, the good wife, spare and angular, patched their clothes and pinched pennies, cooked green beans and potatoes without a smidgen of meat, sold eggs and butter, and rode into the town of Intercourse, Pennsylvania, on the spring wagon, with half a dozen brown-eyed children who never in their lives ate an egg for breakfast.

Much too wasteful, to let a child eat an egg, when they could bring the wonderful price of a dollar a dozen.

Milk fever set in after the birth of the fourteenth child, and Savilla died.

The twins were seven years old, their unruly brown hair bouncing above button noses splattered with freckles, their brown eyes not quite aligned. When they looked at you, they saw not only you, but what was behind you as well.

They pressed around their mother's coffin, swallowing their tears, standing side by side in their grief, the way they'd lain side by side in the double bed at birth.

They knew hunger and cold and filth, that next year. The oldest daughter was overcome with the avalanche of responsibilities. She sat and rocked Baby

Ezra while the rest of them did the best they could, under the tutelage of their sad-eyed father.

When he married Mattie Stoltzfus, she entered the house like a freight train, tall and wide and hissing steam. The twins sat wide-eyed on the worn-out davenport that smelled of cow manure and sour milk, and wondered how they'd manage in times like this.

They knew they disliked Mattie, so they agreed that they wouldn't do what they were told. They never spoke back to her, just stood and looked at her with their curiously unfocused gaze and disobeyed.

Rueben Esh listened to his new wife, found a green willow branch, and switched their thin bottoms, his sad brown eyes filled with resolve.

"She doesn't like us," Harvey said.

"No, she doesn't," Henry said.

The parents made arrangements, packed their clothes into two brown paper sacks, and sent them down the road to neighbors who had only three children of their own.

Rueben stayed in the barn that day, left the parting to Mattie.

December 18, a week before Christmas, they stepped off the porch in their torn shoes into a few inches of snow, through the wire gate and out the lane, past the barnyard and the bare maple trees that waved their black branches in the cold wind.

The boys didn't look back, knowing that what was behind them was something they could never have again.

After the first mile, their feet were cold from snow leaking into the cracks in the soles of their shoes. Their hands were red and chapped from the cold, so they switched their paper sacks from one hand to the other. Their torn straw hats flapped in the wind, and occasionally they took a free hand to slap the top of it. Behind them, their tracks zigzagged through the frozen pellets of snow, but they never strayed from each other, their shoulders meeting again and again.

A buggy passed from the opposite direction. They waved solemnly and kept walking. They were being sent to Ephraim King. They had been told how far to walk on Peters Road, where to turn, and which drive-way to look for, so they recognized the place when they came to it. A low rise, and suddenly, behind the woods, there it was.

Instinctively, they drew together. Their steps slowed. The wind blew cold. They could hear their stomachs rumble underneath their thin coats that closed down the front with hooks and eyes.

The farm where they were expected to live looked much the same as any other Lancaster County farm. A white-sided house with a porch and a *kesslehaus*, a white barn with white outbuildings flanked by patches of woods and corn-stubbled fields, a winding creek with willow trees swaying bare-limbed on its border.

"I guess they know we're coming."

"I hope so."

Unsure which door to enter, they hesitated at the end of the cement sidewalk. No barking dogs announced their arrival, no one appeared at a window, and both doors stayed shut, as if the farmhouse had turned its face aside.

They looked at each other, one's uncertainty mirrored in the other's brown eyes.

"You want to go back?"

"We can't."

Harvey nodded, and together they moved to the front door, lifted their fists, and knocked, first one, then the other.

A patter of feet, and the door opened.

"Oh, it's you! I was watching for you. Thought your *dat* would bring you *mit die fuhr*. Have you walked all this way?"

"Yes."

She opened the door wider, standing aside to usher them in. She was of medium height, and not too thin. On her round face, spectacles perched on her wide nose. Light-colored eyes peered through the polished lenses, her small red mouth like a raspberry. They noticed the row of safety pins down her dress front and the narrow gray apron belt with a row of small pleats across her stomach. The apron was wet, as if she had left her dishwater. She extended not one, but two, warm hands, red from the hot water.

"Well, here you are, then. We are looking forward to having you. My name is Rachel. But I suppose now I am your Mam. You may call me Mam. We have three girls, Malinda, Katie, and Anna. They are in school. They will be home this afternoon.

You are Henry and Harvey Esh, right?"

"I'm Henry."

"I'm Harvey."

She rolled her eyes, raised her hands, and laughed, a long rolling sound that neither of them had heard very much in their short lives. They didn't smile, only watched Rachel with a serious, off-kilter expression in their brown eyes, unsure if they were being mocked or merely laughed at in a kind way.

"I'll never know which is which. Well, what does it matter. Here, give me your bags. I believe we have the necessary clothes in here, right?"

They both nodded.

Four eyes looked at her, two of them not quite focused with the others. Rachel stepped closer, peered into their faces.

"Your eyes. . ."

She straightened, led them to the *kesslehaus*, and showed them where to keep their shoes and hang their coats and hats.

The *kesslehaus* was warm with the steam coming from the *elsa-Kessle*, the great kettle built into the brick oven, with a heavy cast iron door in front, where wood was shoved through to heat the water above it. There was a white Maytag wringer washer with a galvanized tub for rinsing, a painted gray chest, a sink built into cupboards, and a cream separator in the corner by a door. The cement floor was painted gray, slick and shining.

After Rachel took their paper sacks and set them in a corner, she turned to them with a serious expression.

"Now, I will have to check your heads for lice."

Willingly, they bowed their heads as she took them to the white light by a window and lifted their wavy brown hair, peering closely behind their scabby ears.

She said nothing, just took them to the *kesslehaus* and doused their heads well with coal oil, then lifted a bucket of steaming water, added lava soap, and scoured their heads. Retrieving a galvanized tub, she made them bathe all over.

She pinned their heads to her stomach and washed their ears and the sides of their necks, taught them how to use a toothbrush and baking soda, then told them to sit at the table and she'd get their dinner.

They felt pink and scrubbed. They wiggled their toes inside their patched socks, touched their raw scalps, and watched Rachel with solemn eyes.

She had dimples in her elbows that only appeared when her arms hung straight down. Her covering was not as big as Mattie's. Her hair was rolled tight on each side of her head, and her dress was navy blue.

She was making something in a pan that she stirred all the time. It smelled sweet, like cornstarch pudding.

Their mouths watered. They swallowed.

Harvey wiped away a trickle of saliva.

Henry was dizzy with hunger.

Mattie had not given them breakfast, saying the cornmeal was low. But now, past dinnertime, the thin reserve they had was almost used up.

Harvey felt hollow inside, like the bottom of tall grass in the fall when it turned brown. Henry thought he might fall off his chair if he couldn't get the kitchen to stop spinning.

Rachel got down a tin of saltines, spread them with butter, then ladled a thick, yellow pudding over them.

"Do you like crackas and cornstarch?"

"We don't know."

"You never had it?"

"No."

"All right."

That was all she said, then left them alone.

Harvey looked at Henry.

Henry nodded.

They bowed their heads, their hands clasped in their laps. Too shook up to pray, they waited till the proper time to lift their heads, then took up their spoons and ate the sweetened pudding and the salty, buttery saltines that melted on their tongues.

They scraped their plates, and sat, unsure what they should do now.

Rachel appeared, asked if they wanted more.

They nodded, quickly.

She refilled their plates, and they ate until they scraped their bowls a second time. A full stomach was a new sensation, and with the scrubbing with soap and hot water, their eyelids fell heavily. They made their way to the couch by the windows, and fell asleep in bright light of the afternoon sun on the snow.

When the girls came home from school, swinging their black lunch buckets, they stopped inside the *kesslehaus* door when their mother appeared with lowered brows and a finger held to her lips.

"*Die boova sinn do.*"

Carefully, the girls tiptoed to hang up their bonnets, hiding their faces for a few seconds longer than they normally would have.

Malinda, the oldest, was the first to turn, questioning her mother with her small blue eyes.

"Why are they sleeping?" she whispered.

Harvey woke up first, blinked, then sat up quickly, his hair tousled and stiff from the kerosene wash.

Henry followed, clearly ashamed to be caught napping, rubbed his eyes and slid a glance sideways at Harvey, gauging the mood of his brother. He sidled closer, until their shoulders touched.

Katie stood by the rocking chair, small, round and blue-eyed, dressed in a purple dress and black pinafore-style apron, her hair rolled back like ropes, sleek and glistening, her face an open book, revealing eagerness and curiosity, like a squirrel.

The boys gazed back at her, four brown eyes that took in every detail of this girl they would supposedly call their sister.

Anna wasn't interested. She went upstairs, like a wisp of fog that blew through the room and that no one was absolutely sure had been there at all.

Malinda, prodded by her mother, walked over and peered at them, tall, thin, a black apron pinned around her skinny waist with safety pins, her green dress buttoned down the back with small green buttons. She wore black stockings and the biggest black shoes the boys had ever seen, coming up over her ankles, tied with black laces in a row of holes that marched up her foot like ladybugs.

The reason Henry noticed her shoes was because he lowered his face and kept it lowered when Malinda approached.

"Hello."

She stuck out a hand for the traditional Amish handshake.

Henry took it, then Harvey did, but cautiously.

"So you will be my new brothers?"

Two sets of shoulders were shrugged, first one, then the other.

"Can't you talk?"

Two heads nodded.

"What's wrong with your eyes?"

And that was the twins' introduction to a new life in a strange house, doing chores in an unaccustomed barn with a new father who did not resemble their own in the least.

Ephraim King was of medium height, built like a bulldog, massive shoulders and neck, large hands with fingers like knobby branches, legs that bowed out from the knees, so that when he walked his steps looked like a broken pair of scissors.

He was loud, and always talking, or whistling, and sometimes he broke into song, snatches of hymns, but most often, silly little songs that made no sense.

The bear went over the mountain,
The bear went over the mountain,
The bear went over the mountain,
To see what he could see.

That was one. There were many more, so the twins found themselves creeping through the barn, hoping to catch another song. But too often it wasn't worth their tiptoeing, when he was only whistling.

He was always happy, that was one thing sure.

The first few days, Ephraim's happiness carried the boys along, acquainting them to their altered existence. It was all so befuddling, a new bedroom upstairs, the stairway cut in half by a landing, then veering off to the left to continue on its way.

Sent to bed without a light, they both ran into the wall before learning the stairway turned to the left.

In the mornings, they were expected to rise in the stark, frigid air of the strange room, dress and be downstairs at 5:30, walk through the kitchen to the *kesslehaus*, shivers waving over their backs and down their legs, dress in their chore boots and coats by the light of a blue kerosene lantern, already lit and set on the countertop of the sink.

Their appearance inside the warm barn, moist and steaming with the Holsteins' breathing, always brought a cheerful "*Guta Marya, boova.*"

They were expected to answer in the same way, so they did, hesitantly at first. This whole *Guta Marya* thing was so brand new and out of the ordinary, they only mumbled the words in a hoarse whisper.

There were calves to be fed, heifers to give forkfuls of hay, which proved to be more than they could handle. They stood side by side in the dark, frosted morning, when the east was changing from night to a gray awakening that would turn to a splash of lavender and pink, and pondered the problem of the lengthy pitchfork handle, the amount of hay to be moved, and the allotted time they were given to accomplish this.

"Wheelbarrow's too slippy in the snow," Harvey said.

"Wagon's too small," Henry said. "Think the man would get us a tarp to fork the hay on, slide it down?"

"Don't know. We can ask."

They had a hard time calling him Dat. There was only one Dat, and that was Rueben Esh, tall, thin as a stovepipe, sad-eyed and quiet as a forest pool on a still day.

They could not place noisy, whistling, smiley-faced Ephraim in the notch reserved for Rueben.

So they compromised and called him *da mon*.

They didn't understand the tooth brushing, either. All that effort, ramming a toothbrush back and forth, upside down and inside out, with that vile tasting white baking soda on it, just did not seem necessary.

Malinda showed them how to wet the bristles of the toothbrush and hold it in the dish of baking soda. It didn't make it easier.

Another perplexing thing was all the food being carried into the house. How could one family eat so much food?

Harvey asked Henry that night, snuggled together in the big double bed, warm and cozy on the soft flannel sheets that smelled like some flower they couldn't name. The covers on top of their thin bodies were so heavy and warm, they could easily feel as if The Good Man who lived in Heaven had his Hand pressed down at the quilts and sheep's-wool comforter.

It felt so good, to be warm from the top of their kerosene tainted head to their skinny pink toes.

"Why do you think they went away with their buggy and came back with all those paper sacks?" he asked, his voice burry with sleep.

"It has to do with Christmas," Henry answered, yawning.

"Oh."

Then, "Christmas at home wasn't different from any other day, was it?"

"Sometimes we had a *Grischtag Essa* at Doddy Beiler's. Remember we got an orange? It was so sour I fed mine to the chickens. Mam pinched me and twisted my ear."

"Ow," Harvey said, levelly.

"Guess I should have eaten it myself."

"Probably would have been best."

"I miss my mam, sort of."

"I miss her. Dat too."

"You think they think of us?"

"Yes. But they can't afford us."

"I know."

Their breathing slowed and deepened. Their little chests rose and fell underneath all those covers, their forms making barely a bump that anyone could see. The brown pupils of their eyes disappeared beneath the heavy lids that slid over them, as thick, black lashes, like teeth on a comb, lay on their thin cheeks.

A shaft of moonlight found its way beneath the green pulldown shade, creating a patch of light on the heavy rag rug beside the bed. The walnut chest of drawers with porcelain knobs stood guard against the opposite wall, the glass berry set from Ephraim's mother resting on the oval embroidered dresser scarf.

The floor was polished pine wood, smooth and clean in the moonlight. Their only possessions were hung in the closet, behind the door with a white glass knob, the paper sacks folded and stored beneath a can seated on a chair in the corner.

Outside, a heavy, sugary snow lay over the forests and harvested fields of Lancaster County. Roads crisscrossed the landscape like etchings in a pie crust, punctured by dark ponds and waterways not yet frozen, the dark icy water gobbling up the crystalized snowflakes as they fell.

The horses in the tie stalls rested their weight on two legs and fell asleep as the winter's cold deepened. Cows rattled their chains, harrumphing a loud exhalation of breath as their legs folded clumsily beneath them, their massive weight settling around them as they dozed. The hens in the henhouse tucked their pointed beaks under their wings, the straw beneath them soiled with broken egg yolk.

The covered bridge that spanned Pequea Creek snapped and groaned as the moist cold settled into the impressive timbers used in its construction. Below, the icy black waters flowed, swift, deep, and menacing.

Till morning there was an embroidery of thin ice lining the banks, where the water swirled and eddied in silent pools, downstream from overgrown tree roots. Large bass and carp lay dormant, their metabolism slowed to conserve energy, their colors blending with the light and shadow that played on the creek bed. Beneath the silt and mud, frogs and turtles were burrowed, spending the winter months away from the freezing temperatures, to begin the cycle of life all over again in the spring.

Life slowed and hummed around Henry and Harvey as they slept the deep sweet slumber of children.

Displaced, innocent, accepting their lot in life without complaint, they lay side by side, the way they had been placed at birth, without knowing what their life would bring, as children do. Already, they had placed their trust in Ephraim and Rachel, to feed them and keep them warm, the only two things they would need.

Those three girls would just have to learn to like them, being as unimpressed as they were.

Nothing to be done about that.

Chapter Two

THE TWINS WATCHED IN WIDE-EYED WONDER the goings-on in their new home.

Mam, as she was to be called but still thought of as Rachel by both of them, was a flurry of activity sending the girls off to school amid stern warnings: find their own boots and mittens, and no, she hadn't seen a package of pencils, but if they'd learn to keep track of their things they wouldn't have to go through this, finished with a screech about looking at the clock and don't they see what time it is.

Her face was red, her hair frizzy, and her covering sideways as she whirled from room to room with a dustrag, a wet mop, and a bucket with hot, soapy water.

Henry was secretly glad that Rachel told off Malinda; she was only ten, but she acted as if she was as old as her mother, which she wasn't, so he figured it was time she found out.

Teeth brushing and face washing were two of her forms of torture, so if she wasn't put in her place, hard telling what else she'd come up with. But of course, they said nothing, just sat quietly side by side and watched with their slightly unfocused gaze.

Ephraim King thought it would be best to keep the boys at home from school for a week, let them become acquainted with their new surroundings before being introduced back to the schoolhouse in Leacock Township, a large brick building that housed forty pupils and had one teacher. The children were mostly English, and they had an English teacher named Mrs. Dayble.

She was tall and wide and as mean as a *gluck* on her nest. She terrified Henry and Harvey both.

But it was school, and they knew they had to go. They watched their p's and q's, finished their work on time, and watched the teacher with their dark eyes, knowing where she was at every moment. They knew her pinching was painful, so they didn't plan on having their palms rapped with the sharp side of a wooden ruler.

They had watched Benjamin Stoltzfus standing by the privy with his hands in his pockets, blinking back tears of pain, after a few cracks with that ruler.

They sat up and took notice of any behavior that was unacceptable.

Rachel's sister Lydia showed up that morning. Short and round, her apron flaring from her hips, she sailed into the house in a cloud of cheer and good-will, to help *die schveshta* Rachel get ready for the family Christmas dinner.

The family included ten siblings, a mother and father (on the Beiler side), and somewhere between sixty and seventy children. They weren't exactly sure.

Amos and Annie had a new one, little Emma, who was their sixth girl and no boys. They thought Davey and Fannie's little one was already six weeks old, so that made nine for them. Another boy. Was it Manasses or Ephraim? Ephraim, they believed. He was a big one, weighing over ten pounds.

Well, no wonder. Fannie was a chunk herself, so what did she expect, eating all that bread? Ei-ya-yi.

Henry and Harvey were sent to the barn to help Ephraim, so they donned their denim coats, pursing their lips in concentration as they bent their heads to close the hooks and eyes down the front. They sat on the painted cement floor and tugged on the rubber Tingley boots, smashed their tattered straw hats on their heads, and slipped and slid their way to the barn to find him.

"Ephraim," Henry said.

"Dat," Harvey corrected.

"Dat," Henry agreed.

When they found him, he smiled, leaned on his pitchfork, and asked what they were up to.

"We're supposed to help you."

"Rachel sent you out?"

They nodded, together.

"All right. You can sweep cobwebs in the forebay. *Schpinna hoodla* all over the walls. I'll get the ceiling."

So they obeyed, found brooms, and began to sweep the walls. Their brooms were meshed with the spiderwebs in a short time, and their arms became tired long before they were finished. But they kept on working, eager to please Ephraim. Over and over they swept between the sturdy brown timbers that held up the walls of the barn, until there wasn't a spiderweb to be found.

Ephraim came to check on their progress, and smiled. He hooked his thumbs in his trouser pockets, lifted his face to the walls, and gave a low whistle.

"*Gute boova! Fliesichy boova.* You did a good job. Now we want to clean the *vassa droke*."

He showed them what he wanted done—the water carried out in buckets and dumped beside the barnyard fence.

With the high praise ringing in their ears, they lifted buckets of dirty water, riddled with hay and grain and the horses' saliva, straining to carry each one through the door of the barn, across the slippery, packed-down snow to dump it in the low place by the fence, as they had been instructed.

The cold water sloshed across their trouser legs and darkened the fronts of their coats. Their hands turned purplish red. Their mouths compressed with determination, they scurried in and out of the forebay, like two straw-hatted ants, intent on receiving more high praise from their new father.

They scrubbed and scrubbed the sides and bottom of the cast iron watering trough, pebbled and rough, green slime and bits of hay loosening as they worked.

Their stomachs growled with hunger. Slower and slower they wielded the wooden, stiff-bristled scrubbing brushes. Just when they were beginning to wonder if Ephraim had forgotten them, he appeared at the door.

"*Boova, Kommet. Vella essa.*"

He didn't inspect their work, neither did he praise them, so they walked to the house, their heads bent, sober and confused. Had they dumped the water in the wrong place? Was the scrubbing done all wrong?

Henry told Harvey not to worry that he had not checked their work; he would do that later.

They had both been thinking the same thing, and this comforted Harvey, nodding his head eagerly.

The smell of cooking greeted them in the *kesslehaus*, steam rising upward from beneath the metal lid of the "*elsa Kessle*," creating a moist heat that felt wonderful as they shrugged out of their coats and hung them on hooks, slapped their straw hats on top, and bent to wriggle their shoes out of the rubber boots. They took turns washing their hands and faces with the green, gritty, and strong-smelling bar of Lava soap. They dried themselves on the navy-blue roller towel, running a hand through their wavy brown hair, and went to the kitchen.

The kitchen was fragrant with heat and spices. The overpowering smell, sweet and delicious, caused both boys to swallow as saliva rose in their mouths.

They couldn't look at the rows of cookies cooling on the countertop. They had never imagined such a sight. Dark brown molasses cookies sprinkled with white sugar, pale sugar cookies with pink frosting, chocolate cookies that were small and shaped like bells, squares of brown cookies with walnut halves pressed into them.

This was only seen with stolen glances. Harvey lifted his waterglass and drank. Henry did too. They sat back and listened to the grownups, talking about the weather and if there'd be more snow for Christmas.

Was Amos busy?

Oh, he was just *hesslich hinna-noch*. He had spent too much time with the corn husking, now he still had the fodder to gather, which he wasn't going to get done in the snow. Not now anymore.

But she didn't mean to *glauk*, he worked too hard; what they really needed was a good *knecht*.

Ephraim nodded and smiled, his small blue eyes twinkling in his wide face, his brown beard bushy, surrounding his face like the bristles of a soft broom, hanging below his chin in stiff waves.

"I have two of them now," he said, turning to the twins. "*Ach, ya. Die glany boovy.*"

Lydia flushed with pleasure as she eyed them both, her face lined with more smiles as she spoke. Rachel placed a steaming dish of chicken potpie in the middle of the table, followed by one of mashed sweet potatoes mounded high, a river of browned butter dripping down the sides. There was applesauce in a glass dish, pickled red beets, small green cucumbers in another, and slabs of homemade cheese layered on a blue platter, pale golden with perfectly round holes in every slice.

Lydia and Rachel kept talking and Ephraim kept listening. They were discussing the runaway team of horses over toward *Nei Hullant*.

Finally, Ephraim cleared his throat and stayed quiet, which was the signal for the women to finish talking, bow their heads, fold their hands in their laps, and pray silently before they ate.

The boys' plates were filled with heavy, thick squares of potpie swimming with chunks of chicken, carrots, celery, and onion in a smooth golden gravy.

The sweet potatoes in browned butter weren't as good, but they ate the mound that was put on their plates.

The cheese was good too, sprinkled with salt and eaten with the little green sweet pickles.

They sat quietly, their stomachs pleasantly stretched, the warmth of the kitchen coloring their cheeks to a red glow.

They kept stealing glances at the cookies but said nothing. Rachel served cups of steaming peppermint tea, followed by the sugar bowl.

"Just one spoonful," she told the boys.

They dipped their heads, embarrassed now, as if their new mother had known they'd planned on using two or three if that sugar bowl was passed with the tea.

They never had sugar in their tea at home.

And then, like a miracle, she got up and began piling cookies on a dinner plate. Every kind.

"Cookies!" Ephraim said, laughing.

Harvey chose a chocolate one. Henry slowly lifted a sugared molasses cookie, watching the grown-ups' faces for signs of disapproval.

"Surely you want more than one," Ephraim called out. "It's Christmastime. You may try as many cookies as you want."

"Go ahead, boys," Rachel urged.

So they did. They tasted every different kind of cookie. It was amazing what happened to a mouthful of cookie crumbs if you drank tea. Everything melted and blended in with the tea until there was nothing left but a whole mouthful of unbelievable sweetness to swallow. Then you could bite off another bit of cookie and start all over again.

The grown-ups kept talking, so the twins kept eating cookies. The kitchen swam as their eyelids became heavy with the warmth in the room, their full stomachs, and the strenuous work they had done.

But when they got back to the barn to begin their vigorous scrubbing, they felt wonderful. Full of energy, happier than they had been since the day they arrived.

"I think we have a good home," Harvey said.

"I believe we do," Henry agreed solemnly.

"The Good Man must have heard our *Müde binnich*."

"I believe so."

When Ephraim came to tell them their mother wanted them in the house, they laid down their brushes and watched his face for signs of approval.

"Good job, boys. Well done."

Words as sweet as peppermint tea and cookies. Words they had never heard before from the sad-eyed father to whom they had been born.

For a long time after that Christmas, the boys would always look at the sparkling clean water in the cast iron trough, remember all over again how they had done well, the thought lifting their small shoulders and straightening their knobby spines, giving them a spring in their step and a fierce, undying devotion to Ephraim King.

It was the same with Rachel.

The reason she called them in was to introduce them to gingerbread men. Christmas was not complete without children making gingerbread men, and with the family Christmas gathering at their house, she would not have time to allow the girls to help after school.

So the boys got the job.

They concentrated, bit their tongues and crossed their eyes, and tried so hard to cut out perfect gingerbread men. They placed the raisins in the exact position, even became silly and turned the raisins

down instead of up, to form a frowning gingerbread man.

Whey Lydia and Rachel threw up their hands
and laughed with them, they giggled and made a
few more. They watched them come from the oven,
puffed up and spicy, and when they were told to try
one, they passed the hot gingerbread man from hand
to hand to cool it, before biting off the top of the
head, being careful to watch Rachel's face for a sign
that they were doing something wrong.

When the girls came home from school, there was
a general upheaval as they examined the cookies and
fussed about the gingerbread men.

Malinda ate a frowny-faced one, then pretended
to be in a bad mood, the cookie having the power
to do that. Harvey thought she was serious, his eyes
turning bright with shame and unshed tears. Henry
became very quiet and sober.

Anna said she was only joking, but it took a while
till the boys trusted Malinda and returned to their
usual selves.

Katie said they couldn't have done better.

It was almost too much, all this approval. Harvey was not sure it should be this way, and told Henry so.

"I mean, surely soon, something bad will happen. We'll do something wrong, like break a glass or a plate, and then will everything will be as usual."

"Our mam was not mean. Just tired, with too many children."

"Yes. Too many. We were too many children. There were two of us at one time, so we were too many."

They pondered the truth for a few minutes.

"I think Mattie probably misses us. She liked us, all right."

"Yes. Yes, she did."

So they repeatedly assured themselves that it was the fact that they had too many children that they were sent away. Then Harvey declared their own Savilla mother would not have sent them to live with Ephraim King. It didn't matter how many children she had.

"She died, so she doesn't know," Henry said.

"Maybe she does."

"Naw. She's dead. You don't know anything if you're dead."

"If you go to Heaven and become an angel, you do."

"But not to look down here."

"You don't know."

"You don't, either."

"Nobody does."

They solemnly accepted this bit of wisdom together.

They pushed heavy coarse bristled brooms across the rough cement of the forebay. At one time, the concrete floor had been smooth, but with the iron shod hooves of countless horses clattering over it, the surface became pitted. So they pushed the broom, over and over across the same area, until there was no dust or bits of straw and hay.

After that, they were allowed to go sledding in the back pasture. Ephraim produced a long wooden sled with steel runners and a bar across the front that you could push or pull on either side to turn the sled to the left or right. A rope was attached to holes drilled on each side, long enough so you could pull it behind you comfortably.

The sun shone in a cloudless blue sky, the cold was tinged with a bit of warmth in the afternoon, the white slopes stretched before them like a brilliant promise.

They talked and laughed, jerked the sled along as they leaped joyous little bounces of energy, slipped and slid up the hill until they reached the top. It felt like a mountain. They could see wedges of dark forest thrusting into the white corn-stubbled fields, the neighboring farms nestled like toys between them. Roads zigzagged through the snowy countryside, an occasional gray buggy pulled by a trotting horse moved along at a snail's pace.

Harvey laid the rope carefully along the surface of the sled. He looked at Henry.

"Lie down or sit?"

Henry eyed the long descent, pursed his lips with the decision.

"Better lie down."

So Harvey flung himself on the sled, with Henry coming down hard on top of him.

"Don't hit the fence at the bottom," he yelled in Harvey's ear as the sled began a slow coast in the sugary snow. Speed picked up rapidly. The wind brushed their faces with cold. Yelling their exhilaration, they reached up to smooth their straw hats down on their heads, but it did no good. Halfway down the long slope, the wind grabbed the hats and flung them away, to skitter across the snow, rolling like a plate.

Then there was only the heart-stopping speed, the cold rush of air that brought tears to their eyes, making a white blur of everything. The sled's runners made no sound; their ears filled with air and their own shouts.

Harvey leaned on the right side of the wooden rudder, desperately trying to avoid the oncoming fence. They escaped by inches, rolling off the sled at the last instant, sprawled in the snow, their bodies convulsed in helpless giggles.

"Hu-uh!" Henry finished.

"Whoo-eee!" Harvey echoed, pounding the snow with his bare fists.

They leaped to their feet, stuck one cold reddened hand into one pocket of their trousers, bent over and ran back up the hill, their noses running, their faces wet with spitting snow.

"Hey!" Harvey pointed.

Together, they watched a huge, lolloping dog stop to inspect a straw hat, look in their direction before grabbing the brim in his teeth, lifting his head with the treasure he found, and running across the slope.

They took off after him, dropped the rope, and the sled careened haphazardly down the hill, to rest against a fence post.

"Dog! Dog! Stop!"

They ran, shouted, slipped and slid to their knees, jumped up, and resumed the chase. The huge dog stopped, turned, eyed them, but kept the straw hat clutched in his mouth. Dipping his head, he wheeled away with the odd gallop of a big, ungainly dog.

Out of breath, their legs shaking with fatigue, the boys stopped. They looked at each other.

"Whose dog?" they both said at once.

They both shrugged their shoulders and resumed their running. The dog stopped. He dropped the hat, his mouth wide, his tongue lolling, and watched the boys approach. His tail began to wag like a flag waving. As they neared, he bent his front legs, leaped to the side, took up the hat, and bounded away, looking back over his shoulder to taunt them.

They were going farther and farther away from their farm. Woods rose up in front of them, a tangle of briars and tall weeds growing around the trunks of huge trees, their leaves gone, with branches spread to the sky like a giant pattern.

The boys stopped. The only sound was their ragged breathing. The dog stopped, the hat in his mouth. He wagged his long, bushy tail in surrender, sat down and dropped the hat, his mouth spread like a welcoming smile.

Henry extended a hand, wiggling his fingers.

"Here, dog. Here, boy. Be nice and give us our hat."

The dog obeyed.

Harvey snatched up the hat. They sighed with relief, not wanting to return to their new parents with the announcement of a lost straw hat. As it was, the brim was torn, tattered by the dog's teeth. They examined it, shook their heads.

"Dog, now look what you did. *Schem dich*."

The dog was certainly not ashamed. He bounced around on all fours, whining and begging for attention. The boys touched the top of his head, then boldly ran their hands along his back, where the long black hair parted in the middle, falling down on either side in a luxurious flow, like a girl's hair before her mam wet it and rolled it back.

The dog had small brown eyes, set far apart in his head, a huge, grinning black mouth with a gigantic pink tongue that flapped when he smiled. His skin was loose, his feet were huge. Long hairs grew all along his legs to his feet. There was no collar, no sign of anyone owning this dog.

They put their arms around his neck and squeezed. He slobbered his pink tongue all over their faces. They closed their eyes and laughed.

They rolled in the snow, playing with this soft, kindhearted animal. They chased each other in circles, till they all piled in a big heap, took long breaths, and laughed some more.

Together, they retrieved the sled, rode down the hill, over and over, the dog lolloping by their side, then on the sled with one of them.

When the sun cast a reddish glow on the hillside and the air around them turned pink, they knew they'd overstayed. Shamefaced, their cheeks red with cold, their hats smashed on their heads, hiding their eyebrows, they walked slowly into the forebay, the sled resting by the side of the barn, the dog keeping watch, sitting upright and serious.

The milking had already started, the kerosene lantern casting a yellow glow above the backs of the black-and-white Holsteins, the air heavy with their breath, silage, and warm milk.

Ephraim put away his milking stool, dumped his bucket of frothy milk into the strainer setting on a galvanized milk can, and looked at them. The shamed faces and torn straw hat softened his heart. The dog softened it ever more.

He grinned his slow, easy grin, tickled the dog's head with his large round fingers, and said it looked as if they'd found a faithful buddy, now hadn't they?

Chapter Three

CHRISTMAS MORNING ARRIVED.

The boys were awakened by the sound of feet dashing past the door of their room, suppressed shrieks, and small tittering sounds.

Henry grabbed Harvey's arm beneath the covers, hissed a dry-throated question, his heart pounding.

"You think the house is on fire?"

Rapid breathing was his only answer.

Four eyes stared wide-eyed at the ceiling. Four hands clutched the quilts as they trembled beneath them. What could have caused the girls to run that way?

They stayed still, their ears strained to hear any sounds that would help them understand what was going on.

More shrieks.

They heard Ephraim and Rachel's voices, although no one seemed especially alarmed. They sniffed. No smoke, so far.

Then they heard their names being called.

"Ya," they answered as one voice.

"Come on down. It's Christmas morning!"

Bewildered, they dressed, tucking wrinkled shirt-tails into freshly washed trousers, snapping suspenders in place as they went downstairs.

They had never experienced Christmas morning. Too poor to buy or make Christmas gifts, the Rueben Esh family did without presents, although they always received a peppermint stick or an orange from Grandfather Beiler. Never both.

Their eyes widened to see the three girls, Malinda, Katie, and Anna sitting on the floor, brown paper wrappings strewn like fluttering birds around them. Their faces were shining, their eyes bright. Between them was a tiny porcelain tea set, white with delicate purple violets etched on the little plates and cups. The teapot had a little spout and a lid you could take off and put back on. This was Katie's Christmas gift.

Anna was holding a rag doll in her arms, her face bent over the doll's white, upturned face. Black eyes and eyelashes were sewn on the face, brown yarn was stitched into the head and braided into two stiff braids on either side. The nose and mouth were embroidered in red.

"Her name is Lucy. Lucy Miriam Wenger," she announced.

The twins nodded solemnly, their dark eyes showing their respect and admiration to Lucy Miriam Wenger. She was a pretty rag doll.

Malinda cradled a pale blue brush and comb set on her lap. There were scrolls of gold all over the back of the brush and across the comb. It was nestled in a silk-lined box that she could open and close with a very small gold latch. For once, she was quiet, even reverent, admiring her gift.

Anna told them these gifts were from the *Grischt Kindly*. During the night, the *Grisht Kindly* brought gifts of kindness to children.

He had brought a gift for the boys too.

Rachel pushed them gently to the sofa, where they sat waiting till she placed a box on their laps. Each box was about as big as a shoebox, wrapped in brown paper packaging.

"Go ahead. Open it."

They had never opened a package, so they weren't sure how. Their fingers scraped across the smooth top, searching for a splice or dent in the paper.

Ephraim smiled.

"Just rip it off," Malinda said, bossy.

So they did.

The box was red, white, and black, with the words *Canadian Flyer* written sideways across it. When they saw the picture of black figure skates, their heads turned toward each other and they both said the exact same thing: "Skates!"

"Did you ever own a pair?" Ephraim asked.

"Oh no. Never. We could just slide on the ice with our boots. But we watched Danny and Bennie, already."

"Now you can learn to skate. Malinda will show you how it's done."

"What do you say, boys?" Rachel asked, not unkindly.

"*Denke. Denke.*"

"You're welcome."

And then because they were so shy, and receiving this kind of gift was almost more than they could comprehend, their faces turned pink, and they blinked rapidly. This kindness made them uncomfortable, as if the family would expect something in return, and they had nothing. Perhaps in the end, they would fail, horribly, at some major task, something that was expected of them that they could not fulfill. But for now, they would accept the skates and try not to let the thought bother them.

Breakfast was pancakes and maple syrup, eggs and fresh *ponhaus*, stewed saltine crackers in hot milk, and grape juice. It was a breakfast fit for a king, Ephraim said, smiling at Rachel, who sipped her tea and waved a hand to banish the flowery words of praise before she was caught with a case of *hochmut*.

Finally, Henry had the nerve to ask if the dog was still here. Ephraim had done the morning chores by himself, only Rachel helping with the milking, as a treat for Christmas Day.

"Yep, he's still here. I put the wooden doghouse in the corner of the forebay, filled it with clean straw for him. He'll have plenty of things to eat with the leftovers Mama gives him, a dish of milk here and there. If I have to, I'll get a bag of Purina dog food from the mill, although that would be an extra expense, of course. We can't let the dog go hungry."

His face turned serious. "Now I hope you realize, boys, that someone could show up and claim the dog. This is not a common breed, so don't get too attached to him."

They shook their heads no, already sidling toward the *kesslehaus*, their faces attentive to what he was saying. They couldn't get their outerwear on fast enough, stomping around the *kesslehaus* floor to pull the rubber boots up over their black leather shoes.

And there he was. The beautiful, magnificent dog with the long, black hairs on his tail that waved back and forth like a flag of welcome, the smiling black face with the funny brown eyes shaped like a triangle.

"There you are, dog!" shouted Henry. Harvey plowed straight into the big dog with his arms wide open, and closed them somewhere around the region of his neck.

"Dog, dog!" he shouted, squeezing his eyes shut as the enormous pink tongue sloshed all over his face.

They chased each other around the forebay, until the horses began to bang their hooves against the sides of their stalls. They stopped, looked at the frightened animals, and took the dog out in the gray, white morning that hid the sun away from them.

They played all morning. They hitched the dog to the wooden sled with a harness made of bits and pieces of leather and rope they found on the wooden floor of the closet where the driving horses' harnesses hung.

Harvey sat on the sled while Henry led the dog by the makeshift bridle. He ran in circles, trying to see what was behind him, dumping Harvey into the low ditch by the barnyard fence, The dog became tangled in the harness, overturning the sled, and both boys lay on their stomachs, laughing so hard they couldn't get their breath.

"Whew-ee!" Harvey said, letting out all that pent-up air. Henry held his sides. He had to, the way they hurt from laughing.

"He needs a name. We can't keep calling him dog," Henry squeaked, wiping his eyes.

"Puppy?"

"Not Puppy. A dog as big as this?"

"Abraham Lee's have a Puppy."

"That little short haired one?"

"Yes."

"Well, that's different."

Harvey thought awhile.

"What about Bear?"

"Naw. Not Bear. He's way too friendly," Henry snorted.

"I know. Lucky! We're lucky he found us!" Harvey shouted.

"Yeah, Lucky!" Henry shouted, agreement clinched.

So Lucky he was, both in name and adoration.

Christmas Day contained so much joy the twins felt as if they might burst with all of it. For one thing, there were all the cookies, set on the tabletop all day, free, if you wanted one, anytime of the day, even after lunch and before supper.

There was homemade potato candy, made with mashed potatoes and peanut butter, soft little whorls of it spread on the white dough and rolled up like a cinnamon roll. There was some chocolate candy, but only a small amount in a petite glass dish. No more than two, Rachel said. She had to save the rest for tomorrow, which was second Christmas, another day set aside for celebrating that was not as holy as the real Christmas Day. That was when the large amount of aunts and uncles and grandparents and children would arrive.

Henry told Harvey he was not looking forward to it.

Then, after all that ham for supper, they were allowed to pop popcorn on the wood range, and roast chestnuts in the oven.

Malinda said every raw chestnut had a white worm in it, but after it was roasted, the worm turned to powder and became part of the chestnut. You could never eat a raw chestnut or you'd get the worms and die.

Harvey's eyes became big and round. He looked at the tray of roasted chestnuts and rolled one eye toward Henry.

"I am not going to eat them," he whispered.

"They're roasted," Henry answered.

Ephraim cracked so many chestnuts in his mouth, chewed so loud, that Harvey decided the only safe way to spend the evening was to stick with salted popcorn.

Rachel read the story of Jesus' birth from the Bible. The boys had heard it before, of course, with their sad-eyed father gathering his many children about him on Christmas Day and introducing their fledgling souls to the milk of Christianity, which was the Christ Child's birth.

Rachel was a good storyteller.

She said the Baby Jesus was a good baby to be born in the stable with the cows and donkeys and sheep, and He lay quietly in His manger bed filled with straw.

Henry had never thought of that. He elbowed Harvey's ribs and asked what born meant. Harvey didn't know, so he shook his head, told him to be quiet.

They drank cold cider. Ephraim heated his in a saucepan and drank it like coffee.

It was warm and bright in the farmhouse, as the twins sat listening to Rachel's voice rising and falling. They imagined the shepherds in the field, the host of heavenly angels singing to them of Jesus' birth. But as the hour became late, their eyes grew heavy, and they thought only of the dog, Lucky.

The wonderful Christmas Day came to a close when they trudged wearily up the stairs, shed their clothes, and climbed beneath the covers with soft sighs of happiness and contentment. They fell asleep without remembering to say their "*Müde Binnich.*"

Second Christmas arrived a bit differently, having to get out of bed in their frigid, upstairs bedroom, shivering into pants and shirts, then straight to the *kesslehaus* to don their outerwear.

They lifted their faces to the snow that fell sideways, blown in by a steady moaning wind that whipped the bare, black branches in the moonless early morning. They pressed their tattered straw hats on their heads and raced for the warm, steamy barn, closing the cast iron latch firmly behind them.

You'd think Malinda would be friendly, having received that gift on Christmas Day, but she glared at the boys from her crouch on the wooden milking stool, telling them to walk quietly, or they'd scare the cow she was milking, and she'd turn over the bucket of milk if she kicked.

So they said nothing, just went quietly to greet Lucky in the forebay, who wiggled and bounded and jumped all over them, so glad to see his beloved little friends.

They fed the heifers and the horses, by the dim flickering light of the kerosene lantern. Harvey carefully placed two long, yellow ears of corn in the small section of the wooden trough that was worn smooth by the heavy leather halter and the chain attached to each horse. Henry dumped their portion of smooth, slippery oat kernels, and they stood side by side, watching the massive noses in the trough, crunching and chewing.

A horse had an expert way of eating the hard, yellow kernels of corn off a cob. They never ate the cob, just stripped the corn off with their long, yellow teeth and chewed with a steady, popping sound. Some corn fell out of the sides of their mouth, but they lipped it up after the cob was bare.

It was their job to gather up the cobs after the horses were finished and carry them to the tool shed. Ephraim stuck them upright into a bucket that contained a few inches of kerosene, which the cobs would soak up like a sponge. That was what Rachel used to start a fire in the cookstove every morning.

Nothing went to waste on the farm in those days. The twins knew to sweep up every bit of hay to make sure the horses ate all of it. If they spilled oats out of the scoop, they were expected to sweep it up and give it to the horses. Every bit of manure was loaded on the spreader with pitchforks, drawn to the fields with sturdy Belgians, and spread on the land for fertilizer. The gardens and flower beds were also covered with a heavy layer in the fall, where it would decompose, enriching the fertile soil in spring.

Breakfast was oatmeal and toast with apple butter, eaten quickly and quietly. Ephraim knelt by his chair and everyone else followed suit, kneeling by their own bench or chair, as he said the German morning prayer from the *Gebet Buch*. This morning, even his words were spoken faster than usual, with respect to his wife's red face and snapping eyes.

This was the day of the *Grishtdag Essa*.

Dishes were done in double-quick time, the kitchen swept and dusted. Rachel put warm soapy water in a tin basin and proceeded to pull each child's head against her round stomach and scrub. She used no mercy and wasted no time.

The rough washcloth was raked across their faces and around their ears and neck, over and over, her breath above them coming thick and fast.

She felt soft, though, and she smelled of oatmeal and Lava soap. She parted their hair down the middle, removed the snarls with the sturdy comb, patted their heads, and told them to run upstairs and dress in their Sunday clothes.

Harvey stood in the middle of his cold bedroom and explored his ears, from the top to the bottom of his earlobes.

"Guess they're still there."

Henry was pulling on the sleeve of his blue Sunday shirt, trying to slide it off the wire hanger.

"What?"

"My ears."

Henry laughed. The shirt slid off the hanger so he dressed quickly, jumping into the stiff black Sunday trousers. Harvey did the same, then pulled on his black socks.

They stood back and surveyed each other, seriously inspecting their appearance. To be thrust into a world of strangers was a daunting prospect, so they buttoned all their buttons, straightened their collars, and adjusted shirttails and suspenders.

"Should we wear our *chackets*?"

"She didn't say."

They pondered this question.

"Go ask," Henry offered.

At that moment, the doorknob turned and Malinda stuck her head in the door.

"Mam said to wear your *chackets*."

So they did, without answering Malinda.

Now what if they would not have put on their trousers and she stuck her head in like that? Well, they both decided firmly, if that was how she was going to be, then she'd just have to see their thin, white legs and maybe their underpants.

Downstairs, they were told to *raum up* the *kesslehaus*, put away the boots, and sweep any hay or straw that might have been dragged in from the barn.

They obeyed, finished their work, then sat side by side on the sofa, unsure what was expected of them from here on out. When they felt like this, it was always comforting to feel the touch of the other twin's shoulder, each boy knowing he was not alone. That was when Malinda came blustering in from the *kesslhaus* saying the boys had not shaken the rugs.

Rachel was mixing celery into the bread cubes for the *roasht*. She never missed a beat, just flung words over her shoulder, telling Malinda she didn't ask them to do that. If she thought it necessary, she could go ahead and do it.

Katie and Anna were freshly watered down and combed so tightly, they had a surprised look with those lifted eyebrows. On either side of their foreheads, their dark hair was rolled in, stretched into two long rolls and wound around a steel hairpin in the back, forming thick coils of rolled hair with the hairpin centered exactly in the middle, on the outside, with about a dozen more stuck into the rolled coils to keep the hair in place.

The boys thought it must be an awful thing, being a girl and having to go through all that. They remembered their own sisters and missed them, especially Emma and Annie, who were older than both of them.

Henry swallowed, as his eyes turned soft and liquid, wondering if they thought about their brothers often, or if they were already forgotten.

They tried to be brave, but their hearts quaked when the gray buggies began to arrive, filling the house with all kinds of strangers the boys had never seen. At times like this, they wanted to go home, even if it was a sad, poverty-infused home, it was still the home they knew.

So many people, so many voices.

Black shawls and bonnets, children wearing *mondlin*, those lined wraps with shoulder capes that buttoned down the front, a matching bonnet in purple or blue. Babies unwrapped like Christmas gifts, sisters and cousins pawing at scarves and tiny black shawls, peering into brand-new faces to exclaim over the hair or the likeness to Uncle Rufus or Aunt Hettie.

Perhaps Cousin Barbara.

Henry and Harvey remained on the sofa, wishing they could turn into pillows.

No one took notice of them, so they stayed quiet, their dark eyes not quite focused on everyone and no one.

Finally from the din, there emerged an old, old woman dressed in black all over. She was short, bent forward at the waist, round like an egg, with her gnarled old hands spread over her cane like tree roots. From beneath the hem of her skirt, two black shoes shuffled over and stopped in front of the boys.

"*Vell. Voss hen ma do?*"

One of her scary looking hands was extended toward them, so Harvey obeyed his training and put his hand into it.

As scaly as a dry fish. But he shook hands.

"*Schoene boova. Ztzvilling.*"

They looked up into a face so riven and crisscrossed with cracks and wrinkles that it barely resembled a face. There were hairy warts or moles all over the place. One on the end of her nose. Her eyes were almost closed off by flaps of skin, and she had no teeth.

"How old are you, boys?"

"We are seven," Harvey whispered.

"What? Speak up! I don't hear well."

"We are seven."

"Oh. *Sivva.* Do you go to school?"

Rachel disengaged herself from a conversation with a sister-in-law and came to the boys' rescue.

"Boys, this is a great-grandmother. *An gros grus-mommy.* She is 97. Her name is Fronie Stoltzfus."

The boys didn't say anything to that, but thought she must have been in the Garden of Eden somewhere. Ninety-seven years old was so old you could hardly think on it.

They breathed easier when Rachel led her away, relieved to stop being accountable for being only seven and not belonging to this family in the true sense of the word.

Although a constant stream of children paraded past the sofa, no one stopped or offered to play with them. Little eyes watched from behind chair backs, even smaller ones stood in front of them and glared, a thumb stuck into a pink mouth, saliva dripping on aprons or shirtfronts.

They waited a long time to be seated for Christmas dinner. All the men and boys ate at the first table, a table that extended the whole way across the kitchen and into the living room.

Wonderful smells came from the platters of steaming *roasht*, the white mounds of mashed potatoes with browned butter running down the sides, and puddling along the rim of the serving dish. There were cooked green beans, stewed turnips, and sweet potatoes. Celery cooked in a vinegary white sauce, applesauce, shredded cabbage and carrots, pickled red beets, and sweet pickles. Chow-chow and cooked peas. Homemade egg noodles.

The twins sat on the sofa, watched the dishes being passed from one hand to the next. They watched burly red-faced men lifting mountainous spoonfuls of everything, causing them some anxiety.

Would there be anything left?

Mince meat pie, pumpkin pie, and apple pie. Chocolate cake and grape mush. Vanilla cornstarch pudding and strawberry dessert. White cake and spice cake.

Still the men kept eating, talking, and laughing. When they finally folded their hands in their laps and bent their heads to thank God for their full stomachs, Henry sighed with satisfaction.

The dishes were cleared, washed and dried, set back on the table, and all the women and girls were seated.

Rachel and another woman the twins did not know stayed by the stove to serve the table. No one took notice of Henry and Harvey. Again, the dishes were passed, the women ate and ate, served the girls, talked and laughed, and enjoyed themselves immensely.

A lone tear appeared on Henry's eyelash, fell, leaving a wet streak on his cheek. He was hungry, afraid everyone had forgotten them, and did not know how to go about making his presence known without seeming bold. Harvey glanced over, then slid closer, pressing his shoulder against Henry's.

"We'll eat with our Rachel," he whispered.

Henry nodded, his brown eyes met those of his twin, comfort passed and accepted.

And they did.

The table was set for a third time, although only to about half its length. There was plenty of food to go around. Women hovered over them with serving dishes, platters of steaming *roasht*, and bowls of potatoes. The boys lifted their spoons and ate and ate till they could hold no more. Then they tasted the chocolate cake with the cornstarch pudding, and after that, the pumpkin pie.

Rachel smiled so sweetly at them, as she kept pushing more pie in their direction. She asked softly if they had made new friends. They shook their heads, ashamed now.

"It's all right. You will after dinner," she said.

She introduced Cousin Bennie from Kirkwood. He was tall and blond, blue eyed and fair skinned. His hair was cut high on his forehead, but along the length of his ears, it wasn't cut, so that only the tips of his upper ears pushed through the straight yellow hair.

"Hi!" he said loudly.

"Hi!" answered Harvey, then Henry.

"Twins?" he asked.

They both nodded at once.

"I'm Bennie Beiler. My dad is your dad's brother. Aquilla. Well, they say Ephraim isn't your real dad, but you're here now, so we're cousins."

The twins smiled shyly, checking Bennie's face for signs of disapproval. He seemed genuine.

Together, they sat on the *kesslehaus* floor and tugged on their rubber boots. Five more boys came to join them, all aged between six and twelve. Bennie introduced them by age: Homer, Eli, Dannie, Amos, and Gideon. The boys acknowledged each one.

They brought Lucky out from his doghouse and the fun began. Snow swirled around them as they hitched the excited dog to the wooden sled. They raced and rolled and tumbled, the big, loose-jointed dog galloping along full speed, dragging the sled filled with cheering boys, his tongue dangling like a long pink ribbon.

Malinda appeared with a gaggle of scarved girls, who wanted to use the sled to go sledding on the hill. They stood there like different sizes of fence posts with their hands hanging uselessly, waiting and glaring till the boys gave up and unhitched Lucky. They stood there so long, snow accumulated on the tops of their heads and their shoulders, like big grains of sugar. Malinda told the boys to put that dog in the doghouse, he was tired out. Didn't they have any sense?

Bennie eyed her with full-out dislike, reached down and scooped up a handful of snow, packed it in two cupped hands, and let it fly.

Smack!

Bennie knew he was in for it the minute that snowball hit her bossy face. Malinda yelled, scooped up a handful of snow, her eyes streaming with melting snow, unable to focus properly, the snowball yards from her intended target.

That whole afternoon the twins had more fun than they ever had before. They flung snowballs from a fort, ducked and yelled and rolled over and washed each other's faces with handfuls of snow.

Malinda called a truce and gave everyone the same chance to build a proper fort. Henry and Harvey rolled snowballs, wrapped their arms around them to lift them high, packed them together, and smoothed them over. The fort was v-shaped and built for strength.

Snowballs whizzed by, knocking straw and black felt hats off the boys' heads, splattering all over the girls' scarves, splatting into walls and the snow-covered ground in front.

Barn cats scuttled along walls, casting apprehensive glances at the war in the driveway. Lucky whined in his doghouse, but Malinda made him stay there. Bennie asked if she was always the boss, and she said no, but the twins nodded their heads behind her back, creating a look of glee on Bennie's face.

Then they were called in to sing German Christmas songs. Slumped shoulders and quiet groans of protest were followed by disgusted expressions and snowballs flung away without aim.

Singing hymns at *S' Grishtag Essa* was nothing short of a punishment. The house was overheated, the men sat in strict and holy circles of righteousness, while the women spread their skirts across their knees, pursed their lips, and hung their eyebrows at a humble angle, trying to erase the fact that they had gossiped about Amos Fisher's Lena, who turned sixteen in January and would bring her parents to shame.

The children all had to sit still, hold the fat hymn-book as if they could read or understand one word of German. It wasn't so bad when they sang the fast tunes of "*Schtille Nacht, Heilige Nacht*" or "*Freue Dich, Velt,*" but when the men began the slow, laborious plainsong, bellowing out the words of old hymns from the Ausbund, they knew the snowball fight was in the past.

Rachel served grape juice and cider after the children thought they surely wouldn't start another song, only to hear the trembling vocals of yet another uncle. Bowls of popcorn seasoned with salt, then gold popcorn balls, sticky and crunchy with brown sugar and molasses, followed the juice and cider. Once the singers wet their throats with grape juice, they began wailing on, although the children soon recognized their gateway to freedom lay in the heavy platter of popcorn balls. Sure enough, the minute they began to eat, the singing stopped, and they were free to go.

The headlong dash to the *kesslehaus* was halted by anxious mothers who were thinking of the ride home and all that wet outerwear. They helped the children dry their clothes on wooden racks, brought out the checkers and Parcheesi games, served more cookies and warm cups of spearmint tea.

Henry and Harvey draped themselves over the backs of kitchen chairs and watched Bennie beat Malinda at checkers. Bennie was smart. Smarter than anyone they had ever met. He could build the best fort, and move the checkers to just the right spot. Plus, he had a pony, he said. Anyone who owned a pony was smart and rich and luckier than anyone they had ever known.

The Christmas dinner wound down when Ephraim began to watch the clock, stretch his arms above his head, and make strange, exaggerated yawns.

"Chore time," he said.

Reluctantly, the brothers and sisters gathered up their various offspring, braved the cold and oncoming twilight, amid heartfelt thanks and much handshaking, words of goodbye and well wishes.

S' Grishtag Essa was over for another year.

The house was in complete disarray, but with Rachel barking orders, the girls sweeping the floors and washing the dishes, and the twins sent to the barn to help do the chores, life returned to normal before they went to bed.

The best part of winter was yet to come, when they would watch the farm pond freeze over and be able to try out the most wonderful gifts in the whole world: those Canadian Flyers.

Chapter Four

AFTER SECOND CHRISTMAS DAY, THE TWINS finally went to school, carrying their books in a paper bag, a black metal lunchbox containing a slice of buttered bread, a jar of milk, and a sugar cookie.

Their new home was not far from the one where they had spent their first six years, so they went to the same school as their birth brothers and sisters. They were hesitant and shy at first, but before the week was up, they accepted everything as the new normal on both sides.

Mrs. Dayble had not repented of her ill temper, so things remained the same as far as scrunching down in your seat, hoping it wasn't something you had done that made her walk like that. So hopping mad, she rocked from side to side, before twisting misbehaving Emanuel Lantze's shirtsleeve, which was sure to contain the skin of his arm. Sure enough, he clapped his left hand over his right forearm, lowered his shoulders, opened his mouth in a silent howl of protest, then squeezed shut as he absorbed the pain.

Harvey shivered in his shoes watching Emanuel. He bent his head and resumed his studies, muttering "two times six is twelve, two times seven is fourteen," and so forth.

Henry's eyes snapped his disapproval of so harsh a punishment for merely tweaking Helen's pigtails. Emanuel wouldn't do that if she would quit turning around, pointing at his mistakes. She'd told him once that his handwriting was worse than chicken scratch, so she had it coming.

The redbrick school was nestled in a group of maple trees with a slope of pasture rising on each side. The front porch was on the gable end, where the roof came to a V, and there were three windows on either side, with two on the porch. There was a huge cast iron furnace toward the front of the room that often burned red-hot, heating the front half of the classroom but not the back. There was a row of blackboards along the front, a wooden tray along the bottom that contained chalk and erasers. The floor was wooden, wide, thick oak boards that were oiled in the fall before school started. The desks were wooden, varnished to a glossy sheen, with cast iron legs and a hinged seat you could put up or down. The seat was attached to the front of the desk behind, so there was a long row of desks and seats down throughout the room.

Five rows of eight desks, all filled with children.

One teacher.

Her desk was up front by the blackboard, and she stood behind it mostly, like a bald eagle with big yellow eyes with no eyelids, and a powerful hooked beak.

Henry figured she could probably kill a fish with her nose. Of course, he never said that to anyone, not even Harvey. He just thought it.

Mrs. Dayble's classroom was quiet. The children learned their lessons. If they didn't behave, she administered her famous pinch, and if that didn't thwart the problem, the ruler did. If any parent complained about her methods of discipline, she lifted her chin, crossed her arms, and told them to come teach the school if they could do better. No one ever did, and she had taught school in Leacock Township for thirty-two years.

Lucky stayed on. Sometimes when an automobile or a horse and buggy came rolling into the Ephraim

King farm, the boys would peer fearfully out of the barn door, or peek out a window in the house, wondering yet again if it would be Lucky's owner, coming to take their pet.

But it never was.

They had many happy Christmas days at their new home. They grew to think of Ephraim and Rachel as Dat and Mam, while their biological parents faded into a murky background of memories of their very young childhood. They remembered the good times and the transition between families with a twinge, although nothing that would hamper their ability to grow and learn, to become decent, obedient boys who learned to love and respect their new parents. They always understood the Esh family's poverty, being unable to feed the growing number of children, and understood too that Ephraim King needed boys, and they filled that need, which always served to satisfy the questioning inside. That, and the love Ephraim and Rachel had for the boys, constantly showing their caring in many ways.

Lucky was a constant companion. Everywhere the boys went, there was Lucky, the huge black dog lolloping by their side. In the cold of winter, in snow and ice, in the heat of summer, through the scattered leaves of autumn, there was Lucky. It was a rare and special bond, one the Amish folks talked about for years to come.

Five Christmases came and went, creating more happy memories for them as they grew. They were twelve years old that spring of 1941. Lancaster County was pummeled with snowstorm after snowstorm that winter. Belgian horses and trustworthy mules plowed through six-foot drifts, hauling cans of milk to the creamery. For days at a time, no trucks or automobiles could navigate the roads. Men with snow shovels, graders, makeshift snow pushers, and draggers were everywhere.

And then it began to rain in late March, swelling the rivers and creeks to a dangerous brown surge filled with chunks of ice as big as a shed. Patches of slush moved along like lace cloth, bits of wood and dead tree branches roiled and bumped, staying against the trunks of trees, before the current pulled them away, hurling them along.

The Susquehanna River overflowed its banks, the dead water crept past its banks across the road and into the stately homes built along its banks in the city of Harrisburg.

There was nothing to be done but call the situation an emergency and evacuate. Everywhere there were misplaced folks, living with relatives, in empty buildings, or they left the county entirely. The people of Lancaster County had woes of their own. Cows became stranded in pastures on high ground, unable to navigate the many swollen creeks that sluiced their way in brown, foaming currents that looked like dirty dishwater.

Gray clouds hung over the land, repeatedly releasing yet another rain shower, deepening and widening the already overflowing creeks.

Ephraim offered to take the boys to school that morning, saying it didn't look as if the rain had any notion of letting up. Harvey said, nah, they'd walk. "It's not raining now."

So they grabbed their black, tin lunch pails, donned their collarless black coats and straw hats, and were stopped on their way out the door with admonishment to wait on Katie and Anna.

So they did, shifting their weight from foot to foot, watching the door without patience. A robin chirped constantly in the crabapple tree by the *kessle-haus*, so they deserted their post and went to see what all the commotion was about.

Of course, before they found the nest she was building, the girls appeared in their royal-blue bonnets and black shawls, telling them to get down from there, it was time to go.

They had a two-mile walk, which they didn't consider being too far or too strenuous. It was actually a very nice walk on most days, even in winter, with ice to slide on, snowballs to make, walking with Ben Stoltzfus' children after the first mile. So much to talk about with Willie and Rueben. Much the same as all the other farm boys, there were endless discussions about the animals, the pastures and woods, conjuring up half-truths to impress one another, as children will.

This morning, they were not at the end of the back lane that led to their farm, so they walked on.

When a horse and buggy pulled up beside them, Ben's friendly face beamed down at them.

"*Vedta mitt?*"

The girls willingly clambered aboard, but Henry and Harvey looked at each other and shook their heads, both thinking there might still be time to hurl a few branches into the swollen Pequea Creek, by the side of the red covered bridge.

"All right then!" Ben called, pulled on the reins, and chirped to his horse. The buggy rumbled away, spitting gravel beneath the steel wagon wheel rims.

Immediately, the boys took off. They ran gleefully, their mouths wide, their lunches swinging, knocking against their legs. When the covered bridge was in sight, they increased their speed, their breath coming in hard little puffs, their cheeks red with the damp air.

Over the stone wall, down the slippery grassy slope beneath.

"Whoa!" Henry shouted.

"Whoa!" Harvey echoed.

The brown water was right there. Right at their feet. The Pequea Creek spread out like an ocean before them. They stood side by side, their shoulders touching, mesmerized, watching the powerful surge from beneath the bridge. Only a few yards from the base of the bridge and rising. That was when they spotted the little brown dog. Whimpering and crying, thin and shivering, he was stuck on a stone ledge, a small shelf of stone so narrow he could barely stay on, inches above the water. When he saw the boys, he cried like a real baby, begging and yelping.

"Aw!" Henry whispered.

"If we had a stick. . ." Harvey muttered.

"He couldn't hang on to a stick."

"Maybe."

All thoughts of school and tardiness vanished. They were single-minded in their purpose. The dog must be rescued.

They turned, searched the weeds and trees by the side of the road. They picked up and discarded a few puny branches, but nothing that was long enough to reach the poor, frightened animal. They turned as one, both noticed the loose board on the bridge. All it would take was a hefty yank to loosen it.

"Damage to the bridge," Henry said, seriously.

"What else can we do?" Harvey asked.

"Would it be long enough?"

"I believe so."

They scrambled up over the stone wall. Both grabbed the red board and pulled upward, then pushed. The rusty nails groaned. They worked at loosening it, pushing, then yanking sideways, till the board loosened, slid sideways, and fell with a *whump*.

Immediately they picked it up, ran to the stone wall, and shoved it over. The little brown dog's eyes were large and brown and pleading. His cries increased.

The deep brown water roiled out from under the bridge, carrying logs and branches, a dead cat with slimy fur matted to its body, boards, and clumps of brown weeds and brambles.

Side by side, the twins hung over the stone wall above the water, straining to angle the board just to the dog, near enough to be able to guide him up over his dangerous perch.

Only a foot.

"I'll lean over, you hang on to my waist," Harvey instructed.

"Don't, Harvey. What if you slip?" Henry warned. "I'll be careful."

Henry felt Harvey's shoulder leave his. He slid his arm around his waist as he leaned over, straining to acquire a few more inches to reach the whining, stranded animal. He got the board situated on the ledge. The dog lowered its head, ready to step out, when the board slipped on the slick, wet stones, went down with a splash, taking the dog with it.

It overbalanced Harvey.

The weight was too much for Henry.

It happened in the blink of an eye. Harvey tore out of Henry's grasp, leaving him with a hoarse, choking scream and empty arms.

He could only watch Harvey hit the brown water, the red board and the little dog going before him, submerged in the dangerous current that was suddenly wicked, evil. The deep, powerful sound of rushing water meant death and destruction.

Henry left the stone wall and slid in the wet grass. He waved his arms and screamed. He cried. He begged Harvey to swim, swim, Harvey. He saw Harvey's straw hat round the bend.

Harvey's head appeared above the water, his face white, his brown eyes terrified. He thrashed his arms to stay afloat, then disappeared around the bend with the board and the dog.

Henry called and called.

He could not race along the bank to follow Harvey's progress. The briars and undergrowth grew too thick and heavy. The thought that Harvey would make it seized him. He was a good swimmer in the farm pond. Every summer he became a better one. Ben Stoltzfus' Willie said he was like a fish.

Henry climbed over the stone wall, his breath coming in hot puffs of terror. He cried, moaned, muttered to himself. He found he was uttering the word "please, please" over and over, begging for help from a much Higher Power from his soul, without knowing he was capable of such deep immortal pleading.

There were no automobiles or teams, horses and buggies, nothing, that morning.

So Henry ran. He ran to the schoolhouse, often stumbling and falling, till his trousers were torn and blood seeped from his torn kneecap. He burst through the front door, an ashen-faced, terrified specter that stayed in tender children's minds, rendering them unable to sleep, concerned mothers sitting with them as they lay wide-eyed, asking questions about death and God and the reason why He let Harvey Esh slide into that awful brown water.

Mrs. Dayble turned, disapproval for her tardy scholars pulled firmly in place. It melted away at the sight before her.

Quickly, she laid down her hymn book, walked to his side to place a now shaking hand on his shoulder.

"He fell in, he fell in," he said, hoarsely, between panting breaths.

"Who? What are you talking about?" Mrs. Dayble asked, her own breath coming in hard puffs.

"H... H... Harvey."

The class had stopped singing at Henry's appearance.

Thirty-eight pupils, lined up by size, in five rows, stood silently, in shocked disbelief, straining to hear what their classmate was trying to convey. Faces turned pale, eyes grew large and dark.

Mrs. Dayble grasped Henry's shoulder. "Tell me what happened."

Between coughs and panting breaths, the story came out, wrung from Henry's mind by necessity.

Mrs. Dayble straightened, strode purposefully to the coat rack, got down her old beige woolen coat, barked strict orders for everyone to return to their seats and stay there, she was going to use the telephone.

When she let herself out the door, Henry went to his own seat, sagged wearily into it, and began to sob, quietly, restrainedly.

Katie went to him, slid in his seat beside him, an arm stealing about his heaving shoulders. Anna began to cry in earnest, her friend Salome hurrying to sit with her, the childish intuition of providing instant comfort.

The classroom was silent, save for the sounds of quiet weeping. No one asked questions. No one tried to get Henry to talk. They were still absorbing bits and pieces of Henry's words to Mrs. Dayble.

When she returned, the fire sirens had already started, the high, thin wail reaching out an arm and pulling them without mercy into a stark and awful reality. Something had happened. Something terrible.

Henry stayed in his seat, with Katie's support. Mrs. Daybel asked the children to fold their hands on top of their desks and pray that Harvey would be safe.

They came for Henry.

Concerned parents and neighbors showed up, gathered up their children, thanking God for their safety.

Henry stood by the stone wall talking to the men from the firehouse. He told them precisely, in calm, measured tones what had occurred. It was only when Ephraim and Rachel appeared that he lost all resolve and cried deep, groaning sobs of despair.

His sad-eyed father and overwhelmed mother appeared later, when it began to rain. They stood by Henry, said Harvey's time was up, God had chosen to take him. Henry peered up into their faces, squinted his eyes, and said nothing. Ephraim said they would search along the Pequea, perhaps they'd find him alive. He was a good swimmer.

All his older brothers and sisters arrived in buggies, tied their horses to a telephone pole, came to stand with Henry, staring at him as if he had a strange disease they did not want to contract.

No one spoke to him, so he turned his back and looked out over the Pequea Creek that had grasped his brother in its dirty, brown arms and sucked the life out of him. He hated the creek. The feeling dried up his tears of agony and clenched his fists into tense, white-knuckled misery.

When the rain increased, the group of watchers moved under the shelter of the bridge to wait for any word of Harvey's rescue. Ephraim and Rueben left to help with the search.

All day, each side of the Pequea swarmed with firemen, police, neighbors and well-wishers, members of the Amish, Mennonite, Dunkard, Lutheran, and Catholic communities, all united as one to find Harvey.

When night fell, they took Henry home.

Groups of women inhabited the kitchen of Ephraim King, making coffee, serving sandwiches and cookies, as if in sheer amounts they could somehow lighten the shock and pain of this awful happening.

Malinda had not seen Henry, having opted to stay at home till her parents returned. She was the kind of person who dealt with stress of any kind with action. Alone, she milked all the cows, fed the calves, heifers, and horses without getting tired or slowing down, propelled by a nervous, almost manic energy.

Now, she stood in front of her distressed, broken-down brother and said bluntly, "Don't ever blame yourself, Henry. You'll suffer later on if you do."

It was a strange, hard way of greeting, but for some reason or other, those words often rose up like the wings of a powerful bird, to lift him above the wondering and the regret of what had happened that rainy morning on their way to school.

No one slept.

Henry dozed fitfully on the couch, to awaken a few minutes later with the ghost of Harvey sliding out of his grasp like a knife to his senses.

Oh, Harvey. Harvey. How will I ever go through the future without you? It was like reaching the edge of a cliff to look out over an arid, dead landscape filled with gray, jutting rocks and no water. He could see no way of survival.

Hope that Harvey would still be alive afforded a bit of comfort. It was only when reality set in, a grim-faced policeman's arrival to announce the finding of Harvey's drowned form, caught in a pile of debris at the dam, that Henry tore out of Rachel's grasp, sobbing in silent heaves, ran to the barn, pushing aside bystanders and other folks who wished to convey comfort, to find Lucky.

Lucky, the Christmas dog, still the best companion. He threw himself down, buried his face in Lucky's thick, black hair, and sobbed out the despair and pain and loss, taking in the comfort of the faithful friend's warmth and the stirring of love that ensured his lone survival.

If Lucky was here, he was not alone.

Grown men wept.

When they brought the body of his brother back from the funeral home, Davis and Wendell, in the city of Lancaster, Lucky stood by Henry's side, his small triangular brown eyes fixed on Harvey's still, pale face.

The house was prepared for the viewing. Two neighboring couples were appointed to take charge of the proceedings, as was the Amish custom. The house was filled with friends and relatives dressed in black, sober-faced women and somber men, weeping classmates and cousins.

Two sets of parents, both feeling the loss keenly. It was Mattie's way to remain stoic, stone-faced, and silent.

Neighbors questioned this, in huddled groups of whispers, eyes cast accusingly, doubts put forth into the room like an obscuring fog.

Doesn't she care? Has the woman no feelings for her twins?

The truth was hidden away, beneath the pinned black cape that hung well below her shoulders. She cared. Had cared too much, the day the twins were taken away. No one except her husband and children knew of her breakdown, hidden away in the *Komma* as she struggled to maintain her grasping hope of keeping her sanity when the waters of her agony threatened to pull her under. She had died, in a way, like Harvey, locked away in a darkened room, the green blinds drawn behind the white cotton curtains that reached only halfway up the window frame.

Though the children of Reuben's first wife, she had loved each boy, gazing into their perfect, cherubic faces and loving them with her soft mother heart. She had fiercely resisted this giving away of the twins, but, in the end, submitted to the will of her struggling, over-worked, sad-eyed husband, unable to make ends meet.

For she loved Rueben as well.

Yes, she cared.

But she had reached a peaceful plain where car-ing, like her will, was diminished and taken away, replaced by survival, looking forward to the day when her Lord and Savior returned with all His angels to take her home to Heaven, where there was no fear of poverty, only indescribable happiness and singing in gold mansions that He had prepared for her.

The sun burst through the scudding gray clouds on the day of Harvey's burial, casting a bright, golden glow over the graveyard close to Gordonville. The huddled group of mourners dressed in black lifted toward Heaven in spirit as the gray-haired bishop read the closing prayer.

For years, folks talked about the big black dog that stood at the gravesite, Henry's hand resting on his head. The kindhearted bishop had made allowance, seeing how the black dog was the only comfort for the remaining twin.

When the men shoveled the wet clods of dirt onto the lowered casket, it was Henry and Lucky that stood foremost, watching attentively, the dog peering down into the grave with his sad, triangular brown eyes. He whimpered once. Henry reached down to stroke his head, quieting him.

Buds broke forth from sodden, wet branches that day. Robins and sparrows chirped and flitted about, getting down to the business of nest-building, filling the air with their ambitious songs. Horses plodded in pastures, black-and-white Holsteins tore at clumps of new grass, and baby lambs frolicked on ungainly legs between the watchful eyes of their mothers.

Life went on.

For Mattie, it was another beginning, her pain hidden away as the breakdown had been, swept away and never talked about, never brought into the general public, as was the custom.

Rueben took care of his quiet wife to the best of his ability, all their children gathered around their table.

But in Mattie's heart, there remained a special place for her Henry and his black dog.

Chapter Five

GROWING UP, HENRY OFTEN FELT AS IF THERE was only half of him remaining. He became used to looking up from his chores, to show Harvey the biggest night crawler he ever saw, or to tell him about the bass in the pool by the sycamore tree.

The space in his heart occupied by Harvey was left empty, scraped and raw, so that sometimes, he would clutch his shirtfront, pulling the fabric and row of sturdy buttons away from his skin, to ease the pain, to be able to breathe.

It was those times that turned him to Lucky. They would roam the fields and woods together, especially that first summer without Harvey. There was no greater comfort than being alone with the huge, black dog, settling together on the bank of the Pequea Creek, sitting side by side the way he sat with Harvey.

Lucky was trained well. He knew instinctively when Henry was watching for any movement in the deep, amber pool, where the water eddied by the syc-amore tree. If they sat quietly, from time to time, the flash of a fat bass or catfish would catch Henry's eye.

Lucky's ears pointed up then, but no one but Henry knew this, the way they were mostly buried in the thick hair that grew all over him. Lucky was the most intelligent dog.

Even when the fish swam into view, he did not bounce up and down or whine. He stayed right where he was supposed to, waiting politely for a spo-ken command from his master.

Ephraim and Rachel believed Henry should open up about his loss, at least talk about Harvey at times when they could tell he was suffering. But he never did.

It was Malinda who caught Henry talking to Lucky, telling him all about the day at the bridge.

One evening about three months after Harvey's death, she came to her mother on a hot, humid eve-ning, when the sun still felt too uncomfortably warm, even at that hour. The heat still clung to the sides of the house and turned the grass warm and limp.

Rachel sat on the creaking old porch swing, its rusted iron chains attached to the thick metal hooks from the beam in the ceiling, screeching melodiously. Her hands were never idle, so tonight she was shelling a few leftover peas she found still clinging to the decaying vines.

Malinda strode up to the porch in her purposeful manner, eyed her mother, and stood before her with her hands on her hips.

"Mam, Henry talks to Lucky. I heard him. You had better have him checked by a doctor. I'm pretty sure there is something wrong with his brain."

Rachel looked at her daughter, unruffled, acquainted with her theatrics.

"I'm serious. You should have heard him. He had a long story, over and over, about the dog stuck on the stone ledge, the board. He said the water was like a brown dragon that licked up Harvey. He shouldn't be talking like that."

Rachel considered her words, then told Malinda perhaps it was a good thing if he talked to his dog, if he couldn't bring himself to talk to anyone else.

"But it isn't normal," Malinda insisted.

"Perhaps for Henry it is," Rachel said. "You must consider, he is working through a terrible loss, one you and I can't understand. He doesn't feel close to any of us, with good reason, so we need to respect his privacy. Leave him alone when you hear him talking to Lucky."

Malinda cast a sidelong look at her mother before letting herself in through the screen door.

So the summer heat intensified as July came to a close. The large vegetable patch took up most of Rachel and the girls' time, pulling weeds and hoeing, harvesting, and mulching. The tomatoes were hanging in thick green clusters, some of them with hints of orange on their round cheeks. Cucumber vines were thick and heavy with large, medium-size, and small ones hiding beneath the prickly leaves. The yellow ears of corn turned full and sweet, so Henry was told to help Mam and the girls all day. He found himself in the early light of morning, sticky with corn silk and showers of dew from the wide, abrasive corn leaves that slapped against his face and shoulders.

The sun was like a giant orange ball of pulsing heat, already so early in the morning, so Henry pushed through the stalks of corn, ripping off each golden ear with a swift, downward move, held them sideways in the crook of his arm until he had an armload, then made his way down the row to dump it into the wheelbarrow before ducking his head and returning for more.

Rachel was also in the corn patch, a navy-blue kerchief tied over her hair, secured in the back with a firm knot. She worked fast, her face already beaded with sweat. Lucky sat at the end of the row, his wide thick tongue protruding, panting in the morning heat.

In the kitchen, the girls were washing the breakfast dishes, sweeping the kitchen, setting the house to order. No matter what the job of the day would be, Rachel never started a day's work without the kitchen being in perfect neat-as-a-pin condition.

"You can't work in chaos," she'd say. "A *huddlich* kitchen makes the whole day *huddlich.*"

They sat beneath the shade of two maple trees in the backyard, on the metal porch chairs that bobbed up and down like a rocking chair. Henry sat on the edge, so he could pull off the husks in a fast downward motion and brush the silk off an ear before reaching for another one.

Lucky lay panting in the shade, sprawled out on his side, already uncomfortable in the heat.

"Poor Lucky," Rachel observed.

Henry nodded.

"You know his breed comes from a colder climate. Bennie said he's a Newfoundland."

"A what?" Rachel asked, smiling.

Henry grinned, nodding. "The place his type of dog originates from is closer to the Arctic. Bennie showed me on the map, at school."

"Really?"

"That's what he said."

Rachel smiled again, then watched Henry, already showing signs of adolescence, his shoulders widening, growing tall, perhaps a bit of fuzz above his upper lip. Those eyes, she thought, swallowing a quick rise of emotion. Dark brown pools of so much sadness. The slight variation, the turning in of one dark pupil, only added to the picture of being wizened, experienced in years far beyond his actual age. Rachel felt a quick throb of sympathy. She wanted to be closer to him, allowing him an outlet for the pain that must be spreading through him like a dark mass, shutting out the normal lively exuberance of a young boy.

How was he expected to trust in future relationships? So much had been taken from him at such a tender age.

"Henry," she began.

Immediately, his eyes focused on hers, too alert, too defiant.

"I know it's hard for you to talk about what happened to Harvey, but I worry. I want you to know that I'm here for you if you ever need to talk. Surely you must question God, why He allowed this to happen."

For a long moment, there was no response. Just when Rachel was afraid she had spoken out of turn, or words that were hurtful, cutting like knives, he took a deep breath and looked out across the yard, to the vegetable patch.

"Yeah, well." He stopped, grabbed an ear of corn, and began to husk it, tearing at the leaves as if his words could be distributed by his furious work.

Suddenly, he stopped. "I hate the creek."

Rachel watched his face and stayed quiet.

"I hate that awful brown water. It seems as if God wasn't the one who caused the creek to flood."

For a long time, Henry sat, his elbows on his knees, his hands hanging loosely between them, his head bent, so that Rachel could only see the top of his head, the wavy, loose curls, brown shot through with blond highlights.

There was a terrible light in his eyes when he fastened them on Rachel.

"Does the devil have enough power to flood a creek?"

"Oh, no. No. God is the ultimate power. The devil can only antagonize us, and if we're believers, he has no power to harm us."

"Is that true?" Henry asked, hungrily.

"Yes."

"Well, then, if God flooded the creek, why didn't He keep Harvey?"

"God has reasons, Henry. His ways are so much higher than our own, we can't even begin to understand. We don't lean on our own wisdom. God saw the big picture, the reason why He allowed this to happen. Someday, we'll look back, and we'll see it. But for now, we have to accept it and depend on our faith. You know that faith is believing, even if we don't understand? Don't you?"

"Sort of."

He sighed, a long, slow expulsion of breath that seemed world-weary.

"I thought, though, that God makes a way if we have to suffer. I heard that in church. Actually, at the funeral. So that is why I have Lucky. He takes out a lot of the missing of Harvey. Did you know he misses Harvey too?"

"No, I didn't know that."

"He does. When we go to the creek, he whimpers. He makes sounds as if he's waiting on Harvey."

And then his face crumpled, he slid off the metal chair, folded himself in a fetal position, and with both hands over his face, he shook with sobs.

Instantly, Rachel's own tears welled up, ran down her cheeks, and dripped onto her dress front.

When Malinda stalked out of the house toward them, Rachel gathered herself together, sent her back to the house to start a fire in the *kesslehaus* to heat the water.

After that day, Henry began to call her Mam. He never reverted to the old way of using her given name.

For Christmas that year, he received a new fishing pole with a reel, and a small canvas sack containing hooks and bobbers. His eyes shone with the joy of this precious gift.

Lucky and Henry roamed the fields and forests of the surrounding countryside, in every season. They knew where the ten-point buck lay, his heavy white antlers held so still they blended in with the briars and tree branches and yellow grass. They recognized which groundhog would go into which hole in the side of the alfalfa field, the outcrop of gray limestone where black snakes slithered across on their way to the creek. Chipmunks and squirrels became bold in their presence, chittering and chirring at them from fallen logs and tree branches. They knew which rafter contained the barn owl's nest, and when the young owls hatched. They recognized the difference between a raven and a crow's harsh call.

Henry would ride the harrow, bouncing along on the uneven ground behind the faithful Belgians, Sam and Bob, their heads bobbing up and down with the placing of their gigantic hooves. He knew the call of the meadowlark and the flicker, and he knew which bird had red feathers on its underside.

Everywhere Lucky and Henry went, people knew who they were, waved, called out a greeting, smiled, and shook their heads at the wonder of this lone boy's survival. He seemed able to rise above circumstance and place his future in God's hands at such a young age.

Rachel alone knew how much agony he had survived, but she kept these things in her heart. She believed Lucky was sent from God, an angel in canine form, to look after the brokenhearted twin.

But she never said anything.

The summer Henry turned fourteen years old, he became quite skilled with the new rod and reel. He lived to go fishing, the art of perfecting the perfect cast taking up much of his thoughts and all of his free time. He lived by the pond or down at the creek, him and Lucky, when the work was done and Ephraim said he could go.

An afternoon off was a rare thing, but this afternoon they had finished the last five acres of alfalfa,

closed the barn door, and Ephraim smiled, shook his
head, and said, yes, he could go, before Henry asked.

Henry laughed out loud, said, "Thanks, Dat," and
raced off to the *kesslehaus* for his rod and reel.

Lucky bobbed up and down, bounced around on
his front feet with his backside in the air, his tail waving frantically, the way he always did when he knew
they were going fishing.

As they dug worms out of the manure pile behind
the horse barn, Henry sang.

Oh, Lucky, we're lucky.

We're so very lucky.

My lucky old Lucky.

It was a song he often whistled under his breath,
to a tune he'd made up in his mind, and Lucky liked
it so much he smiled the whole time Henry sang the
song.

Tonight it wasn't so hot. There was a whisper of
a breeze, one that ruffled the cattail leaves, swayed
the tall grasses at the edge of the pond. Dragonflies
hovered over the water and mosquitoes. There was a
dark brown movement on the opposite bank, then a
few silent ripples spread out across the surface of the

water, so Henry knew another muskrat had slid into the pond from his den in the bank.

He grabbed a fat night crawler from the tin can filled with soil and baited his hook. Then, taking a deep breath, he tried to perfect his stance, placing his front foot firmly against a tuft of grass, lifted the rod carefully behind his back, and swung with both arms.

The reel sang as the rod released the spooled line, a sound that was like music to Henry's ears. The thrill of landing a squirming night crawler in the intended spot was just so, well, he could hardly explain it, not even to himself. Fishing was something you couldn't tell other people, same as Harvey's drowning. Some things you felt in the heart, closed the door, and kept them there. It wasn't important that anyone else would know about it.

Tonight, he was sleepy. His eyes were heavy as he sat down on the pond bank. Nothing at all was happening, not even a ripple, not the slightest indication of a nibble, nothing. The sun warm on his back, Henry lay back, threw an arm across his eyes, the fishing rod propped up on a stump. A few deep breaths, and Henry was asleep, the deep sleep of the young and active.

He awoke, alarmed by an unknown thought or presence. He blinked in the fading light of the evening sun to find Katie peering into his face with an annoyed expression.

"You better come home if you're going to sleep," she said gruffly.

Henry sat up, wiped the sleep from his eyes with the back of his hand, glanced at his fishing rod that had slid off its prop, and grinned.

"Must have fallen asleep," he said wryly.

"You must have. You can't catch fish like that."

"How do you know? You don't fish."

"I would, if someone would teach me."

"Someone? Me?"

Katie nodded.

Henry looked at her, checking for sincerity.

It was there, in her serious green eyes that slanted up at the corners, surrounded by thick lashes and eyebrows that looked like a high-flying crow turned away from you.

Henry's brown eyes stayed on hers for a while, till he thought he recognized something he hadn't known he missed. It was hard to explain in words, so, of course, he didn't try to say anything to Katie after they looked at each other for so long. But he knew he had discovered a feeling. Was it friendship? Sibling recognition? He just knew that her eyes were green, shot through with brown and gold lines, like the water behind the biggest limestone on Pequea Creek, and that he needed to see those eyes more than once.

Katie was short for a fifteen-year-old. Short and a bit plump, not much, but soft like a marshmallow. She looked like a pillow in some parts of her, which was nice.

When he talked again, his voice shook until he steadied it. He had to do something with his hands so he wouldn't keep looking for those brown and gold lights in her green eyes.

"So if you want to learn to fish, you'll need a pole."

He held up his rod and reel.

"I know. I don't have one."

"Ephraim got me this one."

Katie sat down on the thick green grass, pulled off a long blade, and wound it around her forefinger. Henry watched as she pulled it tight, the tip of her finger turned red.

"Your finger's going to fall off, you keep that up."

"You think?"

Henry nodded.

"Don't you ever say Dat, for Ephraim?"

"Sometimes."

"Doesn't he seem like your father, after, what is it? Seven years? Eight?"

Henry wound another night crawler on his hook. Katie leaned over and watched.

"Eight years, I guess," Henry said, after a while.

"So Dat doesn't seem like your father."

"In some ways. But I'll always know he's not my real father."

"Yeah. Guess so."

A comfortable silence hung between them, while Henry straightened, twisted his body, and cast perfectly into the middle of the pond with a soft splooshing sound. The red-and-white bobbin floated on the surface.

"Are you going to teach me how to do that?" Katie asked.

"I can if you want."

"I do."

"All right."

"Don't I seem like your sister, either?" Katie asked in a small voice.

Henry shrugged.

"What does that mean?" she persisted.

"Well, you're just Katie. I mean, I like you, of course, but no, you're not my sister."

"Now you're hurting my feelings."

"I don't mean to. Here, now hold the rod with this hand, here. Then, place your other hand on the handle."

"Like this?"

"No. You have to put your right hand higher on the pole, like this."

Henry stood behind her, took her hand and placed it in the proper position.

"Now, bring the whole rod back with both hands, like this. Then, let fly. Concentrate on zinging that hook as far as you can."

Katie leaned back into his chest.

Her white covering smelled like starch and flowers. She smelled like the sun on wet grass, and the rose by the porch early in the morning when the dew sat on the yellow petals before the sun was finished rising above the north pasture. When she stepped forward and away from him, he wished she wouldn't have.

This was not good. This was certainly not how a person was supposed to feel about his sister. But she wasn't his sister at all. Henry didn't really know what to do with this unreasonable, misunderstood craziness.

Better to act as if nothing had changed. It hadn't; not really.

Katie laughed, a high, tinkling sound that carried across the pond. "Look at that. Barely away from the bank."

"It's okay, for the first try," Henry said gruffly.

They stayed by the pond till the sky turned from pink and lavender streaks to a night sky. Bullfrogs chugged from their hidden alcoves among the rushes, the nighttime insect choir began in earnest. Both of them caught bluegills and sunfish, put them in on a stringer, and hung it from a tree root.

They sat side by side, Lucky on Henry's side. They didn't know they were reluctant to return home, but they were. It was so peaceful, so filled with sounds of the pond, the water lapping gently between the thick rushes.

"Should we go back?" Katie asked.

"Guess so."

They gathered up the stringer of fish, the bait can, and walked slowly along the cow path that led to the farm, the barn and house merely a silhouette with tiny white stars pricking through the darkening sky. There was a kinship between them now, the love of fishing, the mutual understanding that they both had something to look forward to.

Rachel was delighted with the fish. She told Henry to clean them, and she'd roll them in flour and fry them in lard. They'd have a bedtime snack.

Katie wanted to learn how to filet the fish, so with Anna following after them, Henry washed, gutted, beheaded, and cut the thin filets from the sides.

Anna stuck her nose in the air like a hound dog ready to howl at the moon, saying fish smelled worse than cow patties, then left them to finish the job by lantern light.

Henry laughed and asked Katie if she thought these fish smelled bad.

She looked at Henry's dark brown eyes in the yellow glow of the lantern and said, of course not.

Henry smiled at her, and she smiled back at him, and he felt as if some of the ache of missing Harvey had been erased by a soft, kind eraser. Not all of it, he hadn't planned on going through life without it, of course, but it was as if the part that hurt the most had somehow been erased.

Chapter Six

THAT WAS THE BEGINNING.

It was the start of something new. It brought a light into Henry's life that made his world different, thinking of quiet Katie as a companion for both himself and Lucky.

Lucky was getting old now. There were white hairs on his chest and below his jaw, and he no longer bounced on his front legs with his backside in the air. He walked steadily, in places where he used to run. He no longer catapulted himself into the pond from a perfect standstill, either. He still accompanied Henry everywhere he went. Henry still put both arms around the big shaggy dog's neck, laid his head on his back, and cried when missing Harvey became as heavy as a stone in his chest. No one else understood. No one else sat quietly and knew what he was feeling except Lucky.

The change was not about the dog, his faithful friend. It was the glimpse of a life where there was the reality of something greater than missing Harvey. It was even different than knowing about God.

When Henry had times in his life when the pain became unbearable, he had often felt a caring, like a soft whoosh of breath. At night, alone in the double bed, when he remembered that Harvey would never come back, he shuddered with sobs that came from deep within the stone of pain, smashing his resolve into a thousand pieces.

Usually, when those times came, it was followed by the absolute knowing, the recognizing of God's love and His caring about the missing of Harvey. Sometimes, Henry thought the comfort might be angels, *die engel*, he heard about in church, the angels Ephraim talked about in his evening prayer. He believed in angels. He believed they watched over him, and that they were sent by God. His faith had no beginning and no end. He could never tell where it started. He just knew that he had always been aware of heavenly beings.

These angels had certainly been there when he and Harvey walked side by side down the road to spend the rest of their lives with Ephraim and Rachel.

Harvey had argued with him, when he mentioned this. It was funny about Katie, the way he never noticed her much. Malinda was there, loud and bossy, someone to be reckoned with, and Anna was the playful one, who spent more time with the twins than anyone else. Katie never said much.

Harvey said once that she was someone who was afraid of her own shadow.

Not now she wasn't.

She was a good fisher person.

Till autumn's cool breath chased away summer's stifling heat, she had acquired the art of perfect casting. That was when they became competitive, battling to the finish to see who could catch the most, the biggest, the best.

Henry admired her. His admiration changed to awe when she used cheese on her hook and landed the largest, fattest small-mouth bass Henry had ever seen.

He laughed at her for putting cheese on her hook.

"You wait, Henry Esh," she said. "You wait. Fish have a keen sense of smell, you know."

That fat bass measured twenty-one inches and was full of clumps of roe. Katie fought the fish as it leaped and dived, giving the line just enough slack to let the great fish wear itself out fighting that hook. When her arms became tired with the effort, Henry offered to take over, but she set her jaw, shook her head, and fought on.

Henry cheered, yelling from the stump he stood on, calling directions, which she mostly ignored. Finally, she told him to get down off that stump and quit yelling, so Henry did, but only because she wanted him to.

They caught so many fish, Rachel had to put them on ice in the icebox. They had fish for dinner, fish for supper. They ate fish soup and broiled fish with potatoes and parsley.

Finally, Rachel threw up her hands and asked them to take the heavy stringer full of fish to Henry's parents. They would appreciate a fine meal of fish, she said. Henry looked at Katie, doubt clouding his brown eyes.

The times he had returned to his home were often awkward. It was like being told to turn left and you knew you'd gone right, but it was too late to fix the situation, so you just kept going, blindly, dumbly, as if you could never quite grasp the reason. Like chasing a ball of dandelion seeds that poofed into nothing before you knew it.

It always left Henry feeling inadequate, empty, wrapped in a veil of thin, gauzy guilt that trapped him. He didn't want Katie to see his own family. He told her to stay, he'd go.

"I want to go," she said.

"I don't want you to."

"Why not?"

"Oh, just . . . I don't know."

"C'mon, Henry."

"All right. But, well . . . You see, Katie, I'm ashamed they're my family. They are so terrible poor."

"It doesn't matter."

He looked down at her, allowed himself the pleasure of meeting all those yellow and gold lights that danced in her green eyes.

"Thanks, Katie."

"You're welcome."

He smiled at her, a smile that appeared infrequently. A smile that changed those sad brown eyes for only an instant.

They took the wagon, laid a burlap bag on the bed, then put the fish along the center.

Henry pulled the wagon, with Katie at his side, Lucky walking ahead, the great paws moving in a steady rhythm.

It was a brisk, chilly evening, with the gold of maple leaves setting off the burnt orange of the pin oaks, and the bright October sky showing signs of an overcast tomorrow. Instead of a red sunset, there was a line of gray clouds rising in the west.

"Rain coming," Henry observed.

Katie looked up, nodded.

"Want me to pull awhile?"

"No."

"Tell me, Henry, how does it make you feel when you go home? Don't you wish they would have kept you?"

"I don't know." Henry shrugged his shoulders. "It's hard to explain. I . . . ah, I don't know."

"Tell me, Henry, I'll just listen."

"Nothing."

"Oh, c'mon."

"It's just hard to imagine having been raised there. If I think on it too much, it doesn't get me anywhere. My life is what it is now, so I'll go forward. I mean, I feel like I should love my family, but I hardly know them. I remember feeling ashamed of their . . . their being so poor, in school, in church. And a guilty feeling, I guess, that we have more."

"But you shouldn't be guilty. They gave you away. It wasn't that you asked to go."

"You're right, I guess."

"You haven't had an easy life, Henry."

Henry had nothing to say to this. He looked at Katie, and she looked at him. They said nothing.

The driveway was pocked with puddles, icelike pieces of organdy along the edges. Brown weeds hung over the fence like forgotten slivers of summer's growth, the boards loosened and sagging from post to post. Skinny mules with sides like washboards, their large heads too long and bony to support their monstrous ears, eyed them without interest, the only movement an occasional flap of their lower lip. A few razor-thin barn cats skittered ahead of them, their thin tails held aloft like handles. The deep baying of a coon hound erupted, shattering the crisp, evening air.

Lucky stopped, his ears pressed forward.

"S'all right, Lucky."

Henry's hand spread out on the dog's massive head. Katie moved closer to Henry, placed her hand beside his on the handle of the wagon.

Loose barn doors creaked on the evening breeze. The yard gate squeaked as they pushed it open and made their way up the dirt path to the door. Henry waited, collecting himself, breathing lightly to avoid the smell of sour milk and cow manure that clung to the row of rubber Tingly boots strewn across the porch. The screen door had only one corner of the screen intact, the rest of it hung loose, flapping in the breeze.

When Henry knocked, there was a scuffling from inside before Rueben Esh came to the door, pulling it open slowly, then peering around it, taking a considerable amount of time to say hello, as if he couldn't remember who this tall young man was.

"Oh, it's Henry," he said slowly.

"Hello, Dat."

"Come in."

Together, they stepped inside, with the string of fish held up for everyone to see. Children of various ages, dressed in the same shade of faded cotton, grouped quietly, without uttering any opinion or exclamation. Mattie came from the bedroom, paused, threw her hands up.

"Why, Henry! A surprise that you came by. Who caught all the fish?"

"We did. Me and Katie."

Mattie's eyes narrowed as she looked the young girl up and down, taking in the large eyes, the clean, gleaming hair, the heart-shaped face, the dress made out of *Ordnung*. Too short. Here was a girl who was not for Henry. What were those Ephraim Stoltzfus' thinking, allowing their daughter to traipse around the roads in broad daylight? They were no longer children.

What if Bishop David came along in his buggy and saw them pulling that wagon?

So she frowned, took the fish off the stringer without speaking. Rueben asked Henry about his health, if Ephraim had the corn fodder all in, if the cows were milking good, which Henry answered in polite sentences.

Mattie turned from the sink with the empty stringer, appraised Katie with a knowing look, and without preamble, inquired about her age.

Katie too answered politely.

Well, thought Mattie, she'll be with the *rumschpringa* soon enough, Henry won't have a chance. After this thought entered her head, her smile returned to her face, and she became friendly, keeping up a volley of questions Henry answered dutifully.

When Henry left, Mattie had a spring in her step. Yes, Henry was a handsome young man, well spoken, and well raised. He had nothing to do with Rueben's lack of interest in work or getting ahead. He would amount to something. And the way he bent his straw hat. Down in front and back, so neat, and such a frame for that square jaw and brown eyes. His voice had changed, lowered, to a manly growl.

Yes, Mattie was glad he had been raised by Ephraim and Rachel. He had learned Ephraim's ways of farming, to get up at 4:30 in the morning and finish all the chores before breakfast, the way her own father taught them. And still she loved her Rueben, tuned in to his lack of ambition and accepted him for what he was, creating an aura of peace and honor in the children as well.

But things were tucked away in the recesses of her heart. Thoughts about life, things no one else would ever know. It kept the days bearable, providing joy in the midst of the life-straining poverty.

Henry and Katie walked quietly, pulling the empty wagon, their hands side by side on the handle, Lucky walking close to Henry, a hand resting on his back.

"They seem nice to you, Henry," Katie observed.

"They are."

Henry had seen the narrow appraisal of Katie and the light of pride in Mattie's eyes. She was a true mother, in a sense, and he hoped someday, after he was married, with children of his own, he could visit more often and become a part of her life. But he said nothing to Katie.

"Henry, I'll be joining the *youngie* in the spring."

"I know."

"Before you know it, I'll be married, and then who will fish with you?"

"Anna?"

"Anna! Don't you know how she hates to fish?"

"No."

"She would never bait a hook or pull off a fish."

"Well, then, perhaps I'll just go back to me and Lucky."

"Would you rather?"

Henry considered her question. They both felt the bump and tug as Lucky leaped silently onto the wagon, and sat proudly, his mouth wide, laughing at them.

"Lucky!"

Henry burst out laughing, then let Katie hold the wagon handle while he went to throw his arms around his pet.

"You're tired, Lucky, you old white-haired dog," he laughed. Katie laughed with him.

"He's smart."

"He sure is. All right, Lucky, we'll pull you on home."

"You didn't answer my question," Katie said.

"What?"

"Would you rather go fishing without me?"

"No. Of course not."

"Do you enjoy when I go fishing with you?"

"That's a dumb question. Of course I do."

Katie smiled.

"I guess that means we're fishing buddies."

"It does."

In companionable silence, they turned in the long driveway to the farm, set against the backdrop of brilliant fall foliage and brown squares of land, green squares of fall-seeded rye like a patchwork quilt, the white buildings cast in a golden glow of sunset. The black-and-white Holsteins munched the pasture grass contentedly, the Belgians hung their massive heads over the top rail of the board fence, the white-painted fence that never had a loose nail or a broken board. The barn roof had just been given a fresh coat of silver paint, the garden was cleaned and seeded with rye grass and a good cover of manure. Firewood was stacked as high as a man's head in the woodshed, the cellar was full of fruits and vegetables in gleaming mason jars, the potato bin overflowing with large brown potatoes covered with the fine dust, all that remained of the fertile soil that had been their home all summer long.

Henry felt the blessing. It seeped into a part of his heart and stayed there. He turned to Katie.

"When you're with the *youngie*, will you no longer go fishing?"

"I don't know. Do people change so much after they are *rumschpringa* that they no longer do the things they did growing up, like fishing and sledding?"

Henry shrugged. "I guess that would be up to each person."

"Right. Well, we'll see how it goes."

Lucky leaped off the wagon, jerking the handle.

"Lucky! You just decide yourself when it's time to get off," Katie said, laughing.

"He does what he wants. He's my best friend."

"Better than me?" Katie inquired.

"Lucky was there for me through . . . through all of it."

"And I wasn't?"

"No, not really. I hardly knew you. You were just one of the girls. Malinda, Katie, Anna. All the same to me."

"Now I'm not all the same?"

"Well, no, not really. I mean, we fish and talk. A lot, actually."

"So I'm a special friend? Like Lucky?"

"Yes."

"Good."

"But that will change in the spring when you turn sixteen."

"Why does it have to?"

"You'll be, well, asked."

"Asked?"

"You know what I mean."

"It doesn't matter if I'm asked, if I don't like the person who's asking."

"That's true."

They stood by the yard gate, the sun sliding behind the horizon, casting them in the deepening twilight. A hawk soared close above the treetops, sounding its loud screech, sending a volley of frightened house sparrows spraying through the yellowing leaves like gunshot.

Ephraim came walking up to them, his shoulders hunched, hands in his pockets, the way he walked when he was tired. How well Henry knew him, this adopted father. And loved him. Yes, he did love him. Always glad to see him in the morning, grinning at him as he sat on his milking stool, with his wide smile, saying "*Guta mya*." Anger was rare, and if he was seen in a display of displeasure, it was not the fearful kind, where your mouth turned dry and your heart went galloping in your chest.

Henry thought often on the salt of the earth. He believed Ephraim was a very large jar of salt of the earth, the real kind, the kind that was sprinkled all over the farm, flavoring life for his wife and children, his animals and fields, all his neighbors, English and Mennonite and Amish, plus every person in the church. Ephraim had a flavorful attitude toward his neighbor, anyone he came to know. His friends multiplied each year, his easy chuckle and conversation like a magnet to the milkman, the feed man, the fertilizer salesman. Henry absorbed all these things as he lived among the good attitude, the benevolence with which Ephraim lived his life.

Two Christmases came and went. Two years of absorbing Ephraim and Rachel's ways, learning about the good management of the farm, what made the cows produce record amounts of milk, which lime or fertilizer was needed and when to apply it.

Nothing was wasted, nothing squandered for pleasure. And yet, his adoptive parents were not stingy, always generous with the children's needs, remembering birthdays with a homemade cake and presents wrapped in paper.

Henry turned seventeen, became a member of the Amish church through a summer of instruction classes and baptism. He had no earth-shaking experience, no testimony about the new birth, and no idea how he would go about describing it. But it was there.

God had always been there.

He had always believed that when Jesus died on the cross, He rose out of the grave, defied the power of death and hell, so now this grace was sufficient for him. It had taken Harvey to Heaven, and someday, when God chose, Henry would join him there.

Heaven, angels, God, Jesus, the Holy Ghost, all of it was very real to Henry, and he just always figured that on account of Harvey's drowning, a part of him already was in Heaven.

When he turned sixteen years of age and began his *rumschpringa*, he was tempted same as everyone else—the wild girls and the drinking of alcoholic beverages and cigarette smoking. It was enticing, exciting, forbidden fruit that he did not always resist.

But it held no real thrill. It was an illusion of happiness. It left him empty and ashamed of himself. Heaven and God moved away during that time. Later, he knew it wasn't that God went anywhere. God stayed the same. It was Henry who moved away, drawn by the beckoning finger of cheap thrills and hidden sins.

Katie began to date a young man from New Holland, Benuel Fisher, who was a lot older. Henry thought he might be twenty-three years old.

Henry didn't want Katie to be dating Benuel, but hardly knew what to do about it. He was just a young *schpritza* and not even half good enough for her. Malinda was married now, and Anna turned sixteen that winter, so Henry never considered himself good enough for any of them. Not that he considered Malinda.

She was still as bossy and overbearing as ever. She had better count herself lucky to have a husband at all, the poor string bean Davey King, tall and skinny and obedient. Henry figured the marriage would go well; he would obey while she led.

He felt regret, though, about Katie. He believed he loved her when she was fifteen, the way he loved looking into her eyes. But he was younger, only fourteen years old, and when she was with the *youngie*, she was always being asked for a date with Elam or Abner or Rueben or Enos.

So Henry gave up.

He actually asked God to give him Katie, at first, but that didn't happen. So he swallowed his misery and tried to become interested in Rhoda, but she was too vain and made him feel like a schoolboy who kept repeating the wrong answers to a disapproving teacher.

Through these years, Henry still had Lucky. Old and grizzled now, stiff in every joint, half-blind and arthritic, he still followed Henry around the farm. He still rose from his bed in the forebay of the barn, stretched, his mouth wide in the dog smile, then walked painfully to greet Henry, who always fell on his knees to caress and murmur, to stroke and love his beloved friend.

Chapter Seven

THE SNOWS CAME EARLY AT CHRISTMAS IN 1940. A foot of it fell the day before, followed by a stiff wind that sent billows of it rolling across fields and roads of Lancaster County. The cold deepened, buoyed by Arctic air that came down from Canada, riding on the wind.

Henry was twenty-one now, the age when he was a man. He kept his own wages and decided his course through life. Tall, with the same wavy brown hair and sad brown eyes, he received a good pay from Ephraim now, who counted Henry as a hired hand, worthy of a steady wage each month.

Henry was at an important crossroad in his life. He felt the need for a lifelong companion, a good wife at his side as he began his own life of farming. He simply didn't know who to ask.

Katie had married Benuel Fisher in 1937, when Henry was almost nineteen. He had been in the bridal party in the honored tradition of *nava-sitza*,

trying hard to congratulate the couple. Pushing back
thoughts of being seated across the corner table with
Katie as his rightful wife, he watched her glowing
face as she went through her wedding day dressed in
navy blue with a crisp white organdy cape and apron
pinned to her small waist.

He didn't sleep much the night after the wedding.
He thought of Christ in Gethsemane and knew He
suffered unbelievably; so this was only a blip, a minor
thing.

Till it wasn't.

Waves of longing, memories of the sun shining on
her face, her eyes flashing green and gold lights, her
perfect mouth wide as she laughed, landing a large-
mouth bass yet again. Katie at the wash line, singing
her silly songs. Katie scrubbing the kitchen floor, sitting up, yelling at him to get off that wet floor. Katie
permeated his thoughts like a heady scent of lavender
or roses, lived in every waking hour.

It was in 1940 when he came out to the barn to find
Lucky stiff and cold, lying in his doghouse, on a fresh
bed of straw. Henry had spread it with care, extra

thick, knowing Lucky's joints ached, especially in winter, when the cold crept around the building and seeped into every available crevice.

Outside, the wind roared, smacked against the barn windows like a giant hand, sending a blinding wall of snow across the barnyard. Tears blinded his vision as he drew Lucky from his doghouse and stroked the great, cold head one last time.

Ach, Lucky. Lucky.

Two losses, now. Harvey and Lucky.

And yes, Katie.

Today at the Christmas dinner, there would be Katie.

He watched the numbing snow, the bending of the bare, black branches of the maple tree, whipping back and forth in the grip of the frenzied wind.

He looked down at Lucky.

He had so much with this big, shaggy dog. A real companion. A faithful friend who absorbed all his childhood sorrows and gave back all the love and support he needed. But now he had gone the way of all animals, all humans. Eventually, life came to an end for every living creature on the face of the earth.

The incredible part was that God knew everything, even the fall of a sparrow, and now, of Lucky.

God had stilled the stout heart. It was time for Lucky to go, leaving Henry with an endless stream of warm memories that became a part of who he was.

Another dog?

Not for now.

Ephraim came to see Henry bent over the form of his dog. He clapped a sympathetic hand on his shoulder and said, "Poor old dog." He left Henry to grieve.

They debated the wisdom of setting off for the Beiler Christmas dinner that day, Rachel saying rather than risk a life, they were best off at home. Ephraim took note of the edge of seriousness in his intuitive wife and agreed. They said it was up to Henry if he wanted to attempt the trip, but in these conditions, they may become stranded.

So he agreed, beset the way he was by a sense of melancholy. He laid Lucky on a canvas tarp and dragged him to the implement shed and buried him beneath the wagon, where there was no snow.

It was hard work, but it buoyed his flagging spirits. Outside, the wind increased as the day wore on, turning eastern Pennsylvania and parts of Maryland and Virginia into a howling maelstrom of wind, snow, and ice.

They did not receive the news till Monday morning, the roads impassable by the strength of the blizzard. A snowplow hit Benuel and Katie on their way home from the Christmas dinner, killing the horse and Benuel, hitting the left side of the buggy as they made a right-hand turn, a wall of blowing snow evidently blinding Benuel as he turned.

Katie and the baby were in critical condition in Lancaster at the hospital.

Henry received the news with only a slight lowering of his eyelids, his jaw clenched, square and hard. Muscles in his cheek worked as he tried to contain the news that roared in his head.

How critical?

She would die with her husband.

The baby. What was his name? John. Jonathan. Yoni.

He couldn't think.

Turning, he made his way upstairs, blindly sought the door of his room, sat on the edge of his bed, shook like an oak leaf in a summer storm. His teeth rattled in his mouth. His hand went up to still the trembling. He felt as if he was in the grip of a gigantic beast that needed to devour him, finish him off, fling him aside like a torn rag doll with no life, no flesh and blood.

What was this?

Did God forget mercy where Henry was concerned? What was God's will? How could he know?

He stayed, the edge of his bed holding him up. He shivered and became numb with the cold of the unheated upstairs of the farmhouse.

Ephraim and Rachel left, he could hear them following the town police to their car. Anna was left alone.

Better go down to her, poor thing.

He gathered himself to go downstairs, to find Anna curled on the old davenport in the kitchen, weeping softly. He stood close to the distraught young woman, feeling clumsy, ill at ease, and he didn't know what to do with his hands.

"Are you all right, Anna?" he croaked hoarsely.

She sat up.

He saw the need for a handkerchief and provided it.

She looked at him, said, *Denke*.

He sat down on the opposite side of the couch and stared at his white-stockinged feet. He didn't know what to say.

Finally, when the loud ticking of the clock became unbearable, he rose, checked the fire in the kitchen range, went to the *kesslehaus* for small pieces of wood, stoked the red embers until a flame arose, then replaced the lid. He stood at the kitchen sink, gripped the edges until his knuckles turned white, watching the wind's half-hearted attempt at blowing the edges of the crested snowdrifts. The sun was brilliant, casting blue swirls of color in the pristine landscape, where the hollows created shadows. Pine trees swayed in triumph, waving green banners of bare branches the wind had freed from their load of snow.

Grace and mercy, grace and mercy, tumbled through his mind. Spare Katie, dear God. You know I have loved her. Have always loved her. I love her still.

And now, if she lived, he would have another chance. But he should absolutely not think this thought. Selfish. Unholy. Profane.

Forgive me.

He felt Anna's presence, a cooling shadow to his fevered thoughts. She placed a hand on his arm, where the long sleeves were rolled up, halfway on his thick forearms. Her fingers were small, white, and tapered, as soft as a snow bunting on a winter snowdrift.

"Could you just hold me for a minute?" she whispered.

Henry started. He looked down at her. Yes, down. She was so tiny, so blonde.

"You mean . . . ?"

Henry had never held a girl in his arms. When other young men had taken the "wild" girls for a fling, he had always held back.

For an answer, she stepped close, put her small arms around his waist, laid her head on his chest, and wept softly, a womanly sound of grief that was unbearable.

Henry couldn't hear it.

He folded his strong, young arms around this slight girl and held her. Strong emotion welled up, feelings he could not decipher. He wanted to keep Anna there, where she was, till the end of time.

Mentally, he shook himself. He was distraught, that was all. Anna was nothing to him, and never would be. It was Katie he loved.

Too soon, she sighed, stepped back, her head bent.

"I'm sorry," she whispered.

"Don't be. It's all right."

Almost, he pulled her close, but she looked up. Her eyes were red from weeping, but they were very blue, the blinding light of the sun on the snow revealing silver lights like music notes of feeling in their depths.

Henry was shaken, unable to tear his own eyes from hers. His hands hung clumsily at his sides, the world spun sideways, then righted itself. He heard the clock's loud ticking, winced when it slammed out the hour in its tinny crescendo.

He swallowed, slowed his breathing.

"I'm sorry about Lucky," she said, soft and low.

Henry could only nod and watch her face. Skin like a porcelain doll, a nose so perfect, and full lips.

He tore himself away, shrugged into his coat, slapped his hat on his head, and went to the barn, fast, without looking back. He had a childish longing to turn around, to see if she stood at the window now, watching him. He wanted to wave, smile, shout, and skip the rest of the way to the barn.

He fed horses, swept the aisles, fed the heifers without ridding himself of her.

Anna!

Little Anna. He had never thought of her, much less noticed her. She never said anything. Not to him, hardly ever.

He reasoned himself into sensible plateaus, high places of rationality he could view from a firm footing, alone in the barn. Lucky dead, which had served to weaken his resolve, his best ability to stay strong. The tragic news, his thoughts running ahead of God's ways.

Anna meant nothing. She was only seeking comfort. She had not tried to convey anything other than that. It was all his runaway emotion at a time when defenses were down.

Ephraim and Rachel returned late that night, after Henry and Anna had done chores together, awkwardly, silently, giving each other a wide berth.

Katie entered into her rest less than a week later, the baby the only survivor.

Little Yonie, not yet a year old.

It was a time of darkness for Henry, a time when he moved through the valley of the shadow of death in the truest sense of the verse. He could not regain his footing, no matter how valiantly he struggled. Anger, questions, frustrations, the inability to accept her death, raged within him like a storm, obscuring the way, hurling him into an outer darkness that felt as he imagined hell to be.

He lost weight, his face grew pale, with ever increasing circles darkening beneath his eyes.

He didn't have Lucky.

Ephraim scoured the countryside for a Newfoundland. Would have paid an exorbitant price.

Rachel cooked his favorite dishes. Anna returned to her former shadowy self.

They took in the baby Yonie, of course. Their son, their grandson, whose roly-poly little body had the power to erase the worst of their grief. A happy baby, chortling over the wonders of a spool of thread or a wooden block.

Spring came early.

The earth exploded with color and scent, as wild strawberry blooms, purple violets, and buttered yellow dandelions pranced onstage, showing their ability to cheer even the most downhearted. Bluebirds appeared on fenceposts, trilling their beautiful song, woodpeckers pounded the trunks of trees like accompanying drums.

Life resumed its normality. Henry plowed the north lot, turning over the rich black soil like a row of giant worms, then bounced over them with the disc and the harrow, the squeaking of leather harness in tune with the thumping of the steel teeth that tore into the soil.

He thought he saw a coyote, at first. No, he decided, a fox. Too big for either one. The low, bent hindquarters. Triangles for ears.

A German shepherd.

He stopped the team. Crouched down and snapped his fingers, calling to the dog.

That was the wrong thing. The dog planted his feet firmly, his ears like two large triangles, head up, then took off in one leap sideways, ran low and hard until he disappeared into the pine woods.

Henry shook his head, stayed on the plow, and resumed the day's work.

The sun shone overhead, the spring warmth like a comforting blanket after winter's harsh exposure. Everywhere he looked, there were marvels of creation, myriad birdsong, flocks of geese in their perfect form, honking their raucous spring cry on their way to build nests in the bulrushes by the edge of the pond.

The geese's cry was only another reminder of Katie, the way the sun caught the highlights in her hair, the way it turned her tanned face into a golden glow, her eyes alight as she expertly landed yet another fish.

Why hadn't he asked her? What had held him back, if he knew she was the one love of his life?

Cowardice. Plain old shrinking away of his own audacity to imagine she would ever come to love him.

For who was he?

A remaining twin, given away like an extra kitten, from a family wallowing in poverty. Skinny old Rueben Esh. Never amounted to a hill of beans.

That, he had overheard at an auction.

So now, would he ever amount to more?

Or would he, unknowing, become his father?

He was unworthy, still, and had been back when his love for Katie resided like a burr in his heart, uncomfortable, prickly, but unable to be removed. Thoughts were burdensome, heavy things that sat in your head with a dead weight if you allowed them to do that. Better to think thoughts of spring, the warm air, the sunshine, although, it too brought a deep longing, a cry from within, almost a painful reaching for some mysterious thing he could not name.

A bittersweet wanting, as if the past and the future were all wrapped up in one unknowable yearning.

One thing was sure: the heart must always long for God, first and foremost. One of his favorite verses in the Bible was the one about not leaning to your own understanding, but sincerely ask to be shown Thy way, direct my path.

Henry bowed his head.

Tears coursed down his face as he cried out silently, groaning from the depth of his soul, asking God to do just that.

Direct my path, show me Thy ways, O Lord.

The horses were sweating now, the white foam appearing wherever the harnesses rubbed against their bodies. Their noble heads kept bobbing, their thick muscular necks straining against their collars, and still they kept going.

Time for a break.

Henry pulled on the reins, shouted, "Whoa, whoa there, Bob," to the lead horse.

Heads lowered gratefully, strong necks distended, stretched. Nostrils dilated, their breath coming in strong puffs, their sides heaving. They rested, their faithful doelike eyes watching Henry as he flopped on his back, threw an arm across his eyes, relaxed in the fresh spring grass that grew abundantly along the edge of the field.

Every day the dog appeared, watching Henry with frightened eyes. Every day, Henry tried to befriend him, but each time, the dog leaped, panicked, and ran.

He told Ephraim about the dog, at the supper table. Ephraim shook his head, swallowed, raised a forefinger and shook it in Henry's direction.

"German shepherds aren't to be trusted."

"Especially strays," Rachel chimed in.

Anna said nothing, as usual, her head bent slightly as she buttered a homemade dinner roll.

"I can't get him to come to me, so nothing to worry about," Henry said, laughing.

"I could," Anna said, unexpectedly.

Henry looked at her, raised his eyebrows.

"How would you do that?"

She smiled. "I won't say."

Her parents watched their quiet, youngest daughter. At nineteen years of age, she showed no interest in dating, never related any of her weekend activities to her mother, went about her life in so much silence, so much solitude, that Rachel often worried.

Was there something wrong with her?

Rachel was well aware of the two grown children at the dinner table not being blood relatives at all, but as far as she could tell, they were brother and sister in the truest sense of the word. They simply lived in the same house, worked in the same fields and in the barn, barely speaking to each other.

So when Anna showed an interest in the dog, everyone was surprised, but, wisely, made no fuss.

Henry looked at her.

"Well then, if you won't say, maybe I'd better watch, so I can learn something."

"No, I don't want you to be there."

Henry nodded, raised his eyebrows, then bent to his second helping of mashed potatoes and beef gravy.

Anna ate her buttered dinner roll, and nothing more was said.

Henry forgot about Anna's words, having finished the plowing of that particular field, and starting another on the south end of the farm, closer to the pond.

The day was gray, lowering clouds bunched together as if they were conferring when to let loose the downpour that was sure to come. The air was chilly with a penetrating dampness that found its way through Henry's light denim coat.

There was movement to his left. Instantly he thought of the dog.

There.

Black, dark colors.

To his amazement, he saw first Anna, dressed in a dark scarf and black coat, her navy-blue dress mostly covered by the black apron.

Henry leaned back on the reins. "Whoa, whoa!"

By her side walked the German shepherd.

"Anna!" Henry shouted.

She put a finger to her lips. "Shhh!"

Henry remained on the plow as they approached. The dog stopped, his eyes intently rooted on Henry's face. Anna's hand went to his head, her fingers spread in much the same way Henry had always cupped the skull of the massive Lucky.

"He doesn't trust you," Anna said, her voice low and even.

Henry got off the plow, but stayed where he was. "I can see that," he said.

It seemed like long moments, when nothing was said, the dog refusing to sit, standing alert, eyeing Henry with brown eyes, large and unfriendly. The heavy tail did not wave. Yet there was Anna, waiting without fear.

Henry watched the dog's face, the way his legs remained stiff, ready to spring.

"He doesn't like me," he said, finally.

Anna nodded.

"I think he's been mistreated, probably by a man. So I suggest we walk with him, on a leash. I'll take him back to the barn, to Luck . . . the . . . doghouse, then later, when chores are finished, we'll win you over."

That was a long speech from the quiet, unassuming Anna.

Henry watched the dog.

He was a fine specimen. A good bloodline, evidently. He was, in fact, beautiful, for a German shepherd breed. The coarse hair on the back of his neck stood up. A low rumbling came from his throat. But he stood at attention, with Anna's hand on his head.

Henry realized his holding back, the reservation with which he assessed this dog. It wasn't Lucky.

The eyes were too big, protruding from his head, not small and triangular and almost buried in thick, silky, black hair. His mouth wasn't laughing, and his skin did not roll around on his enormous frame when he walked so that he seemed to frolic.

This was simply the wrong dog.

Anna saw the struggle on Henry's face.

That was all right.

She was the wrong girl too. She knew this. Always had. She turned and walked away, without a sound.

Henry went back to his plowing with a sense of defeat. What was up with Anna, anyway?

When Katie died, he had been shaken to the core with the possibility of having loved the wrong girl. Anna meant more to him than he ever thought possible.

But now, everything he'd dreamed of had died out, like an untended fire. He shrugged, lifted his face to the sky as the first raindrops began to fall, turned the team, and made his way home.

Chapter Eight

HENRY WATCHED ANNA WITH THE DOG, watched her walk him on a leash, throw balls and sticks, watched him unleash ferocious power, gathering his hind legs under his body like a panther, his bright eyes watching every single move she made, till the ball or the stick was flung into the air in a wide arc, and he was off.

Tremendous power and speed. Agile as all get out. Henry sometimes shook his head in wonder.

But still Anna did not invite him to join. By all accounts, the dog was hers alone.

Henry went fishing by himself.

He often looked back over his shoulder, looking for Anna and the dog. He still thought she might want to join him someday, learn the art of casting the way Katie had. All through spring and now into summer, he had no reason to believe he even existed, as far as Anna was concerned.

She named the dog Colonel, pronounced like a kernel of corn, a hated word that had the upper-grade boys snickering when he pronounced it the way it was spelled.

But he had to admit it was an impressive name, given to an impressive dog. He was beautiful now, under Anna's care. She sneaked an egg from the hen-house; Henry had seen her do it.

Colonel was filled out, his coat sleek.

Henry felt pangs of unwanted jealousy.

But still she didn't invite him.

The whole thing was frustrating. She had told him that day on the plow that *they*, not just her, would walk him on a leash. And yet, he had never been asked to accompany her.

Last night on the porch swing, Anna sat on one corner, so small she hardly took up a fourth of the swing. She was wearing a pale blue dress, the color of the evening sky, and no apron, the heat hanging over the countryside till late.

She was reading, never looking up at his approach. He asked if he could sit. She barely took her eyes from the book, nodding in an absent way.

He sat on the opposite end of the swing, looking out over the yard and the garden, watching the shadows creep up behind the implement shed, the fireflies blinking their tiny yellow lights as darkness approached.

All was quiet from the reader.

Henry glanced her way a few times, but she was so absorbed in her book, he didn't want to disturb that concentration, the way her eyebrows were drawn down by the intensity on her face.

He breathed deeply.

She smelled like soap and flowers and the dew in the morning. Her hair was like corn silk, but shinier.

He didn't know what to do about either one, so he sighed again. He realized if he wanted to get to know this girl, he'd have to do what came so hard for him. Make advances, take the lead, talk to her, ask questions. With Katie, she had done all that. Until she hadn't. The thing was, he was woefully inept. Everything he said came out wrong, his words tumbling into the air like half-dead flies that were annoying and all you wanted to do was swat them away.

He blurted out, "Where's Colonel?"

"In his bed." And back to the book.

"What are you reading?"

No answer. Was that a blush that crept up over her cheek? Clearly flustered, she blinked furiously.

"Nothing."

Henry watched her, sized up the profile. Her nose. That nose was so small and flat, she hardly had one. What would happen if he told her that?

All summer long, she had been a kind of torment; he realized that now. All he wanted to do was look at her, to get her attention somehow. Nothing worked.

He wanted to snatch the book, slam it to the swing, grab her by the shoulders and make her look at him, to really look into his eyes and notice that he was there.

But what he did was get to his feet, wish her a good night, waiting for her answer the whole way across the porch and through the kitchen door.

Now here he was, fishing half-heartedly, watching the field lane for any sign of her. He knew it was futile, but still he watched.

Finally, he gave up, took the last bluegill off the hook, flipped it back into the pond, and watched it swim away into the deep blue-green depth, wishing he could free himself from his attachment to Anna. Hooked. He was hooked. He grinned wryly, bent to close his tackle box, picked it up with one hand, threw the rod over his shoulder, and walked away from the pond.

Verdant growth was all around him. Summer rains and blazing sun had produced heavy, dark-green stalks of corn, a veritable forest of it, growing ten feet tall, already pushing large yellow ears. The alfalfa was a vast rippling sea of short, round-leafed grasses, with a hint of lavender blooms.

Third cutting would be necessary soon, but already the bays were full on each side of the barn. Walnut trees sprouted the cluster of young walnuts forming along their branches; the chestnuts would produce clumps of burrs, the prickly outer coverings that housed the fragrant chestnut. Pumpkin vines were hip high, small lime-green pumpkins already forming beneath them.

God was blessing Lancaster County's rich, brown soil for yet another summer. He was an amazing, benevolent father who so richly gave mankind all things to enjoy.

So, Henry thought, after all my prayers, there is always God's love, His presence surrounding me. His ways so far above my own that I can't even begin to decipher them. So I will trust, cast all my cares upon him, and lean not to my own understanding.

Perhaps Anna was not the one God intended for him. Perhaps he was meant to be alone on his journey of life on earth, only to be reunited with Harvey some glad day when his own walk of life was over.

Who could know?

There would always be unexpected twists and turns on life's pathway. The important thing was to meet each new bend in the road with faith and courage.

All these thoughts spun through his head like a stiff whirlwind, the kind that appeared out of thin air on a sultry summer day and displaced corn stalks or leaves or dust, anything in its path.

Courage he did not have. That was the only sure thing.

Deep in thought, he was jerked back to reality by a high keening sound, followed by a series of yelps that traveled up and down the scales from pain to terror and back again, a cadence that sent chills up Henry's spine.

He dropped his tackle box and fishing rod and took off running in the direction of the sound. He followed the field lane where it made a Y; to the left led to buildings on the farm; to the right led through a maze of corn and alfalfa, then to woods bordering the property.

As he neared the woods, he realized twilight had already fallen, so he would find the wooded area even darker.

The yelping ceased for a moment, then resumed. He followed the sound to the dark form of Colonel, who was down on his stomach, turning his head from side to side, trying to rid himself of the hateful quills embedded in his face. A porcupine! Poor Colonel had tangled with the dreaded creature that protected itself by loosening these barbed quills of misery into a prying dog's nose.

He dropped to his knees, talking all the while. The yelps faded to whimpers as Henry stroked the suffering dog's back.

Where was Anna?

Nowhere in the woods. So he'd have to get the dog back to the house for a pair of pliers, by the look of things.

Henry stood up. "C'mon. Come here, Colonel."

He snapped his fingers, wheedled, coaxed, and did everything he knew to get a dog to move, with no response.

Exasperated, Henry tried lifting him, but quickly set the dog back on the ground after the series of yelps started up again. Well, there was only one sensible thing to do, and that was to leave him and go get the pliers and Anna.

He found the tool he needed on the workbench in the shop, lit a lantern in the milk house, then went to the house for Anna, who had already gone upstairs.

He called her name.

She appeared on top of the stairs, her face registering nothing.

"Your dog tried to get acquainted with a porcupine. He's crying and setting up an awful howling in the woods. I need you to come with me."

"Be right down."

By the time he retrieved the lantern, she was there, her eyes on his face.

"What happened? I thought he was in bed."

"Evidently not."

"Where were you that you heard him?"

"Fishing."

She had to run to keep up with his long, swift strides, her skirt swishing about her legs, her bare feet flying across the grass of the field lane.

The lantern bobbed up and down.

They heard the dog's yelps before they found him. Anna fell to her knees, murmuring to herself or the dog, Henry couldn't be sure, then lifted her face to Henry.

"There's a whole bunch of them. What are we going to do? How do we get them out?"

"Pliers."

She put a hand over her mouth, wide-eyed, as Henry knelt, held the dog's face to the ground, clamped the pliers on one end of the long, hollow quill, and pulled.

Nothing.

Colonel must have known this was the only way to rid himself of the awful quills, so he stayed quiet;

only his eyes spoke of the agony surrounding his nose and face.

Henry attached the pliers again, and yanked. He was rewarded with a quill clenched firmly in the mouth of the pliers. Anna held the lantern, without speaking, while Henry worked in the damp heat of the woods, until every quill had been safely removed.

Colonel sprang up, then bent his forelegs to rub his face in the soft moss and moist earth on the forest floor.

He emitted all kinds of strange noises.

Anna laughed outright.

Henry laughed with her.

"Poor thing, he must have suffered terribly."

"He did, sure. Look at this." Henry picked up a quill to show her the barbed end that had been embedded in the dog's face. "A dog never makes the same mistake twice."

"I believe it. These quills are like fishhooks, really."

"Smaller hooks, but yes, they are. Is that why you don't go fishing?" Henry asked, looking down at her in the glow of the lantern.

"No." Anna pondered his question for a long while, then took the plunge. "I didn't learn to fish because you liked Katie."

Henry became very still.

He could hear the chirping of the robins calling their children to bed, the chirring of an excited squirrel, and knew this was the perfect chance. Like nature, like the ways of the woods and God's creatures, it was time.

So he said, "I did. I loved Katie, but she was not God's will for me. He took her away."

Henry stood openmouthed with surprise, watching Anna take off, like a bird in flight, her bare feet making no sound, distancing herself from Henry with every step, Colonel bounding by her side.

He clutched the lantern in one hand, the pliers in the other, and followed slowly, shaking his head.

Well, chalk one up for speaking at the wrong time, sticking my foot in my mouth, ruining everything once again. I don't talk at all, then when I do, it's out of time.

Ah, better to forget all of it. Women were something he would never understand. Better that he stay single. Didn't the Bible say it was better to stay single, for some? When a man married, he cared for and loved his wife, taking away that single-minded service to the Lord.

The minute he stepped into the forebay, all that rational, spiritual thinking went right out the door. There she sat, weeping softly, her dog's head in her lap, swabbing at the wounds with an antiseptic solution dissolved in a bowl of warm water.

Henry's heart was touched beyond any restraint.

He dropped to his knees, set the lantern to the side, and placed a hand on her small shoulder.

"Don't cry, Anna. He'll be all right."

Anna sniffed, but continued swabbing at the torn spots.

"He's suffering terribly," she whimpered.

"Not like he would be if we'd have left them in there."

"You're right. But isn't there an easier way to remove them?"

"I have a feeling the veterinarian would have done basically the same."

She looked up at him. The porcelain sheen of her skin with an underlying blush beneath her cheek made him take away his hand. It had a mind of its own, and he wanted to touch her cheek to see if it was real.

But of course, after that first bumble, never, never.

"Do you want me to stay here with you?"

"Oh, you need your sleep, Henry."

What was this?

She thought only of him, of his comfort, and agreed with his point of view about the dog. It all came as naturally as breathing. And this tender weeping?

"I'll stay here with you," Henry said, softly.

The only answer was the hiss of the lantern, an occasional rattle of the chains attached to the Belgian's halters when they dragged them up over the wooden trough to reach for another mouthful of hay. Somewhere, a cow lowed quietly. From the shadows, a yellow barn cat appeared, curious, then melted back into the night.

Anna kept the dog's head in her lap, stroking, easing the pain with her soft words.

Finally, Henry spoke.

"I spent a lot of time out here, with Lucky, after Harvey died."

"I know."

"Yeah, I guess you do. You were here."

"I missed Harvey. He was nice to me."

"He was nice to everyone."

"You both were. You know, Henry, I've often thought many boys like you don't turn out well. They feel misplaced after they spend their years growing up with another family."

"Yes, I can understand that. But it's hard growing up with your real family if you know the weight of poverty. I mean, we were happy; children usually are, even in dire circumstances. But you finally come to see where it was for the best. My father was never a happy man. I never told anyone my whole life, but I overheard my parents more than once, from the register cut into the kitchen ceiling. It was the grate to allow heat to circulate upstairs, and if you knelt there, it was like being in the same room with them. I can still hear the . . . I don't know. He was saying how often he doesn't want to continue with life, how easy it would be to leave this earth, and, well . . ."

Henry's voice faded away.

Anna's eyes became large and frightened.

"He wouldn't have taken his own life?" she whispered.

Henry shook his head.

"These things are not talked about, Anna. You know that. It is a shameful subject. They don't have funerals for someone who does that. But I'm not sure he wasn't tempted. He may have tried something at one point. My stepmother . . . well, there's no use talking about it now."

"But isn't it a condition? Something wrong, if a person feels like that?"

"My sister used to say it was the devil."

"We don't know, do we? It is sad, when someone like your father suffers from a feeling of hopelessness."

"I think, although I was only a young boy, I always knew there was something wrong with my father. He told us many times it was only a matter of days before Hitler's army would storm Lancaster County, and we'd all be taken to Germany."

"You believed that?"

"Sometimes."

"But that was an awful weight for a young boy."

"Harvey and I were close. We assured each other that it wasn't going to happen. And it didn't."

She looked down at the injured dog, gently pushed him off her lap, and began to rise.

"You should go in, it's getting late," she said.

"Think Colonel will be all right?" Henry asked.

"I think so. He's tired. He'll sleep."

Together, they rose, walked to the house.

The night was still, and the humidity clung to the night air. Henry smelled the roses that grew in profusion up the post at the edge of the porch. He dreaded going inside, to the stuffy upstairs bedroom that held the heat like a thermos bottle.

"Let's sit here on the swing for a while," he said.

She said nothing, but made her way to the swing and sat at the farthest corner. Henry took up the opposite side, shoved softly to put the swing in motion. Heat lightning rippled across the dark sky.

"Anna, why did you run off when I mentioned Katie?"

"I don't know."

"Tell me."

"No."

"Please?"

She hesitated. He could see her small hands pleating the folds of her dress, restlessly searching for a purpose.

"I don't know," she said again.

"Did I say something wrong?" he asked gently.

"No."

"What is it, Anna?"

She took a deep breath. "It's just that I spent so much of my life wondering if you loved Katie, and when you said you did, it was really hard, I guess."

"Why?"

"Don't ask that question."

"Is it because you cared about me?"

"I always cared about you. You were my brother."

"*Ach*, Anna, I'm not your brother."

Henry strained to hear her words, but he knew she said them, so he hesitated, unsure how he would answer.

"It would be better if you were," she said.

Now what did she mean by that? Confused, Henry didn't know what would be the proper response.

Afraid to open his mouth, Henry looked out toward the barn, the night deepening around them.

Finally, he asked. "How would that be better?"

"Just better, I guess."

"You're not being clear."

"All right, I'll tell you what I mean. I have always been the quiet one, the one who was in the background. My sisters have always overshadowed me, especially where you were concerned."

"But. . ." Henry floundered.

"No, let me finish. Growing up together, my devotion to you and Harvey bordered on worship. But Katie was the one you noticed. She was better at everything. Remember the skates you received that first year? Remember how it was Katie, not Malinda, who taught you how to fly across the ice? It was always like that."

Suddenly, Anna placed a hand on his arm.

"Why did you never ask Katie to be your girlfriend?"

"I wanted to. Just never could summon enough courage. She was so much more than me. Of course, it hurt when she began dating. But, I don't know, perhaps it wasn't meant to be. Do you think God controls all matters of the heart?"

"That's a tough one. Obviously, people get married for all the wrong reasons, and spend a lifetime of mostly being unhappy. So you think, 'They made that choice; they brought it on themselves.'

"Or did they? I believe God allows everything to happen, for a higher purpose, in so many ways we don't understand. We can't figure it all out by ourselves, so we do the best we can, from day to day."

Henry nodded.

He was deeply touched by Anna's wisdom, for a young girl who had always lived a sheltered life on the farm.

"If I were to say that I wanted to begin dating you, would that mean I would have to move?" he asked, his heartbeat accelerating to the point where he was sure he would slide off the porch swing in a faint.

"Are you thinking you might say that?" Anna asked.

"Well, that all depends on what *your* thoughts might be on the subject."

He actually was frightened now; the possibility of hyperventilation or fainting loomed ahead. He knew he could not move from this swing without asking her if she was interested in him, but was hopelessly mired down in the bog of pretense.

All he had meant to do was test the waters, like sticking a finger in a pot of liquid heating on the stove, and he found himself unable to tell her he was serious.

What untold agony was this courage, or lack of it!

Anna, in her kindness and wisdom, reached across the great divide and spoke gently.

"If we are becoming more than a brother and sister, which I believe is happening, then yes, you will no longer be able to live here with us. The ministry will never allow it, neither will our parents. So let's both pray about it, and let God lead the way."

Henry nodded in the dark, opened his mouth to say kind, appropriate words of agreement, but there were no words, only a long intake of life-giving breath.

Chapter Nine

IT WASN'T LONG BEFORE BOTH EPHRAIM AND Rachel became aware of the budding romance that played out right under their noses. Till the autumn winds blew, Ephraim helped Henry inquire about renting the old Tom Adams place close to Gordonville. He also gave Henry a team of horses and a sizable loan to begin raising hogs and chickens, and to start up a small dairy.

The farm was everything Henry had ever dreamed of. Where the road took a turn down a steep hill, then to the right, the Pequea Creek was wide, close to Rohrer's mill. The drive that led to the farm turned left, after you passed the mill, nestled between two hills, with woods on either side, set back from the buildings far enough to frame them with a curtain of gold, red, and orange.

The house was small, built in the traditional two-story "cracker box" farmhouse style, its narrow porch built by someone whose top priority was frugality. The absence of a *kesslehaus* was no big deal, as long as Henry lived there alone, he'd do his laundry on the porch.

Sparsely furnished with leftovers of Rachel's and some dishes Malinda brought packed with newspaper in a cardboard box. He had a cast iron frying pan, a blue agate coffee pot, a good hunting knife, and a potato masher.

The wooden panes on the windows were falling apart, some of the pieces of glass missing, so Ephraim taught him how to repair windows with penny nails, panes of glass, and putty.

The barn housed the horses at one end and cows at the other. There was no real cow stable, no cement stanchions, and certainly no gutter, so Henry cleaned the cow stable every day without complaint. It was more important to save every dollar toward a cow stable and more cows than to have everything handy.

The small barn was built into a hillside, called a bank barn, allowing the horses and wagons to pull hay and straw into the second story without a problem. It was sturdy, built with good timbers, attached to each other by round, wooden pegs. There were remnants of feed sacks, drifts of old hay, corncobs, and rusted equipment covered with thick spiderwebs like lace handkerchiefs draped over everything.

Nothing deterred Henry.

He awoke before four o'clock every morning, milked five cows by hand, strained and cooled the milk in galvanized cans, set it in the cold water or a mechanical cooler, then cleaned the cow stable, fed the six young hogs and twenty-four chickens.

He worked till late in the evening, cooked a pot of bacon and beans, or corn mush, washed it down with homemade root beer or ginger ale, and went to bed.

He tilled the fields, sowed fall oats, and hauled manure under lowering November skies, dreams of the future taking up most of his waking hours, thinking of the time when he would bring home his lovely bride, Anna.

He often shook his head, muttered to himself, and even laughed. If someone could have observed him bouncing along on the harrow, they might seriously think of having his sanity checked by a good doctor.

It was all so unbelievable, so incongruous, the way his life was taking shape, everything falling into place like building a brick wall. Much more than he deserved.

Or didn't he?

His thoughts infused by a heady glow, past sorrows and trials swam away to a forgotten recess of his heart. The lid on the small aluminum stockpot had to be pressed down on all the dollar bills that accumulated there. Almost enough to put in the cement work of a decent cow stable or another cow. The chickens were still laying good for November. A young gilt was about to give birth. He asked Abner Beiler for one of his golden retrievers as soon as Betsy had her pups.

Ten dollars, he said.

It was too much, but Henry missed the companionship of a good dog. Nothing would ever replace Lucky, no dog or horse or cat, but he missed the sight of a good dog rising from his bed of straw in the morning, come to greet him with the affable waving of a plumelike tail.

He built a new chimney, with Ephraim's help. He had pronounced the old one unsafe, saying it was better to spend the money to replace it than lose the house some cold, windy day.

Henry felt capable, basked in Ephraim's praise, soaked up his girlfriend's adoration, and went to bed feeling blessed, thankful for all the talents and gifts God had bestowed on him.

All he remembered when he woke in the predawn darkness of the frigid bedroom was the undeniable thought that there was something wrong, something terribly amiss.

His mouth had gone dry as sandpaper, his eyes wide, staring into the now-hostile dark, the inky void filled with heart-stopping portent. His heart hammered like a frightened bird in his chest, his thoughts exploded like sparks, igniting a fear the likes of which he had never known.

He felt as if he might lose his mind. He had to get out of bed, to do something, but he was so consumed by dread that he thought the floor might open and he'd fall through it.

He took a deep breath, inhaled sharply, then exhaled slowly. He did it again.

He tried to pray, to summon God's presence, but his words seemed to go no farther than the plaster ceiling above him.

He tried to steady himself, to wait and take stock of this odd happening.

Like a flash, it all came back to him.

A dream.

A vivid dream, in which the Pequea Creek had risen, brown and turbulent and muddy, roiling along, laughing at him in an evil fashion. He stood rooted to the bridge, much taller than he actually was, the wind roaring, pushing at his back with a fierce power. He knew he would topple into this laughing, beckoning water if he didn't stop growing taller, but he had no power to keep this from happening.

Then he saw Harvey, crying out for help. But it wasn't really Harvey; it was Anna.

His precious, beloved Anna.

He cried out, into the darkness surrounding him, more afraid than he had ever been.

Dear God, please tell me. The only answer was the suffocating darkness, rife with unanswered questions.

He spoke to Anna, he told Ephraim. They both assured him it was only a dream. Likely he had overworked himself and was tired out, having done without good nutritious meals for too long.

"Don't put any stock in dreams," Ephraim said.

"They are *fer-fearish*," Anna said.

Rachel cooked a roast of beef, made lima beans and potatoes with the skins on, for their vitamin and mineral content. She gave him a bottle of cod liver oil to take, and chamomile tea.

He may as well have chewed on a raw fish as taken the disgusting cod liver oil. He left the tea in the brown paper bag and never touched it.

The thing was, he didn't believe what Anna and her family told him. He had a deep inner conviction, an unspoken need to find out what God was trying to say. Hadn't He spoken to men of old? Look at Samuel in the temple. Called over and over when he was a young innocent boy.

The snow came the first week of December. At first, soft fat flakes came down and melted on the brown grass, but the temperature dropped, the wind picked up, and the fat flakes mixed with icy pellets that rattled against the barn windows as Henry forked hay to the cows.

He wished he'd brought more wood in from the woods. It was unlike him, this lethargic feeling that drew sleepy cotton over his eyes in the morning. He had no appetite, so he opened a can of beans and ate them cold, standing against the white metal sink, one foot crossed over the other, shedding straw and manure, still wearing his barn coat.

The dream was a harassment. It took away his peaceful days, his energy, and his bright-eyed eagerness for the future. He plodded about, distracted, doubtful. He jumped at the slightest provocation. His face turned pale, his eyes sunken.

Anna became alarmed, that Sunday evening in December. They were sitting at the kitchen table, drinking coffee, toying with the sugar cookies Anna had brought out on a pretty platter. Normally, Henry would have consumed three or four of them immediately.

"Henry," Anna said, her eyes dark with worry, "can't you tell me what is troubling you?"

Henry shook his head.

"If I would know, I would tell you. I don't know."

"Is it still that dream?"

"No. Yes."

Anna looked at him in disbelief.

"It still bothers you."

"Yes, it does."

"But you know my parents and I don't believe God talks to us through dreams."

Henry lifted agonized eyes to her face. "But it was so real, Anna. It's infused into my senses, and I can't shake it. I think about it all the time."

"That is a weakness, Henry. You must rise above it."

"I disagree."

There, he finally had the courage to stand on his own two feet. Not to belittle her, or argue with her, but to voice his own opinion on an extremely important matter. Yes, he was only Henry, but he had a right to say what he believed in.

They parted that evening with a polite handshake, an air of disagreement tempered by Anna's wisdom and quiet demeanor. They had agreed on the kind of courtship that would include no physical affection. Anna felt very strongly there was a special blessing in this, to remain chaste and pure before marriage.

At first, Henry had been hurt and angry, wondering what was wrong with an occasional hug or a kiss. Everyone did it, but he respected Anna's views, adopted them as his own, and looked forward to the day when they would be married.

It was that night, a few days before Christmas, when Henry was woken from a sound sleep. There was no fear, no dry-mouthed terror, only the knowledge that he was fully awake, the darkness around him cold, but pleasant. It was a friendly darkness, a darkness that gave its approval of him.

And then, like a soft sigh scented with every imaginable flower that grew all over the world, he understood the dream. As soft as the falling of a spent rose petal, the releasing of a daisy's white flower drifting to the ground, his mind was instilled with the sweetness of what God wanted him to know.

He had grown too high in his own eyes. God had work for him to do, someday, somehow. It was so simple, so sweet and reassuring.

He never told Anna. He just resumed his vitality and his plans for the future, but gave all the honor to God, and not to himself.

Christmas dinner was held on New Year's Day that year, everyone bowing to Malinda's wishes. Her husband's family had too many dinners and Christmas singings going on, and she couldn't take it. She was only one person, and she couldn't take all the clothes *rishting*, the washing, getting the children off to school on time, before preparing for yet another event.

Their family was growing with a new baby at regular intervals. Malinda being in charge, things went well on a daily basis. But when the holidays rolled around, the Christmas spirit was hard for her to grasp.

Henry drove in to the home farm, the sun glinting off the silver barn roof, the snow like a sparkling pristine blanket of white, every pine and bare bough coated with a layer of fluffy snow.

The sun shone, the air was still, life was beautiful for Henry. God was everywhere for him these winter days. He felt the presence, which was drawn closer by the gratitude that came from a heart filled with praise. He felt he had been rescued from going down the slippery path of self-honor, when everything unfolded just the way he wanted.

So there was a spring in his step, a healthy flush to his cheeks, a glad light in his eyes when Anna surprised him at the door of the forebay.

"Hello, Anna!"

"Hi, yourself."

"You're not in the house?"

"No actually, I had this Christmas present to take care of. I think he's a little more than I can handle."

Henry led his horse to a stall, tied him, and hurried out to see what she meant.

Sure enough, a brown ball of fluff, a golden retriever puppy, wriggled into her arms from Lucky's doghouse. Anna scooped him up, held him so tightly he grunted, her face breaking into a picture of pure delight.

She giggled as the dog licked her face. "You name him," she said, smiling up at her future husband.

Colonel trotted into the barn, stopped, and sat on his haunches, gazing up at the new puppy with the weirdest expression.

"Jealous, aren't you?" Anna chortled, bending to hold the puppy to Colonel, allowing him to sniff him all over and become acquainted.

Henry watched her, fascinated with her lack of fear and her understanding of Colonel's personality. He wasn't sure he would have held the puppy to the large German shepherd quite as freely, but Colonel seemed to accept and even welcome the newcomer.

"You sure have a way with dogs, Anna."

She straightened, held the puppy to her shoulder, then smiled at him.

"You're serious?"

"I am. I'm not sure I would have trusted Colonel."

"Oh, he's all right. He would never hurt the puppy. Most dogs are very social, only the ones who are mistreated have a problem."

"But, didn't you say Colonel was?"

"Sometime, yes. But he seems to have outgrown it."

"Hopefully," Henry said.

Normally Henry would not have been invited to the Christmas dinner if he was dating Anna, as courting was kept a secret, mostly, in the 1940s. But Rachel felt differently, saying Henry was their son, and Anna a daughter, so of course, he would be present.

They did not acknowledge each other throughout the day. Henry visited with the men in *die gute schtupp*, while Anna stayed with the women.

Besides Malinda and her rowdy crew, there was Uncle Levi King, Ephraim's brother, Abner Beiler and his wife, Rachel's sister Lydia, plus dozens of nieces, nephews, and cousins.

Outside, the snow fell softly, hushed by the lack of wind, the flakes drifting down to cover tree branches and bushes, the graveled driveway, and the brown grass in the yard. The men's hats were dusted with soggy snowflakes, melting as they stomped into the *kesslehaus*.

The kitchen window was propped open with a small piece of trim, steam rolling from the vast kettle of boiled potatoes, Rachel shaking in a teaspoon of salt, while her sister-in-law wielded the potato masher, her round, gold-framed spectacles steamed, obscuring her view. She yanked them down, peered over the top to continue stomping the potato masher up and down with a certain fury. Behind her, little Rachel and Lydia watched, fascinated, at the jiggling of her hips, the flapping of her big arms.

Henry sat with the men, a cup of strong black coffee at his elbow, his long legs stretched out before him. He was content to take no part in the conversation, just sit in the warmth of the house and absorb the news, the latest prices from the New Holland auction barn, the price of feeder pigs, and the accident on Route 340.

He sat up and took notice when Uncle Levi described the latest design in hay balers, wondering how long until these wonderful pieces of equipment would become widespread, easily available, or *alaupt* by the Amish church.

Uncle Levi was known as a progressive, unafraid to voice his rather strident opinions, but an interesting warmhearted chap whom Henry had always liked and admired deeply.

He watched Abner Beiler pick up a fat little girl, as cherubic as an angel, smile down into her face, and hold her on his knee. She leaned back against her father, her bright brown eyes like two polished stones, wedged between the fold of soft baby fat on her cheeks.

Henry smiled at her.

She turned her face and buried it in the folds of her father's vest, then peeped out at him a few seconds later.

Henry smiled again.

He felt a stab of joy. This was exactly what he wanted, a life belonging to a group of people who were like-minded and dwelt together in unity and love.

Mostly.

He wanted to raise a family, on a farm, his own farm, repeating the cycle of the seasons, over and over, his Anna by his side, supporting him in his work. He hoped he would not expect too much of her; he knew Amish housewives worked hard and shouldered responsibility much more than he had any idea. Anna was so small, so petite, somehow he felt a need to protect her and help her with life's burdens.

She was so childlike, so trusting of him.

Henry sat in the living room that Christmas Day, his last one as a single young man, emotions spilling from him, through him, in ways he could not always comprehend.

Like the horn of plenty, the cornucopia of assorted fruits and vegetables, the bounty of earth's plenty, so he savored this living room, a haven of Christmas comfort and joy. The apple of a grateful heart, the clump of grapes his safekeeping through the years of difficulty, the oranges and carrots, the fleshy, glossy green peppers and red-cheeked tomatoes. He lifted each one, examined the gifts the Lord had so kindly bestowed on his life.

Rachel and Ephraim.

Anna, the most dear.

Even Harvey's death, and Katie's. Each one a stepping stone on the way to maturity and a closer walk with God. His own sad father, also a gift, though perhaps a bitter one, to understand each time he also felt downhearted without reason. He was, after all, his father's son.

Anna gave the dog the dubious name of Buford.

"Why Buford?" Henry asked.

"Look at his eyes. He just looks like a Buford. Buford Esh."

She giggled, snuggled the brown, doe-eyed puppy to her face, and sighed contentedly.

He had never loved her more.

The seasons came and went. Till November of the following year, the Ephraim King farm had been cleaned and painted, scrubbed and washed, so every available surface was sparkling clean for Henry and Anna's upcoming wedding.

The trees were bare by the end of that month, except for a few scraggly brown oak leaves that clung to the branches extended over the porch roof, like a clean-shaven face with a few skipped bristles.

Rachel had a fit about them.

She worried about all of them letting loose and falling on the yard and sidewalks the morning of the wedding. She was no sloppy *hausfrau* and never would be, and she had no intention of being one now.

Ephraim made fun of his perturbed wife. But he watched good-naturedly from the barn as Henry set a ladder against the porch roof, climbed up with a feedbag, pulled those leaves off, stuffed them in the bag, and climbed back down.

Rachel told Anna she was, indeed, marrying a winner. Any man that bowed to a woman's foolish whim was worth praising.

Anna smiled her secretive little smile but chose to keep her thoughts to herself.

It rained on their wedding day, November 24, and turned to ice before the service was over. But the gas lamps hung from their hooks in the ceiling sputtered cozily, and the warm air was permeated with the rich smell of chicken filling and mashed potatoes. An uncle who had been a bishop for many years preached the sermon. Each word that fell from his lips was inscribed on Henry's heart. He took all the old stories very seriously, especially that Adam was lonely in the Garden of Eden, and God created a beautiful woman for him to be his friend, his partner, his lifelong companion.

It was so simple but so true.

Henry had experienced that himself. Everything had gone so well for him on the rented farm he called his own, and still there was an element missing, a piece of the puzzle incomplete. After today, the house would be filled with the essence of a woman, the one for whom he had waited so long.

As was the custom, Henry and Anna did not move to the farm till March. It was an old tradition, to allow the young groom time to prepare his home, while the bride stayed with her parents, sewing, preparing quilts, hooking rugs, crocheting doilies and pillowcases, and so on.

They visited the home of every guest who had been at their wedding. In below-freezing temperatures with billows of snow borne on the harsh winds of winter, they traveled from one corner of Lancaster County to another, visiting people, collecting the *haus schtire*, the wedding gift.

None had been brought to the wedding. The gifts were withheld until the *yung-Kyatte* came for a sumptuous meal. Newlyweds were highly esteemed, the visit considered a great honor, the table loaded down with many home-canned or home-cured delicacies.

After the meal, they would sit in *die gute schtup* and hold lively conversations while Anna produced a canvas top, with different colors of yarn to be pulled through, creating a unique pattern of flowers, or a design of tulips to be sewed for a pillow top that would be placed on the cane-seated rocking chair in Henry and Anna's *gute schtup*.

When it was time to leave, the hosts would proudly bring a shovel or rake, perhaps a heavy wrench or sharp saw for Henry, a blue agate canner or a sturdy potato masher or a stainless steel bucket for Anna.

As Henry went to hitch up the horse, Anna shrugged into her heavy black coat, pinned the black shawl snugly around her shoulders, took off the white covering and placed it in a small, overnight suitcase, her *coppa-box*, donned a heavy woolen headscarf, and placed the home-made black bonnet on top. Over her face, she wore a thin black scarf, wound around and around, leaving only a narrow opening for her eyes. After she pulled on heavy gloves, she was prepared for the long ride in the roofless, one-seated courting buggy.

Her feet encased in large rubber boots, bricks heated in the oven and wrapped in towels, she stayed half-warm, as long as the distance was not over ten miles.

There were times, however, when the distance was closer to twenty, and that was when Anna's teeth clacked together uncontrollably, like castanets, her body shivering with the cold, and her feet were like blocks of ice.

These were the times that tested her endurance, her strength, and the much-touted submission to her husband.

Chapter Ten

IN MARCH, THE GLAD DAY FINALLY ARRIVED.
Ephraim and Rachel deemed it was well and good
that Anna would be a proper *hausfrau*.

The wind whipped the women's skirts to one side
and sent the men's hats rolling across the yard. The
horses' manes blew off their arched necks, whipped
to the opposite side, their tails streaming to the same
direction. They pranced, champed at the bit, made
many false starts, halted by irritated movers with a
loud, "Whoa! Ho there, Fred."

The wind was only a minor annoyance.

Henry laughed as cardboard boxes wobbled across
the yard, slammed drunkenly up against the fence. He
ran after wildly flapping pieces of newspaper, securing
them with a chaotic churning of his arms and legs.

Nothing could alter his high spirits. Nothing.

The wind was harsh, yes, but the buds were pushing on the trees, the spring peepers had sounded

down by the creek, that high, shrill call of lonely males doing their best to attract a mate.

The red-winged blackbirds had arrived, showing the trimmed red wing as they took flight, calling out the beloved, "Birdie-glee, birdie-glee!"

Henry knew the moist soil would be loaded with nitrogen from the heavy load of winter's snow. The roots and stems of winter wheat were pushing, as was the new seeding of alfalfa.

Anna received a new table, made by deacon Amos Esh, and four chairs from the Mennonite named Abel Horning.

They were sturdy, well-made chairs, with acorns and oak leaves painted on the back.

They were given an icebox, a used Servel, painted blue, one Aunt Lydia had in her *kesslhaus* for years. It worked well, and for twenty dollars, you just couldn't beat it.

After they all wended their way down the winding driveway, Henry and Anna sat side by side on the new davenport, surveyed their house, with satisfaction, a sense of awe.

"Somebody pinch me," Anna murmured, laying her head on Henry's shoulder.

He drew her close.

"I'm relieved to hear you say that, Anna. I was so afraid you'd miss your mother the first evening."

"Oh, my, Henry. I've waited for this moment for so long."

Before going to bed, Henry got the *Gebet büchly* from the desk top, and looked at Anna with a question in his eyes.

"You planned on saying the *gebet* together, as we've taught our whole life?"

She nodded, a small smile on her lips, her eyes filled with trust.

They knelt side by side, in front of individual kitchen chairs as Henry opened the book to a German evening prayer. He read fluently the words written by men of old, in a low well-modulated voice that carried well.

Anna shivered, chills creeping up her spine. It was if he had been reading German prayers all his life, and with a women's intuition, she knew.

She pondered all this, her heart accepting what her mind did not.

Henry was special. He had suffered more than some much-older folks, and suffered well, without self-pity or drawing attention to himself. Anna knew that he valued his walk with God even above his love for her.

She smiled a small, secretive smile. She would see what she could do about that.

That spring, life was poignantly sweet for the young couple, their days filled with rewarding hard work, their evenings spent sharing their innermost thoughts, dreams, and hopes.

Henry was prone to continued conversation, now that his beloved Anna sat by his side, listening, nodding her head, occasionally adding a word of correction, or one of wisdom.

As the days grew warmer and the evenings longer, Colonel and Buford would join them on the porch, splayed out, their tongues lolling as they wound down from the day's activities.

Buford had grown into a beautiful, silk-haired retriever with the fine curtain of silky hairs on his underside and down the back of his legs. He had taken second place to the alpha Colonel, who had established himself as Buford's guardian when he was a puppy.

Colonel walked over and rested his head on Anna's knee. Crickets chirped beneath the wooden floor of the porch. A barn cat slunk around the corner of the well house at the end of the sidewalk. The barn rose up beside the driveway, peeling red paint hanging in shreds from graying boards like blisters. Behind the barn, the ridge showed brilliant shades of new green, small purple Judas trees flecked among them like lace.

The field lane wound up behind the barn, a narrow, brown track that led to the back thirty acres. Robins dived through the air, clumsy with haste, calling raucously to their wide-mouthed babies that huddled hungrily in their nest.

Henry pushed Buford aside to get up and go to the kitchen for a drink. Buford lifted his head, blinked, then lowered it on his paws.

Anna watched Henry go.

The one and only sadness of her life was that he had never really accepted Buford or Colonel. Outwardly, he put on a good show, but she knew he would never love these dogs the way he had loved Lucky.

Henry was not aware that Anna saw through the thin veneer of his pretense. Oh, he liked the dogs; he just didn't love them. She would come to accept this in time, and she was determined to never let him know how she felt.

In time, Henry gave his patient wife a detailed account of his companionship with Lucky. The dog had been like a sponge, a soft, warm, silky recipient of all his grief, tears, and loneliness.

Lucky understood human suffering in a way other dogs did not. Henry had spent hours brushing the silky long hair, seated on a bale of straw, before he went to school.

He told Anna that when he cried, Lucky felt his pain, the way he laid his heavy head on his knee and looked straight into his face as the tears puddled in his eyes, then ran over, down his cheeks and off his chin, sometimes dropping on Lucky's head.

"You see, Lucky was baptized by my tears. He was a special dog sent from God. I don't doubt that one instant. When Lucky showed up in that snowy field, God already knew he would replace Harvey. So he was a miracle."

Anna listened, drying a stainless-steel saucepan at the sink, her towel going round and round. Henry was seated at the kitchen table, with the last of his coffee growing cold in the cup, the way it often did.

"But you do like the two dogs we have now?"

"I do. Oh, of course, Anna. But they're not Lucky."

"I know. I notice things."

"What?"

"Well, you just don't enjoy them the way you enjoyed Lucky."

"Yes. Yes, I do. The farm would be so empty without either one. Especially Buford."

Anna nodded, smiled, and the subject was finished.

She was very wise, her womanly intuition right on the mark, more often than not. It was something Henry would always hold in high esteem, the way she sensed his moods. Indeed, she was a woman worthy of his praise.

She kept an immaculate house and garden, took on her share of the milking, and helped Henry in the fields whenever he needed her. Every day, Henry thanked God for his lovely wife, their health and happiness, and the ability to serve Him.

When their first baby was born the following year, they named him Ephraim, after Henry's adoptive father, and Anna's.

He was a scrawny, red-faced little fellow, with a shock of light hair like long peach fuzz. He was like a starved bird, his mouth always open, his yells of outrage powered by an extraordinary set of lungs. Like bellows, they were.

Henry tried his level best to be a patient, understanding husband, hovering over poor Anna and her squalling infant in anxiety, wanting to clap his hands over his ears and run out the back field lane to get as far away from these frightening screams as he could.

"Your milk has no food value," Rachel said.

"He's hungry," Aunt Lavina said.

"His stomach hurts," Mattie said.

"Paregoric," Daddy Beiler said.

Definitely chamomile. Peppermint. Catnip. Goat's milk.

Hold the baby upside down.

Bewildered, Henry milked all the cows while Anna stayed in bed for ten days, then dressed and rested on the sofa or a rocking chair.

Uncle Levi's Rebecca came to stay, a mild-mannered sixteen-year-old with no experience and a stilted aversion to dogs and men.

When told she would be expected to help with the milking, she told them politely, her words laced with steel, that she never milked a cow in her life and she had no intention of starting now.

Henry ate burnt eggs. How could you burn an egg? They were actually charred.

He washed them down with scalding cups of tea, ate the white bread she served instead of toast, and charred sausages that were pink everywhere but the outside.

He never said anything but was always kind, praising her ability to manage the washing and ironing.

But he was met with a hostile stare and her feet planted firmly with toes to the side like an ostrich.

Wasn't the birth of a baby a joyous event, one that tied the bonds even firmer, love multiplied by three? What had gone so wrong?

Anna seemed foreign, far away, dark circles under her eyes, going about her days grimly, the shouts from the baby increasing as weeks turned into months.

Where was the relief? Where was the joy?

But as these things go (as Rachel soothed and held and patted and encouraged), it only lasted for a while. With a smile on her face, she told them, "This, too, shall pass." And it did.

By the time Baby Ephraim was six months old, he was a chubby, rosy-cheeked boy who ate anything they fed him with seemingly no ill effects from the contracting stomach pains or the lungs that had been used to the limit.

Anna smiled and laughed and swept up her baby, kissing him from the top of his head to his toes. Henry found out about the joy and love of babies. It had just been delayed for a while as little Ephraim worked through bouts of colic.

A few years later, Levi was born, a solemn-looking child who weighed two pounds more than their first-born. He slept all night and most of the day. Ephraim toddled around and stuck his finger in the sleeping baby's eye, or pulled on the thatch of brown hair and said, "*Ich gleich net ihn.*"

Henry laughed, received the full amount of joy, and praised God every day for the miracle of babies. He told Anna they'd have a dozen more if they were all like Levi.

Anna beamed. Her blue eyes shone into her husband's adoring gaze. She said she would love to have many more babies, until their table was filled with children.

"Blessed is the man whose quiver is full," Henry quoted, while Anna nodded in agreement.

And then, old Solomon King passed away at the age of seventy-nine. A leader of the Gordonville district, a *diener zum buch*, he was mourned by everyone. He was a pillar in the church, a staunch supporter in time of need, a powerful speaker who never failed to lay wisdom on hearts. The church prospered beneath his tutelage.

There was talk of ordaining a minister to take Sol's place, but no one took it too seriously, least of all Henry and Anna.

They were too young, they assured themselves.

A year later, an announcement was made. In communion services, they would ordain a minister.

Votes were taken, and five men were in the lot, Henry among them. He was the chosen one, selected by God from the five. Henry bowed his head and felt completely undone, inadequate, and unable.

They drove home in near silence, Anna's hand resting on his forearm, without saying a word. After the flurry of well-wishers had gone, they spent a sleepless night, alternately praying and crying, talking and holding each other while the boys slept peacefully, unaware that their father had been ordained a minister.

Their family grew again, with the birth of baby Rachel. Henry walked into church services with the ministers and the deacon, learned to preach in the manner of the Amish, and read German scripture with ease.

They bought the farm, built a cow stable, and milked ten cows by hand. The fields produced abundantly, and the mortgage dwindled as each year passed.

Ephraim and Levi, at the ages of ten and twelve, could help with chores now. Two more boys had been born after Rachel, Enos and Harvey, then Anna. Four boys and two girls in all.

The years were kind to Henry and Anna. They worked hard, enjoyed the children, and spent many days together, working side by side.

Colonel and Buford were both old and stiff, but close companions to all the children, a constant sight around the farm.

When Henry was ordained bishop, the family accepted their lot with grace, bowed their heads, and asked for wisdom to lead the church.

Henry was a gifted speaker, well known throughout Lancaster County. He had known sorrow and pain, had sympathy for the suffering and the poor in spirit.

Harvey's death seemed a far-away memory.

How could he ever have thought of Katie, when Anna was so obviously the perfect helpmeet?

God's ways were fascinating, his love beyond comprehension. Henry grew in spirit and kindness and love.

Anna's days were blessed beyond measure.

When Christmas came that winter, Anna bought another Newfoundland puppy from a dealer. They hid the large, floppy dog away for two days, until Christmas Eve.

They waited until Henry was in his study, his German scripture and his copy of the German and English dictionary open on his desk, his head resting on his hand, his eyes half-closed as he struggled to stay awake.

He heard the scraping, the tittering and giggling, before the door burst open, and shouts of "Merry Christmas, Dat!" erupted from all the children, grouped around a cardboard box, with Anna in the background.

"My, what is going on here? A surprise? A Christmas surprise?"

They jumped up and down, and squealed and shouted. Into the chaos, Henry dived, laughing, pulling off the top of the cardboard box to find a bored-looking miniature Lucky sitting in the middle, his small, triangular brown eyes quizzical, as if to say, "Why were you making all this fuss?"

Henry was completely taken by surprise. He didn't know there was a black Newfoundland to be found for hundreds of miles. The children watched wide-eyed as Henry lifted the puppy, held him to his face, then sat with him on his lap, stroking the silky hairs, reminiscing, remembering those years with Lucky.

His eyes filled with tears.

"Thank you, everyone. You thought of the perfect Christmas gift."

When Henry was ordained bishop of the north Gordonville district, he felt the weight and respon-sibility without an ounce of strength. Drained, con-fused, unable to see his way, the path too steep and too rocky, he groaned from his innermost soul, beg-ging God to be by his side, show him the way, and he would not lean to his own understanding.

But he had Lucky now. A gift from his children and his beloved Anna. And from God.

The years passed, with Henry growing in spirit.

His beard was streaked with gray, his wavy hair thinning, but he was still a stalwart figure, tall, wide, with an arresting face.

What was it about that face, people thought.

They listened, rapt, as he preached in his kind, compassionate way. He visited the sick, spoke words that were meaningful, and was held in high esteem by the members of his congregation.

He often returned to that night of terror, the dream like an unspeakable dragon, the meaning crystal clear as he traveled through life as a minister, and then, *da full dienscht.*

To God goes the honor. All good and perfect gifts come from above, from the Father of lights. Love for Anna grew in ways beyond his imagining. On her forty-second birthday, their last child was born, making an even dozen. A daughter named Mary.

All the children gathered round his table, and he could honestly say his quiver was full.

Seven sons and five daughters.

Each one brought up by Anna's quiet discipline, her everlasting patience and love. If the children did well, he gave his wife all the credit. And he still loved Lucky, padding around the well-kept farm in his funny rolling gait, the loose skin with the abundant silky black hair, the only kind of dog that would ever touch his heart.

He often knelt in the haymow, away from prying eyes, clasped his hands, and prayed for God's wisdom, His strength and guidance, with Lucky sitting by his side, listening to the sound of his master's voice.

Side by side, just the way he sat with Harvey as a small boy, given to the Ephraim King family.

Side by side.

The End

A Horse for ELSIE

Chapter One

ELSIE STOOD AT THE METAL YARD GATE beneath the old white oak tree, one foot tucked up under her purple skirt, the other planted solidly on the fractured cement sidewalk, and glared at the pony and cart trotting gaily past their driveway. The pony was perfect—small, round, and compact, the way all Shetland ponies are. But this pony was special in the way he arched his thick, short neck and raised his hooves high, looking as regal as could be.

He was driven by Elam Stoltzfus, a boy from seventh grade, one grade above her own. Elam was bold, as proud as his pony. She had asked him once if she could drive the pony, but he had told her airily that anyone who had no experience with ponies could not drive this one. He'd give her a ride sometime, but no, she could not drive.

His little brother, Benny, sat beside him today, his straw hat smashed down so far Elsie could only see a nose and a chin. What was the point of going for a ride if your eyes were stuck behind a straw hat? Boys were strange creatures with idiotic ideas—especially Benny. He claimed there were turtles as big as a cow that lived to be a hundred years old. Then, as if that wasn't hard enough to believe, he said they lived on an island she couldn't hope to pronounce and couldn't think of spelling, so she had tried to look it up in the *World Book Encyclopedia* but never found it. He was making it up, she was sure. She wasn't about to ask him how to spell the name of the island, either.

And there he went, sitting beside Elam driving that perfect pony. Elam was older than Benny but just as much of a know-it-all, especially when it came to horses. Elsie had read *Black Beauty* and all the Marguerite Henry books in the school library, so she knew a lot more about horses than those two thought she did.

The thing was, her family was poor. They could hardly afford hay and grain for their one stodgy old driving horse, let alone feed a pony or any sort of horse just for pleasure. So, Elsie never dared talk about wanting a horse of her own. When Elam talked about all their horses, she hung around to hear what he had to say, correcting him on occasion, but mostly thought he was too proud, even arrogant, boasting about that barn full of beautiful horses.

Elsie was the oldest in a family of five children, all girls—except Amos, who was only a year old and the biggest pest anyone could imagine. He was always underfoot, his nose ran constantly, he fell and hurt himself at least a dozen times a day. And who was yelled at to go rescue him? She was.

They all lived in an old farmhouse that wasn't their own place, the way other Amish people bought their homes. Elsie's father had been in a car accident on the way to work at the pallet shop in Kinzers and lost most of his right arm. Ever since then, he'd struggled to find work he could do that paid well enough to support the family. He was cheerful and thankful, appreciated the cheap rent, and loved the old farmhouse and the dilapidated barn that housed his old horse and rattling secondhand buggy. He loved every one of his children and said he was grateful for each day here on earth. He could have been killed that day, and then what?

Which was true.

Elsie couldn't imagine life without her happy father. He was everyone's sunshine, the spark that ignited all the good times. And there were plenty of good times. But being poor was a constant disappointment. When the other girls had new dresses and black aprons, brand-new name-brand sneakers and baseball gloves, Elsie knew she looked dowdy with her sneakers from the consignment shop on Strasburg Road, dresses that were her cousin's hand-me-downs, and a baseball glove that was too small and weathered to a dull brown, the laces loose and broken. When lunch boxes opened at dinner hour in school, she eyed the fancy granola bars in their shining wrappers, the bought containers of yogurt and Jello and pudding, the individual bags of Cheetos and potato chips, and did her best to hide her white American cheese sandwich in both hands. The bread was always homemade and crumbly, leaving telltale crumbs all over her lap and on her desktop. She had become an expert at swiping them onto the floor before the other children took notice.

Her mother made a fresh popper of popcorn almost every morning, unless she bought a huge bag of stick pretzels at Creekside Foods. She only did that when they were on sale. Popcorn worked really well, though, especially if it was seasoned with sour cream and onion powder. Rosanne Esh, in eighth grade, loved Elsie's popcorn and traded all sorts of delicious things to get her hands on it. Once, she handed over a ziplock bag containing chips that were stacked together, perfectly uniform and shaped like little cups. Too proud to ask what they were, Elsie merely reached into the bag and ate them one by one. It was the most delicious snack she had ever eaten. It was a big mystery, how anyone could make potato chips that weren't greasy or salty and that fit together so precisely.

Elsie was always impressed that the other girls had fancy new lunch boxes every year. Actually, some of them were like little purses with their names written on the front in fancy lettering. They said their mother bought them at a 31 Party. Whatever in the world that was, Elsie thought.

At recess, Elsie forgot about being poor. She was an avid baseball player, naturally athletic, with long, thin legs that propelled her around the ball diamond faster than the boys. She scooped up hard-drive grounders, caught flies, and threw the ball with amazing precision to yelling, hopping outfielders. It was a known fact that Elsie was always chosen long before some of the upper-grade boys, which usually sparked a few martyred sniffs from Elam. Oh, she knew what he was thinking. Girls should never be chosen to be on a team before guys, no matter how good they were.

Elsie always flashed him a triumphant look, before bouncing over to the team that had chosen her. *You drive your fancy pony, Elam. I get chosen before you, so there.*

Elsie guessed if she had not been born to an Amish family, she would be a player on some important team, wearing a uniform and a ball cap pulled low on her forehead, her hair in a ponytail. Wouldn't that be exciting? But she was Amish, and she loved her world, her people. She was fine with flying around the ball diamond in her faded green dress, the pins that held her black apron around her waist mostly intact, her hair in the bun on the back of her head loosening steadily as recess wore on. Mostly, she was content.

Except for this chafing ambition to own a pony, a harness, and a cart. Not just an ordinary pony, but one that ran down the road the way Elam Stoltzfus's pony did. Like a show horse. It gave her chills.

Someday, somehow, she would have a Shetland pony that ran as beautifully as Elam's pony, Cookie. Now what kind of name was that for a pony? A cat should be named Cookie. A pig or a parakeet, maybe. Not a pony. If she had a pony, she would name him something more inspired, like Lightning or Whiz or Dreamcatcher (Dream for short).

She turned when she heard a high-pitched sound coming from the sandbox beside the house. There was little Amos, his face lifted to the sky, screeching like a hyena, his eyes closed tightly, his mouth an open hole that emitted desperate sounds of agony. *Now what?*

Elsie turned and ran, flung herself on her knees, and reached for him, streaming nose and all. She found his hand stuck firmly inside the small opening of the metal watering can.

"Here, hold still. Stop yelling. Shh. Hush."

Nothing helped, so she tugged, twisted the child's

toy first one way, then another, until she freed the trapped, reddened little hand.

His yells increased with her efforts until they escalated to short, horrible shrieks of panic.

"Hush, Amos. It's all right."

Her mother's worried face appeared at a window, a moment before she dashed through the screen door, letting it close with that familiar slapping sound. She bounded down the steps and to the sandbox, holding out her arms, already crooning her baby nonsense that made Elsie's toes curl.

"*Komm, komm.* Poor little chap."

She lifted the corner of her gray apron to wipe his face, leaning back to blow his nose as he turned his head.

"I don't know why you do that. Use a handkerchief," Elsie said drily, swallowing her disgust.

"Oh, it's just baby mucus. Just a little bit. Right, Amos?"

He dug his half-wiped face into his mother's shoulder before popping a sand-covered finger into his mouth, opening his eyes wide with astonishment and beginning another fresh chorus of howls.

Elsie stalked off. Her baby brother was so different than her baby sisters had been. He pulled cats' tails, got scratched on a regular basis, then sat there and howled exactly like this. The next day he would do it again. He ate dirt, swallowed dimes (Mam found one in his diaper), emptied out cupboards and trash cans, played with shovels and trowels and scissors if he could, and hardly ever played with toys.

Elsie secretly believed there was something seriously wrong with him. He probably had some sort of handicap that wouldn't allow him to go further than third grade. She planned to have a serious talk with her mother about it.

Elsie never understood why her parents couldn't have stopped at four girls. The girl babies had sat in their bouncy seat and played with their toys, or smiled and cooed, blowing little spit bubbles. They also had hair—a nice amount of dark brown fuzz that grew from their scalp like a velvety bonnet, framing their features perfectly. Every one of her younger sisters were good babies—Malinda, Suvilla, and Anna Marie.

Then along came Amos, shattering the well-ordered life of the Esh family. He weighed almost ten pounds and was bald as a volleyball and red as a caramel apple. He never stopped howling unless he slept. So between Elam and Benny being so full of themselves and a baby brother that drove her to distraction, Elsie decided she'd rather not have boys in her world.

Her father wasn't like boys. He was tall and strong and happy, with a shining stainless steel hook protruding from his nearly empty sleeve. It was attached to his shoulder with a series of bands that opened and closed the hook with a rolling motion of his shoulder, so that he could use it like a thumb and a forefinger.

Sometimes he would play games with the little girls, pretending he was the big, bad wolf, snapping the steel hook open and shut like jaws, sending the little girls shrieking up the stairway or into the pantry. He would make awful growling noises as he crept through the house, his back bent double, his head turning from side to side like a hungry predator until even Elsie felt as if she should hide behind the couch.

No, her father was a beloved figure, a whistling person who brought a light into Elsie's world and illumination to all the good things surrounding her she may have missed otherwise. She admired him immensely for the way he soon accepted the loss of his arm, never spoke a word of self-pity, and certainly never turned moody. Sometimes Elsie tucked one arm to her side and kept it there, for hours, just to see how it would feel to be her father. She could pull weeds, but not use a hoe. She couldn't tie the bib apron around her waist, and she certainly couldn't tie her *kopp-duch* under her chin. She couldn't sweep the kitchen, but she could wash dishes, only it took much longer and they weren't too clean.

So who knew, perhaps Amos would grow up to be wonderful like her father someday, but that didn't seem likely.

The house they lived in was close to Gap, a fairly small town in the heavily populated Lancaster County. It didn't seem as if they lived in a bustling area, at home, anyway. The house was built on a rise, among trees, surrounded by farmland. You could barely see Gap off in the distance. At one time, there had been a barn, but a fire had destroyed it in 1937, which was so long ago you'd get tired if you tried to think about it. There was a heap of brown stones, some of them blackened, in a tangle of blackberry vines, thorny as all get out. There were snakes back there, large, slippery-looking black snakes that gave you chills of delicious fright.

The house was actually a farmhouse, but if there was no longer a barn or fields belonging to the house it couldn't be called that. So it was just a house.

Emanuel Lapp owned the two acres of property. He was an older Amish man with a white beard and white hair and more money than President Trump, Elsie decided. He must have, because he owned four farms. He didn't charge them much rent, just enough to let them keep their pride. He hired workers to put on new white siding and new windows with white trim. They cemented the porch floor and added new vinyl posts, which made the house look scrubbed and clean.

Mam planted geraniums and petunias, put in a garden, and trimmed the ancient boxwoods in front of the house. She never complained about cracked linoleum or peeling wallpaper. She put contact paper on the old shelves in the pantry and in the kitchen cupboards, so she could wipe them down with strong Lysol soap. They set their furniture along the walls of the house, painted the steps gray, and lived in it just the way it was.

Sometimes Mam's face would harbor that wistful expression when church was held in some nice home or other. She would run her fingertips along the smooth cupboard doors when no one was watching, or stand in awe of some fancy bathroom done up in a dusty shade of lilac and beige, the shower curtain the identical twin to the window curtain.

But she never mentioned any of it to her husband. How could she? Why hurt his feelings so badly when he was doing the best he could? They had shelter in winter, food to eat, and best of all, each other.

Elsie helped her mother with Amos, washed dishes, and folded laundry. She learned the proper way to hoe, learned how to run the cultivator, and how to pull the small weeds without hurting the vegetable plants or loosening their roots.

She picked peas and beans, shucked corn, picked cucumbers and tomatoes. All summer long, there was the garden, that enormous patch of earth that spilled all kinds of vegetables from the stalks. When April arrived, they ate new spring onions and radishes with fresh homemade bread and butter. When enough warm May sunshine ripened the peas, they bent their backs over endless rows and picked bucketfuls, pouring them into plastic Rubbermaid totes, then sitting on the porch and shelling them for hours. Elsie grumbled and complained, ate raw peas by the handful, and said she didn't know why the minute school let out, the peas were ripe. The truth was, she missed baseball already. What was she supposed to do all summer, with no pony and only long, skinny cats and a screaming baby brother?

They didn't have a trampoline or a swing set. She was too big to play in the sandbox, and besides, that's where the cats did their business. She'd caught them at it. Filthy animals. Cats ran a close second to boys as far as being annoying, but her mother said the cats were here to stay, that the younger girls loved them.

After the peas were all blanched and put in the freezer, the hulls scattered among the peavines for compost in the soil, the green beans and cucumbers got ripe. They brought more backbreaking work, requiring Elsie to bend down and move the beanstalks aside to find the elusive beans hanging underneath.

By the month of June, the sun was hot, hot, hot. Mam did not like the beans to be picked early in the morning when they were wet. Mam's mother always said if you handle the beans when they're wet, they'll get rusty. Whatever she meant by that. How could something become rusty if it wasn't metal? Old wives' tales, Elsie thought, shaking her head. But then, her grandmother was old, so she might have known what she's talking about. Elsie went down to the garden in secret on one dew-filled morning and picked a few handfuls of beans and fed them to the driving horse named George. Sure enough, a week later the next growth of beans was crisscrossed with brown spots. Rusty.

By July and August, Elsie gave up and stopped complaining. The heat was like the roaring furnace in the Bible and the corn and tomatoes and peppers and lima beans were all ready at once. Amos developed a painful-looking heat rash followed by days of loose bowels until his little backside was as red as his face and you could hardly tell which end was which. Mam was constantly in the kitchen, chopping vegetables and mixing vinegar and sugar and pungent spices so that the kitchen took on a sharp, acidic odor, like unwashed underarms. They froze two thousand ears of corn, Elsie told her mother. She laughed, said, "No, no. Now, Elsie. We sold some to the Hoffmeiers down the road."

Mam's face was also a perpetual shade of red. All summer long it stayed that same alarming color, as if the blood vessels beneath her skin were all rising to the surface, ready to explode with tension and heat.

"How old do I have to be before I can get a job?" Elsie asked her father one night, after the sun had left nothing but twilight and a few stars had poked their light through the navy blue curtain of night.

"How old are you now?" he asked.

"Eleven."

"Oh, by the time you're fourteen, you could help Aunt Lydia at market, probably. But remember, Amish children give their wages to their parents. If you make a hundred dollars, you would have only ten to put in your savings account."

He shifted his weight, spun his glass in a circle to stir the mint tea, then looked at her with an expectant gaze.

Elsie's eyes flashed her irritation.

"If that's the case, I'll never have a pony. Never."

"Elsie, I wish you could have one. But even if ponies were free, we still couldn't afford to feed it. We must be sensible. Lots of children don't have ponies. I never did. Neither did your mother. We grew up to be responsible adults, I like to think."

He smiled at her, that happy, childlike smile that let her know she was loved and everything was right with his whole world.

"But I want a pony."

"Not just a pony," her father replied, "but a cart and a harness and a halter and a lead rope, and enough money to buy two scoops of feed and two blocks of hay. Every day."

"That's right."

Elsie drew up her knees, pulled her skirt tightly around them, then wrapped her hands around her legs, her fingers interlaced. She watched her father's expression, hoping to find his solid reserve crumbling, even a bit.

"Listen. I would love to see you have a pony. But your mother is in dire need of necessities she never mentions. If there is any money left over, ever, we need a new mattress set and a lawn mower that works. They don't require feed and hay. So for now, you'll have to be reasonable."

Elsie knew what he said was true, but that didn't take the sting away. She felt trapped. Even if she worked hard at the market or as a *maud*, she'd never make enough to buy a pony if she had to give so much of the money to her parents. Still, she was determined. She'd figure something out, eventually.

Chapter Two

LUNCH AT SCHOOL WAS ONLY FIFTEEN MIN-
utes, and she stayed at her desk, eating whatever her
mother had packed. She unwrapped her cheese sandwich and ate it quickly, mostly to hide the whole
thing before anyone saw there was no ham or bologna. She never turned sideways in her seat and put
her legs in the aisle to socialize like the other kids did.
They didn't have to see what she got out of her faded
old Coleman lunch box, crisscrossed with scratches
and scruff marks.

"Hey."

Elsie didn't turn, didn't expect to be addressed at
lunch hour.

"Hey, Elsie."

She put back the sandwich, turned and raised her
eyebrows.

"You're not on my team today, are you?"

Now what? Elam never acted as if he cared one
way or another whose team she was on. She knew he

disapproved of her ball-playing abilities, so what did he care?

"I don't know."

"Well, Artie here thinks you're on his team, and he hasn't won a game for so long, he doesn't even know how to be a winner anymore."

Artie was short for Arlen, and Elsie avoided him as much as she could. He came from a wealthy family who lived in a beautiful house about half a mile away. They went to Florida every winter, taking the children for a few weeks and calling it "educational."

"So whose team were you on yesterday?" Elam asked.

"Yours."

He turned to Artie gleefully. "I told you."

That was puzzling. Why would Elam think her being on his team was a good thing?

Elsie shrugged. You could never tell what boys thought. Likely they had some sort of bet going on that she would never find out about.

Elsie's tattered glove was like a shot of caffeine. Pure adrenaline. And it was a perfect day for baseball—barely a breeze, the sun warm but not too warm, the air clear, tinged with the smell of autumn leaves, acorns, dirt, and dying weeds.

She took her place on first base and watched Artie as he walked to the pitcher's space. He had all the confidence in the world, a slight bounce in every step. Rosanne was the catcher. Why they'd put her there was beyond Elsie, seeing how hard it was for her to bend over and stop grounders, given her size. Not that Elsie would ever say that out loud.

Samuel, a fifth-grader, was up to bat and lopped a perfect grounder to Artie, who threw the ball to Elsie. Samuel made a wild lunge for first base, but dropped his shoulders dejectedly when Elsie playfully tagged him.

She smiled. "Nice try."

"Thanks."

Elsie made two home runs, racking up points for the team, caught fastballs on the outfield, and threw with razor precision. No one ever said much to her about her ball-playing abilities, though she got a lot of high fives on the field. The girls seemed almost embarrassed that she was so good—like maybe it wasn't proper to be that much better than all the boys.

Today, Elam grinned at her. "Poor Artie. Whooped 'em."

She smiled back, too shy to speak. She felt the blush in her face, hoped no one would see.

At the end of each school day, Elsie always felt a sense of loss. Going home meant working for her mother at an endless round of weary jobs—getting laundry off the line, sweeping the kitchen, picking up toys, or worst of all, peeling potatoes. She hated plodding around like an ordinary housewife.

Elsie had no plans of becoming a housewife. At twenty-one years of age she could keep the money she earned, all of it. She'd find the hardest, most challenging job she could find and work herself up to manager, maybe running her own stand at the bustling market in New Jersey that Rosanne talked about. Then she would put all of her money into a savings account until she could buy a pony. Just one perfect Shetland pony with an arched neck and shining, well-kept hooves and a shower of light-colored long hair, thick and clean that hung down the side of his neck, a portion of it down the front of his face.

She would name the pony Cliff, for the tall hills and ravines of their native country.

The cart would not be painted black, but varnished natural wood with a sheen like water. It would have a red upholstered seat with a comfortable back and red pinstripes on the wheels and along the shafts.

Elsie's daydreaming was what kept her going as she swept the broken linoleum with the scraggly broom, washed the dishes in soapy water, folded cloth diapers, and ironed the Sunday handkerchiefs. Never once had she taken into consideration that at twenty-one she might be too tall, too adult, to be driving a Shetland pony.

Church services were announced to be at their house that Sunday, which meant no one would relax for two whole weeks. It always sent a thrill down her spine, though, to hear her father's name—Levi Esh—announced in church. It was a reminder that they were an upstanding family, capable of hosting services in the garage attached to their house.

Being Amish meant there was no church building with a steeple and pews the way countless English folks enjoyed. You took your turn about once a year, sometimes more, depending on the size of the congregation. Amish folks only went to church every other Sunday, the in-between one meant for Bible study and German lessons with the family, a day of relaxation and rest. Most people went visiting or had company, or went to a neighboring district to church.

Amish families were sectioned into districts, from twenty to forty families in each district. If the congregation grew too large, they would decide on a boundary, dividing the church into smaller sections, which was more manageable to host services. That meant ordaining new ministers, casting lots to select men who were ordained to spread the gospel. This was a sacred thing, and one Elsie didn't fully understand. She had overheard her parents' conversation about how hard it was for Ben Zook, being only twenty-seven years old and so shy and humble. He took it hard when he was chosen, but his wife, Sarah, would be a great help.

In the days leading up to church, Elsie went to school, came home, and worked. She scoured the bathroom and ironed curtains, polished floors and raked leaves. She was old enough now to notice the walls that needed a good cover of paint and the uneven, pockmarked cement floor. There wasn't much she could do about those things, though, and she figured people understood. They knew her family didn't have much money and that it wasn't for lack of hard work or due to frivolous spending.

She helped her mother bake dried-apple pies on the Saturday morning before church services would be held in the garage the following day. First, Mam put the dried-apple *snitz* in a large, sixteen-quart kettle, poured a fair amount of water into it, and set it to boil. Flavored with brown sugar, white sugar, and cinnamon, thickened with granules of minute tapioca, the pie filling was wonderful.

Years ago, dried-apple *snitz* was the way church pies were made, but along the way some enterprising person had proved to have a faster method, using apple butter and applesauce, instead of peeling, slicing, and drying apples, storing them, and cooking them down. It was much easier to dump two gallons of applesauce and one of apple butter and flavor it, and it tasted about the same. But there were many apples in the old orchard, and unwilling to waste any of them, Elsie's mother always picked them up and peeled, sliced, and dried them on an old window screen placed on a rack on the stove. They often wound up with more dried apples than jars of applesauce or apple butter, so they still made *snitz* the traditional way.

Elsie brushed the tops of the crusts with beaten egg, sifted a handful of piecrust crumbs over that, then washed dishes and kept Amos away from the hot stove.

She was secretly proud of her mother's beautiful pies. It took away the sting of not being able to serve sliced ham or bologna, which her parents could not afford. Aunt Mamie was bringing ten dozen red beet eggs and Aunt Annie had said she'd bring a box of seasoned pretzels. The ladies from church would bring cheese spread, peanut butter, and marshmallow spread, loaf after loaf of homemade bread, and cakes and desserts.

Her Saturday was perfect. The weather was beautiful, the air nippy enough that she needed a sweater to mow grass. The leaves were raked and burned, the flower beds cleaned out, the borders cut perfectly with the string trimmer. Windows gleamed after their washing, the siding was free of dust and fly dirt, and the floor of the garage was washed and dried, the carpet laid, and tool shelves covered with old white bedsheets.

Her father set the benches, carrying them in from the racks built into the bench wagon, the large gray homemade enclosures on steel wheels that brought the benches, dishes, and hymnbooks to the home where services would be held. Anna Marie bounced around like a little rabbit, slapping the rows of benches as she dashed between them. Suvilla chased her up and down the long rows till Dat made them stop. It was exciting to host church services, especially for the children.

Elsie leaned into the push mower, down at the lower end of the yard, where the grass was so thick and hard. She had reached the end of the row and turned to lean on her mower handle to catch her breath when she heard the familiar *clip clip clip clip* of a pony's small, light hooves. A horse's feet went slower, and clopped heavily, where a pony's feet moved more quickly, creating a staccato sound.

Just her luck. Here she was, standing beside the road, and here they came, that Elam and his strange little brother, Benny. There was no avoiding the arrogant brothers today. She contemplated diving into the undergrowth beside the yard, but figured they'd already seen her, wearing the bright red dress, black sweater, and white scarf. They couldn't miss her.

She leaned into the mower, without stopping to look or allowing herself the privilege of watching the pony in action.

"Hey!"

She heard the hello, but kept on going, not wanting to give Elam the satisfaction of her longing. She'd never have a pony, so why should he get to look down on where she stood, gazing admiringly at his beautiful Cookie?

"Hey, stop!"

She stopped and glared with what she hoped was an icy look. At least condescending, as in, *Can't you see I'm busy? And it doesn't matter one tittle that you can drive that beautiful pony while I push this clunky old mower around.*

"Elsie."

"What?"

"I'm getting a horse. A paint. Black and white. My dad says I'm too big for a Shetland pony. Ask your dad if you can buy Cookie."

For a moment her heart leaped, but just as quickly reality came crashing back. "Yeah. Well, you know."

"What?"

"We couldn't afford to keep a pony."

"It's that bad?"

Elsie shrugged. "S'what my father says."

"Too bad."

"Yeah."

Benny lifted his face to wipe a trail of mucus from his nose with his coat sleeve.

Elsie swallowed. Gross. *Use a handkerchief,* she thought.

"You look like a red-headed woodpecker," Benny announced, after a second swipe at his streaming nose.

Elam threw back his head and laughed so loudly he sounded like a blue jay. Elsie narrowed her eyes and told Benny she didn't see how he could see at all with that hat over his eyes.

Elam interrupted before Benny could send back another retort. "Well, if I get my horse, bring your sisters to see him. I'll give them a ride with Cookie."

He lifted the reins and moved off without a backward glance.

Elsie watched them go, the up-and-down rhythm of the cart, the pony's hooves hitting the macadam in light, quick succession, then turned back to her mowing.

She would. She'd take her sisters to see his new horse. He'd probably only said it because he pitied them, not because he actually thought they'd come. But why shouldn't she? She didn't want him feeling sorry for her. She was happy and led a good life with loving parents and sweet sisters. Well, there was always Amos, but he couldn't really help how he acted, being only one year old. So Elam could stop pitying her, if that's what he was doing.

Her mother praised her efforts, said the yard looked wonderful, so green and evenly cut, and that she didn't know what she'd do without her help.

"You're so capable, Elsie. Thank you."

Her dat's smile was the sweetest icing on the cake, and Elsie thought no pony could ever mean more to her than her parents' kindness.

The following morning they all got out of bed at five o'clock and ate a hurried breakfast of oatmeal and toast. Then Elsie washed dishes while Mam did the little girls' hair, dressed them in colorful blue dresses with black pinafore-style aprons of black capes and belt aprons, pinned their white coverings on their heads, and told them to sit quietly now, don't go get yourselves all wrinkled and *schtruvvlich*.

Elsie changed Amos's cloth diaper, then dressed him in a little white shirt with a black vest and trousers, attached the hooks to the eyes of the vest front, and told him he looked like Dat.

"Da. Da," he said proudly, marching around the kitchen on short, fat legs.

"Better get your hair done, Elsie," Mam said, glancing at the clock.

So Elsie went to the bathroom, got out the brush and fine-toothed comb, the plastic spritz bottle of water, and set to work. Her hair was heavy—dark brown with a reddish undertone. Mam said it was auburn, but no one else said that. Her round face was tanned, so the smattering of freckles was barely visible. In winter, when the tan faded, the freckles looked like bits of dirt someone had thrown in her face, and stuck. She hated her freckles.

Her eyes were big and green as a dill pickle. She didn't like her eyes, either. She looked a lot like a frog with her eyes so far apart, but there wasn't much you could do about that.

No one ever said anything about her looks, so she had no idea how one went about evaluating oneself. The girls her age in school didn't really include her when they discussed dress fabric or new shoes, where their mothers shopped, or what color their bedrooms were, which was just as well. She didn't have her own bedroom, and her mother never shopped for clothes. As far as she could tell, their clothes were all bought at yard sales or thrift shops, which was fine with her.

She pulled on the fine-toothed comb, drew the heavy tresses back at the desired angle, then clipped the bobby pins on each side. She gathered her hair into an elastic ponytail holder and wrapped it expertly into a bun on the back of her head. A few pumps of water, an overhead shower of hairspray, and Elsie was finished.

She slipped the blue dress over her head and her mother brought the white cape and apron and quickly pinned them in place, muttering about her growth spurt, the apron a good two inches too short. Elsie placed the white covering on her head, and she was ready.

Mam took a second look, a bewildering appraisal that would follow her repeatedly through her days. Mam looked as if she might cry, or laugh. She actually looked a bit hysterical.

"You look nice, Elsie," she said gruffly, and turned away.

She wondered if she did look nice. She even went to the bathroom mirror to check, but she looked the same as she always had.

Fast-stepping horses pulled freshly washed carriages up to the house, dropped off the women and girls, then moved on to the barn, where the men would unhitch and tie the horses to the wooden flatbed wagon her father had set in the barnyard. Blocks of hay were scattered along both sides, so the horses could have a snack after their bridles were removed and comfortable halters slipped over their heads.

Elsie often thought those horses could easily drag that wagon off, a sort of mutiny, a horse rebellion, but they were all docile creatures, well trained and obedient, standing there tethered to the wagon to work till they were untied and led to the carriage, backed between the shafts, and ordered to pull the family home. But that wasn't the only reason she loved horses. They were beautiful creatures with soft, expressive eyes that showed a good spirit, ears that flicked from front to back, and gorgeous flowing manes that rippled the way she imagined prairie grass did, or the ocean waves. "Splendid" was the perfect word to describe a horse.

Elsie filed into church services with the bunch of single girls, quietly, seated by age, the way all Amish girls were traditionally seated. At first, she looked down at her lap, shyness washing over her like a wet shower, but later, after the singing had started, she looked up to find a whole row of ministers, single boys, and young fathers staring at her. Well, they weren't actually staring at her, but it seemed as if they were. Some of the older girls were chewing gum, whispering, or flirting with a few of the bold *rumschpringa*-aged boys. Most of the girls sat decently, listening to the rising and falling of the preacher's voice.

When they began to sing the last song, Elsie rose and made her way along the long line of girls to help her mother, grandmother, and aunts prepare the food for lunch. They set out fourteen Styrofoam bowls of pickles and fourteen of pickled red beets with the purplish-pink hardboiled eggs nestled among them. There were also seasoned pretzels, spreads, jelly, butter, and pie.

Elsie helped stack towers of homemade bread slices on plates, then turned her back to spread a bit of cheese spread on a crust of bread, quickly gulping it down in a few bites. Breakfast had been a long time ago.

The rest of the day was spent in the company of her cousins, her grandmother Malinda, and all the chattering aunts. Elsie was always genuinely happy to be among them, a part of a growing circle of belonging, new babies and new husbands or wives added every year.

She didn't mind the absence of sliced ham. Not until Rosanne complained about it. The crust of bread stuck in her throat and she coughed and took a drink of water, deeply ashamed.

Elsie heard Rosanne whisper, "We never have ham here. They're poor."

Nothing to do or say about that, so she left it where it belonged. With them.

She figured sliced ham and a pony were no match for kindness, happiness, and contentment, which they had. All three of those things. So much they tumbled out of a container, ran out, and dripped on the tabletop. But you couldn't tell people things like that without sounding boastful.

She had been helping with the tables and had to eat last, with the aunts and mothers. A few boys had not yet eaten, so they were seated at the same table. She found herself next to Elam Stoltzfus, his little brother Benny opposite, hardly recognizable in clean Sunday clothes and without the smashed hat.

Benny sized up his brother with Elsie and said in

a much too loud tone of voice that they looked as if they were getting married, then honked and wheezed at his hilarity, receiving a withering look from Elsie. But from Elam he got a wide grin that pretty much amounted to a home-run high five, which set him to chortling in glee.

Chapter Three

AFTER CHURCH SERVICES WERE HELD IN THE garage, everything was put back in order. Dat worked at putting the benches back into the bench wagon, with Elsie's help. Mam scrubbed floors and dusted, took care of all the leftovers, washed the front porch, and had a long nap with her little ones snuggled by her side.

That Saturday, Elsie and two of her sisters, Malinda and Suvilla, walked over to the Stoltzfus farm. Elsie's desperation to drive a pony overrode any unwillingness she might have had to accept Elam's invitation. It was time she experienced holding the reins, being in charge of the high-stepping pony drawing the lovely cart.

Of course, she'd have to admire the new horse, too, which was annoying. That was all she ever did, it seemed. Admire Elam's horses and his ability to drive them.

Well. Things were about to change.

She marched up to the front door and talked to Elam's mother, who was a good friend of her family, a comfortable, middle-aged woman with spreading hips and a loud voice.

"Yes," she said, "go on out, they're out there in the barn with the horses." Then she handed Malinda and Suvilla lollipops, those big ones with Tootsie rolls inside.

Elam met them at the barn door.

"What's up, Elsie?"

"I came over to see your horse."

"Good. Benny, hitch up Cookie to give the girls a ride."

"Sure. Come this way, girls, you can help me hitch him up. Hey, where'd you get those?" He pointed at the lollipops.

"Your mam," Malinda said quietly.

Elsie followed Elam to a box stall and waited while he opened the gate and led a horse out to the forebay. It was a vision, like a horse from her dreams. It was mostly white, the back a dazzling, glossy black. It had large, gentle eyes, a shapely neck with a small head and curved ears, and a black mane and tail.

Elsie was speechless. She stood and stared at that horse with huge green eyes, her mouth open but no words coming out of it. She wanted to act cool, as if this horse wasn't anything special, she'd seen hundreds just like him, but she couldn't do it.

Finally she said, "He's really nice."

"Right?"

Elsie nodded, dumbfounded.

"You want to ride him? He has a mind of his own. You have to let him know who's in charge."

Elsie shook her head.

"No, I can't ride in a dress."

She waved a hand self-consciously over her skirt.

"My sisters do," Elam said.

"But they probably wear something, don't they? I mean, you know, under their skirt."

"Yeah, they do."

Elsie put a hand on the beautiful paint's neck, slid it slowly to his head, the side of his face. The horse lowered his head, so Elsie stroked the perfect ears, ran her fingers through the long black hair that hung over his forehead. When the horse laid his soft nose against her sweater, she looked at Elam in disbelief.

"He likes me."

Elam grinned. "Looks like it, doesn't it?"

Elsie placed both hands on the horse's face, one on each side, and whispered, "You lovely, lovely creature, you." She glanced at Eli. "What's his name?"

"Haven't named him yet."

"Do you have an idea?"

"I'll think of something."

He didn't ask her for suggestions, so Elsie stepped back as Elam led the horse away. Elsie felt a decided sense of loss and wondered how long it would be before she could touch the satiny neck below the heavy mane again.

She drove Cookie that day. She sat in the driver's seat and held on to the reins with both hands, Elam to her left and Benny sandwiched in between. The feeling of sitting on the upholstered seat, her feet pushed up against the front of the cart for balance, the reins in her hands, the smell of the leather and pony, the up-and-down rhythm of the cart, was beyond description.

Most of all, the ripple of energy that snaked along the reins from the bit in Cookie's mouth was unlike anything she had ever experienced. To turn to the right or left took a slight touch, only a gentle drawing back on either rein. She imagined the tender mouth, the alert, intelligent pony who could feel the modest pressure on the iron bit in his mouth. She kept a steady tension on the reins, turned him perfectly.

That was when the real thrill began.

Sensing he was homeward bound, Cookie's ears pricked forward, his steps increased, and Elsie steadied her hands and applied more pressure.

"Hold him," Elam said evenly.

Elsie bit her lip, didn't answer. She was so intent on doing just that, she barely heard his words. Realizing her hands were not where they should be, she gripped the reins with one hand till she was able to hold them farther out, away from her body, in order to apply all her strength.

Cookie bent his neck, took the bit in his teeth, and ran. His heavy mane flapped up and down, his neck was arched, his ears turned forward, his legs churning as his little hooves pounded the macadam.

Blip, blip, blip—the staccato sound stirred an unnamed emotion in her. She drew her mouth into a straight line, her lower lip caught between her teeth, to stop the shameful tears that came to her eyes.

This was unreal. This was pure, heady joy.

A great love for the spirited little animal welled up until she was afraid her breathing would be stopped.

"Hold him!" Elam yelled.

Elsie didn't answer, just kept up a steady force on the leather reins, her arms extended, her back straight.

Benny yelled something unintelligible from beneath the crushed straw hat, but Elsie stayed quiet, concentrating on driving the energized pony.

There was the Stoltzfuses' driveway. Going at this rate, there was no possible way to make the turn. She used all her remaining strength to slow Cookie, but it was no use.

"Just keep going," Elam said, laughing.

So she did. Soon enough, the pony slowed, and Elsie could turn him around easily, then trot into the driveway at a decent pace. In spite of the diminished speed, the wheels were pulled sideways, scraping a wide arc in the gravel.

To approach the barn contained another sense of

loss. Elsie sat on the cart, reluctant to hand over the reins. But she knew she was being selfish, so she did, without meeting Elam's eyes.

"Thank you," she said quietly.

"You're welcome."

Malinda and Suvilla were given a ride, then it was time to go home. Elsie had a dozen questions to ask, but felt too shy, not wanting to be a pest. So she gathered her little sisters and they thanked Elam again.

"Right-o," he said. Then, "You're a good driver, seeing that was your first time."

Elsie mumbled something unintelligible and left, herding her sisters out the drive and down the road.

After that day, Elsie's passion for horses took on a new intensity. She planned and schemed and connived the best possible approach of acquiring a pony. Or a horse.

She worked hard after school. She mowed the grass for the last time, raked leaves, and washed the porch floor with soapy water and a stiff broom. She walked to the neighboring farm for milk, watched

Amos on Saturdays while her mother went to town for groceries, and never complained about any job, no matter how difficult.

She asked her father again.

"You still haven't given up on a pony?" he asked, laying aside a copy of the newspaper that was thrown in their yard twice a week.

"No."

"We shouldn't have allowed you to go to the boys' place."

"Why?" Elsie asked, already touching the substance of his refusal.

"Well, it certainly didn't help with your pony obsession."

He reached over to retrieve his coffee cup, slurped the hot black liquid, and replaced the cup back on the light stand. "If you'd never driven that pony, you wouldn't know what you're missing. It's just like being Amish and driving a horse and buggy. If you never own a vehicle or learn to drive one, you remain content, and that's as it should be. You know how often I've told you, Elsie—the funds simply aren't available. When you're older, the income you'll bring in for your family will be a welcome boost to the household finances. I can't help my handicap any more than you can help being born into a family like us."

He hesitated. "Not that there's anything wrong with us. We have more than enough—we're rich, compared to many people. I have to give up every morning to having only one hand, and you will have to practice giving up your own will as well. Giving up at a young age is essential to becoming a well-grounded, mature adult. You must learn to be happy without everything you think you can't live without. Material things are not important, Elsie."

Elsie sniffed, toyed with the fringe on the old granny-square afghan that always lay on the arm of the green tufted sofa. Elsie hated that afghan. Mam had dug through the free box at a neighbor's yard sale, pulled it out with shining eyes, and held it up for Elsie to admire in all its hideous, pilled, musty glory.

"But ponies and cars are different. Ponies are allowed," she said, her voice already hushed as she struggled to accept her father's words.

Later, she talked to her mother while they washed dishes.

"Oh, Elsie, do you have any idea how gladly I would give you a pony? I can see it in your eyes, and it hurts to see you standing at the gate, watching Elam and Benny. But what your father tells you is the truth, and hard as it may be, it's better to say no than to try to hand over everything you girls ask for."

"Well, we never ask for anything, so how do you know?" Elsie burst out, and then saw her mam's strained expression and wished she'd kept her mouth shut.

Winter came with a fierce blast of icy Arctic air and gray clouds that churned and boiled above them like woolen sheep. Mam hurried to pull the last of the turnips and carrots, the woodstove in the living room crackled and burned, and the baseball games came to a chilly end.

Standing shivering in the frigid wind and stomping their feet to stay warm took away the thrill of popping flyers and catching grounders. The Ping-Pong table was set up in the middle of the classroom, and serious competition ensued.

Christmas excitement was in the air, especially after the teacher handed out parts for the Christmas program. The pupils giggled behind their copies, raised hands, and asked dozens of questions until the harried teacher became red-faced and impatient, snapping at her overenthused troupe and efficiently deflating the Christmas spirit.

Elsie walked home from school, her Christmas poem in her lunch box, her head down, her feet shuffling. Ahead of her, Malinda raced in circles with her friends, not yet touched by the burden of being poor, of being different than everyone else.

Elsie dreaded Christmastime. With each passing year, it got worse. Eating her cheese sandwich, listening to the upper grades chattering on about their wish lists, the shopping, the wrapping and gift giving, the final blow the tallying of mounds of different items they received. Of course, Elsie never participated.

She imagined herself seated beside Rosanne and Lydia Mae, talking about her new pony named Dream, or the coat her mother had found at Target. What was Target? She had no idea. At least there was a big meal to look forward to. There was always *roasht*, mashed potatoes, candied carrots, and home-made noodles with plenty of rich brown gravy. There were cookies and homemade candy, Rice Krispies treats, peanut butter fudge, and chocolate-covered peanuts and raisins. But they each received only one gift—a doll or a pair of warm slippers. Never both.

And so when Christmastime came, Elsie caved inward, became quieter and more reserved. She was who she was, and accepted it, but it still rankled at times, like a burr stuck in her sock. You suffered the itch until you took the time to reach down and extract it, which was actually a whole lot easier than extracting this jealousy, or whatever you called it when you stood on the sidelines and knew you amounted to the grand total of zero.

By the time Elsie had completed eighth grade and had been given a diploma saying she had successfully passed to vocational class, she had driven Cookie a number of times, but never came close to acquiring a horse of her own.

Elam became different, then.

He didn't help her hitch up Cookie anymore. Benny did. Elam was always busy on the farm. He never looked at her anymore, either, just sort of swung his gaze behind her head and looked at whatever was back there. He blushed. Furiously. His face turned dark red and he blinked so rapidly he hardly knew what to do.

That was a mysterious thing to Elsie, but she figured he pitied her for not being able to have a pony and didn't know what to do about it. Boys were like that. She had observed this phenomenon many times, watching them get softhearted with sympathy or admiration and covering it all up with a hard exterior.

So she didn't think about it much, just let Elam go his way, and she went hers.

Benny became her funny little friend, though. He didn't try to be funny, he just was. He hardly ever took that straw hat off, even in winter. The brim had torn along the crown, from Benny yanking on it so much, so when it was really windy, the front of his hat would be blown straight up, which acted like a sail and tugged even harder, causing Benny to run around the farm with one hand smashed down on top of his head.

When Elsie turned fifteen, she was through vocational class and ready to look for a job. She had four options: working at the market, helping at one of the many local dry-goods stores, housecleaning for English ladies, or being *maud* to Amish housewives who had a new baby, were housecleaning, or simply needed an extra hand at canning or freezing the garden produce. Elsie shrewdly calculated hours, the price paid per hour, and how many days her mother would allow her to work. Though housecleaning paid the most per hour, working at the market would bring in the most money, since the days were long.

So her mother called Amish market stand owners until she procured Elsie a job at the Reading Terminal Market, a place teeming with city folks and hundreds of vendors hawking their goods inside an old railroad station converted to a farmers' market. She would be working for Eli Beiler, starting at a hundred dollars a day, being picked up at 4:00 a.m. Sharp. "She has to be ready," Eli had said. "If we stop two minutes at everyone's house we lose fifteen to twenty minutes to get to market. Can't do that."

That scared Elsie. She pictured a king on his throne. A slave owner on horseback holding a whip in one hand.

Her mother hitched the old horse to the buggy and they went to the fabric store to buy cloth for three new dresses. She dug through the large cardboard box on the porch that was marked "Clearance" with a fluorescent yellow sign. Some of the fabric just wasn't selling well; most had a bit of a flaw imprinted into the weave or a few snags.

Mam picked up a bolt of blue fabric with tiny checks in it.

"It's a little fancy," she mused, "but at this price . . ."

Elsie shrugged. She was glad for the new clothes, but would have preferred to use every bit of extra money toward a pony.

"Do you like this?" her mother asked, holding up a bolt of green with a puckered surface.

Elsie gave a noncommittal nod. "Whatever you think. I'm going to look at books."

Mam chose plain white fabric for two new bib aprons, saying her dresses all had a bit of a pattern in them so they'd have to be toned down a bit with the white aprons.

Elsie shrugged again. If she was honest with herself, it wasn't just that she'd rather spend the money on a pony. The thing was, most girls wore pretty new dresses, hoping to get the attention of some boy or to impress the other girls, even if they didn't admit it. She knew she wasn't going be popular, whether she had a fancy new dress or not. Especially now that school was over and she hardly ever saw the other kids her age. She intended to spend as much of her time working as she possibly could—not socializing, and especially not with boys. Elam was the only friend she cared about as far as boys went, but he had turned into an awkward, pimply, blushing creature she couldn't begin to understand, so that was that.

She picked up a romance novel with a horse on the cover and turned it over. $13.99. She read the paragraph on the back, was stabbed with intense longing, but placed it back on the shelf. You could get all kinds of books at yard sales for a quarter, fifty cents, or a dollar. Mam rejected every one that looked vaguely intriguing, said they weren't fit. None of her girls were ever going to fill their heads with that romance stuff. It wasn't true, anyhow.

That left Elsie to wonder how much her mother felt slighted by her father's mishap. Or maybe she had just let love and romance wither and die, leaving only bitterness and a sour attitude.

But no. Her mother and father sincerely loved each other. There was too much happiness and love in their house to think such thoughts. Her parents truly loved each other, no doubt. So with books, like horses, Elsie gave up. She obeyed, didn't question, stayed within the boundaries her parents set for her.

Mam sewed the three dresses, allowing Elsie to sew the top of one, the least expensive. Elsie found it frustrating, setting the sleeves properly, learning to sew in a straight line, but with her mother's encouragement, she didn't do too badly. The bib aprons were harder, so Mam sewed them herself, pressed them, and let Elsie slide one over her head and tie it behind her back.

Elsie stood back, turned slowly for her mother's benefit.

"All right."

That was all she said.

Just all right.

Elsie thought she looked at her with a strange light in her eyes, but that was probably from bending over the sewing machine all day.

She was surprised when her mother came into her bedroom after the lamp was already extinguished. She carried a small battery lamp, her old, faded housecoat swishing as she moved across the floor.

"Elsie."

"Hmm?"

"I want you to be aware of yourself at market. Not all men are honorable. Some might do you harm by wanting you the way a man is not supposed to want a young girl. Here is a book for you to read. It's about how to conduct yourself in a Christian way when you're out in public. You have grown up in the past year, so I think you need to be aware of the proper behavior for a young girl."

With that, she left the room, closing the door softly behind her.

Obediently, Elsie read the thin booklet. It changed

her life forever. She was so deeply shaken she read her *Black Beauty* book for an hour before falling into a restless half sleep that left her tired and irritable in the morning.

When her mother asked if she had read the book, she threw a withering look in her direction and went to the washhouse to begin sorting dirty laundry.

Chapter Four

AND SO ELSIE ENTERED THE VAST, BEWILDER-
ing world of the farmers' market, thrust into an
atmosphere of hustle and bustle, a fast-paced energy
that carried her in its unwilling arms and spilled her
on the cracked cement floor, struggling heroically to
maintain a smidgen of composure.

She knew nothing of piecrusts and rising yeast rolls.
Eli Beiler said they would train her. Ha. The "training" composed of being yelled at by a fat, domineering
woman with thin black hair, a unibrow, and, perched
on a sausage nose, heavy glasses with lenses so thick
they made her eyes appear like little black marbles.

She was vast. Huge. Her white bib apron was so
tight the strings that were knotted around her waist
were completely hidden in rolls of flesh. They called
her Rache, as if she was too busy to finish pronounc-
ing her name. If you tried to call her Rachel, she'd be
through the swinging doors before you could say the
last syllable.

Elsie was given a recipe, a few basic instructions on the mechanics of a huge electric mixer, introduced to a girl named Lillian, and told to take a fifteen-minute break at ten o'clock.

Lillian was short, blond, and almost as loud as Rache. She was also extremely fancy, wearing a pink dress with tight sleeves and a hem that scraped the soles of her shoes. She talked nonstop, chewed gum and snapped it with regularity, drank Pepsi from a plastic cup filled with ice, and ran around on her Nike-clad feet, darting everywhere like an anxious bee.

"OK, here. This is what you do. You dump this out, like this."

She was interrupted by a screech from the mountainous Rache.

"Lillian, stop doing everything for her. She'll never learn. Elsie, here, step up and get that pile of dough onto the kneading table. Lillian, step back, there."

So Elsie dumped, heaved, and learned by bitter trial and error. Lillian was basically very kind, she was just so terribly speedy and outspoken. Rache grumbled all day about being stuck training these new ones, Eli sending them in as innocent as babies.

She eyed Elsie and asked who named daughters that anymore. Poor thing.

Kindhearted Lillian took up for her, said Elsie was old-fashioned, it was cool. "I'll call you Els."

Rache snorted and popped half a custard-filled doughnut in her mouth.

"Elsie, don't wad that dough up like that. These are dinner rolls, so they have to be handled lightly. Use more of that oil spray. These rolls will stick to the pan if you don't."

Elsie was lightheaded with hunger and fatigue by lunchtime. Her ten o'clock break had consisted of hiding in the bathroom for fifteen minutes, ashamed to let anyone in that bakery know she didn't have money to buy snacks. Mam had said she could eat bakery items, but she was too shy to ask for a dough-nut or a whoopee pie. Lillian brought back a few bites of a cheeseburger and some limp fries with wet ketchup stains on them.

"You want this? I'm full."

"You sure?"

Nothing had ever tasted quite as good as those soggy fries and that tepid burger.

All day they mixed, kneaded, shaped, and baked bread, dinner rolls, sandwich rolls, and sticky buns.

Rache yelled at them about the size of the sandwich rolls. "Who was shaping these? Elsie, you need to use more dough."

Not once did Elsie venture into the crowded aisle ways. It seemed like a human stampede, a place where all manner of humanity would walk all over you, crushing you in the process.

She had nothing to eat all day, except the few bites of Lillian's leftover food. She rode home in the back seat of the fifteen-passenger van, crossed her arms over her empty stomach, and didn't talk to anyone.

She burst into tears the moment she spied her mother's face, the story of that awful day coming out in bits and pieces.

"Ach my, Elsie. I had no idea. I am so sorry. Here, sit down."

Elsie shook her head, blew her nose, said she wanted a long, hot bath first. When she returned, her hair dark and wet and wavy, the fine dark smudges of fatigue below her large eyes, the freckles like a constellation of beauty dust, her mother kept the astonishment at her daughter's budding young beauty to herself.

She ate a steaming bowl of vegetable soup with saltines and applesauce, a thick grilled cheese sandwich made with Velveeta cheese and margarine, and sliced peaches and ginger cake for dessert. Then she handed her mother a fifty-dollar bill, two twenties, and a ten. The sensation of gratitude was an unspoken pact.

"Here is your ten dollars, Elsie."

She folded it and put it in the small cedar chest with the horse painted on the lid. She received five more dollars to buy food the next day at the market, then went to bed and slept so deeply her alarm clock's jangling threw her rudely into a strange and alien world.

The second day at Beiler's Bakery was no worse than the first, but didn't prove to be much better, either. She accidentally dropped a heavy plastic dishpan of dough, which set Rache to yelping like a frightened puppy. She came at them like a steaming locomotive, saying she couldn't put up with any of this nonsense, she had too much on her mind.

"You mean your hips," muttered Lillian.

Elsie caught her eye and grinned.

At lunch she realized she'd have to brave the crowded aisles to buy food. She stepped out timidly, staying near the wall as much as possible, and bought a hot dog and a drink, plus a bag of potato chips, all for $2.50. She would pocket the remaining money and add it to her savings. She was given an apple by the white-bearded Amish man at the produce stand and a chocolate cupcake by Eli Beiler himself.

He asked how her day was going.

"All right. OK, I guess."

"Good." And he was off.

He didn't care, Elsie reminded herself from time to time. Neither did Rache or Anna or Judy, the English lady who sat at the cash register. In the world of profit and sales, it was each man to himself. Or each girl. So Elsie learned not to expect praise, to be seen without being noticed, to work hard and do her best, just like at school.

Lillian helped her comb her hair to complement her face. She told her she could actually be very pretty if she learned a few things.

"You have gorgeous eyes. You should let me shape your eyebrows."

Elsie was horrified. She had never heard of such a thing.

"You just pull out some of those stray hairs from your eyebrows."

Mam noticed the hair immediately.

"Elsie, how you comb your hair! Now, this is not *alaubt*. Absolutely no way will any girl of mine comb her hair like that. You look awfully worldly. Now you go upstairs and roll your hair back the way I have always taught you. Now go."

Mam fussed. Dat's eyes twinkled at her in a happy, dancing way, so she knew her father understood what it was like to be young and wanting to be a part of something. What it was exactly, Elsie could not be sure, but it was there. A possibility. A tentative knowledge that she would not always be the lone girl who said nothing as she ate her cheese sandwich hurriedly, before the others could see the cheese and homemade bread.

As the weeks turned into months, Elsie's little bundle of money grew. Twenty dollars a week for twenty-four weeks amounted to over four hundred dollars. She had spent some on new coverings and a new pair of sneakers that Lillian bought for her when she went to Rockvale Square, a place Elsie had never seen.

So by the time her sixteenth birthday was a month away, Elsie was one of the best workers the bakery had ever hired and was fast friends with Lillian, who was planning on introducing her to her set of youth. Lillian had taken it upon herself to coach Elsie into popularity, telling her she needed to buy a new pattern for her dresses and redecorate her bedroom, that she should smile when a cute boy came to the stand, and that she needed a particular cream to clear up the occasional blemish that appeared on her jawline.

Sometimes it irked Elsie. She would never fit in, whether she smiled at the right moments and spent all her savings on new things or not. She didn't even have her own room. How was she supposed to redecorate it? She had never chosen her bedroom color or the furniture and she would never ever be allowed to go away in cars with other youth on Saturday evenings. Lillian had taken over her life, telling her what was cool, how to dress, how to act, what to say and think and do, as if programming a robotic person.

She spoke to her parents, who said there was nothing wrong with Lillian, that they just were not quite on the same level. They knew Lillian's parents, in fact. Mam had gone to school with her father. But they had always hoped Elsie would join the group that most of the church girls belonged to, which was not the same group that Lillian went to.

Elsie didn't particularly want to go to Lillian's group, but she also didn't want to disappoint her one friend. She agonized over standing her ground, telling Lillian she would be joining the more moderate group of youth.

She wasn't sure she wanted to join either group, really, but she supposed she'd have to eventually. Part of it was that admitting she was old enough to join the other youth meant admitting she was too old for a pony. It didn't seem fair that she had outgrown her childhood dream without ever having had the chance to own even a cheap, old little pony she could hitch to the express wagon. It seemed to her as if the best years of her life were gone, the rides with Benny and Cookie and her sisters only a memory.

It probably wouldn't be long before Benny started blushing and disappearing right off the face of the earth, the way Elam had. Boys were as strange as they'd ever been.

All you had to do was watch Amos, and you'd know boys were strange and disturbing creatures. Amos cut earthworms with his little sand trowel and ran after the skinny barn cats screeching like a mountain lion. He ate raw beans from the garden like a guilty little rabbit, his nose twitching with pleasure, but if you tried to get him to eat cooked vegetables with mashed potatoes, he threw himself back against his highchair and pounded the footrest with his heels. He wasn't even close to potty trained, and it was disastrous every time Mam made a feeble attempt at achieving it.

"He needs a brother," Dat said.

"He needs discipline," Mam said.

Amos said he didn't want a brother, and he didn't want that other thing, either.

Everyone laughed, which set Amos into all kinds of ungainly antics, until he wore himself out and sat on the couch with his hands clasped in his lap, breathing hard.

A few weeks before Elsie's sixteenth birthday, Lillian bounced into the bakery and announced the fact that Jason Riehl had asked her for a date on Saturday evening. Her face was flushed and her eyes shone as she accepted everyone's congratulations.

Suddenly she turned to Elsie, her smile fading. "Sorry, Els. Since I'll be dating, I guess I can't bring you to my group."

Elsie couldn't have been more relieved.

"That's OK, Lillian. I'm . . . eh . . . joining the group my friends at church go to. I just hadn't told you yet."

"Oh, great! Wonderful. That's good."

Elsie was thoroughly hugged, wished the best.

Rache lumbered in with a shipment of yeast. "What's this I hear?"

"I have a date! With Jason. Jason Fisher."

"Who's he?"

"You wouldn't know."

And with that, the day swung into motion. By now Elsie was so accustomed to the mixer, the dough, the time to bake rolls and bread, it seemed as if she could do it with her eyes closed. The bakery was her friend now, her supporter of dreams. She figured by the time she was eighteen years of age she'd have a few thousand dollars, which would enable her to purchase a horse. A riding horse. Then she'd have to pay for the feed.

She hummed as she worked and smiled at Lillian as she relived the evening of the big question. It seemed like she'd been waiting for ages for Jason to ask her, and now he had.

"Well, I don't want a boyfriend," Elsie said, feeling more confident. "I want a horse."

Lillian's mouth fell open. "A horse? Seriously? What for?"

"I love horses."

"You love horses. Hm. That's different for a six-teen-year-old. I mean, isn't it? If you were English you could ride competitively, like girls doing the barrel-racing thing. Hey, did you ever go to that horse thing in Harrisburg? You know, I think it's in February."

Elsie shook her head, then left to bring another fifty-pound bag of flour from storage. Lillian had no clue. Their lifestyles were so completely different, you could hardly begin to compare the vast underlying separateness of their everyday existence. If Lillian guessed that Elsie's family didn't have much extra, it wasn't because Elsie had said anything. She had learned in school to say nothing, to listen, to show happiness for others.

But being sixteen would hold its own new challenges. Elsie could not be expected to compete with any of the other girls. Things like dresses, sweaters, coats, shoes and purses, money to pay drivers or purchase Christmas gifts or wedding presents would have to come out of the amount she was saving for a horse. The horse was far more important than any number of dresses or shoes, she confided to her mother, who responded with raised eyebrows, an incredulous expression.

"But, Elsie, how do you expect us to pay for all your needs? Surely you want your room painted, with new curtains? I thought perhaps we could find some decent furniture at an estate sale, or a moving sale. Suvilla can move in with Malinda. They won't mind sharing a room. And you'll need new dresses, of course."

"I don't care about that stuff."

And she didn't.

Elsie insisted that they not celebrate her sixteenth birthday. It would simply cost too much to buy that enormous cake and gallons of ice cream. She knew her parents murmured in the living room, each one on their old recliner, reading and relaxing before they retired for the night. Both of them thought it inappropriate, this refusal to enter her years of *rumschpringa* without the traditional party, but Elsie remained adamant.

Shortly after her birthday, she received a substantial raise from Eli Beiler. He told her she was carrying the workload of two girls. Elsie blushed furiously, her gaze fastened on her worn thrift-shop sneakers, having no idea how highly Eli Beiler thought of her.

Here was a rare girl. She deserved every penny of the large raise. It wasn't just the fact that she was a hard worker, it was the efficiency of her movements, her quiet, friendly demeanor, her conscientious fifteen-minute breaks that meant she always appeared back at her workplace a few minutes before it was time to start.

She had even won over Rache, which was no small feat. He had often fancied getting rid of Rache, but knew she was indispensable. He needed her to help manage the place, especially the ordering and distributing.

Elsie told her parents about the raise and offered them the amount she had received. In the end, they allowed Elsie to keep thirty dollars instead of twenty, which they declared only reasonable, seeing how she had pleased her boss, been a good example.

"You have truly honored your father and mother," they told her. Now there was thirty dollars. Twenty for the horse, and ten for what she was slowly accepting as necessities for teenagers.

So, at the urging of her mother, Elsie went to the thrift store in Strasburg. She had no idea what color she wanted the walls of her room painted and couldn't have cared less about curtains or any kind of bedspread, quilt, or comforter. Why spend money on things no one would see, things she didn't care about? But she accommodated her mother, agreed to the packaged quilt and shams (what were shams?), and watched a small child throw a temper tantrum about a Ziplock bag containing small items her mother did not allow her to have, while her own mother chose filmy white curtains yellowed with age, mumbling to herself about homemade lye soap and the power to turn anything snowy white.

They left with bags of good items and went to the paint store, where she paid far too much for one gallon of paint the color of a horse's muzzle—the part that was velvet. She swallowed her annoyance at the expense, knowing this decorating brought her mother more pleasure than herself, definitely. And she couldn't take this away from her.

They painted the walls and gave the old woodwork a fresh coat of white. Mam said it didn't matter if the paint was left over from painting the porch posts and said "Exterior" on the side of the plastic five-gallon bucket.

As they worked, her mother gave her sage advice, talking in a breathless tone as she plied the roller. There were many things to learn about *rumschpringa*, she said, stopping to look into her daughter's eyes.

"Things have changed since your father and I ran around. You will belong to a supervised group, where you won't have to worry about some of the improper behavior that used to be tolerated. Well, not really tolerated—there was plenty of concern, sadness, whatever, but no one really knew what to do about the low morals that had crept in over the years."

"So how did things change?"

"Well, a group of parents and ministers took it on themselves to make a change. And you know how hard it is to do that among our people." She shook her head, rolling her paint roller up and down the corrugated roller pan. "But change has come. There are still plenty of *ungehorsam*, but I think this group is a good one. They're decent kids who care about their future, who seemingly want what is right. So when the time comes to begin dating, I want you to think deeply, pray that God will lead you in the path of righteousness. For one thing, you will be expected to spend your evenings in the living room with your chappy, and not upstairs, the way we did."

"Stop saying 'chappy,'" Elsie said.

Her mother laughed, a deep, happy sound that always made Elsie laugh with her.

"Oh, well, that's what we used to say."

"I know. Don't worry about a chappy for me, Mam. I have no intentions of becoming interested in any young man in the near future. Or the far-away future. I want to keep working until I can get a horse and be able to buy feed and hay, a saddle, and a bridle."

Her mother looked doubtful, but she couldn't help but notice the way Elsie's eyes shone as she talked about her long-held dream.

Chapter Five

BY THE TIME ELSIE REACHED HER SEVEN-
teenth birthday, she had learned the ins and outs of
rumschpringa, the do's and don'ts, why there were
popular girls and girls who were not. She learned to
avoid eagerly amorous suitors, too.

Already, she had been "asked" by more than one
nervous, bright-eyed young man awash in thoughts
of romance, wanting her for their girl. She felt coldhearted, cruel, but knew it wouldn't work. She simply had no interest in any of them and was rather
perplexed that they had an interest in her. She had no
idea of her outstanding beauty, her grace and charm.

She understood the girls' room thing now. Her
friends spent many hours visiting each other, sitting
on the bed, happily gossiping, giggling, dressing up.
She enjoyed the time together, reveling in friendship,
the kind that brightens existence for each other. And
her bedroom was pretty—everyone said so.

"Where did you get this unique furniture?"

"It's really lovely."

Her parents had acquired the furniture at an estate sale, a dull brown thing without a headboard for the bed, a mirror that was broken, and drawer pulls that were so loose they came off in her hand. Her father measured and adjusted, fixed and nailed things together, while her mother applied layers of white primer and paint and glaze. The results were amazing. Her parents did not tell her the weeks of penny-pinching that followed, but she knew, and loved her parents even more.

They made this sacrifice for her.

She was in the garden when he stopped his horse, slid the buggy door aside, and said hello.

Elsie straightened, wiped the back of her hand across her forehead, leaving a brown smudge, and smiled.

Elam. All grown up now, his hair cut fashionably, wearing a white polo shirt and no suspenders, his shoulders wide, his face tanned and chiseled, his eyes deep and dark. Elsie noticed all this fleetingly, her eyes going to the magnificent horse hitched to his buggy—black, huge, and powerful, the neck thick and arched, with a wavy mane that rippled in the evening sun. The horse's feet had long fur around the hooves, in the back, so that his graceful legs looked as if he wore boots.

He stood at attention, his head held high, both front hooves aligned perfectly, his ears flicking, swiveling easily, alert for a command from his master.

Elsie's mouth formed an O of admiration, but there were no words.

"You still looking for a horse?"

Dumbly, she nodded.

"I think I know of someone who has one for you."

"Serious?"

"I think so."

"Where is he?"

"It's a ways off. I thought maybe you'd enjoy a ride over to see him."

Elsie nodded. "When?"

"How about Friday night?"

"You mean, with . . . ?"

She could only incline her head in the direction of the horse hitched to his carriage.

"Yeah, this one can travel twenty miles without becoming winded. His stamina is amazing."

Almost, she echoed him, saying, "He's more than amazing!" But she was certain Elam knew what he was driving, so why gush and exclaim unnecessarily?

"You'll go?" he asked.

"Yes. I certainly will."

"OK. I'll pick you up around five."

She didn't get home from market till seven. It would be too late.

"Uh, I'm sorry. I don't get home till seven."

"How about Saturday night, then? Five?"

"I could do that."

"Good. I'll see you then."

He tugged slightly on the reins and the horse lifted his feet with perfect fluid grace. The steel rims of the buggy wheels moved, crunched on gravel, and he was gone, the gray buggy top, the black underside and wheels with the slow-moving vehicle emblem and row of reflectors shining in the sun.

Elsie turned back to her hoeing, wondering how he knew she still wanted a horse. After school was over, they had parted ways, in every sense of the word. He worked on a construction crew, had joined another youth group, and hardly ever attended church services, likely going to church with buddies who were in other districts.

But he must have remembered.

She bent down to retrieve a long-rooted dandelion from among the cabbages, wondering what had become of Benny. Certainly, the straw hat would be gone from his head, as he approached the age where young men thought about their appearance. Who knew, though? He might still be wearing a hat below his eyebrows, squinting at the world with his altered eyesight.

Elsie smiled to herself, then began humming.

Was it possible her dream may be coming true? A real live horse. Elam had not elaborated on the breed, the place, or anything, really.

She pictured a stable. One of those huge, standing-seam, metal-roofed barns with siding stained to a cheerful yellow-brown color that resembled logs, huge paddocks and riding arenas, a lush pasture dotted with excellent horses. Equine paradise.

Elam would know a good horse when he saw one, so there was no sense in worrying if the animal would be appropriate.

Perhaps, if she was lucky, she'd have money left over for a used saddle and bridle. She thought of the beautiful hues of color on the Navajo-inspired saddle blankets thrown in heaps at the harness shop in Gordonville. To own one of them would be a stroke of good fortune. She loved to follow her father to this shop, the odor of leather and dye, oil and horses, the air sharp with the smell of new nylon ropes and halters. Even as a small child, she had followed her father into the dim interior and stood mesmerized, tracing a design on a brand-new saddle with a forefinger, stepping up as close as possible to the layers of leather harnesses and sniffing deeply. The bio-plastic harness had no smell, which was quite sad, but Dat said they were lighter, better.

Elsie didn't agree, but never said so.

Her anticipation mounted as the days went by. Friday seemed so far off. Lillian was preoccupied, grouchy, if it came right down to it, so there was no happy banter, no Jason this and Jason that. At least Lillian's happy prattle made the day pass swiftly, every week. Finally, Elsie told herself to stop watching the clock. If she checked every fifteen minutes it seemed as if the day would never end.

Rache lumbered into the yeast bread corner, carrying a handful of silver trays.

"Hey you, Lillian. Elsie, that last batch of hamburger rolls was too small. I mean, the rolls. You have to stop skimping on the dough. That's not going to help our sales."

When there was no answer, she cleared her throat.

"Just so you know."

Then she turned on her heel and moved away.

"Good. You didn't talk to her, either," Lillian commented.

"I couldn't think of anything to say. I guess they were too small."

"Puh. She isn't happy if she doesn't pick on someone."

And so Elsie picked up speed, tried to correct the problem, and stopped watching the clock. In spite of her best efforts, the day seemed endless. Her shoulders ached, her feet hurt, and she was upset at Lillian.

Saturday was even worse.

Finally, she found her coworker in a corner, her back turned, wiping her eyes with a crumpled Kleenex, her nose red and swollen.

Without thinking, Elsie slipped an arm around her waist, and whispered, "What's wrong, Lillian?"

Without answering, Lillian tore away from her, knocking down a pyramid of bread pans that clattered to the floor, creating a sound that brought Rache immediately.

"Seriously, Lillian," she said, in a low, threatening voice.

Red-faced and flustered, Lillian bent to gather up the pans, keeping her face averted without giving Rache the satisfaction of a reply.

"Try not to let that happen again."

Lillian straightened, her eyes shooting sparks of outrage.

"It was an accident, OK? So go mind your own business." Then she muttered "Fat cow" under her breath, or what she hoped was under her breath, but

Rache caught the nasty slur and went crying to Eli Beiler, and Lillian was let go that day.

Fired.

Elsie was horrified. She felt awful about Lillian and worried for herself. To be fired from her job would be complete annihilation of her dream. A popped balloon.

She couldn't afford to be in ill spirits and must certainly never vent her feelings about a coworker. She must pay close attention to details. If there was no market job, there was no horse.

The thing was, Rache was indispensable. She was the queen of the bakery. So there was no use denying her superior position, or fighting against it. Elsie felt a stab of pity for Lillian, her unnamed troubles, and the stinging humiliation of being fired.

Rache confided in her, then. It wasn't just the slur; Lillian had been slacking off in her duties, which Elsie was carrying, until she was easily doing three fourths of everything, and it wasn't fair.

Rache sat down, braced her tired back with her palms clipping her knees, a cup of cappuccino at her elbow, and said she had been trying to get her niece to take Lillian's place for a while already, but wasn't having any luck.

"She isn't interested." She sighed, took a sip of her hot drink, grimaced, pried the lid off, and blew across the top. "Hot, hot, hot," she said.

"Do you have anyone in mind?" she asked, after swirling a mouthful like Listerine mouthwash, then bending for another slurp, more grimacing.

"Perhaps my sister Malinda. She's not sixteen yet."

"You have a sister? Perfect. I'm going to tell Eli. Oh, here. Here he is. Eli!" she bellowed, wagging a finger like a rope sausage. When he appeared, Rache pointed at Elsie.

"She has a sister. Could we hire her?"

Eli whistled, low. "I would say so."

Elsie nodded, said she'd bring her along the following week.

Her parents agreed immediately. But Malinda smiled, shook her head, and said no, she didn't think she'd enjoy bakery work, but thanks for asking. That brought one raised eyebrow from Dat, pursed lips from her mother. After a brief discussion, Malinda agreed to go.

Not that she did so without complaining to Elsie, though.

By the time Saturday evening came, Elsie stopped thinking about the bakery and Malinda's coming introduction to all of Elsie's own trials and mistakes, and focused entirely on the upcoming ride to an undisclosed location with Elam Stoltzfus.

She didn't worry about the color of her dress and had no time to fuss with her hair and covering, having arrived home only thirty minutes before five. She didn't think Elam would notice her appearance. He was merely doing this to help her find the long-awaited horse, which was thoughtful and very kind.

She gasped when he drove in, sure she felt like any English girl if someone had picked her up in a very expensive, foreign-made car, one you seldom saw and, of course, never had the opportunity to drive.

The horse bounced, all grace and strength, lifting his front hooves high, his neck proud and powerful. The buggy wheels flashed as if there were water on the spokes, the gray canvas top flawless.

Nervous now, Elsie smoothed a palm down the front of her black apron, inhaled a steadying breath, told her mother goodbye, and walked through the door, down the steps along the cracked, uneven sidewalk.

Elam sat in the buggy and watched her descend the porch steps, wondering how Elsie seemed never to notice how perfect she was. She was as fresh as an April shower, and as invigorating.

When she slid in beside him, he looked into her eyes once, then found himself immediately tongue-tied, all the clever words he had planned on saying evaporated like steam off the apple butter kettle.

"Where are we going?" she asked eagerly.

"North of Ephrata."

"Way up there?"

He nodded, could not think of one word to say. They rode side by side, too close, yet too far away, in an uncomfortable silence. Elam was dry-mouthed, horrified. He tried to remind himself that this was Elsie—the expert ballplayer who was tall and skinny, put in the background by the other girls. He'd known her most of his life.

Elsie was too shy to lead the conversation. This was Elam Stoltzfus, the Elam of good fortune, who owned ponies and horses and never allowed her to drive. Or hardly ever. He was so far above her in everything—knowledge, prestige, wealth, a good, solid name in the community, and now, very, very good-looking.

She leaned against the soft seat back, crossed her arms, and relaxed. If he didn't talk, then there was no reason to become upset. Besides, she could sit and watch the black horse run for miles and be content.

The buggy seemed light, like an afterthought to the horse, or as if it had never been there in the first place. This horse ran for the joy of running, creating a flowing motion where the buggy seemed to be a part of the horse.

Elsie couldn't help but compare him with the only tired old Standardbred they owned. He trotted along with his loose ungainly pace, creating a jerking motion as soon as the road inclined, then slowed to a walk, which resulted in being tapped with the tip of the frayed old whip. As soon as he felt the whip, he jumped, lunged into his collar, only to slow to another walk a bit farther down the road.

This created plenty of movement, being jerked forward then slammed back against the seat, the seat itself lifting a bit from time to time.

"So, what do you do?" Elam croaked finally, then grimaced inwardly with the pain of the lame attempt.

"Do? You mean, as in work?" she asked, her voice low.

He nodded, too miserable to search for further words. What was wrong with him? He felt beads of perspiration form on his forehead, but was far too embarrassed to lift his left hip to fumble for his handkerchief. As long as she didn't look in his direction, he'd be all right.

"I work at the Reading Terminal Market. In the bakery."

"Do you like it?" Oh my. See Jane run. Run, Sally, run. His words were completely predictable, as if he'd read them from a first-grade reading book. He cringed, sniffed with misery.

"I do, actually. I like my boss, Eli Beiler from the Cattail area. Do you know him?"

"I don't believe I do." Whew. That cliff-hanger was done. Now what was he going to come up with?

The long ride was turning into an excruciating form of mental endurance. He had always prided himself on being the suave conversationalist with all the girls he knew, so this shake-up had not been foreseen. Ill-prepared to meet an unexpected rush of awe, never associating plain, poor Elsie with the girls who were usually seated beside him, he was floundering like a hooked and landed fish.

She asked how much they were asking for the horse. "I have been saving money for over two years, but I give most of my wages to my parents. Hopefully, I'll be able to afford the horse you have in mind."

"You will."

"How do you know?"

Once on the subject of the long-awaited horse, conversation came easier, although it was far from relaxed.

The summer's evening was perfect, the air heavy with maple leaves, undulating telephone wires, the manic wheeling and flocking of an assortment of small brown birds, traffic coming and going in myriad colors of blue, white, red, and black. They passed immaculately groomed lawns with colorful arrays of petunias, dahlias, marigolds. Fields full of corn growing like small trees, thick-stemmed, broad-leafed, the large, firm ears formed and yellowing. Fourth cutting alfalfa. Soybeans and pumpkin and tomato patches.

As they approached the town of Ephrata, Elam turned his horse south. Here the houses thinned some, open farmland turning to patches of woods and narrow township roads with decidedly cheaper, older dwellings. There were mobile homes and double-wides with cars parked in unmowed sections of lawn, weeds growing around them like unkempt fur.

Elsie thought it might be just a short section of these types of properties. Soon they'd emerge into an open vista of level farmland, an area where the land was cared for, well-maintained horse farms.

A German shepherd lunged on the end of a sturdy chain, barking in short, angry barks, his collar tightening. A small dog tumbled off a set of steps, flew across the yard with furious yips, his legs churning beneath him. A heavy, balding man lowered his bare feet from the porch railing and set up an awful volley of commands to both dogs, who went on with their insane howling and yelping. They traveled past that canine threat, only to find themselves surrounded by another pack of dogs of unrecognizable breed. Large brown dogs with matted coats, their ribs showing like teeth on a large comb, tails hairless with skin diseases.

Elsie couldn't help herself.

"Where are we going? These poor dogs. Surely the horse isn't here, in this . . . this area."

"Actually, he is."

He wished he'd never come, wished he had never set foot in this place. Thinking of Elsie had all been a horrible mistake.

They turned right, down a steep gravelly incline, fissured with deep, washed-out ruts, patches of weeds down the high center. The buggy tilted and lurched, threw Elsie against Elam's shoulder. The horse picked his way down as gracefully as he did everything else.

The passed a patch of woods to the right, a brown field to the left, overrun with spots of brambles and overgrown millet stalks, an old golf cart with one tire removed, holes in the roof and tufts of white insulation protruding. There was an array of rusted vehicles, like gloomy harbingers of worse times to come.

A crumbling shed that had been red at one time but was brown now, with only a hint of pink between the rotting boards.

Elsie fought back despair.

What had Elam been thinking? How had he ever found this derelict place? No horse coming from this barn would be worth even a hundred dollars.

He stopped the horse, handed the reins to her, and said he'd go talk to Mr. Harris, the owner. Elsie watched him climb from the buggy and walk through the assortment of used kitchen appliances that lay half hidden in a growth of weeds. She thought this must be some cruel joke someone had thought up.

Chapter Six

To hold the reins that led to the mouth of this wonderful creature diverted her thoughts as Elam returned with an aging man, stooped at the waist, shuffling through the weeds with a pair of shoes like rowboats, laces riffling along, untied.

Without speaking, Elam led the horse to a fence, placed his hand on the post to check for sturdiness, then unhooked the rein, allowing the horse to lower his head, stretch his neck. He came back to the buggy, reached below the seat for the neck rope, tied the horse, and motioned for her to come with him.

"Elsie, this is Charlie Harris. Charlie, a friend of mine. Elsie Esh."

Elsie was sized up by a pair of rheumy eyes that still held a brilliant blue color. He wore no eyeglasses, and his nose was crisscrossed with purple veins and pockmarks like the moon's surface. A yellowed moustache hung above his puckered lips, the coarse white hair tangled and ungroomed.

"Hello, Elsie Esh. Pleased to meet you, I am." His voice was soft and whispery.

"Hello. I'm pleased to meet you, too."

"Well, good. Then we'll go see the horse."

Together they waited while the old man unhooked a two-by-four from a cast-iron brace, the only thing that held the door in place. When he swung the door back, the stench was overpowering, burning, an acidic odor of old, stale manure and fresh urine.

Elsie coughed, brought a hand to her mouth.

The light from the door was thrown unmercifully on the most pitiful sight Elsie could imagine.

"He's only four years old. A magnificent palomino. My granddaughter's. Barrel raced. Rode him at the Ohio State Fair with the Angels. He's a wonder, this horse."

The soft, breathy voice went on, explaining the loss of his granddaughter, the many events where she had shown the grand horse. Bewildered, Elsie tried to imagine this horse being ridden anywhere.

Elam stood, his thumbs hooked in his trouser belt, nodding, his eyes taking in everything.

The neck. Elsie had never seen a neck so thin on a

horse. His head was much too large, like an oversized lollipop on a stick. Coarse hair hung from his skeletal body in long, loose tufts. His thin mane hung in sections, with burrs parting the small amounts, cruel barrettes of nature.

"His name is Gold," the old man whispered.

Elsie looked at Elam, his face half averted, the light from the open barn door illuminating the pity in his eyes.

"Are you serious?" she whispered to him.

"Oh, yes. He was gorgeous."

"But he's not now."

"Do you know what can be done with a horse like this? It's why I brought you!"

He turned to face her, his eyes meeting hers squarely. She questioned. He answered with his sympathy.

Because we're poor, she thought. *You brought me here to show me this was all I could afford. That this place reminds you of ours. I have almost two thousand dollars. I can afford a nice horse.*

She swung her arm in the direction of the opened door. "You know I don't have the means to pay a veterinarian, or expensive minerals and top-of-the-line horse feed. So why think you can pawn this half-dead thing on me?"

Elsie was close to tears, and Elam was caught off guard. Misery piled on misery. It had begun badly and was ending worse. Old Charlie Harris, hard of hearing and blissfully unaware of anything amiss, kept talking in his soft breathless voice of the blue ribbons and prizes, the photographs.

When the granddaughter passed, victim of a fiery auto accident, he had taken on himself the well-meant responsibility of keeping the horse. He thought he could do it, but had fallen ill, his mental capacity deteriorating along with the aging body. The results were one broken horse who was fortunate to receive hay and water once a day, the floor of his stable rising higher with his own waste, piled in corners, turning acrid, liquid without bedding. Clots of dirt and manure stuck in his overgrown mane and tail, his beautiful legs were stained and discolored with the filth.

Elam looked at Elsie, saw the heaving chest, the passion in her green eyes, and understood. He'd had no intention of reminding her of her parents' lowly station—and what was lowly, really? Did this girl measure everything around her by the material wealth of others? Compare her own life to every situation that arose?

"Elsie."

She swung away from him, walked through the door, out of sight.

Well, nothing to do but the reasonable alternative. Turning to Charlie Harris, Elam made him an offer, which was accepted.

"Now, I know the horse needs some care. I must have forgotten to feed him a few times. Don't have the strength for the mucking out. Yes, yes. You'll do him justice. The young lady doesn't want him, then?"

"No."

"Well, that's all right. Quite all right. You'll do right by this horse. He's a winner."

Elam nodded.

The ride home was painful for them both. Quiet attempts at conversation died before they could be ignited, leaving them with a keen sense of having failed. He berated himself for the oversight. She blamed herself for having been gullible enough to be led like a blind sheep.

Before they arrived home, she had to know.

"Are you buying him?"

"Yes."

"For . . . for yourself."

"Yes."

She stepped out of the buggy before he had a chance to make amends. Never looking at him, she mumbled a goodbye and stalked into the house on legs like stilts, slapping the screen door behind her.

She went to her room and sat down hard on the edge of her bed, releasing an expulsion of pent-up frustration.

She'd always be poor Elsie, who had no taste, no smarts, not even a mind of her own. Dumber than a box of rocks. Good for nothing but winning baseball games for him. All this being "asked" was the same thing. Every young man wanted a meek and submissive wife who would hold her husband in high esteem, calling him Lord. And lordly he was, this Elam Stoltzfus. Even Benny of the smashed hat looked up to him in constant hope of being acknowledged and accepted.

Well, this drive with him had uncovered what Elam truly was, which revealed the fact that he had never changed. The same kid who wouldn't allow her to drive the Shetland pony. So arrogant. Look how he sat in that classy buggy with his wide shoulders and those solid, tanned arms covered in dark hair. She wondered what they felt like.

What? Why was she thinking about his arms? Elsie began to cry. Her face puckered and large salty tears trickled down her cheeks. She cried for every day in school when she'd eaten her cheese sandwiches facing the blackboard so no one would see. She cried for all the times she'd known the answer to difficult questions but was much too inhibited to speak up in a classroom ripe with superiority. Mostly she cried trying to figure out why Elam's arms affected her so deeply. Young men simply did not do that to her. None of them. So why now, when it was so obvious he thought of her as nothing but the poor girl down the road who could only afford a half-dead horse?

It was his nose that set her into fresh, subdued wails of wretched feelings. His nose was wide and short and blunt. It was a perfect nose set above a wide mouth with lips that were not too thin and not too full, dry, and masculine, and—oh no— really nice. She couldn't allow herself to think of his eyes that were not brown or blue or green, but the color of dried oak leaves in the fall. When an oak leaf got rained on, when it became wet, it took on a chestnut hue, a color that was not the color of anything else.

This thought brought on a fresh river of tears, until her eyes were rimmed with red and her cheeks looked like a map of the world, splotched with red and pink and purple.

She honked into a wad of toilet tissues, threw it on her nightstand, and thought of his even white teeth when he smiled. She went to the mirror above her dresser and pulled back her mouth in a grimace, her front teeth protruding like a—well, those of a horse. She broke into fresh sobs.

She sat in church with her eyes still slightly puffy, watched the long line of young men and boys file in and take their seats on the long wooden benches, Elam among them.

Determined to change everything she felt the previous day, Elsie opened her *Ausbund* with the rest of the girls and kept her face lowered as she sang, never once looking up. The fact that Elam was far too close, facing her way, made it almost impossible to raise her eyes. He must never know how much she had suffered. Was suffering.

Did he have the horse in the barn at his home? She wished she could be a hawk or an owl, to glide across the barn or perch on a window ledge, to see if the sad horse had already found a new home.

And if he was there, was he happy? Surrounded by all those high-steppers Elam's father owned, how could he be?

She knew he'd feel like her, eating her cheese sandwich, staring at the blackboard. The horse would be much more comfortable alone with Fred in their humble barn.

Horses had feelings, too. Elam wouldn't know that.

Now she was more confused than ever. If the horse was so pitiful, and she had refused to take him, how could she hope to save him except by swallowing her pride and asking Elam?

Now she had gotten herself into a gigantic, irretrievable mess, and to extricate herself meant admitting it was all her pride that had made her refuse him in the first place. She would never let Elam see this. The horse would just have to learn to be happy where he was.

She couldn't stop herself from visualizing the poor, broken-down horse, standing on three legs, the hip bones protruding like clothes racks, one leg bent, neck outstretched, that long, thin neck that just grabbed you, with the long, hard face of a much older horse, his eyes half closed in shame as the other horses kicked and stamped and whinnied, eyeing him with bold unwelcoming eyes.

Elsie tried hard to put it all behind her, to focus on the minister's face, to take in the surroundings. But everything blurred, colors running together in otherworldly chaos. When the minister spoke of kindness, she thought of the horse. When he spoke of the crossing of the Red Sea, she thought of the poor horse's inability to keep up with the throng who walked on dry land to the other side.

Then, to complicate matters even more, Elam's sister, Barbara, invited a group of girls to her house for the afternoon, Elsie among them. There she would be, not far away from the barn, unable to see for herself. If she remained quiet, perhaps Barbara would say something about the horse, and no one would ever know what had occurred.

They made soft pretzels, dipped them in cheese sauce, drank iced meadow tea, and giggled and talked before taking turns using the shower before they dressed to attend the youth gathering a few miles away.

Elsie had just stepped out of the bathroom, a white towel like a turban around her head, the cape pinned to her dark gray dress, barefoot, carrying her small piece of luggage. She felt the handle loosen and sag, looked to see if she had remembered to zip up the outside pocket, while walking hurriedly. There were more girls who needed to use the shower. That was why she plowed into a solid form, bumped the towel against it, releasing the twist on top of her head, resulting in a loose towel that slid sideways, followed by a thick, heavy ripple of gleaming wet hair.

Annoyed, she drew up short, straightened, dropped her bag, and caught herself by grasping two heavy arms covered with silky hair.

"Oh."

"Sorry."

"I . . ."

"You . . ."

She meant to let go of his arms, but she didn't.

Elam's face was very close and the hallway was in shadows. There was no one else around and everything, everything was filled with possibility. Flowers and butterflies could grow out of the walls and music could waft up from the floor.

"Elsie . . . I . . ."

"I'm sorry."

She let go, picked up her bag, and tried to push past him, but he caught her. Slowly he brought his hands up to touch both sides of her face, touch the wet hair that cascaded on either side. There were no misunderstandings, no divide of poverty or wealth, no broken horse named Gold, only two young people on the cusp of a strong attraction but kept at bay by their upbringing, by their parents' admonishing of right and wrong, and most of all, what was conventionally acceptable.

With a small cry, Elsie broke away and dashed past him and into Barbara's room, her face ashen, the wet towel lying on the hallway floor.

"What happened to you?" Florence asked.

"You're white as the walls."

Elsie laughed, a quick, breathless sound foreign to her own ears. "Guess the water was too hot. Sort of felt like passing out. Happens sometimes."

"Yeah, it can."

They went back to their hair brushing and spraying and clipping back with bobby pins and barrettes, capes pinned to a perfect V on their necklines, aprons pinned snugly around slim waists. The smell of girls' cologne stuck in the air as thin stockings were wriggled into.

Barbara walked down the hallway to the bathroom, saw the crumpled towel, found Elam lounging in the doorway of his bedroom with a slack jaw and a vacant expression, and thought, *Aha. Shower wasn't that hot. Something going on here or I'll eat this towel.*

She knew about the horse, had noticed Elam like a midwestern tornado ever since he'd taken Elsie for a ride to see him.

She'd have to help God along a bit, here. Elam had a strong admiration for Elsie now, same as he had in school. He'd told Barbara she was quite an athlete, for an Amish girl. He'd bet anything that if she wasn't Amish she'd be professional in baseball or volleyball. If she had a chance.

Which she didn't, Barbara had reminded him.

But she had forgotten all this, till now. Elam had basically lost track of Elsie over the past few years. Didn't even belong to the same group of young people.

You watch. You just watch, Barbara chortled to herself.

After the episode in the hallway, the youth gathering held no charm for Elsie. It felt like a bowl of Corn Flakes without sugar or milk. A jigsaw puzzle with no border pieces. The sun without the moon, the moon without the sun. A land without rain.

The whole atmosphere was drained of vitality. It was hard to understand, this sudden loss. If she had never known Elam, there would be no loss. But she had always known Elam. Elam and Benny. Cookie and his new horse. But that was a different time.

How could you link the two times? This Elam was like a warm campfire in a dark, cold forest. This Elam took up all your senses and threw them into the sky, where they turned to stardust, little pinpricks of dazzle in a dark sky you didn't know needed light. And having seen this transformation, you could never think of Elam as the same person driving Cookie, with Benny beside him.

She felt helpless, carried along by a deep, churning current headed straight for a high waterfall. She cried when she found a dead kitten by the side of the road. She didn't like cats, never had. But the kitten was so little and so thoroughly dead.

Her work at the bakery was like a speeding train threatening to derail. One moment her rolls were light and buttery, the sweet dough turned out to perfection. She loved her job, her coworkers. The next minute she wanted to hurl a mass of dough out a window, watch the glass split and break, tinkle to the ground in dozens of sharp sections, the dough coming to rest on top of it.

In short, everything was an unexplained mystery.

A month passed. Two.

She saw Elam in church only twice. He was never at her youth group's events, which was what she had hoped for, without admitting it even to herself. She missed something, but didn't know exactly what it was.

Sometimes she felt as if she were trying to catch white feathers that were drifting down like snowflakes, only to hurl them away the minute she touched them.

Then he showed up, knocking on the wooden frame of the screen door one evening when the cold, damp air that crept in from the northeast carried a promise of winter.

Dressed in a black peacoat and a gray stocking cap, his hands shoved in his pockets, he stepped back when Elsie opened the door.

"Hello, Elsie. How are you?"

Here he was. The border to her puzzle, the rain to her drought. The sun and the moon. But that was supposed to be God, not Elam. All this zipped through her mind as she pushed open the screen door.

"Hi. Come in, it's too damp and cold tonight."

"How are you?" he repeated.

"Fine. Good."

Now that you're here, she thought. Flustered, she tucked an imaginary *schtruvvel* from her hairline behind her ear.

Elam stepped into the bright, overheated kitchen, the woodstove at the far corner producing a steady glow. The old propane light in the cabinet by the recliner hissed steadily, throwing more heat.

He greeted the family. Her father spoke at length about the weather, saying there was to be a wintry mix till morning. He'd been hoping for a solid layer of snow for Christmas. Her mother smiled, inquired about his mother. Amos told him he was four, soon, and he was getting a trike for Christmas.

"Not the same color as my old one. Rusty-colored is my old one. My new one is red."

Elam laughed, then bent to pat his head.

"You are growing, Amos. Really growing. You better tell your mother you need a bigger tricycle."

"Trike."

"Trike," Elam agreed.

After that exchange, Elsie was weak-kneed with the understanding of what was wrong with her. It hit her like she'd been slammed into a wall.

She loved Elam more than anything or anyone else. He was her hero, her promised one, her meant-to-be.

Here he was, standing in their plain, dreary kitchen with the old appliances and torn linoleum, the scuffed chairs and faded oilcloth on the table, and everything, everything became impossible. The flowers and butterflies turned black and fell off the wall, leaving large porous holes that no amount of drywall compound or paint could fix. They were poor and crippled. The only reason he stood inside that old front door was to pity them. Maybe to offer the old horse for a few hundred dollars.

He turned to her.

"Elsie, would you like to walk over with me to see the new horse? You haven't seen him since he's been in our barn."

She stood with her pride on one shoulder, her love on the other. She accepted without a rational thought in her head and went to comb her hair and grab a warm white scarf and her heavy coat and flew down the stairs, her eyes alight with hope.

Hope that stuffed back the impossibility, kicked away the dead flowers, but planted new seeds and would wait for the first green shoot, the first sign of activity.

They set off at a brisk pace, the night gray-black and impenetrable. Oh, lovely world. Lovely, lovely night filled with stardust and falling stars! Comets and asteroids, whole planets zipping and spinning along, filling the night sky with the wonder of all of life.

Chapter Seven

TO FIND THE HORSE LOOKING SO DIFFERENT she would not have known it was the same animal was a shock in itself, but when Elam asked her if she wanted him now, she all but fell over.

"I can't take him. Not after you've done so much for him."

"One thousand dollars," he replied.

Elsie's eyes narrowed. "How much did you pay for him?"

"Exactly that. One thousand dollars."

"Are you sure?"

He was treading on thin ice, pride and poverty and remembered school days.

"Would I lie to you?"

"Well, no. I guess not."

"So do you want him? Saddle and bridle?"

"I do. But . . . I have only ridden a horse once, maybe twice. How can I be expected to show any kind of good horsemanship? I guess, to be honest,

I'm scared. How can I compete with that old man's granddaughter?"

Elam laughed.

"You take this horse home, make friends with him, he'll do anything you say. He's sweet-tempered."

Elsie hung her arms over the side of the heavy wooden plank that made up part of the stall. She watched, took in every muscle, the rounded sides, the glassy coat, and, most astonishing, the well-proportioned head and neck. The filth and manure stains were gone, the legs were groomed to a sheer white, turning into a honey color, which spread to the horse's entire body. The mane and tail were lighter in color, as if those sections had been spun and pulled into the color of homemade taffy.

There was, however, still a droop to his eyes, as if he were still sleepy, or exhausted. The long brown lashes drooped over the deep brown eyes that seemed to glisten with tears.

"He seems tired," she said.

"Go in to him," Elam suggested.

The horse merely lifted his head and eyed her with the same tired gaze. To touch that glossy neck was like a benediction, but when he turned his head to nuzzle the front of her coat, Elsie gave in, threw her arms around the horse's neck, and hugged, tightly, laying the side of her face against his mane.

"You lovely creature. I can't believe the difference in a few months' time."

Elam stood at the gate, smiling, taking in what he had accomplished.

Elsie cleaned out the extra horse stall, swept cobwebs, washed windows, swept the old pocked concrete forebay. Malinda helped her dump the plastic half barrel that served as a watering trough and scrubbed the sides and bottom with wooden brushes and refilled it with cold, clean water. There was a rack for the saddle, a large nail for the bridle, the special feed Elam used in a fifty-pound bag that rested against the cement block wall. Minerals were in a square yellow bucket. A pickup truck delivered the best hay.

She wrote a check to Elam Stoltzfus for the wondrous sum of one thousand dollars, a check to the feed mill for $52.00, and one for $310.00

to Ronald Sanders for hay. Which meant she had spent $1,362.00, years of work at the bakery. She had a little over $800 left, which would melt away fast, buying good horse feed. Elam walked through the snow, leading the golden horse with a fairly long rope. Elsie watched them approach from the open barn door, her heart thudding against her rib cage.

What a striking figure he made. And the horse was unbelievable.

She smiled, put out a hand for the rope, and introduced Gold to Fred, who became quite animated, hopping and bouncing around in his stall like a half-grown two-year-old.

"Ach, Fred, you old geezer," Elsie laughed.

"Hey, he has a new friend. Nothing wrong with that."

Elsie saw the red ribbon braided through the mane, the bunches of greenery.

"It's lovely. How do you braid that through this coarse hair?"

"Barbara did it. I have no clue." He shrugged one shoulder. "She'll teach you."

They heard the slam of a door, and were soon surrounded by a gaggle of sisters making quite a fuss about the horse, followed by Elsie's parents and Amos.

Her father said the horse would continue to improve, that he appreciated what Elam had done for Elsie. Anyone that loved horses the way she did should have the opportunity to own one. As always, he never complained about his own lot, never referred to the loss of his arm, turning the spotlight on Elam instead of his own misfortune.

Elam lingered in the dimly lit forebay after her family had returned to the warmth of the house.

"Whenever you're ready for riding lessons, let me know, OK?"

"First I need to purchase something to wear under my dress."

"Barbara wears those stretchy things."

Elsie laughed. "Now how would I know what those stretchy things are? I'm new at this, you know. I'll probably learn to ride on my own. For a while, if you don't mind. I don't want anyone watching, knowing I'll be a genuine klutz."

"You were never a klutz at anything, Elsie."

The note of seriousness in his voice surprised her. He was not sincere. He couldn't be.

"You're making fun of me now."

"Never. I'd never do that."

"You used to."

"Not intentionally. I was always amazed at your ability in sports. I can't imagine horseback riding would be any different for you."

Elsie was speechless, flustered, and so painfully ill at ease hearing that compliment from the one she, well, she adored.

She didn't say thank you and she didn't smile or look at him. She merely shoved a sliver of wood with the toe of her boot, as if her life depended on maneuvering the small piece into exactly the right position, her eyebrows drawn down in concentration.

She heard his husky laugh, too close. She looked up, found his nearness alarming. She stepped back, grasped one hand with the palm of the other.

"Elsie, you're amazing. You'll do well," he said.

"I'll probably fall off and break my leg, or my neck. What if the horse doesn't like me?" She was babbling now. After all, she was not amazing. She was raised on coffee soup and fried mush and cheese sandwiches and never once owned a new pair of shoes and had only nine or ten dresses instead of forty. Or fifty.

She had nothing except a repainted secondhand bedroom set and a good job that paid her parents well. Well, and now she had a pretty amazing horse.

But why would Elam stand there now and act as if she were actually what he'd said?

"You don't believe me, right?"

She shook her head.

She spoke so quietly he had to bend his head to hear.

"It's hard to believe you're speaking the truth, when . . . you know, I remember what a big difference there was between us in school. And that difference has not changed."

Her words were so soft and quiet, he could barely hear, but he sensed how hard it was for her to say them.

"It's all right. We're older now. The things that mattered so much in school aren't important. It makes no difference to me if you live in a hut or a million-dollar home. It's you that fascinates me."

"Fascinates? You mean like watching a tobacco worm chew on a leaf?"

He laughed, a long, genuine sound of delight.

"Do you ever look in the mirror, Elsie? And look what happened at your job. You're a beautiful, special, talented girl, and I would love to have you for my girlfriend."

Even more quietly, Elsie whispered, "Oh, but it wouldn't work."

"What? I didn't hear you."

"Well, what I mean. Well . . . . you can't want me. Not to date. Not for a girlfriend. Not seriously."

The lantern light ebbed slowly, turning the barn even darker. The light from the snow outside formed rectangles of white against the blackness of the barn walls. The wind blew loose particles of snow across the highest places, and around corners and under doors.

Elsie shivered. She was thoroughly miserable, after messing up every nice thing he had said. But the truth had to be spoken. Heartbreaks cost too much. They were the most expensive thing on earth, if pain could be counted in dollars.

She couldn't imagine her love blooming, allowing herself the freedom of loving Elam, only to have him tell her he "didn't feel right." Or he was confused, which would mean he was bored with her, was distracted, had found someone who intrigued him. So there you go, cast aside, forgotten, huddled like a beggar on the street with your heart slightly damaged forever.

Hadn't she listened to Anna Mae for hours on end? David had loved her. He had, she insisted. And then, out of thin air, his words like hatchets, he told her he didn't feel right. His feelings for her were no longer the same. Like a balloon, the air had slowly leaked out until there was nothing left but a tired, senseless little heap of nothing. Anna Mae couldn't take it. Her mother took her to see a doctor and she was put on an antidepressant to help her through the worst of it.

Elsie shook her head, the decision becoming a solid thing.

"The answer is no," she said firmly.

There was a space of silence. Old Fred snorted through his nose, rubbed his shoulder on the old wooden feedbox. Outside, the wind blew bits of snow against the barn, causing a scouring sound, as if the cold could clean the remaining slivers of paint off the drying boards.

"Can you explain the reason why?" Elam asked softly.

Elsie's thoughts scrambled, stirred together like cake batter, pride, memories, his superiority, everything, coming apart, breaking into pieces that floated around in a restless void.

She grasped at anything, one good reason that would not hurt him but would save her from exposing the smallness of her own world.

He was just too much, too wealthy, too many horses, too sought after by every girl she knew, too kind and polite and assured in his own station in life.

"I'm not good enough for you."

"Elsie, I . . ."

"No."

He left after a soft "good night." Elsie stumbled through the snow and the wind and let herself in quietly, and to bed, where she lay shivering, dry eyed.

Every girl's dream was to fall in love with a kind, talented, handsome young man like Elam, like a fairy tale, living happily ever after.

But it wasn't that easy. There were so many paths that twisted and turned, a labyrinth of feelings that always led to the same swamp of low self-worth, where she inevitably got bogged down in the mire and could see no way out.

How could he love her? He hadn't said he loved her, only that he wanted to be her boyfriend. Perhaps it was the horse, the ability to teach her how to ride, how to feed him, how to . . . well, everything. No, the match would be too uneven. Like three-fourths of a pie, her share only one fourth.

She learned to ride, through the snow and the cold.

By the time Christmas festivities began, she had already acquired the good posture, the sense of being one with her horse, who was well trained, never showing temper or disobedience.

Each day his appearance improved even more as Elsie brushed his coat, pampered and fussed with the thin mane and tail, which were showing signs of new, heavy growth. She stroked his velvety neck, under the mane, where the renewed muscle was becoming heavy and rounded. A bond of the kind that is only apparent when a human being loves an animal from the heart developed between them, and Gold responded like dry leaves to a flame. He gave his all for his new master, the girl who had replaced his first love.

The barn was the only place Elsie felt true contentment. She washed the windows with a clean rag dipped in soapy water with a dash of vinegar. She held the old porch broom to the rafters, plying it across the cement block walls and the vertical boards above it to remove cobwebs. The stalls were mucked out every day, a wheelbarrow load spread across the old barnyard, on the large garden, in the fields, anywhere there was a need for some of nature's fertilizer.

Her father grinned good-naturedly, joked that he would have gotten her a horse a long time ago if he'd known how much work she'd put into that old barn. Her mother shook her head, smiled, shrugged. They all knew that would not have been possible. But times had changed for the better. Two girls working at the bakery now meant their household income had gotten a serious raise. No longer did depleted supplies of ordinary necessities give Mam a lump in the throat, although she had always kept a brave face to her husband and all who knew her.

Christmas in the Esh household was first and foremost a celebration of the birth of Jesus Christ. Elsie and her sisters had learned at a very young age to understand the coming of the baby Jesus, the stable and the animals, the shepherds in the fields, the coming of the Wise Men to follow the star in the east. The gifts the family exchanged were simple, the Christmas dinners at the grandparents' the highlight of every holiday season. There, the cousins, aunts, and uncles brought joy, togetherness, a sense of belonging, the small gift of a book or a set of handkerchiefs a token of Daddy and Mommy's love. Elsie still had most of those books, the inside covers inscribed with the same words: "To Elsie, Christmas," followed by the year. Sometimes, there was a coloring book and a brand-new package of Crayola crayons, the yellow box still square and polished. Inside were twenty-four sharp, brand-new crayons, the greatest delight. If you colored a picture with new crayons, you could color without coming out of the heavy black lines. After the Christmas dinner, the girls spent hours coloring around the kitchen table, chattering happily, comparing colors and talents, denying the ohs and ahs of admiration from each other. They often received homemade doll clothes from their parents—little Amish dresses and black pinafore-style aprons or new flannel nightgowns for the dolls they had received years before from the thrift or consignment shops.

They exchanged names at school for trading gifts, which was a source of angst for Elsie, knowing the gift she would give would be inferior to what she received. She dreaded the opening of those packages. Sometimes she received twice, three times as much as she had given. She knew the children were all admonished to be grateful, no matter how small the gift they received from the David Esh family, so there were never any cruel remarks, only kind appreciation. But she knew.

When Elsie became older, there was the exchanging of names among the youth, but she had her own small stash of money and could buy her own gift, which meant accompanying a gaggle of shrieking girls to the expensive stores her mother never entered.

This year, Mam informed Elsie it was the first Christmas ever that she felt a sense of freedom, having the girls' market money to buy more gifts than she had ever thought possible. Her face appeared younger, unlined, uplifted, with a glow of Christmas joy. Her father's happiness was always apparent, but now he had a spring in his step, an eagerness to hitch up old Fred and accompany his wife to the Amish stores scattered along the many roads of Lancaster County. Snow drifted lazily across the countryside, already turning the brown fields to a dusting of white, like talcum powder. The macadam roads became slick, so the cars traveled slowly. They kept Fred to the right side, on the wide shoulder of the road provided for slow-moving horses and buggies, the snow spitting against the windows, settling on Fred's back, slowly melting from the body heat and sliding wetly down his sides, turning the hair on his haunches to dark streaks. It was a magical day for David and Mary Esh, gratitude filling their buggy with Christmas warmth that permeated every aspect of the joyous festivities.

For Elsie, the money she handed to her parents was no sacrifice. She had the one thing she had worked so hard to earn: her horse. The hours spent in the cold learning to ride, her face red, her eyes shining as she loped across the fields, could not compare with anything she had ever experienced. It was beyond her biggest expectations.

Now if she could only deal with this Elam Stoltzfus episode.

She told her mother about it as they coated peanut butter crackers with chocolate. Her mother stood at the opposite end of the table, her face glowing with inner happiness, a Ritz cracker spread thickly with peanut butter put together with another one on top, like a whoopee pie. She threw it into the large stainless steel bowl of melted chocolate that rested on top of boiling water, turned it with a fork, tapped the handle on the side of the bowl until the excess chocolate dropped off, then gently deposited it on the waxed paper spread on a cookie sheet.

"Oh, imagine, Elsie. Wilbur's chocolate. It's

so expensive. And I had enough, oh, more than enough to purchase it at Creekside. This is the best Christmas, ever."

"For me, too, if Elam Stoltzfus wasn't ruining it."

The tapping stopped.

"Whatever!" she exclaimed, borrowing her daughter's words.

"I mean it. Mam, he said he wants me for his girlfriend. He said I'm amazing. He did. And you know it's not true."

"Elam Stoltzfus said that? Well."

The tapping continued, but a pleased smile spread across her glowing face. She placed a coated cracker carefully on the waxed paper, then faced Elsie squarely.

"And why is this not true?"

"Well, I'm not. We're . . . I am just me. None of that is true."

"I think it's true. I think he was sincere. He's been like that even when you went to school. Remember how he hung around here with that pony of his? Candy, or Cookie, whatever his name was?"

"He never let me drive."

"Elsie, you can put more peanut butter on that cracker. I have another jar in the pantry. A bigger one." She spoke with so much pride and happiness, not having to spare the peanut butter. Then she continued, earnestly. "To have someone like Elam say such a thing would not be easy. I know there is a divide in our way of living, but money has nothing to do with love. God's ways are not our ways, His thoughts far above our own piddling ability. You are an amazing daughter, talented in so many ways. In fact, everything you attempt, you excel in. Not everyone acquires their dream the way you have, through sheer hard work. You have to rise above everything that has always been our lot in life. To be poor is nothing to be ashamed of. Your father is handicapped, but rich in everything that counts. Do you realize we could be swimming in wealth, with an angry, self-absorbed father who shows no love or respect to his family?"

She picked up a tray of freshly coated crackers, a spring in her step as she carried them to the counter.

"So, what did you tell him?"

Elsie just shook her head.

Chapter Eight

THE BAKERY AT MARKET WAS CONTROLLED chaos, with Rache circling the entire area with lowered brows and a voice like a bullhorn, wedging her way between girls with clipped words of remonstration, egging them on to do more, even when it was impossible to do so.

Tray after tray of Christmas cookies was baked, arranged, wrapped, and sold. They couldn't keep the shelves filled, which resulted in harried customers lined up in frustrated rows wearing perpetual frowns of impatience. The cash register dinged endlessly as women marched off with boxes of pies, dinner rolls, loaves of bread, trays of cookies and cupcakes.

Through all the clatter around her, Elsie worked steadily, her sister Malinda at her side. Nothing distracted them from producing perfect yeast breads and rolls as they concentrated on the task at hand. It was important to allow the yeast dough to rise to the correct level, to bake the loaves just long enough in the huge commercial oven, to watch carefully that quality would not be compromised in spite of the frenzied pace around them.

It was eleven thirty, and still they hadn't had a break. Rache slammed back to the yeast dough area, flopped on a folding chair with all the force of her questionable poundage, set down two coconut doughnuts and her cup of endless cappuccino, and said she couldn't take this anymore.

"This corner is the only one that knows what they're doing. The rest is all one big hurricane. That Sheila is going to be fired unless I miss my guess. She doesn't know the meaning of the word 'hurry'. Oh, did you have your break yet?"

She bit into her coconut doughnut, closed her eyes, and moaned.

"It's almost a sin to eat something this good. Did you have your break?"

"Not yet."

"Well, go. You'll fall over, skinny as you are."

"We can't. We have to watch the proofer and the oven."

"Seriously, girls, it's not legal. You have to go. I'll watch. Go."

She stuffed the remainder of the doughnut into her mouth, pointed toward the aisles teeming with Christmas shoppers.

"Go," she said around the unbelievable amount in her mouth.

They ordered ham-and-egg sandwiches and apple juice, bent their heads in prayer, and bit into the heavenly warmth of the steaming food.

"Mm. These are the best," Elsie murmured.

Malinda nodded, her mouth full.

"I could have fainted, I was so hungry."

Elsie laughed. "Let's get another one quick. Split it. I'm never going to be full with one. I'd get an order of hash browns, but it takes that restaurant forever. We have five more minutes."

Their spirits lifted by the good food, they returned to work, not a second late.

Rache looked at the clock, shook her head.

"You girls are the best. I'll tell you. You should be paid double."

And until the Christmas rush was over, they were.

Their eyes wide, they counted their bonus, counted it again. Eli Belier thanked them both, then leaned close to ask them to keep it a secret.

"Nothing destroys a peaceful workplace faster than comparing wages. I do thank you. You continue to do an outstanding job, the biggest factor being the responsibility you take so seriously. I never worry about the yeast dough corner. Never. Don't forget our Christmas banquet the twenty-ninth, girls. Bring your boyfriend, Elsie."

She grinned, waved him away. He laughed and hurried off.

Bring your boyfriend, he'd said. Huh. If she accepted Elam, she would have that option.

On Christmas morning the girls slept in, having crept into their warm beds with limbs like soft butter, weary beyond anything they'd ever known, their Christmas bonuses tucked in a drawer. It felt almost wrong, having so much cash in an envelope.

They woke to the happy clatter from downstairs, the younger children having opened their presents early.

Elsie grabbed her robe and hurried downstairs to find Amos quite beside himself, roaring over the train set he had discovered in the large square box. Dat and Mam sat together on the couch, coffee mugs in hand, laughing, their eyes shining, allowing him to make all the outrageous sounds he wanted.

"Un train! Un train! *Gook mol*, Elsie!"

His worn flannel pajamas were red, and by the time he was finished whooping, so was his face. Elsie scooped him up, trying for a hug and a resounding kiss, but his desperate struggle to free himself prevented any affection.

The living room was warm with the crackling fire in the old black woodstove, the smell of bacon and breakfast casserole wafted from the oven, and candles glowed on the windowsill with pine boughs on the sideboard. It was Christmas.

Elsie opened her package to find fabric for a new dress, a lovely shade of green, somewhere between olive and a crayon green.

"Oh, it's really lovely, Mam. Such a different shade of green. Thank you."

"There's more," Mam said, beaming.

Elsie dug into the white tissue paper to find a small bottle of cologne, something she had never owned.

She had watched her friends spritz all kinds of floral scents liberally while she busied herself doing her hair, adjusting her covering or apron, aware of the fact that she had never been able to own something so unnecessary,

"It's too expensive," she breathed.

"Not this year," Mam said, then laughed outright, an uninhibited sound of joy and pleasure Elsie had never heard.

"The boys will notice you now," Dat said, his eyes shining over his coffee cup.

As if they hadn't already, Elsie thought, a lurch in her stomach, a stab of remembering Elam, followed by her mother's words.

Could she claim that large chunk of self-worth as her own? How did a person go about believing they were amazing? Such a thing was far too slippery, like the catfish she had tried to catch with her bare hands in the deep, dark pool in the creek. The fish looked fat and old and lazy, but the minute her hands touched the slimy scales, the fish shot away like a torpedo.

Amazing was too much. Too strong. Too hard to live up to. But Christmas cheer worked its magic and

the heavy cloud of Elam and every insecurity that
came with thinking of him soon vanished.

The breakfast table was boisterous, happy, with
excited voices chiming into other voices until a general bedlam broke out, complete with the pinging
and clacking from the battery-operated train. And
then gradually they settled down to enjoy their new
gifts. Anna Marie worked to complete the potholder
from the new loom, plying nylon strips from one
metal hook to another, her eyebrows lowered in concentration. Suvilla was wrapped in a cuddly throw,
the new book from her parents held only inches from
her nose.

Elsie threw on an old coat and scarf and let herself
out the front door to her horse, taking deep breaths
of the pristine air, the gray-white world of winter,
when the sun was hidden behind a thick layer of
clouds. She squinted against the white light from the
snow and shivered inside the coat.

The interior of the old barn was cold, damp, but
so clean. It smelled of fresh new hay, oats and corn,
leather, the rusty old hydrant by the half barrel, a
smell she would never tire of.

"Hey, baby."

Gold swung his head over the rough planks of his box stall, shaking it up and down a few times, as if to nod, his way of saying good morning. Elsie caught his nose, bent her head to kiss his face. She caressed his velvety ears, stroking the forelock of blond hair that hung between his eyes.

"How are you? You're a good boy. My baby," she crooned. She went to the shelf for the currycomb, opened the door to his stall, and began the daily ritual of a thorough grooming. She washed the white hair above his hooves with an old rag, then combed out the snarls in his mane and tail.

As soon as she'd be able to purchase ribbon, she'd learn how to braid his hair, the way she'd seen a horse's mane done in a magazine called *Western Horseman*. She'd been at the dentist's office and had become so lost in the world of horses and girls wearing cowboy hats that her mother had to call her twice before she looked up, the hygienist waiting patiently by the open door.

Elam would know. Not that she'd ask him, though.

She jumped, the currycomb falling from her nerveless fingers, when the door opened abruptly, letting in a rectangle of gray-white light onto the dim concrete floor of the forebay.

"Hey."

There stood Elam in the doorway of the barn.

"Oh, you surprised me."

"I bet. Didn't mean to. Sorry."

"It's ok."

"What are you up to?"

"My usual morning chores."

Elam walked past her to prop his elbows on the top plank. He whistled.

"Wow!"

Elsie smiled a very soft, hidden smile behind the hand she put up to her mouth.

"It's amazing."

"Is that your favorite word?" She was suddenly ashamed. She shouldn't have said that.

"Why, sure! It is amazing to see a transformation like this in any animal, but especially a horse. You still feeding the minerals?"

"I just ordered another bucket."

Nothing was said about the cost. Elsie appreciated his silence. It made her feel as if she were normal, ordinary, able to pay for something she needed with no questions asked.

"I haven't watched you ride him."

Elsie blushed. "You won't."

He laughed.

Then, "Do you have a ride to the Christmas singing tonight?"

Warily, she eyed him.

"No."

"Can I take you? The singing is over at Emanuel Lapp's and I'm hitching the two Belgians to Dad's bobsled. Thought we could take the field lanes, mostly dirt road. It's hard to use sleighs or sleds with the road-clearing crews at work as soon as it snows. You want to ride behind two Belgians?"

"When did you get Belgians?"

"We've always had them. These two are really showy guys, though. My dad and I bought them together. Terrible price. We'll raise colts, see how it goes."

"Why Belgians?"

"You'll see."

He knew her well enough to know she would
be thrilled at the sheer size and beauty, the massive
strength of these beautiful horses bred for hard work.

"Who else is going?"

"Just us. But I'm putting bales of straw and blankets in the sled so we can take spins around the
fields."

She expected herself to pause, to stall and figure
out how to politely answer no. Instead she said, "All
right."

That afternoon, she told her parents she was going to
the Christmas singing with Elam. Her mother raised
one eyebrow in question from her chair, but said nothing. Her father grinned openly, in that unaffected childlike manner. But, mercifully, no one said anything.

She dressed in red, for Christmas. Her dress was
a deep burgundy, a pretty shade on a fabric that
draped across her shoulders with a velvety softness.
She found herself humming, her cheeks flushed, as
she skipped downstairs to ask her mother for help
with her cape.

Malinda accompanied her back up to her room, sat on her bed with her skinny knees drawn to her chin, her eyes shining.

"Oh, I just can't wait till it's my turn to be sixteen. I simply can't wait. I'm counting the weekends. Ada and Sallie are looking forward to it as well."

"I wish you the best. I really do. It's a good time in our life, or a hard time. Whichever we choose to make it."

"You seem to be doing all right."

"I am. It's just . . ."

Elsie bit her lower lip.

"Sometimes, you're faced with hard choices."

"Like what? Guys, you mean?"

"Well, yes."

"Elam."

"Well, yes."

They laughed together, sisters enjoying the secrets and romance of *rumschpringa*.

"Elam would be my pick," said Malinda. "Except he's . . . well, you know. He's pretty sure of himself and his horses. You can see it in the way he walks and talks and drives, just everything."

"Remember Cookie?"

"Remember how mad you got?"

Elam was right on time. Bundled in her best sweater and woolen coat, a white head scarf and heavy gloves and boots, her covering preserved in a Tupperware box, her purse slung across her shoulder, Elsie hurried through the twinkling light from the scattering of stars overhead. Little dots of light decorated the snowy landscape, and there was the smell of cold and pine and bare branches, of decaying cornstalks.

"Hello again, Elsie," he called.

"Hello."

There were no headlights, only battery lamps attached to each side of the massive bobsled. The Belgians were the largest, heaviest horses Elsie had ever seen. She had often seen them from a distance, plodding along in some endless field, drawing a plow or harrow, their noble heads in a powerful arc as their leg muscles worked to do what God had designed.

Depending on what type of farm equipment they were pulling, there were only two, hitched side by side. Sometimes there were four, and if the plow or the liquid manure spreader required it, there were six.

But these looked like show horses, not real farm workhorses, with all this prancing and sidestepping, as if the energy had never been directed to any menial task, certainly not drawing farm equipment.

Elam didn't say anything. He was too busy trying to hold them both to the standstill that was required until he tended to the heavy lap robes.

"Woah there, Captain. Stand still."

Elsie arranged the heavy robes herself, tucking them in beneath her legs. Laughing, she told Elam to drive, she'd be fine.

"They're quite a handful."

"I can see they are."

When he finally did loosen the reins, they lunged, but not in tandem. The left horse leaned into his collar a few seconds before the right one, which caused a jerky, uneven movement that tilted the makeshift seat, resulting in Elsie grabbing for the dashboard to keep from being thrown backward.

After that, they trotted together, their massive hooves making a dull *thlock thlock* of sound in the heavy snow, the wide bobsled runners whispering long behind them, as if the *sshhhh* was meant to quiet the world around them.

The cold stung their faces. The edge of the woods appeared dark and deep, with black etchings of tree branches like crocheted lace against a lighter sky. The moon was only a sliver of cold, as if it only appeared to let the stars know who was the ruler of the skies.

Elsie shivered. She thought she had dressed warmly, but this cold, going at a fast clip against it, drove through her woolen coat and sweater, leaving her with goose bumps up her back and down her arms, her teeth clacking if she didn't press down on them.

"Cold?" Elam asked.

"No."

Not really the truth, but oh well. What could he do if she told him she was miserable?

"Want to drive?"

"We're almost at the singing. I can't."

"Why not?"

"My arms aren't strong enough."

"Sure they are. Here."

Without further words, he presented the reins to her, held them out like a proffered gift, a challenge to see if she would accept. All right. She would.

The first time her fingers closed around the heavy leather reins, she felt the magnificence. The power. It moved from those massive mouths, traveled through the steel bit and along the reins, tugged at her arms with every jingle of the harness.

It was better than riding, better than flying above the earth, better than soaring through unknown heights like a falcon. Or an eagle. It was simply indescribable, perched high on this bobsled seat, knowing the whole magical harmony of those two horses was in your control. As if for the first time in her life, Elsie felt a sense of leadership, of being the one who was able to direct these beautiful animals, in control.

She laughed out loud, a rich sound of pealing bells.

Elam watched her face and felt the despair of her resounding "No" all over again. Well, there was a reason for the old-fashioned "courting." It was the process of winning a heart. It didn't always happen immediately and he certainly wasn't about to give up that quickly.

When had she become this amazing young woman? She'd been the skinny classmate that stood at the gate in her faded, patched dresses and glared at him with those big green eyes without lifting a hand. He'd felt like a prince riding by, someone far superior to her, with that perfect Shetland pony.

The baseball in school was the beginning. She was the most graceful, coordinated girl in school, with the ability to throw a ball farther than the boys. Now she had blossomed into this beautiful girl, with so many God-given talents, he was in awe of her.

"Hold them, we're going downhill."

She nodded, concentrated on using her strength to its full advantage as the horses arched their necks, felt the slight push of the bobsled as they started down the gradual incline.

The cold winter air rushed by, numbing her face. Her fingers were stiff beneath the woolen gloves, shaking like a leaf. But she wouldn't trade the discomfort for any other sensation on earth. This was exhilarating, pure freedom.

The last stretch to the barn was level, so the horses naturally slowed their pace. Elsie put both reins in one hand, shook the other to increase circulation.

Immediately Elam offered to drive.

"No. I'll park them," Elsie said.

And she did so expertly, driving up to the circle of gray and black carriages, with dark figures unhitching horses or just standing in the cold winter night, talking, laughing together.

The bobsled slid to a halt and Elsie handed the reins to Elam. She hopped off immediately, started unhooking the traces.

"They're barely breathing faster," she observed.

"No, these guys can go all day, although at a slower pace."

"They're enormous."

"We want to do a six-horse hitch for the Ohio horse sale next year."

"Sell them?"

"Maybe. We keep buying and selling. We're always changing horses. You could come over on your days off to work with them. Learn how to braid manes, wash the fetlocks, get them in shape for shows, or whatever we need. Potential buyers or photographers are always coming around."

"You mean . . . ?"

"We'd pay you, of course. My sisters don't show much interest. They're scared of anything bigger than Cookie."

"You still have him?"

"Of course. He'll die in our barn."

"You're forgetting I'm new to the horse world. There's a lot I don't know."

"You'll learn. You can do anything you set your mind to. And you really love horses."

"I do."

"Well, then . . ."

Elsie smiled in the light of the battery lamps. Their eyes met and held. Her smile widened, and she laughed, a throaty sound of glad emotion that broke the spell. She stepped forward, clasped her gloved hands to his forearms. He felt the pressure, his heart beating so furiously he was certain she could hear.

"I'll do it."

The rest of the evening was a merry-go-round of lights and singing and faces. Colorful packages were exchanged, shouts of Christmas merriment erupted. There were Christmas cookies, meat and cheese trays, and hot chocolate. But all Elsie thought about was the huge barn filled with Belgian horses and the challenge it presented.

Chapter Nine

SHE DROVE THOSE BELGIANS THE WHOLE way home, sitting on the right, in the driver's seat, her back straight, her hands on the reins, with Elam beside her, allowing her the privilege of doing this on her own.

They did not speak, leaving the wonder of this Christmas night to engage their thoughts with the quiet tenderness of the season. Distant lights shone across the white fields, the border of trees like a dark frame surrounding a magical photograph. The stars overhead seemed to wink at them, as if they, too, knew and understood the extraordinary spirit of the night.

The whisper of the runners on snow sang the song of the ages when a young man's heart turns to thoughts of love. Elam wondered if his father heard this song, his grandfather before him, and his great-grandfather before him. How did they know who was the one they longed for? From God, that's who.

The mystery of true love couldn't always be deciphered, so you just took it, appreciated it, and didn't try to make sense out of it.

For Elam, there was no one but Elsie. Plenty of girls had let him know in the way most girls do that they'd be happy to accept him whenever he felt inclined to ask them for a date. But it had never felt right, till now.

Skinny, unadorned Elsie, sitting in her desk with that old battered lunch box, ashamed of her food, her dress, her coat. And yet, when it was time to play baseball, none of it mattered. Intent on winning, her sportsmanship took over, as she turned into another person, the one who sat beside him now, concentrating on the handling of these horses that were powerful enough to run off out of control, spilling them out on the snow like corks, light and helpless.

The jingling of buckles and snaps, the flapping of leather on the horses' bodies, along with the steady, muted sound of the great hooves running across the snow filled the air. The smell of the horses' warm bodies mixed with the fresh paint of the bobsled.

Elsie's laugh broke the spell.

"The horse on the right is getting tired. He's not pulling his share," she exclaimed.

"Really? How do you know?"

"My left rein needs more pull."

He could not think of a sensible answer. If he hadn't known her his whole life, he'd have thought her a much more experienced driver.

"You can walk them."

"No, they wouldn't like that."

He opened his mouth to ask how she knew that, but closed it instead, quickly deciding he'd allow her the confidence of driving. How did she know? She was a born horsewoman. The thrill of this discovery increased his need to step back, give her time to acknowledge this talent on her own. She did not accept flowery compliments well, the ever-present lack of self-worth raising its hideous, unwanted visage.

Their arrival at her home seemed like a loss. He did not want this magical evening to be over, but was afraid to ask if he could come in for a cup of coffee. Besides, the dilapidated little barn wouldn't hold these horses, and he was positive she'd say no.

She hopped off the bobsled in one swift move-ment, still holding the reins, then turned to hand them over as he slid across the seat to the driver's side.

Her eyes glowed in the light of the battery lamps.

"Thank you," she said simply.

"You're welcome."

"May I thank the horses?"

"Of course."

She went around to the massive heads, stroked and murmured as they obediently lowered their noses into her gloved hands.

He strained to hear her words, but knew they were not meant for his ears.

"They're great horses. Like gigantic teddy bears. They're filled with goodness, aren't they?" she asked as she made her way back to the light from the lamps.

"I never thought about it, but yes, they are. They would never hurt anyone."

Her happy laugh rang out, like bells.

"I can't wait. When do you want me to come over?"

"You work at the bakery the last three days of the week, right?"

"Yes."

"So why don't we try for Tuesday evening?"

"Will your parents approve of having me in the barn? They won't think it's odd?"

"Why would they?"

Flustered suddenly, she tried to erase the question with a shrug.

"Oh, I don't know. Maybe your dad would think I'm too bold."

"He's not like that."

"All right. I'll be over. Good night."

The darkness swallowed her as she made her way to the house without further conversation.

Reluctantly, Elam lifted the reins, chirped to the team, and they moved off smoothly. All the Christmas cheer disappeared like the puffs of steam from the horses' nostrils.

Now why did he feel like an amateurish klutz, suddenly? *The left horse needs more pull. They wouldn't like that.* He felt the need to establish his own horse sense, make sure she'd know he was the one who would be teaching her about these huge animals. Not the other way around.

There, she'd done it again. Amazed him. In school, it was no different. He'd never seen a girl throw and catch the way she did.

He'd have to grasp his sense of superiority back as fast as he could if he meant to impress her.

Dressed in her everyday chore clothes, without adornment, the way she'd been in school, she strode up to the barn with a purposeful step, a glad light in her eye when she spied him.

"There you are!" she said, panting slightly.

"Yup. How are you?"

"Great. Excited."

"Good."

Her eyes scanned the long row of doors, the clean, wide aisle in between, the horses standing quietly behind their own partition.

"Why didn't you ride?"

"I won't ride when you . . . well, no."

"What is that supposed to mean?"

"I'd be far too self-conscious to ride when you are watching me."

"Why?"

"I don't know." She shrugged.

"Well, then we won't ride. We'll work on getting the Belgians ready for the sale in Ohio."

Her eyes shone. She clasped and unclasped her fingers. The door opened, letting in the cold white light of the winter day. His father came through the door, rubbing his hands, shivering.

"Why hello, Elsie. It's good to see you."

"Hello."

"Elam says you'll be helping out with the Belgians. Good. We're glad to have you aboard."

He noticed a strange look on his son's face and wondered.

And so began the evenings that bound them together. Elam taught her all the ways of grooming, braiding, washing and oiling fetlocks, waxing hooves, all of it a labor of love for Elsie. The best times were the hours of hitching them to various wagons, learning the proper handling of these awesome creatures.

Her favorite was the one they called Captain, or Cap for short. He seemed to take an instant liking to Elsie, responding to the slightest command spoken in her soft voice. She drove him in the high two-wheeled cart, alone, and with his partner, Caleb.

When the weather was unfit for driving, they polished harnesses, trimmed manes and tails. She proved efficient in the art of braiding colorful ribbons into the heavy manes as well as grooming the bodies of the great beasts until they shone with a deep copper glow.

Elsie and Elam talked as they worked, about everything and anything. She learned many things about him, including the insecurities he harbored about being what his father expected of him, which came as a surprise.

"I didn't think you knew what it felt like, trying to live up to someone else's standards," Elsie remarked, stopping midstroke to stare at him, her arms hanging loosely at her sides, the currycomb in her right hand.

"You don't know my father. He's a very precise person. When you think you've managed to come up to his standards, he raises the bar."

She noticed the flicker of self-doubt in his dark eyes, the slight twitch of the corners of his mouth, as if he were remembering a past episode that brought unwanted emotion. His face was becoming a familiar map, one she scanned so often she was coming to know every contour, every flash of his eyes, or the softening of them. She knew by the sound of his voice when he was frustrated and when he was pleased. She knew when the pressure was on, like today, that he would always bring up the subject of his father.

"We're driving four at the horse sale. Four. Cap, Caleb, Doll, and Dominic. I want you to do it. He says I have to, but I know you're better. He won't accept it."

Elsie's mouth hung open in disbelief, her eyes wide as she gazed at him.

"You think I can?" she whispered.

"You've done it."

"Two. Never four."

"Today, we'll do it. I'll show him."

His mouth was set in a determined line.

The February weather accommodated the hitching up, the sun warm on their backs, a brisk wind in their faces. The horses were full of energy, prancing, sidestepping, lowering their noses to the piles of gray-white snow scattered across the wide area in front of the barn. Elsie's skirt was tugged first one way then another, her headscarf threatening to leave her head. They worked together, calming the horses, fastening traces, checking and rechecking the harnesses, every buckle and snap.

Elam told her the horses had to learn obedience perfectly, so they made them stand still, in spite of the wind and their own high energy. It was a thrill to be able to master these powerful animals' will, to know that a spoken word would enable both of them to stand back, admire the clean silhouette of this amazing hitch.

At the last minute, Elam's father came out of the house, buttoning his coat, his walk purposeful, as if he regretted having allowed this without his supervision.

"You didn't tell me you were hitching four," was his greeting.

"I think I told you this morning," Elam replied.

He looked over the team with a trained eye.

Elsie watched Elam's face for any sign of fear, but there was none.

"I thought Doll worked best behind Dominic," his father said.

"Behind? They're a team," Elam answered.

"As long as you know what you're doing."

With that, he strode off, leaving Elam with a flicker of doubt, a waning confidence. He turned to Elsie. "You drive."

For only a second, she sensed the little boy's disappointment in him. He had not quite come up to his father's expectation. Did he ever?

To see this in the one who always showed absolute confidence, perceived as arrogance more than once, was astounding.

So he was not as sure of himself as he would have the world believe.

She took a deep breath and looked at the four massive horses, their flanks quivering with the cold and the eagerness to run. This wagon was no bobsled. It was twice as high and glossy, the wheels like wet pine wood, the color of caramel. The body of the wagon was painted a deep burgundy, with the same caramel color repeated on the seat. The first time she'd seen the wagon, she'd gasped in disbelief.

She had never imagined anything like it, didn't know such beauty existed in the form of a horse-drawn wagon. It was borrowed from Bailing Springs Stables for the show.

She shook her head. "I don't know about this."

"You won't until you try."

He handed the reins to her. She scrambled up the wide iron steps. He stayed at Captain's head, watching intently as she took a deep, steadying breath.

"You OK?"

She nodded.

He came around to the other side and was up beside her.

"Gloves?"

She nodded.

She had never been so afraid in all her life. This was different than driving two, and that in itself inspired awe.

When she loosened the wide leather reins and called the command to start, her voice was high. Her breath came in quick gasps.

She did not feel the cold, or the warmth of the sun. Everything faded away, leaving only the backs of the horses, the black symmetry of harness, buckles, rings, and polished adornment.

She concentrated on the four arched heads and necks with the intricacy of the woven manes, the red ribbon intertwined with the oatmeal-colored manes. Sixteen massive hooves crunched on gravel, the huge wheels moving effortlessly. They had moved off together in a perfect rhythm, which was amazing. But she knew they'd spent hours being trained for this.

The road loomed like an insurmountable hurdle. Could she make the turn?

Elam didn't speak. He gave her no instruction, merely sat watching for traffic as if this were an occurrence that happened every day for both of them.

All right.

She remembered the softness of a horse's mouth. She eased into the drawing of the reins, her hands light, but feeling the power and obedience.

"Car," Elam said softly.

Her first impulse was to haul back on the black reins with all her strength, but she pulled lightly, concentrated on distance, the ability to stop before the car's approach.

She waited, the car went past, and she loosened the reins, drawing slightly on the right. She couldn't make a tight turn, so she allowed a slight maneuver.

The horses responded as one.

The turn was executed flawlessly.

"Perfect!"

Elam was grinning, watching Elsie, who never took her eyes from the team, her back straight, her hands held at the proper angle, her profile showing pure concentration.

"Great. You're doing great."

She said nothing, allowed no smile of recognition.

Traffic almost stopped. The occupants of passing vehicles gawked like schoolchildren. Cell phones were held out of windows as their picture was taken repeatedly. Cars pulled to the side of the road, motorists scrambling to record the massive four-horse hitch on their phones to show the world.

Elsie was not distracted. She kept her eyes on the horses, her hands steady on the reins as they moved along the country roads of Lancaster County, making a huge circle before coming from the opposite direction, slowing to make the turn into the Stoltzfus driveway.

They drove up to the barn, where the dark figure of Elam's father emerged immediately, a scowl on his weathered face, his hat pulled low.

"Why'd you let her drive?" was his way of greeting.

"She'll drive at the sale."

"Not without my permission."

There was nothing to say to that, so they climbed down, one on each side, beginning to loosen traces as they averted their eyes. He watched, without comment, then turned away and left.

Benny came flying out of the house, his coat flapping behind him as he struggled to shove his arms into the sleeves. He had long since abandoned the torn straw hat, but his long bangs took the place of having to peer at his surroundings through the brim of his hat.

"Hey, you guys!" he shouted. "Why'd you leave without me? Huh? Sneaking off so I don't get to ride. I bet you got your picture taken? Huh? I could have been on there."

"Too bad," Elam called, grinning at his younger brother.

"Can I drive next time?"

"Probably not."

"Is that right? I'll ask Dat."

"Look, Benny, you don't have an interest in these horses. There's a lot more to it than having your picture taken. You're never with us, you have no idea how to drive, or hitch them up or anything."

Benny changed the subject. "I'm going for pizza. Wanna come with me? Me and Rueben."

Elam lifted his eyebrows to Elsie.

The truth was, she was starved. She'd been too nervous to think about eating all day. But with Benny and his sidekick? She nodded.

After the horses were rubbed down, stabled, and fed, and the wagon shoved into the garage, they cleaned up in the house. Elsie was shy and quiet, borrowing a clean apron from his sister. She tried not to gawk at the immensity and beauty of the house. Elam and she were still worlds apart.

"You have to get in the back," Benny informed them, after he led his horse and buggy up to the yard.

Elsie stiffened.

She wasn't aware of any young man having a back seat available. Normally, the youth crowded in the front, the back full of all the paraphernalia young *rumschpring* carried with them.

"Why do you have Dat's carriage?" Elam asked.

"My brakes are shot. Came down Welsh Mountain and burned them out over the weekend."

There was nothing to do but climb into the back and submit to the intimacy of the back seat of a buggy, which is a small space, at best, knees shoved up against the front seat.

Benny was a terrible driver, talking nonstop, lurching to a grinding halt, then chirping and shaking the reins over the unsuspecting horse's back, causing the buggy to be yanked forward. He drove off the road repeatedly, resulting in a clunk as the right wheels dropped off the macadam, onto the gravel shoulder, throwing Elsie against Elam, who took full advantage of the closeness, wrapping an arm protectively about her shoulders.

Rueben was picked up and the two started in with their constant jokes. Elsie laughed so hard, tears ran from her eyes as she bent forward, which enabled Elam's arm to tighten even more.

The pizza was delicious, the dim light another

intimacy with Elam painfully handsome beside her. Everything seemed surreal, the giddiness of having driven the four-horse hitch successfully, the joy of looking forward to the sale in Ohio, knowing she would soon ride Gold with Elam on his riding horse, as all her insecurities and inhibitions melted away in his company.

And later, she blushed to think that, yes, when that arm came around her shoulders on the way home, she had leaned in slightly—maybe more than slightly.

Oh, the feeling of being wanted and protected, though. She had never imagined the quiet assurance of growing into something she labeled "like." She liked Elam. Love, the heart-throbbing captivity of falling in love, was too much. This kind of friendship was perfect.

Chapter Ten

FOR ALL THAT YEAR, THEIR FRIENDSHIP DEEP-
ened. They fed horses, braided manes, cleaned stalls.
They stood in box stalls ripe with the smell of fresh
horse manure, leaned on pitchforks as they talked.
Sometimes they argued, when Elsie could not control
her tongue, when she felt passionately against one of
Elam's decisions.

They rode together, sometimes holding hands, the
creak of leather, boots in stirrups, the nodding of the
horses' heads, the ring of an iron-shod hoof on rock.

And still they did not date officially. He never
asked her out on a real date, so no one knew about
the developing relationship.

Elam's father watched with a wary eye, but never
said a word. His mother knew, but figured it was best
to stay quiet. That girl had more horse sense than
anyone she'd ever known, and if horses were what
it would take to get those two together, then so be
it. Elsie was who she wanted for Elam. Unspoiled,

taught in all the ways of submission and obedience, she would be the perfect match for Elam's strong will and spontaneity.

Sometimes they spent a weekend together, but always with a group, never giving away the friendship that had developed already. She drove the four-horse hitch at many events, Elam beside her, her gloved hands soft but firm and capable. She looked forward to each event, but concentrated on extra training beforehand, doing the work, inspecting harnesses, braiding and rebraiding manes until they passed her expectations.

She grew to love the crowds, the yells, the hat throwing, the thunderous cheers. Her confidence increased every time they made successful drives around the ring, which pleased Elam. She had even taken to standing up to his father. There was never anything done quite right, always a buckle too loose, a strap too tight, a braid not bound tightly enough. Small, irritating things she had hurried to correct, before. When the horses were loaded into the comfortable trailer, tethered, and given sufficient attention, he stood by the gate as they raised it, stern and imposing, as always.

"You should have loaded Dominic first."

"Why is that?" Elam asked, clapping his hands to rid them of dust, then bending to brush off his clean black trousers.

Elsie stood waiting.

"He's the most aggressive."

"And why would it make a difference when he was loaded?"

His father's eyes met those of his son, the thread of dislike decipherable by the pronounced scowl on the elder Stoltzfus, and the downward twitch, the vulnerable arc of the sides of Elam's mouth that always tore at her heart.

Elsie stepped forward, her arms crossed loosely across her waist.

"Dominic does best on the right, at the very front, on account of the traffic. That's why he's loaded there."

She could see the arrival of his taunt, his dismissal of her judgment, could see the correcting of it, the instant smile of condescension.

"Ah yes, Elsie. You're learning fast."

"I am. And I do appreciate that you allow me to work with the horses. It's a lifelong dream."

"Just make sure you take 283, and not 30," he said gruffly, and strode off.

Elam muttered something about him not being the driver. The driver had his wife along, which meant they would share the second seat of the dual-wheeled pickup truck with the immense trailer attached to it. They talked the whole way, conversing in Pennsylvania Dutch, mostly about the relationship with his father.

"I mean, come on. Why would we take 30, with four horses? That route is OK if you're not in a hurry, but what was he thinking? He always manages to make me feel like I'm ten years old."

"I think it's most fathers and their oldest sons. I really do. It's normal. He knows you're better with the horses than he is. He knows we've taken these horses to a level he never thought possible."

"You're right."

"So don't worry about it. He needs to feel as if he has accomplished all this, not us. It's a man thing. I can tell he hurts you with his words, but let him have that sense of authority by picking on little things. It makes him feel important."

"He needs to grow up."

"So do you."

"Harsh words."

"Necessary words."

Their eyes met and held. They both smiled. It was a smile that made Elsie feel wanted, respected, accepted, elevated to a position of absolute trust. They knew each other so well, could openly discuss every situation, every slight feeling of annoyance or anger, every joy, every accomplishment.

And yet, it never dawned on them that they probably should be dating in the conventional way. Perhaps if they did, all this would be lost, this shared intimacy of building a perfect four-horse hitch. They made the wide curve from Route 283 to the Pennsylvania Turnpike entrance, slowed while the driver positioned the EZ pass scanner, then resumed their speed as they traveled west.

"Another few hours and we'll be there. Altoona isn't more than a hundred miles, maybe a hundred twenty."

Elsie sat back and enjoyed the view of the wide Susquehanna River, the towering apartment and office buildings in Harrisburg.

Three Mile Island was steadily spewing the steam from the nuclear plant, with other, smaller islands dotting the river like moles on a face. Elsie loved the river and wished she could camp on that largest island; she pointed it out to Elam.

"I'll take you camping sometime. But not here, on these islands. You wouldn't be allowed."

"Seriously?"

For Elsie believed everything Elam said. He was the wise one, the knowledgeable one. But when it came to the horses, she was his equal. And finally, she knew it.

Her work at the bakery was no longer a challenge. All she really cared about was Elam and the horses, and not necessarily in that order. To be able to groom them, braid the manes, and oil the fetlocks was nothing like the repetitive motion of doing hundreds of yeast rolls and bread, cinnamon rolls like an expanse of sweet dough she automatically peppered with cinnamon and brown sugar, her hands flying effortlessly while she talked to her sister Malinda.

Rache, the eagle eye of the entire business,

confronted her before the Christmas rush. In her normal abrasive manner, the ever-present tall cup of cappuccino clutched in her sausage fingers, she stood without speaking, a huge and intimidating presence.

"So, what are your thoughts about your job?"

Confused, Elsie stopped rolling the length of dough. She turned to look at Rache, one eyebrow arched in question.

"What do you mean, my thoughts about my job?"

"Well, you're awfully preoccupied. Your thoughts aren't on your work. I asked for two batches of iced raisin bread, and what did I get? Only one."

Elsie blushed, stammered.

"Surely not."

"Yeah, it's true. Now there are only two loaves on the shelf."

"I'm sorry."

"Sorry isn't going to correct the problem."

"I'll do another batch."

"You can't. You have all you can do with the iced cinnamon rolls. I don't know what Eli will say."

Elsie felt the heat rise within her. The old Elsie would have quivered in her shoes, frantically apologized, afraid she'd lose her job, at worst. But now, she felt a new confidence. The same backbone she felt as she climbed effortlessly onto the high wagon seat and took the reins in her hands, looked out on the beautiful symmetry of those four wide backs and the colorful, intricate weaving of the manes, and knew those magnificent creatures trusted her as she trusted them. She held the power to make them obey with the reins in her hands, knew when one horse was nervous, jumpy, and knew what to do about it.

Now, she knew Rache was used to the power of the upper hand, knew she could display all kinds of authority, being Eli's right hand, and reveled in it.

Elsie knew, too, that one batch of raisin bread was not a big deal. Not even close to what Rache was hoping to make it.

"I'll do it. No problem."

"It is a problem."

Malinda worked furiously, her back turned, her head lowered in submission.

Elsie drew herself up to her full height, her hands on her hips, and looked at Rache squarely. Her eyes

were like wet raisins in mounds of dough, shining
with grease.

"As soon as you remove yourself from this space,
I can get to work on it. If you need to tell Eli, go
right ahead. For all the years I have worked here, he
has never complained about my work, and I'm sure
I have made more mistakes than one batch of raisin
bread."

Elsie lowered her hands and made shooing
motions, to get her to remove herself.

"Go. I need to get started."

"Growing up, are we?" was her parting shot, but
she moved off, like a great lumbering ox, holding the
cup of cappuccino like a sword.

"Elsie!" Malinda hissed.

"Sorry, Malinda. But it's time she knows I am no
longer afraid of her."

The bakery fairly sizzled with activity as Christmas
approached, and Elsie did her best, the way she
always had.

Somehow, she knew the old ways to please Eli and
to astound Rache with her abilities were faltering.
Like a gasoline engine that was running out of fuel.

Her heart simply was no longer in the work at the bakery.

Yes, she needed the money. Her feed bill came regularly every month, and her parents depended on the extra amount, now doubled by Malinda's pay. Her mother had confided in her about being able to "put away" a rather large sum for her cedar chest made at Dannie King's woodworking shop. She would buy towels and sheet sets in January, when some of the local dry goods stores held their sales.

"Maybe even Walmart." She spoke reverently, with a hidden delight at being able to do as other mothers did, to fill the hope chest with linens, tablecloths, and kitchen towels, the marriage of a daughter like northern lights in a dark sky.

She was in awe of her daughter Elsie. But still, lovely though she was, it was necessary to stay humble. She could be dating now. She'd heard from her sister that a half dozen boys, if not more, had asked her.

She turned them all down, crazy to be with those Belgians on the Stoltzfus farm. Or was it the son?

Well, she'd go ahead and get that hope chest filled up, a luxury she could not have dreamed of before the wonderful high-paying job at the bakery.

God would provide, she'd always said. And now He had.

Elsie knew she did not want to live the remainder of her years providing for her family. She longed for a home of her own.

To be able to get up in the morning and make breakfast for someone she loved, to do laundry, clean her own house, work in her own garden, the added bonus of being able to work with the horses. . . .

What? Where had that thought come bubbling out of? To daydream about her own home had nothing to do with the Belgians, or Elam. Did they? Did it?

Oh, but it did. Elam and the Belgians and Gold, Cookie, old and graying around his nose, all of it, everyone was included in her hopes for the future. It was all she wanted.

And yet, he had never popped the question: "Elsie, may I take you home? Elsie, may I ask you for a date?

May I pick you up on Saturday evening? Around seven?" Since that night she turned him down so long ago now, he hadn't once broached the topic.

As time went on, she came to believe their friendship was merely that, a friendship and perhaps a professional partnership.

The weekend in October when they trucked the riding horses to Mount Gretna to go trail riding in the mountain with the colorful foliage was a bit of heaven on earth. They'd talked of their relationship, how well they got along, how one knew what to expect of the other, even laughed about it. The look in his eyes contained an ownership, a pride in her, so that her heart quickened. She was so sure he would turn the conversation to serious plans of beginning a formal courtship.

Sometimes, he held her hand when they rode, their knees touching as the horses walked in rhythm, the creak of stirrups and saddles whispering their close feelings.

On the trail ride, he told her she was beautiful.

That was all, though, which was much like drinking unsweetened tea—it was good, but she had hoped for more.

And here was the Christmas season again, a time of joy in the savior's birth, the giving of gifts to one another to follow the tradition of the wise men, and she was left with the impending wisdom that she'd have nothing from Elam but a tall glass of unsweetened tea. And another and another.

There were no horse shows or sales till January. The Belgians were in top-notch condition, so Elsie stayed home in the evening, pampered Gold, took her brother, Amos, for rides, sitting astride like a mighty little warrior as the cold wind scoured the brown fields, sending bits of corn fodder aloft, whirling madly in any direction.

Amos loved the golden horse, spent all his time at the barn with Elsie, jabbering away in his lisping voice.

He told her that if he ever got married, he and his wife would have a llama farm with horses to chase them around and a red Farmall tractor to haul the dead ones away.

Elsie threw back her head and laughed.

"You funny boy! Now why would your llamas die?"

"A fox would get them."

Elsie laughed again, a deeper, richer sound.

And then he was there, his dark form filling the lantern light, a wide grin on his face. Elsie saw him and stopped laughing.

Amos said sternly, "Elam's here."

"I see."

It was all Elsie could think of. He appeared different, somehow. His face was pale, drawn, as if he were not feeling well. His eyes were serious, dark, as if he had experienced a sobering event that he needed to share with her.

"I had a ride on Elsie's horse," Amos told him. "We just got back. We're cleaning up the forebay. Where's your horse?" Amos asked, his face like a cherub peering out from the lowered stocking cap.

"I didn't bring my horse. I walked."

"Not even Cookie?"

"I wouldn't fit on Cookie too well these days," Elam replied. And still he did not smile.

He said, "Can I talk to you, Elsie?"

She gestured toward Amos, raised her eyebrows.

Elam nodded toward the house.

"Bedtime, Amos. I'll take you to the house."

"Why?"

"It's late."

When she returned, Elam was finishing the job of sweeping wisps of hay. He looked up, his face still a set mask, like a wax figurine.

"That didn't sit well with him," she said, hoping to lighten his mood. "He wanted to tell you about his llama farm."

Elam merely lowered himself onto the old express wagon, as if his knees would give way if he stayed on his feet a minute longer.

"Sit down, Elsie."

He patted the seat beside him. She bent to scrape away the wood chips and bits of bark left on the wagon from hauling wood from the shed into the house.

"What's wrong, Elam? You don't have the flu that's going around, do you?"

"No, I . . . I'm all right."

A silence hung between them like a veil, the only sound the steady grinding of Gold's teeth as he chewed the good hay.

The battery lantern shone steadily, its white light illuminating the shabbiness of the old barn, the cracked windowpanes, the one replaced by a piece of plywood, the blue plastic half barrel set on cement blocks for a watering trough.

She felt the old misery of being poor, of having this half barn, half shed as a shelter for the beautiful Gold. And Fred. Fred, the old, plain Standardbred driving horse with his discolored halter, torn on one side.

Well, this was who she was. Plain Elsie. Davey Esha ihr Elsie. Handicapped Davey, with one hand and most of his arm missing. And they were doing well. They had remained independent, had made a living, even if it had always been a bit hardscrabble. They had risen together as a family, buoyed by love and kindness, tremendous caring for each other, and Elam would simply have to look for another girl if she would never be good enough.

"Elsie. I miss you."

"Well, I'd be over, but it will be another few weeks till Christmas is past. We're really busy at the bakery."

"No. I miss you more than I can say."

"But . . . I don't . . ."

"I can't go on another day without telling you how I feel about you. I'm not good with words, OK?"

She nodded, dumbfounded.

"Do you ever think of me in the way that . . . I mean, do you come over to help with the horses for just that? The horses? Or do I count?"

"Well, I . . ."

Why aren't you dating? Most of your friends are."

"I just never wanted to."

"You still don't?"

For a moment that seemed like hours, Elsie did not give him an answer. Who was she to tell him? He would not understand.

"I guess not really, or I would have accepted."

"Accepted who?"

"You know. The ones that have asked me out on a date."

"Yeah. I guess. Why didn't you take them?"

"I don't know."

This was going all wrong. Elam had the distinct sensation of being bogged down in unrelenting mud, with no available help.

Elsie wanted to tell him she wasn't dating because she could not accept anyone except him. His beloved face was the one she wanted to see when she woke up in the morning, the face that would be across the table from her at every mealtime. He was her friend, her confidant, the one who knew everything about her, every dream, every goal, her attitudes both good and bad.

"So you won't be dating anytime soon?"

Elsie took a deep breath to steady herself, embracing the clear and precise feeling of flinging herself off a cliff, abandoning all convention and common sense.

"I can't date anyone when it's you I love," she whispered.

She felt him draw back, heard his sharp intake of breath.

"What did you just say?" he asked hoarsely.

"I love you, Elam. No one else."

"Elsie," he said thickly.

He stood then, and reached for her hands. He drew her up, his eyes never leaving her face. He dropped her hands, his going to her face.

"Beautiful, talented girl. I can't believe what you just said. Elsie, you are the love of my life. A love that grew so big it was way out of proportion, and became scary and, well . . . I'm not much of a man, I guess. After that first time when you turned me down, I never had the nerve to tell you how I felt."

And then he drew her close, found her lips, and kissed her with a great tenderness, a quiet longing. Elsie was carried away to the place of a love that was real, a hundred times more than she could have imagined.

The old barn with the leak in the roof became a haven for the two people who felt the beginning of a love that would last a lifetime. The kind God gives freely to those who love Him, the enduring love that rides on the wings of admiration and respect.

Outside, the first snowflake of the season settled on the rusted old roof and winked at the two of them as it slowly melted into a tiny rivulet of winter. Christmas bells rang deep and true across the land, some evening service coming to a close as the silvery snowflakes came down in earnest, blessing the two as they remained in each other's arms, a declaration of the wonder of love.

The End

The More the
MERRIER

Chapter One

IT WASN'T THE FACT THAT SHE WAS LEFT alone after Eli died that was so hard. It was caring for eight children in 1931, those bleak years of the Great Depression, when neither hard work nor skillful financial management made much of a difference, seeing how there was no money to manage and no jobs to be had.

Sammy was the oldest, at sixteen years of age, hired out to Jonas Beiler over toward Strasburg, working on the farm from sunup to sundown. He was a strong, curly-haired youth with an outlook as sunny as possible considering his father's passing. So that left seven children for Annie to feed and clothe, and no matter what she did, life had turned into a scramble for survival.

A small woman with an abundance of thick brown hair, wide green eyes that held a shadow of sorrow, and a wide, full mouth compressed with the hardship of daily life, she mourned the loss of her husband and

wondered what God meant by casting her in the role
of widowhood. But still, she bowed her head and said,
"Thy will be done." She kept the cows, but sold two
of the pigs to pay the feed bill, and acquired twenty
chickens and a sick calf that she nursed back to health.
Suvilla and Enos, ages fifteen and thirteen, helped milk
the cows by hand every morning and every evening,
and helped lug the monstrous milk cans onto the low
flatbed wagon and haul them to the end of the drive
for the milkman. They cleaned cow stables, forked
loose hay and straw, fed the chickens, and ate coffee
soup and fried mush for breakfast, a lard sandwich for
lunch, and potato soup for supper. Curly-haired and
big-eyed, their cheeks blooming with pink color, the
children shed a few stoic tears for their father, and then
tried to go on with their lives. Everyone had to die at
some point, some earlier than others. That fact didn't
exactly make it easy to say goodbye to their father, but
they did their best to accept the simple words of their
mother: "His time was up."

Ephraim was eleven years old, solemn and
wise, and he instructed the smaller children in the
way of life and death, repeating the words of the

minister from the funeral service. Ida was barely a year younger, and like twins, they spoke and thought alike, although she hung on to every word from his mouth, an adoring younger sister whose devotion to her brother bordered on worship.

Emma, Lydia, and Rebecca were often referred to as "the three little ones"—six, four, and nearly three years old with thick brown curls plastered severely into rolls along both sides of their heads, the heavy tresses pinned into coils in the back. They were young enough to accept without question the disappearance of their father, feeling only the small portion of grief God allows for little ones.

It had been six months and twenty days since his passing, Annie counted as she sat on the back stoop with the sound of children playing mingling with the wind in the maple trees, the clucking of the chickens, and distant barking of dogs. She was weary to the point of exhaustion. Early spring, the time of plowing, harrowing, and planting, had always taxed her strength, even when she had worked alongside Eli, his sturdy frame ahead of her walking behind the plow, the reins secured behind his back.

This year she had Sammy at home for a few weeks, but the work was still more than they could reasonably manage. The seed corn was bought on credit, which was a weight on her mind and shoulders. What if there was not enough to pay it back? She envisioned losing their home. Did people go to jail for unpaid debts? No, the church wouldn't allow it. She'd have to make a humiliating trip to see Amos Beiler, the deacon, but so be it.

She watched the three youngest race across the lawn, marveling at their strength and energy after the meager soup in their stomach. The potatoes were all gone, even the smallest one, wrinkled like an old man's face. They'd gone down cellar, broke off every sprout to ensure the potatoes' well-being, but they knew the supply would run out in April or May, and the new crop would not be ready to dig till August.

There were canned tomatoes, green beans, pole limas, and corn left, but none of those vegetables satisfied hunger like solid, starchy potatoes. Cornmeal was good, though, and she roasted one ear of corn after another. She filled the oven of the solid range with the heavy ears of corn and allowed the odor of it to fill her with fresh hope. As long as they had roasted, ground cornmeal, they wouldn't starve.

The sun's rays slanted between the dancing maple leaves, creating a pattern of light and shadow. There was a blaze of color in the west, brilliant orange and timid yellow, a soft lavender that melded with the weightless blue of early spring. It was the kind of evening that made her feel as if everything was manageable. Possible. That she'd be all right in spite of the huge obstacles she faced. She leaned back, rested her weight on her elbows, stretched her feet, and watched a blur of small birds whirring across the sky in a frantic synchronized spiral of movement that took her breath away. Well, if God knew each sparrow that fell, and designed the ability of tiny birds to fly like that, then he would surely favor her with his kindness.

Yes. He would.

Dear Heavenly Father, guide me along this path you have prepared for me. Help me to make good choices, to protect my children. Give me strength for today.

She got to her feet. She was a small woman and wore the traditional purple dress with a black apron pinned around her narrow waist, her substantial white organdy head-covering revealing only a thin strip of her abundant hair and hiding most of her ears. She was a stalwart and modest figure that moved purposefully across the lawn, then bent to examine the rich dark soil for signs of onion tops pushing through. She straightened. Her eyes roved the perimeters of the yard searching for little ones, and, finding none of them, she turned toward the barn to come upon the three little girls on their hands and knees, poking a long hoe handle beneath the woodpile.

"He's in here. I saw him go," Lydia said excitedly.

A vague question of what was meant by "him" brought a smile to Annie's tired face. A mouse, rat, snake, earthworm? Which of God's creatures was hiding beneath that pile?

Suddenly there was a shriek from Lydia, a roar from Emma, a hurried scuttling followed by a mad dash in her direction. The smallest one, Rebecca, was toddling after them with howls of outrage. Annie brought her hands to her hips.

"Here, here," she said, speaking with authority. "Lydia, what is under the woodpile? Stop your *greishas*."

Small hands clutched at her side, her waist, tugged at her apron, with dusty shoes dancing around her own feet. She bent to scoop up Rebecca. "Shh. Shh. Hush."

"It's a snake. A black one as thick as your arm. It turned around and was going to bite us!"

"They don't bite, Lydia. Stop saying that. Snakes are good—they eat mice and rats."

She turned to go back to the house, the sturdy white dwelling with long, deep windows, a porch along the front, and a smokehouse off to the right. A cement sidewalk separated the green lawn like the part on the top of someone's head, with a Y that led to the smokehouse. Another block of cement contained the cast iron water pump with a tin cup attached to it, hanging on a piece of thick string. Everyone drank from the cup, without the benefit of even a weekly wash with the rest of the dishes in the house, so the handle was darkened by the repeated insertion of two fingers curled around it—fingers stained with soil, manure, tobacco leaves, hoe handles, and sweat.

A few yews grew in neatly trimmed rectangles along the front of the house, with a climbing rose attached to a trellis on the right. The windows were without light, the house as if everyone was remembering the loss of its owner, shrouded in grief. Never again would his joyous footsteps announce his arrival. Annie would never again turn from the cook stove to greet him, or walk with him to sit on the old davenport beneath the double windows in the kitchen. He had been taken from her by the freak accident that she had relived over and over in her mind—runaway horses that took a wagonload of firewood down a steep embankment. They'd uncovered his body by clawing at chunks of it, but his actual death had been by drowning, half in and half out of the icy Pequea Creek.

Annie herded her gaggle of little ones into the house, closed the door firmly against early spring night temperatures, then went to the cook stove to lift the round lid from the glossy top, before bending to grab a stick of firewood to keep the red coals from dying into the bed of cold gray ashes. She smiled to herself as three little ones tucked their feet under their skirts, leaning over the edge of the couch to make sure the black snake had not followed them inside.

One by one, the older children trickled into the house, fresh-faced and windblown, every one with a headful of thick brown hair in a variety of waves and curls, and wide green eyes that were always curious and full of life.

Ida and Ephraim were chattering like magpies, the words tumbling from their mouths punctuated by exclamation or giggles, eyes wide with disbelief or eyebrows lowered in concentration. They bent their backs simultaneously to untie the shoelaces on their high-topped leather shoes, peeled off their black cotton socks and stuffed them back into their shoes, then set them neatly in a row along the wall in back of the cook stove.

"Time for bare feet, Mam!" Ida trilled.

Bowa feesich. To be rid of cumbersome leather shoes, to wiggle toes and feel the delicious softness of grass and soil and pine needles, was a pure pleasure for all children between the ages of two and fourteen.

"No bare feet until you see the first bumblebee, Ida."

"Bumblebees have nothing to do with bare feet. Why do you always say that?"

Annie thought for a second. "I guess my mother said that, so I do, too."

Ephraim's round green eyes gazed into his mother's with no guile, pure and innocent as a forest pool. At eleven years of age, he was unusually quiet, reflective, a lover of school work and books. Annie lay awake at night considering how he hadn't shed one tear after the death of his father. While the remainder of the family allowed their sorrow to spill out at the funeral, Ephraim stood dry-eyed, his eyes unfocused, as if he had gone to another place that was happier.

"Ephraim, where were you?" she asked.

"Down by the creek."

"By yourself?"

"Yes."

"What were you doing there?"

"Watching the tadpoles."

Annie smiled at him, then turned to the stove again. She felt torn in so many directions since her husband's passing. With eight children and only one parent, how could there ever be enough of her time to meet each one's needs? For one moment, despair crept into her thoughts like an unwelcome virus, an annoying pain that she knew she must endure.

Each child was an individual, each one with her special personality, his own needs to be met, and Eli had been so good with the boys, such a strong leader, with clear and unflinching authority like a beacon of light to guide their feet. Yes, sometimes she thought he was too hard on them, and there were times when his words seemed suddenly harsh, catching them all off guard. But discipline was important for children, and he was carrying a lot of responsibility. The stress would get to anyone now and then.

Now he was gone.

Reality hit her repeatedly. Grief was a constant companion, an unwanted presence that sucked all the oxygen out of the atmosphere around her, often leaving her gasping for air, feeling numb and half-dead inside. It was for her children that she lifted her head from the pillow every morning, got through the dark days of winter. Now there was a promise of spring, with its bursting of new life; each blade of grass that sprouted was a harbinger of hope.

Taking a deep breath, she turned and spoke.

"Bedtime."

"We're hungry."

"There will be plenty of breakfast in the morning." She said it with confidence, but wondered how long children could stay healthy on coffee soup and fried mush.

The anxiety raised its visage once more, but she gave herself up to God's will, steeled against the fear, and spoke the necessary words.

"Ephraim, get the water ready."

She hoped her voice carried the proper authority. To get the water ready meant setting the agate dishpan on the bench by the back door, adding a good amount of cold water from the cast iron spigot in the kitchen sink, grabbing the teakettle that was always humming on back of the wood range, and dumping enough boiling water into it to produce a nice warm temperature for face washing before bedtime. With a wash rag that hung from a bed and a bar of lye soap, the night ritual was complete.

One by one, they bent over the soapy water, washed faces and hands, swallowed against the emptiness in their stomachs, and sat waiting till their mother produced the black prayer book, then turned to kneel at a kitchen chair. Who could tell what went through each child's mind as the soft voice of their mother replaced the deep, strong voice of their father, reciting the words of the old German prayer that had been written hundreds of years ago? Fluent in German, she read well, her voice rising and falling, comforting to the children's ears.

When they rose to their feet, she put the prayer book back on the shelf, sighed, and wished the children good night: "*Gute nacht, Kinna.*"

The children answered in unison before turning to wend their way up the staircase, their bare feet soundless on the wooden steps. The usual scuffling in the boys' room was followed by a scattering of voices, bedsprings creaking, a few footfalls in the girls' room. And then silence spread like a mist through the house.

This was the time Annie dreaded most, the long evenings that moved toward the stroke of midnight punctuated only by her soft sighs, whispered prayers, and shifting for a better, more restful position. This was when his absence felt as if someone had literally done her physical harm. A knife slash in her chest, a stray bullet grazing a section of her midriff, leaving a wound that wasn't deadly but one that would never heal.

She had loved so deeply. Eli had been the one she had always noticed, yearned for, as a youth. But she never thought he would acknowledge her presence, and certainly never want her for his wife. Tall, well built, too handsome for his own good, he'd broken a few silly girls' hearts before turning to the quiet, stone-faced Annie, bringing the smile to her lovely mouth, the glistening to her green eyes.

But as marriages go, theirs was not a perfect union. He was demanding of her physical love, and she the proverbial shrinking violet, needing her rest and the energy to feed yet another infant. He was robust, with a strong personality, a man who needed a social life, visiting friends, inviting them for an evening meal on a Sunday, going to barn raisings and livestock auctions, lingering at the local feed store to banter politics with *"die Englishy,"* where Annie would have been content to stay home with the children.

Now, after his tragic accident, the house seemed lifeless, dead.

She had never realized the life he had breathed into his family's existence. Like fresh air and the light of the sun, his laughter had rung out through the rooms, fulfilling every child's need for a bit of merriment when times were hard. A good sense of humor quelled her worrying, effectively making her world a lighter place, so with his absence came the demons of her inability to cope with the hard task of providing for all of them. Occasionally she remembered the darker moments, when he would enter their home with a dark cloud over his head, barking orders and refusing to meet Annie's questioning eyes, but thinking of those times only brought a pang of guilt to her heart. She should have been more forgiving, quicker to meet his needs while she still had the chance.

The children were growing fast, thin and wiry, with seemingly bottomless stomachs. The milk check barely paid the bills, with two cows gone dry. The hay supply in the barn was alarmingly low, and it would be a few months before more could be cut. She would have to talk to Jonas Beiler, soon. He'd look for another hired boy even if she desperately needed the three dollars her eldest son brought home every week. She could not handle two freshening cows, the hay to be cut, the corn planting, not to mention the birthing of the sows.

Yes, she knew the Amish community would never let a widow and her children starve, of course, but she had her pride. There was no reason she could not carry on alone, even if it meant tightening their belts and sending the children to bed a little hungry.

Some days she had gathered dandelions and boiled the succulent new leaves in salted water. She put a bit of lard in the hot cast iron frying pan, stirred a cup of flour into it, watched it thicken, then added milk and the greens with a few hardboiled eggs stirred into the thick creaminess. Without bacon, it was bland, but the children said nothing, bending their heads and shoveling the life-giving food into their mouths with appreciation. Empty stomachs that have been in that state for too long can be easily filled, Annie reasoned. Soon there would be new onions and radishes, tender green lettuce to make creamed lettuce with onion and hardboiled egg. Meat was so low she could hardly remember cooking a large piece of beef or pork. To butcher a chicken meant the waning of her egg supply, and she needed the eggs to sell at the local grocery.

She'd have to send the boys to the creek soon. The trout would be hungry and she could make a fish stew. There were still dried navy beans in the cloth bag on the pantry floor, and flour. Salt, coffee, molasses, and cornmeal. Milk and eggs. The lard can had been emptied a few months ago, so she'd resorted to buying it, something she had never done while Eli was alive. There had always been the butchering of hogs, in the fall when the frost tinted the grass and days were filled with the winds of oncoming winter.

The weight of her responsibilities was crushing. She could have told the deacon in the church and received help, but it was not Annie's way. Stoic, long-suffering, and proud, she lay awake at night without the comfort others would readily have provided. She would keep the farm somehow, even if it meant sacrificing food and any earthly pleasures. Headed to the stairs, she caught sight of Emma's and Lydia's shoes, which seemed to mock her determination. They were much too small, and the soles were already separated from the shoe. Well, at least it was warm enough to go barefoot most days now.

Chapter Two

IN THE MORNING, AFTER A DEEP SLEEP CUT short by the harsh jangling of the windup alarm clock, things took on a new perspective as she made her way to the barn to milk, the translucent glow of the waning moon lighting her way. She got down the oil lantern from its wooden peg, set it on the board provided for this purpose, struck a match, tilted the glass chimney, turned the wick, and proceeded to light it. The small orange glow emitted enough light to see the seven cows in a neat row, tied to their stanchions, their tails swinging idly as they turned their heads to look at her with soft, liquid eyes.

She hung the lantern from a hook that swung from a heavy beam, grabbed the three-legged wooden milking stool and the heavy steel bucket, pushed on Marigold's hipbone, and sat down to milk. She tugged on the swollen teats after wiping them clean, then began the steady rhythmic squeezing of the front quarters, her hands clenching and unclenching as the milk flowed in thick streams, hitting the bottom of the bucket noisily.

Now where was that Enos? He knew the cows should be given their feed while she milked. It always kept them content. When Suvilla opened the cow stable door and let herself in, shivering, Annie asked where Enos was.

"He's not my responsibility," she answered sharply.

"Suvilla, I'm in the middle of milking. Go to the house to see where he is."

Without bothering to reply, she went, obeying her mother in spite of her reluctance.

Annie continued milking, working through the normal tiredness of her fingers till she had the first cow stripped clean of her milk. A blush of color appeared on her cheeks. She felt invigorated, ready to tackle any job, no matter how strenuous.

"Good morning, Enos, sleepyhead," she called out when he stumbled into the warmth of the cow stable.

He grinned sheepishly, stretched and yawned, then propped the palm of his hand on the rough wooden post that supported the heavy beams above them.

"I was tired."

"Well, you need to feed the cows, quickly. Bessie needs an extra half scoop, she's milking heavily since she calved, alright?"

He nodded and ambled off, his lanky frame already showing promise of being tall and strong.

The tinkling of streams of milk hitting the bottom of Suvilla's milk pail, accompanied by the rasping of the feed leaving the metal scoop, the pungent scent of cow manure, ground corn, and loose hay, the grinding of the cows' teeth, were all familiar sounds that held the promise of her world righting itself and settling comfortably on strongholds of hope. The long night with its talons of fear was a thing of the past.

Pleased to see the second galvanized steel milk can fill to the brim, she set the strainer aside, set the lid on top, and tapped it firmly in place with the rubber mallet. Then she helped Suvilla lift it into the cold water of the cement cooler. There would be five full cans to be rolled on the back of the wagon and taken to the end of the farm's drive for the milkman to pick up.

She cooked breakfast that morning with a song on her lips, whistling low under her breath as she boiled the strong coffee, sliced the congealed cooked corn mush into neat rectangles, and fried them in shimmering hot lard. Suvilla sliced bread from the high loaves and placed a slice in each soup bowl, only half a slice in the smaller children's bowls. Annie added milk and a bit of maple syrup to the coffee, then called the children to breakfast before flipping the slices of mush, standing back to avoid the needles of spraying lard.

Her mouth watered as she slid the pans to the middle of the stove, using her apron as a hot pad. She got down the hook to lift the round stovetop lid and reached for a few sticks of wood. The fire was dying down, and to fry mush properly you needed plenty of heat.

Rebecca was crying as she made her way down the stairs, her bare feet creating the uneven rhythm of a small child's descent. Annie had no time to comfort her, so she told Emma to go see what was wrong, then got down two plates to hold the golden rectangles of fried mush. She ladled the milky, sweet coffee grounds that had settled on the bottom of the kettle, then slid into her chair and bowed her head with her hands folded in her lap. The children followed suit without being told, lifting their heads after Annie lifted hers. The silent prayer was always a time of gratitude for what was placed before her, but it was also a time of discreet observation of each of her children's obedience or lack of it.

Suvilla used to be extremely devout, her head bent so far down that her chin grazed her thin chest, her eyes closed in concentration as her lips moved in prayer. Lately there were times when she seemed to not be praying at all, her head barely bowed. Beside her, Enos's eyes roved across the table, turning slightly to check the amount of wood in the wood box behind the stove, his thoughts very obviously not related to food in any way, while Ephraim was praying quite piously. The smaller children all bowed their heads, some more than others, but all were obedient to the unspoken rule of "patties down."

When Annie lifted her head, she had a clear view of the white barn. She blinked, then took the back of her hand to wipe her eyes, thinking the mist by the cow stable window was a blurry vision. A wisp of fog? But the morning was so clear, so painfully bright and lovely and windy.

There it was, though.

She half rose from her chair, her eyes wide.

"What is it, Mam?" Suvilla sked, her spoon halfway to her coffee soup.

"I'm not sure. Enos, look. Does it look like something is in front of the cow stable window?"

He turned halfway from his seat on the bench, then swung his legs over before getting to his feet, then hurried to the window.

"It . . . it looks like smoke?"

It was a question he already knew the answer to.

He was out the door without further words, Suvilla and Ephraim on his heels, followed by a white-faced Annie, running as best she could with the loose sole of her shoe flapping.

When Enos yanked the barn door open, it was the draft of air that gave vivid life to the smoldering flames that licked along the wick of the kerosene lantern they'd thought to be extinguished. The flame had crept along the glass after it had fallen from its precarious perch on the board along the wall, finally reaching the small tank and erupting into flame, flames that licked greedily at loose hay and dry boards, bits of sawdust and dried fabric feedbags. With no breeze, it burned lazily, cleanly, a line of low flames snaking out from the contained kerosene fire on the cemented walkway where the lantern had fallen.

The cows mooed now, tugged at the restraints, danced from foot to foot. Their eyes rolled in terror as the heavy smoke increased to a dense black cloud.

"Let the cows lose!" Annie screeched, her voice a roar above the crackling flames. She plunged directly into the stinking black smoke from the kerosene lamp, now fanned by the rush of cold wind that blew through the opened door.

The cows were panicked now, bawling and jerking back on the leather collars around their necks, their hips and legs swaying first to one side of their stalls, then another, trying in their own clumsy way to free themselves from the oncoming flames, which made it extremely difficult to loosen them.

Her eyes watering, coughing and gagging, Annie tried desperately to find an opening between the first two cows, but their agitation made it impossible. The moment a panicked cow felt a hand on her hip, she leaned into it, squeezing the limited amount of air from her already tortured lungs. She heard coughing, tried to cry out to Enos and Ephraim.

"Get out! Go back!" she screamed, now that she felt the immensity of the smoke's evil power.

She was awakened by a distant noise, someone calling her name. Immediately she found herself retching and heaving, giving in to the thick slime in her throat. Unable to open her eyes, the burning like a living worm encrusted with pinpoints, she lay on her back with tears from her squeezed eyelids creating tracks through her smoke-blackened face, gasping for breath, before turning to retch again.

"Mam, Mam!"

She heard the agonized cries from Suvilla and wanted to answer, but was overcome by wave after wave of crushing nausea. She was aware of Enos and Ephraim, wanted to raise a hand in protest, but could do nothing but turn her head and heave weakly into the cold, windblown grass.

Dan Beiler had gone to the small town of Intercourse to the hardware store known as Zimmerman's, having run out of two-penny nails when he was in the middle of remodeling his kettle house. His horse was feeling his oats, which was a nice way of putting it, he thought grimly, as he hung on to the reins and hauled back with all of his strength. He didn't know where the line between running away and merely running was drawn, but he knew this old hack he was driving didn't feel as if it would hold together too much longer, at this alarming rate of speed. After he had the creature under control, he decided the horse needed a longer run to rid him of all this excess energy, so took the long route between New Holland and Intercourse by way of Smoketown along the Old Philadelphia Pike, and allowed the crazy horse to stretch out and run until he played himself out.

He could see the billows of smoke even before he heard the fire alarms, tugged on the right rein, and turned onto the next road he figured would take him to the fire. Someone might need his help.

The farm was set back from the road, a clump of maple trees surrounding the two-story white farmhouse, a white barn that was in the throes of an evil fire licking at it from within, by all appearances. He had no idea whose residence it was, but he passed men on foot, drove into a field as fire engines screamed behind him, then hurriedly tied his lathered horse to a fence post and ran all the way to the fire.

On approaching the burning barn, hearing the agonized bawling of tethered animals, he remained reasonable, and stayed away. He was on his way to offer his services to the firemen instead when he found the small group on the grass behind the smokehouse, the terrified children grouped around a blackened person half sitting, half laying against the side. He could see she had been inside the burning building, as had the oldest children.

"Is she alright?" he asked, squatting beside her to look into her face.

Suvilla replied, coughing between words. Her hair was singed and her face streaked with black. "I think she got kicked, but we dragged her out. Somehow . . . ."

She looked a little dazed. "Wow," Dan answered solemnly. "You saved your mother's life. Has a doctor been called?" He looked around, wondering why none of the firemen had come to help this woman.

Suvilla nodded, said someone was coming.

He looked at the woman's face, reached out to touch her shoulder as she opened her eyes. He was met with a depth of sorrow and suffering that spread through his soul.

"I'm alright, I think," she whispered.

And still she held the light in his eyes.

"Where is your husband?"

The three little girls were huddled on the ground with their mother, and spoke as one.

"He's in Heaven."

Dan nodded. Small, blackened, defeated, she was like a flower beaten by storms, stomped on and mangled. A great pity welled in him, an empathy that filled his chest until he couldn't speak. He merely bowed his head and allowed her pain to be his own. He knew exactly what she had gone through, was going through. He'd been down that road himself, only three years ago.

He steadied himself with a deep breath.

"Let's get you into the house."

She shook her head. "I can't walk."

He looked around, saw the flames, the exposed beams, the fire trucks, the crowd, heard the crackling and hissing. He asked the children to step aside, then slid one arm beneath her shoulders and another one beneath her knees and easily picked her up off the ground and carried her into the house, one arm dangling.

She protested quietly, but she was weeping, so words were difficult. He put her on the old davenport, pulled the green blinds, and told her to stay inside with the children. He instructed Suvilla in getting a hot bath for her mother, and how to fix a bracing cup of mint tea with milk and honey. When the doctor arrived, he left quietly, suddenly feeling out of place and useless.

The barn and all its contents were completely destroyed. The pigs in their pigsty and the twenty chickens in the henhouse survived. The horses were out to pasture and stayed there, but one of the wooden wagons parked in the haymow burned to the ground with the rest of the barn.

Dan Beiler went home to his children and told them the story of his almost runaway horse and the subsequent fire, the widow and her eight children. He could not get her image out of his mind—those sorrowful eyes that were the color of oak leaves beginning to turn.

He went to the barn raising when the whole place was swarming with women bringing copious amounts of simple food, burly men and skinny teenagers working side by side to erect a new barn for the widow and her eight children. When he was on the highest rafters he found himself trying to get a glimpse of her, but he saw only her children. Where was she? Was she still recovering from the smoke inhalation? Perhaps she was more seriously injured than he had thought. But surely the men would be speaking of it if that were the case. He wanted to ask, but he knew if he did, eyebrows would be raised immediately, and that was the last thing he wanted. A widow and a widower. Aha.

Dan thought back over his last three years of emptiness and grief. The first year had been like living in a dense black cloud. His world had become a gray landscape that contained only enough oxygen in the atmosphere to keep him alive. His only reason for living was his six children: Amos, Lavinia, Hannah, Emma, Joel, and John, starting at age twelve and continuing every other year except for Hannah and Emma, born only a year apart.

He'd carried the vulnerability of self-blame for his wife's death for too long. Pneumonia was common, but some recovered. She had not. A long winter of arnica, onion plasters, mustard plasters, comfrey tea, kerosene and brown sugar, turpentine, pills from the doctor that had given her relief for a few days, before she fell victim to her agonized coughing, her lungs full of infection and bacteria.

He had loved her with a quiet, gentle, undemanding kind of love, a husband who made life a bit cozier in hard times. The children knew nothing but a home that was a safe haven with an atmosphere of harmony and understanding, so when they were plunged into a sea of grief and dreadful emptiness, Dan had his work cut out for him, balancing the farm and his bewildered children adrift in a new world.

Almost, he'd married Bertha Zook, a sweet woman who had been too busy caring for her ill parents to ever date or marry. Urged on by his family, stating the need to acquire a mother for his children, he tried to love her the way everyone was sure he would. They had sat together in her parents' kitchen, and he found her intelligent, well spoken, certainly with a loving heart. But something was missing, and after several months he decided it was wrong to drag the relationship on any longer. He knew for certain he was never going to ask for her hand in marriage, and so he told her that any man would be blessed to have a wife such as she, but that he was not ready to remarry, and that she should not wait for him.

Nothing stirred him emotionally as far as friendship with a woman went, so he was shocked to find himself thinking so much about the widow Annie.

Annie had, in fact, spent a few days in the hospital in Lancaster until her lungs cleared up. Her mother and sisters stayed with the children until she was well, and later cooked food for the barn raising. They had no doubt she'd be all right. The Amish community would band together to help her; a poor widow touched the hearts of everyone around her.

The church paid for the barn, her father provided cows, the sun warmed the earth and the rain replenished it. Potatoes and peas went into the soil, and sprouted in long green rows like small soldiers lined to attention. Annie could hardly grasp what the folks around her had done to help. It was almost too much. She had no choice but to let go of her pride and simply let the gratitude-filled tears flow. The morning of the fire became a painful blur in her memory. She pushed it aside, knowing if she dwelled on the horror of that day she'd never accomplish all the tasks at hand. Though she did sometimes wonder about the man who had carried her to the house. Or had she just imagined that? She had been in something of a delirium for those first twenty-four hours. But the voice . . . she remembered his calm, soothing voice so clearly. She could ask her children, who had miraculously been unscathed, but no, that would not be proper.

Chapter Three

THE SUN CONTINUED TO WARM THE SOIL OF Lancaster County through May and into June. Warm breezes that formed across the eastern shore danced their way into the mainland, bringing humidity and rain, enough to produce abundant pea vines, glorious cucumbers, and bush beans clumped so heavily, one hand rummaging among the leaves easily produced a fistful.

Sammy came home to live and work through the spring and early summer, which turned out to be an enormous help to Annie. He was a carefree spirit, laughed easily and often, took his father's death as a chastening from God, and went on with his life. He had a host of friends and ran around from home to home in an old roofless courting buggy with torn upholstery and a tricky lid with misaligned hinges on the box behind the seat. To see Sammy with his friends brought Annie a vague feeling of discontent, a bittersweet nostalgia of her own years of *rumschpringa.* At these moments, any little thing could produce tears of sorrow for her beloved Eli—a blooming rose, the sinking of the sun in its fiery glory, which brought a longing to sink along with it.

Life was hard. To greet company with a semblance of happiness, to pretend she was even vaguely interested in the voices around her, to answer when a question was asked, was sometimes more than she could accomplish. So when visitors came and went, they had good reason to be concerned.

"She looks bad," they said quietly to their husbands.

"Mark my words, she'll have a nervous breakdown."

"It's been almost a year, and I don't see much change."

"I pity those children with that *unbekimmat* mother."

As folks will do, they passed judgment without the necessary cushion of compassion, so Annie was perched on a hard pedestal in the view of surrounding friends and family, her face white and drawn, her contribution to conversation nearly nonexistent.

Didn't she appreciate the new barn and all the help that had put her back on her feet? She was like a sad dark shadow of her former self, and it was indeed high time she snapped out of it.

But they didn't know about the times they were not with the family. The times when her love for her children was like the cup that was filled to the brim and running over, supplying the sole reason for going on. It was the reason she worked from dawn to dusk, milking cows, driving the two-horse hitch in the wooden farm wagon, forking hay and cleaning stables. She chopped wood, heated water in the iron kettle, poured it into huge galvanized tubs, did her laundry with homemade lye soap, pegged it on the line, and was proud of the dazzling whites. She hoed in her garden, picked vegetables, and canned them in mason jars. Every bean and cucumber and tomato was preserved. So were the peppers and apples and watermelon rind and the corn and small potatoes. Red beets were pickled in their own juice, with sugar and salt and vinegar, a dark burgundy color that added variety to the green and yellow on the shelves down cellar.

The children all worked alongside their mother, and their childish banter lifted her above the grief that so easily consumed her. Her children were her life, all that she needed. The children and her faith in God, who sat on His throne in Heaven and directed their lives as He saw fit. "The Lord giveth and the Lord taketh away, blessed be the Name of the Lord." The Bible verse meant so much to her, was often whispered just under her breath as she turned the crank on the hand wringer, fed the worn cotton dresses and the patched underwear through the rollers, then rinsed them in hot vinegar water before starting the process all over again.

Her arms were like steel, her legs strong and muscular, yet she retained her womanly figure. She had no time to think about her appearance; she merely arose every morning, pulled on her dress, and pinned a gray apron around her sturdy waist. She combed and twisted her luxuriant hair into a tight coil on the back of her head, set the white covering over it, and faced the day.

It was hot. The heat shimmered across the hayfields like some strange dream, the scorching wind rustling the leaves on the stalks of corn, turning the children's faces a deep shade of brown. *Like little acorns*, Annie thought, as she watched them shrieking and tearing across the lawn, in pursuit of some unwilling barn cat. She smiled to herself, then. A smile that lifted only the corners of her eyes, but it was a beginning of the end of the debilitating grief.

She viewed the rows of bright jars on the can shelves in the cellar, the reward of days of backbreaking labor, and felt the smile deep inside of her. The rays of happiness were like the sun that only appeared occasionally, the scudding dark clouds of her grief obscuring it. Now, though, it seemed to happen frequently, and she knew the truth of her mother's words: "Time is a healer. This, too, shall pass."

Then one day she received a white envelope with no return address and masculine handwriting amongst the other mail. Annie took it silently from Emma and thanked God it had not been Suvilla who brought the mail in. She lifted her gray apron and discreetly put it in her dress pocket, then flipped through the other mail, opening the letter from her sister in Berks County.

She sat on a kitchen chair, the afternoon humidity building like a furnace in the house, wiped her face with the familiar square of muslin, and read the pages with enjoyment. She smiled, she frowned, she cried. She breathed deeply, shifted positions, then lowered the pages to her lap and stared into space.

Sarah thought she could move to Berks County and live alongside her and her husband. Life would not be quite as hard without that mortgage on her farm. Annie tried to imagine it. She loved her sister Sarah, knew without a doubt she would be a huge help, both emotionally and spiritually. And financially, for sure.

But the children. They were so well adjusted here on the farm, in the school, in the church.

She put the letter in her desk. Eli's desk, as she always thought of it. She turned and began to pour water into a bowl for a batch of bread. She'd have to think about it, discuss it with the children.

After everyone was upstairs, she stood in the middle of her kitchen, the oil lamp creating a yellow glow, the heat lingering long after the heat of the sun had disappeared. Her heart began the quickening thud of agitation. She exhaled sharply, then drew a deep breath to steady herself, before slowly retrieving the letter from the depth of her pocket. The thing had been like a rock, begging her to open it all day. It could have been from anyone, of course, but somehow she knew, the way women sometimes do, that there was something important about this particular letter. With fingers that were slightly unsteady, she tore a corner of the envelope, inserted one finger, and ran it along the seal.

It was one sheet of lined paper.

Dear Friend,

Greetings in Jesus' Name.

I was there with you when you experienced the tragedy of losing your barn. I am hoping your health has been restored.

My name is Daniel Beiler and I am a widower with six children. My wife, Sarah, passed away three years ago. She had pneumonia.

I have prayed at length, and still feel the
same, so I am taking it as God's will for my
life. Would you consider starting a friendship?
I would like to know you better. If it is alright
with you, would September the fifteenth be
acceptable to meet?

You understand, it would be late, so the
children are asleep.

Please honor me with a reply.

In Jesus' Name,
Daniel Beiler

Annie didn't know what to do, so she cried. She
sobbed and hiccupped. All the pain of parting with
Eli crashed down on her head like crumbling plaster. And then, as if that weren't enough, she felt a
deep shame. For the fact was, she wanted a husband.
She wanted to wake up in the morning with another
warm human in the bed beside her, someone to talk
to, to share her responsibilities, and yes, to touch,
and to love, and to cherish the way she had cherished
Eli. Surely it was too soon to want another man.

Another man . . . those words in her mind brought a fresh wave of tears.

Of course, there were the children to consider. What about Suvilla? Sammy? They were old enough to have a voice in this very serious matter. What would they think of their mother starting a friendship with someone new? Should she ask them, or was that improper? This was a whole new world to navigate. She wished there was someone trusted that she could seek out for guidance, but of course there wasn't. For a moment she wished she had the kind of mother she could turn to for advice, but that was simply not the kind of relationship they shared. Where Annie was sentimental, her mother was practical. Where Annie welled with emotion, empathy, deep feeling, her mother kept stone-faced, never shed a tear that Annie could remember. Annie often felt ashamed that she couldn't keep her own emotions better in check. She knew her mother disapproved of crying—but then, she disapproved of most things. Likely that came from Annie's grandmother— but she was the last person Annie wanted to think about now. She actually shivered, the image of her grandmother bringing with it a cold wave of anger, disgust, and then, just as quickly, guilt. She should respect her elders, she knew.

Her thoughts came back to the letter and she wept on. She cried until she felt ill, then laid her head on her folded arms atop the kitchen table and allowed all the anxiety and indecision to overwhelm her. She tried praying, but it felt like the silent pleas for wisdom and direction didn't make it past the ceiling. She felt alone, intimidated, undone.

Slowly her tears subsided, her breathing returned to normal. She lifted her head, wiped her eyes, blew her nose in the sodden handkerchief, then got up and threw it across the kitchen in disgust.

Six children. *Six!* She had enough to do with eight of her own. This whole thing was just ridiculous. Why was she obsessing over it? It was too soon since Eli's death, fourteen kids would surely put her over the edge of sanity, and she knew nothing about this Dan Beiler. He was probably just lonely and overwhelmed with all those children and wanted a *maud* that he didn't have to pay. She should just reply with a polite no and be done with it.

She remembered then, in spite of herself, the feeling of his strong arms carrying her into the house, the gentle voice he used in instructing the children in her care. So she hadn't imagined him. And apparently he'd been thinking of her ever since then.

She slept only a few hours that night and dreamt restless dreams that made no sense, leaving her with a vague sense of foreboding and a serious headache all morning.

The next day her mother came to help her pick green beans and cucumbers, wearing her stiff black bonnet and no shoes, her bare feet walking across stones, rough cement, and prickly grass as if she was wearing invisible shoes. Austere, a formidable figure complete with a high forehead and hawk-like features, the large green eyes missing nothing, she put Annie on the defensive immediately. Her greeting was short, clipped, and to the point, wasting no time on niceties, certainly no sympathy.

"No help unhitching?" she called from the washhouse door.

"Oh, Mam. Sorry. I didn't hear you pull in."

"How could you miss it?"

"I must have been in the back bedroom."

"No matter."

But Annie was left with the distinct feeling that it did matter very much. She sighed.

"The yard needs mowing." Coming from her mother, it was a rebuke more than an observation.

They walked together toward the house, her mother surveying everything she passed with a critical eye. Annie wished she'd had time to sweep the entryway, which she now saw had clumps of dirt, a stray feather one of the children must have found and then dropped on the floor. There were a few plates and a coffee mug in the kitchen sink.

"Sammy had to help out at Jonas Beiler's," she explained. "So that left the girls, and they were busy with the cleaning. We had four bushel of tomatoes to tend to."

"On Saturday?"

"Yes."

"You should have done them on Friday."

Annie had no energy to delve into a detailed account of Friday's work, so she said nothing.

"What's this?" Her mother's voice was curious and accusing at once.

Annie's heart took a nosedive. The letter. How could she have been careless enough to leave it out? Had any of the children seen it? Thank goodness they were now all outside and wouldn't hear whatever her mother was to say next.

Her mother's thin hand raked it from the desktop, her eyes following the obviously masculine curve of the handwriting. She read it quickly and then held it out in front of her, disgusted, as if it contained a forbidden fruit.

Annie swallowed. She clasped and unclasped her hands behind her back, watched in disbelief as her mother waved it angrily.

"You will not, Annie."

Annie nodded, felt as if she'd been caught in some unforgivable sin.

"Your husband is gone only seven months. Who is this man?"

"It's ten months, Mam."

"And you are receiving offers? Have you no shame?"

"Mam, it's only a letter. It is not an offer of marriage. I can refuse. It came only yesterday and I haven't had a chance to respond yet."

Her mother's eyes narrowed. She turned and placed the letter back on the desktop before turning slowly, her eyes going to her daughter's bewildered ones.

"You think I'm being too hard on you, but you need to think of the children. You have a big responsibility, so don't fall for some overeager suitor who has no feelings for the children. You need to wait. And *six children?*" She made a snorting noise, as if having so many kids was some kind of sin, evidence of bad character.

In reality, a large family wasn't so unusual in the Amish community. Children were a blessing from God. Annie didn't remind her that she had eight of her own children, a fact that her mother had considered an excellent thing prior to Eli's passing.

Instead, Annie just nodded again. "Yes, Mam."

They worked side by side the remainder of the day, cleaning out the last of the bush beans, plucking the prickly cucumber vines. Seeing all the remaining tomatoes, they decided to cook the vegetables separately and make vegetable soup.

Carrots, onion, parsley, celery, potatoes, corn, and green peppers were all cleaned, sliced, chopped, and added to the copper kettle of boiling tomatoes and parsnips. Navy beans and a large beef bone from the butcher shop, salt, pepper, and some dried chives were dropped into the mix, resulting in the most pleasurable aroma from the kettle house door.

The incident with the letter was pushed to the back of Annie's mind as she focused on the work at hand, and with the girls all helping to wash jars, chop vegetables, and of course, to take turns mowing the grass, the day turned out to be so much better than she had expected. Suvilla was a willing, able-bodied worker, which impressed her grandmother deeply, while Ida chattered happily with her innocent lisp, bringing an occasional smile to the narrow face.

Row after row of glass jars containing the bright vegetable soup filled the counter that afternoon. They ate big bowls of it for lunch, with slices of dark wheat bread spread with the pungent yellow butter that had formed by the steady sloshing of the wooden paddles in the glass butter churn. There were no strawberry or raspberry preserves, and there wouldn't be any deep brown apple butter in the fall. Sugar was a luxury, used mostly for preserving, so the only sweetener was the dark molasses or the amber maple syrup, both of which would have to last till spring. But there was the heavy ginger cake, and fresh peaches from the orchard, with plenty of rich, creamy milk, cups of mint tea with a dollop of maple syrup, and more milk.

Her mother sat back, her stern features mellowed from the full stomach, an occasional smile flickering as Ida kept up her lively flow of words.

"Do you have firewood for winter, Annie?" she asked, as she carried plates to the sink to be washed.

"Not yet. I mean, there is some, of course, to cook with, but the winter's supply hasn't been tackled yet," Annie replied, pouring boiling water from the teakettle into the dishpan.

"*Ach*, Annie. Perhaps I'm too harsh. It must not be easy, this going on by yourself. We don't realize how very much we depend on our men for so many things."

Oh mother, you have no idea, Annie groaned inwardly, but she just gave a soft smile.

"But be very careful of marrying that second time."

"I will."

Warmed by her mother's kind words, she told her about her sister's offer to have the family come live near them.

"After everything the church has done to get you back on your feet here?" Her mother asked, incredulous. "Really, Annie. I'm surprised you'd even consider it."

Annie quickly assured her she wasn't really considering it, that she was just telling her how thoughtful Sarah was to suggest it. Inwardly, she wondered why she hadn't seen it that way before. Yes, she'd been quite ungrateful and would repent. She'd write to her sister tomorrow to thank her and decline her offer.

As she watched her mother drive the horse and buggy down the lane that led to the main road, she turned and shook her head sadly. No, there was no way her mother could know this road of solitude, with its unpredictable twists and turns, the desperation when a cow became sick, the anxiety over the unpaid bills, the lurching of her stomach when winter's chill crept through every available crevice around windows

and doors, but the damper was turned low to keep the
firewood supply from dwindling too fast. The times
when they wore coats to sit in the living room, drew
their feet up under blankets, the temperature in the
house far below what was considered comfortable.

To pay down on the feed bill meant cooked and
fried mush for breakfast, tea and saltine crackers
soaked in milk when the coffee ran low. It meant
dried navy beans boiling on the back of the stove until
the smell of them was no longer appetizing, because
the beans would fill their stomachs so they could fall
asleep. Annie knew what it meant to be hungry and
cold, but figured times were hard for everyone, so
there was no sense in mewling complaints like a weak
kitten. But her mother's words rankled.

Who would fell the trees and chop the wood?
Who would shovel the snow and manhandle the
milk cans, feed the horses and chickens and pay the
bills, clothe the children and put shoes on their feet
before they turned red and calloused by the cold? She
would, she supposed. With Suvilla and Enos.

And so she put the letter out of sight, out of mind.
For a few days she mulled over how to reject his

request kindly, but then the busyness of her days and exhaustion of the evenings took over and she realized a week had passed, and then a month, and by then it seemed less rude just to let it go unanswered. Likely he'd started pursuing someone else by then, anyway, she figured.

Daniel Beiler waited and waited, eagerly checking the mailbox, only to be disappointed time after time. When the heat of summer was blown away by the winds of early autumn, the frost covered the low places like a veil of diamonds, and the pumpkins turned huge and orange on the vine, he sat down at his desk and wrote her another.

She read the letter, sighed, stared off into the distance before looking at the calendar. Six days before a year had passed.

Ach, Mam. Would it be so awful if he simply paid me a visit?

It had been a tough day—the three youngest spent the bulk of the morning arguing over a corn husk doll, Suvilla was beginning to develop a disrespectful attitude that Annie didn't understand and didn't have time to address, two of the cows seemed to be sick, and there was still the matter of chopping enough firewood for the quickly approaching winter. Without the time or energy to obsess over what to do with the letter, she made a quick decision. She wrote a letter in her fine hand, with blue ink on a scrap of paper from her black composition book. Yes, he could pay her a visit on the fifteenth of November. She felt bold, strong. She was a grown woman and could make her own decisions. Look at everything else she was handling on her own!

But she spent the night without sleep, stumbled into the cow stable long after Suvilla and Ephraim had started milking, and began to cry into her bucket of milk before stumbling back into the house, saying she had a stomachache. She sat in a kitchen chair staring at the opposite wall until Suvilla came in, glancing at her mother with something far too close to disgust, and then set to work preparing breakfast, waking Annie from her exhausted reverie.

Chapter Four

WHEN HE SHOWED UP AT HER DOOR ON THAT November evening, there was a raw wind driving icy rain against the north side of the house. It dripped off the edge of the roof, sloshed into low places in the yard, banged loose shutters, and created a sea of slick, half-frozen mud.

The knock was slight—so soft, in fact, that she couldn't be sure she had heard it at all—but when she opened the door, he was there, dressed in the heavy black-capped overcoat, the wide-brimmed woolen hat dripping water. She stepped back, told him to come in. He towered above her, all wet wool and formidable height and width. He shook her hand and held it a fraction too long. She lifted her huge green eyes to his kind ones and he was seized by a sense of belonging, a sense of rightness that could only be described as coming home. He felt himself letting go of the immense loneliness that had been his constant companion for too many years.

She had baked molasses cookies and brewed a pot of spearmint tea. She showed him into the kitchen, wishing she'd had time to scrub the floor. They spoke in soft voices so as not to wake the children sleeping upstairs. He was gentle, relaxed, kind—a combination that was in surprising contrast to his physical height and strength. It was hugely attractive. She didn't try to resist the pull of his gentle voice, but instead allowed it to sustain her, carry her along as the evening unfolded.

He had six children, the oldest being twelve years old. Four were in various grades in the elementary school they attended in Leacock Township, and the two youngest, Joel and John, were at home with him and the *maud*.

"Who is your *maud*?" Annie asked.

He sighed, waved a hand in resignation. "Whoever I can get for the week or the month. It's really hard to find a dedicated girl, although a few of them have stayed longer than that. John was only six months old when Sarah died, so he doesn't remember his mother. Joel says he remembers her, but I doubt it."

"It must be hard."

"Probably not harder for me than it is for you."

"That's very kind, but my children have me in the house providing their needs, whereas for you . . ."

Her voice fell away, suddenly quite shy. She hadn't meant to insinuate, to suggest.

His soft laugh put her immediately at ease.

"Look, we may as well be honest. I need a wife, and have not found anyone suitable in three and a half years. Then I followed my horse to your burning barn, and you were overcome by smoke, remember?"

"Yes," she whispered.

"I have not forgotten that day. The barn raising was a huge disappointment . . . I had so hoped to see you. But I couldn't exactly walk to the house and boldly ask the women, so I let it go. Except I couldn't really let it go . . ."

Annie didn't know what to say, so she sat in silence, suddenly feeling awkward.

"Your new barn looks good," he said, bringing the conversation back to a safe topic.

Annie shook her head wryly. The lamplight cast a soft gleam on her thick brown hair, created contours beneath her lovely green eyes.

His heart thudded, thinking how tired she appeared, the drooping of her heavy lids over the gorgeous green eyes. He wanted to smooth the hair away from her forehead, erase the dark circles below her eyes with his kisses.

It had been so long.

"Yes, the church has been more than sufficient. I will never be able to repay, if I live to be a hundred years old. The alms I have given this year would barely pay for one door. No, the hinges on that door."

He nodded, his eyes never leaving her face. "Times are hard," he murmured.

"Do you think things will get worse?" she asked.

"I think the worst is over."

"Really?"

He forced himself to continue the small talk. "It will be slow, the return of people's trust in government and the large banks. We will remain fearful for a good many years. But with our land and the ability to raise crops, we should be all right. The cities are much worse off than we are."

She nodded, suddenly grateful for every jar down cellar, every potato and onion, the covered cabbages and the celery that remained in the garden, banked with good soil and horse manure.

She took a deep breath, then smiled a small, hesitant smile. "Thank you for reminding me I have so much."

He nodded, then let the silence linger for a few moments.

"What was your first husband like?" he asked abruptly.

"Eli? Oh, he was a good husband and father. Good to the children, a good provider. I had nothing to complain about. We had a good marriage, one I have never regretted."

"So you had a bad time dealing with his death?"

"Yes, I did."

"So if you were to marry again, would that second husband always be compared to the perfection in Eli?"

Annie shook her head. "No, no." Should she tell him about his stormy moods, his angry outbursts? She considered it, but then he was speaking again.

"For me it was quite different. Sarah was . . . well, let's just say she was not always stable. She fell when she was a baby, they say. Her relatives said she had a fractured skull but they never took her to a doctor, so she bled in her brain. I think she was afflicted with a mental condition, but since I am not a doctor, I couldn't say for sure. She was extremely happy and noisy one day, and sunk into a deep sadness the next. Having her babies was always a difficult time, but she loved the little ones, so they kept coming. I washed a lot of dishes and clothes, changed diapers and packed lunches for the school children. Sometimes it was tough, but I had to keep going for her sake. Her mother helped out, and her sisters, but most of it fell on me. But you know how we promise to care for each other, in sickness and in health, so I tried to do my best."

His voice trailed off, infinitely weary.

They spoke more freely after that confession. She told him of the times when Eli was demanding, putting his needs ahead of her own, although she felt bad, even now, mentioning something so trivial.

He saw the good in her, the willingness to submit to a loving husband, while she saw the amazing supporter he had been to a wife that might have been afflicted with a disease of the mind.

"Bad nerves," they called it. Many were institutionalized, incarcerated under unthinkable conditions, so he had done all he could to prevent that.

"Her pneumonia? She ran away in an icy storm, hid in a neighbor's shed till the following day, and almost froze to death after a long and tortuous emotional battle she fought after John was born. I blamed myself for years, but finally found peace in the forgiveness of our Savior."

His voice broke.

"The children never knew. They carried on when their mother had the blues, sang with her on the good days. There was harmony in our house as far as anyone could tell. They thought it normal to see Dat doing the washing or the dishes. For that I am grateful."

Annie felt a great empathy, then. She was in awe of this kind and gentle man who had lived with so much pain and disappointment without complaint.

"Why did she run away?"

"She said I didn't love her, which was what she often said when she fell into depression. I did love her, Annie. The best I could."

"I believe you."

"You do?"

"Yes, I do."

Their eyes met and held. Love was exchanged that night with unspoken communication and mutual admiration.

Rain continued its cold lashing against the north side of the house, replenishing the water table below the rich soil, filling the streams and ponds. Dark clouds railed against an inky night sky, hiding the face of the moon and the stars, but inside the widow's house, a soft warm glow of love and understanding began to flourish.

Lonely hearts were fertile ground for the sowing of love, and the night had already turned toward morning when he silently crept out of the house and drove his horse slowly and without the benefit of lantern light until he was safely out of sight.

"Someone was here last night," Suvilla announced at the breakfast table.

Annie had her back turned, making tea at the stove, so she stayed there until she felt the color leave her face. Then she turned slowly but didn't meet their questioning eyes.

"Well?" Suvilla queried again.

Enos shrugged his shoulders. Ephraim said she was dreaming. Ida cut her corn mush and ignored them all.

"It sounded like a man's voice, Mam. You were talking, too."

Suvilla was old enough to know, and to speak her mind, so Annie slowly lifted a finger to her lips, drew down her eyebrows to mimic the "sh." Suvilla's eyes widened, but she closed her mouth and said nothing more.

When they were alone, Annie told her, haltingly.

"What? Who is he? Does he have children?"

Suvilla drew back, staring open mouthed at her mother in disbelief. Annie stumbled over her words, but answered her questions honestly, trying not to show embarrassment. She explained that he was the one who helped her on the day of the fire, that he had six children, that he had requested that they start a friendship.

"*Six* children?"

Annie nodded. Suvilla shot her a look of disbelief, but swallowed any other comments. Children were expected to obey their parents in the Lord. Annie ended the conversation and went about the chores, knowing that if she were apologetic or dragged the discussion on it would only give Suvilla opportunity to voice rebellion. No, it was better to maintain her role as parent—to be loving but firm, not to burden Suvilla with decision-making responsibility beyond her years. It was better for children to have clear boundaries, to follow the Ten Commandments, which included respecting their parents. It gave them a sense of security, even in their teenage years.

After Suvilla found out, she lay awake listening every time Daniel Beiler visited. She resisted the urge to wake Ida, who lay beside her, the cold beginning to creep across the floor and through the uninsulated walls. She couldn't make out most of the words, but she heard the drone of Daniel's voice, the soft answer in her mother's, and imagined how her mother must feel. She was old enough to know the shy glances of young men, to dream of "going steady" someday.

But it was odd to know her own mother was possibly falling in love.

It was toward the end of November when he asked her to marry him. Still, only the oldest children were told, and none of their friends or extended family. The marriage would have to wait till March, as they had to sort through logistics such as the sale of the farm.

Annie walked with a new spring in her step, a new light in her eyes. Daniel was everything to her now. His proposal had been so kind, so gentle, so full of promise. He was concerned about her welfare, the immense responsibility of the combination of their families. "Fourteen kids," he said wryly, and she giggled softly. He took her small capable hand in his and asked her if she was really ready for that kind of challenge.

"With your help, yes. I am."

He would never forget the immensity of those words.

Annie butchered the fattest chicken for Christmas dinner. She made traditional *roasht* with it, roasting the chicken until the meat could easily be pulled off the bones, then mixing it with bread cubes, celery, onion, eggs, salt and pepper. The skin of the chicken was put through the meat grinder, for added richness of flavor. The liver, heart, and gizzard were all ground as well, minced into the other ingredients until it all came together in a savory stuffing dotted with pieces of dark and white chicken, returned to the oven to bake until it was golden brown. There were plenty of potatoes that had been dug in the good, dark earth and then carried carefully into the cellar to be stored in the bin. So Annie peeled and cut a plentiful amount and put them on the back of the cook stove to boil while she used the chicken broth to make gravy. The cabbage had been shredded, mixed with what sugar could be spared, salt, and vinegar, and set in a cool place. There were sliced turnips, lima beans cooked with salt and butter, tiny sweet pickles and dark red beets pickled in a brine with their own juice.

She made two pumpkin pies using molasses and maple syrup for sweetener, and put a sprig of holly on top of each. It wasn't the Amish way to adorn their homes with Christmas trees or wreaths, but the children decided that Christmas that they would take their mam's pies over any fancy English decorations. Each child got one wedge of the smooth, creamy pie, and they savored every bite.

The woodstove crackled and burned, giving the warmth that spread cheer throughout the house. They heaped their plates with the fragrant *roasht* and the mounds of buttery potatoes and thick, rich gravy. Dan had tried to give her money to buy the children gifts, but she had declined, said it wouldn't be proper—especially before they were married. They had never done gifts for Christmas anyway—it wasn't a tradition she had grown up with, her mother having thought gifts distracted from the true meaning of Christmas, the celebration of the Christ child. So there were no gifts on that cozy evening, but the children felt as if it was the best Christmas ever.

Chapter Five

ALL ACROSS LANCASTER COUNTY THE SNOW blew in from the northeast, tiny particles that made a swishing sound as it was driven across metal roofs, hard-packed frozen earth, and ponds. The wind moaned in the pine trees, whistled around the eaves of the house, and threw particles of frozen snow against window panes like sand. The atmosphere was heavy, gray, with a yellowish cast that seemed ominous.

Annie lifted her face to the sky as she made her way to the barn, the driven snow like pellets against it. This was a real January blizzard, and she was prepared, reveled in it. She loved the snow, the purity of winter scenery, when weeds and mud and unsightly puddles were all hidden under the beauty of white, white snow, with blue shadows in hollows and beneath trees that made the whole world seem magical somehow.

And now she was so happy. Her future had changed from the gray of care and responsibility to a wonderful life with a man she loved beyond reason. He was everything she had ever imagined any man could be—kind, caring, soft-spoken, and so pleasant to look at. She loved his eyes, the straight, fine nose, the mouth that curved into a beautiful smile when he arrived in the evenings.

She lifted her arms and gave herself up to the joy that coursed through her veins, skipped a few steps, then reined herself in to a sedate walk. Oh, but it felt wonderful to experience joy again. To feel loved and desired.

Two more months till her wedding day.

It was sobering, thinking of these six children she had never met, but she would love them to the best of her ability. As he would love her own.

The breakfast table held the hum of anticipation as the children looked forward to the snow and all the sledding and sleigh rides. The boiled cornmeal was served with molasses and milk, the bread toasted in the huge cast iron pan on top of the stove. The coffee was steaming hot and so good laced with plenty of cream.

There was firewood in the woodshed, staples in the pantry, enough to keep the hunger away. Annie felt blessed beyond measure, filled with an appreciation for God's kindness, the love he bestowed on them, the richness of life.

On Saturday evening Daniel handed her twenty dollars and told her to buy fabric or shoes, whatever they needed for the wedding.

Annie told him she couldn't take it. "No, no. It's too much. I have a good Sunday dress. It's blue."

She didn't tell him it was eight or nine years old, had been sponged and pressed numerous times, worn thin at the underarms.

"No, Annie. Take it. I want you to have a wedding dress."

She blushed, a gentle rose color that spread like a rose across her cheeks. This time she accepted, not wanting to disappoint him.

They made the decision to move to his farm, as the house was larger and would better accommodate fourteen children. They would add her eight cows to his herd. They would butcher the pigs, add her chickens to the flock.

Annie had never seen the farm, had only a vague idea of where it was located. She would be moving out of her home and the church district she had always known, but that was all right. She would be Mrs. Dan Beiler, mother of fourteen children, able to hold up her head as a woman and mother in the community.

Annie smiled at Daniel, and he smiled back.

They did not touch, only communicated what they felt with their eyes.

They had both been married before. The kisses would wait.

She was taken to his farm to meet the children only a week before the wedding, after the public announcement had been made in church. Now that their secret had been revealed, they would be able to travel together in broad daylight, to be seen in stores or to visit family. Her parents had been told, and though her mother had raised her eyebrows with a mixture of surprise and disapproval, she had kept her tongue quiet as she cleaned the house and made sure she had cabbage and potatoes down cellar for the wedding meal. Annie would butcher her old hens to make the *roasht*.

Daniel's children were shy, peering at her with curious eyes. Amos was a small version of his father with straight dark hair, the wide mouth. Annie took his politely proffered hand, said, "Hello, Amos." Lavina, Hannah, and Emma were like three peas in a pod, all born only a year apart. Dark-haired, dark eyes, curious, their faces were open and honest. Annie gripped their hands and felt a surge of tender love for the motherless trio.

"Hello, hello," she said, smiling warmly.

The three girls responded to Annie's warmth with hungry eyes, wide and lonely and searching. For too long their lives had contained no mother, no solid, unchanging figure they could depend on, no one to cuddle and cherish them, to listen to their little girl woes and joys. There were maids who came and went, washed clothes and dishes and floors, ironed and cooked and baked. Most of them were pleasant, but distant. It was their job to meet the children's tangible needs, but not to love them with the tenderness of a mother.

So when the genuine interest shone from Annie's eyes, they absorbed the warmth of her love and felt rescued. They stood side by side, their eyes never leaving her face. Annie felt reassured that their families would meld easily, that they'd become one just as she and Dan were becoming one.

Joel and John were old enough to know there was tremendous importance in this woman. This was not another *maud*; she was to be their mother. They weren't too sure about someone actually marrying their father and living there, but they remained seated on kitchen chairs, shook hands when it was expected of them, and observed.

"So now you have met your future Mam," Dan said eagerly.

Amos nodded. The three girls responded with hearty smiles and a vibrant yes. Joel and John merely stared, wide-eyed.

"You know she has eight children of her own. You will meet them before the wedding. We will all live together here, so we'll have to make arrangements where everyone will sleep."

Amos shifted from one foot to the other, flicked the straight dark bangs on his forehead.

"Is there someone my age?" he asked timidly.

"Enos is thirteen," Annie said.

Amos smiled. "I'll be his friend."

Annie smiled back, but winced, thinking of Ephraim and Ida's inseparable bond. Would they open up to include Amos? Well, she'd tell them that's what was expected of them, and they would obey. They were good children.

She sewed a new blue wedding dress. Her old black cape and apron would do. The children were equipped with new dresses or trousers as needed, but they did not all have something new to wear.

The farm was sold to Henry Blank for his son Josiah, who would be bringing his new bride in the fall. Annie spent a few hours in tearful nostalgia, then she straightened herself up, realizing a door in her life had been closed and a new one was opening. God had mercy on her existence and was ushering in the beginning of a new life, and she was thankful. She would take this in stride, be a mother to his six children, and never look back.

Her mother was a hard worker, a strict overseer of all the wedding preparations, which was a relief to

Annie. She spent a few days helping with the house-cleaning, but had a huge amount of work herself, preparing for the move to Dan's farm.

The wedding would be held in her parents' large farmhouse, which meant every piece of furniture would be moved into the adjacent woodshed to make room for the setting of wooden benches. And woe to the *hausfrau* who was caught with rolls of dust or spiderwebs beneath bureaus or cabinets, resulting in unmerciful teasing from the men in the family. No, Annie's meticulous mother would never be caught with a job half done. The furniture was cleaned and polished, upended and swept underneath, and the living room rugs were hung over the clothesline and beaten until no dust puffed off of them. The kettles were scoured and polished, for no worthy woman would be caught at wedding time with less than a mirror-like gleam on all the cookware.

The celery was banked with manure-rich soil, the cabbage round and full, but that had been in the fall of the year. By March, what had been harvested in the fall had been consumed out of necessity, celery and cabbage being quick to rot. So her mother made a trip to the greengrocer in Intercourse and handed Dan Beiler the bill with pursed lips and narrowed eyes. Vegetables in March were dear, she told him, standing by while he wrote her a check in his careful hand.

Annie's children, all eight of them, were properly introduced to Dan and his six sons and daughters, a quiet, awkward meeting that all of them were relieved to be done with. It was just so strange, looking at a group of children who would be living in the same house for the rest of their youth.

None of Annie's kids were too sure about Dan. He was large and different, his voice too soft and pillowy for a father. Their real father, the one that died, had been smaller and quicker, his voice loud. If he said something, anything at all, they knew he meant business.

So when this new father was soft-spoken and kind, smiled a lot, and addressed each one individually with gentle words, they weren't quite sure what to make of it.

They were married on a cold, windy day in March, when the sun shone weakly behind scudding clouds and wind bent the trees into perfect C's, whipped bare branches in a frenzy, sent men and women scurrying between house and barn, shawls flapping, men's hands plopped on hat tops.

But inside there was light from gas lights, warmth from the woodstoves, voices, laughter, and an aura of celebration. The house was filled to capacity with voices rising in plainsong, the slow rise and fall of old German hymns from the heavy black *Ausbund*. They were pronounced man and wife by his uncle, Stephen Beiler, from over toward Leola, a bishop who was well known for his fiery sermons.

The fourteen children sat on benches with varying degrees of attentiveness, but all had the same bewildered expression, a vacant wondering of the future created by the joining of the two people who sat side by side in the minster's row, looking as if this was the most serious moment of their lives.

But later they all enjoyed the festivities, the plates of good, hot chicken filling, mashed potatoes, and gravy. There was plenty of cake, pie, doughnuts, and cookies, with cornstarch pudding and grape mush. The children sat in a respectful row, ate with gusto,

and tried not to think too much about how different
their lives were about to be.

And so life began for Dan and Annie Beiler in
1932, on the farm he inherited from his parents on
Hollander Road. He had inherited money from them
as well, and had managed it well so that it had grown,
despite the Depression. The house was substantial.
Built of gray limestone, the mortar was as thick as
seaworthy rope and the walls were so thick the win-
dowsills easily held a variety of potted plants. There
were six bedrooms upstairs, with a staircase along the
front of the house and one in the back. The wealthy
landowners who designed and built the house at the
turn of the century, in 1798, had built the narrow
curved staircase in the back for the servants' use.

The kitchen ran along the side of the house that
faced the large stone barn, with cabinets built by
a German Baptist named Wesley Overland, well
known for his distinctive style. There were polished
hardwood floors and rugs scattered throughout the
house tastefully. The furniture was far better than
anything Annie had ever owned, so she appreciated

the cherry sleigh beds and the heavy ornate dressers and bureaus. There were plenty of bed linens, patchwork quilts and heavy comforters made with sheep's wool. They stretched the long kitchen table to add even more leaves to accommodate the eight children and their mother. There was an indoor bathroom with a porcelain commode, but no bathtubs—at that time they were frowned on in Amish homes and pronounced an unnecessary worldly luxury.

Annie could hardly believe this magnificent dwelling was now hers. She had never imagined an indoor facility to use the restroom, and certainly not in an Amish home. She realized Dan was a bit of a progressive, living in such comfort, plus the way he was outspoken about other modern inventions.

She cleaned and scoured, made up freshly washed beds with sheets and pillowcases just off the line. Dan told her to paint rooms wherever she felt a need, but she was appalled at the thought of spending money only to change the appearance of a room if it was perfectly serviceable without. She washed the walls, though, with a bucket of soapy water and a heavy cloth, wiping and scrubbing till her shoulders ached with fatigue.

When she was finished, she took stock of her situation and thought it quite manageable, really. Suvilla slept with Ida in a big double bed in the front room toward the barn. Lavina, Emma, and Hannah slept in the other front room, across the hallway.

Annie allowed Dan's girls to stay in one room, and her own girls to stay in another. They had enough to merely become acquainted without having to share a bed. She put Amos with Joel and John, who all fit together in one bed nicely enough. She thought twelve-year-old Amos might appreciate being responsible for his smaller brothers.

Sammy was reserved a small room in the back, the former servant's quarters, with only a single bed and dresser. He was more than pleased with this arrangement, having easy access to his own staircase to sneak in and out of the house whenever a bit of mischief beckoned.

Enos and Ephraim were tremendously happy to be allowed a room of their own without having to host Amos. Amos the Intruder, as they called him when they were alone. They knew it was wrong to think of him in those terms, but that's what he was. He was always trying to get in on their private jokes or games, and it was a hassle to have to stop and try to explain everything.

The oblong room was left for the other Emma, Lydia, and Rebecca, the three little girls who were delighted to sleep in a sizable room together. There were two beds with a small stand in between, a place to put handkerchiefs and water glasses.

So that left one small room in the back for guests. Every respectable Amish home needed a comfortable guest room for overnight visitors, folks who traveled twenty or thirty miles with a horse-drawn carriage and needed a place to stay before they could make the return trip. To cook a delicious meal, to stable and feed the weary horse, was an honor. Most Amish families looked forward to receiving visitors. The parents would share stories and news over the dinner table as the children eyed one another with shy glances and listened with intrigue. Plus, company was a good excuse to bring out the sack of white sugar and bake a golden pound cake with brown sugar frosting.

Of course they would be getting visitors after their marriage, so Annie whipped everything into order in a few weeks' time, just in time to drop seeds into the well-worked soil. The garden had been plowed to double its size, with nine more hungry mouths to feed. The flower beds were dug with fresh cow manure, the lawnmower sharpened and oiled, before the lawn was neatly mowed and trimmed.

The bedroom downstairs contained the furniture Annie had brought, with one of her quilts made up neatly on the high, iron bed frame. There was a rather large sampler on the wall, done in cross stitched embroidery, with the words "East or West, Home is Best" done in heavy black lettering with a design of roses in a myriad of brilliant colors. The frame was made of natural wood by Eli's own hand, so Annie cherished this bit of frivolity more than anything she had brought.

Dan was gentle, caring, all she could ever want or need. To lie in his arms with the shrill cheeping of the spring peepers down at the pond, the breeze from the soft spring night like a balm from paradise, knowing she was loved, cherished, and so very appreciated was the closest thing to Heaven. But in the morning, there were challenges in the form of six children who were expected to accept the eight of her own into their home and lives. They sat in out-of-the-way corners and glowered when she became happy or silly with one of her own. She tried her best to draw Amos into a lively morning discussion, but he retaliated by his sullen look before letting himself quickly out the door. If Enos or Ephraim—at Annie's prompting—tried to win him over, he thwarted all attempts at companionship with handfuls of thrown dirt and hurled swear words.

As problems arose, they dealt with them, although Annie had days when she wondered why she had ever thought another marriage was God's will for her life. Especially days when the two Emmas locked horns, fighting and arguing and then pouting, disobeying her orders simply because they felt so miserable inside. "Emma One" and "Emma Two," they called them. Neither one thought it was amusing. Each Emma wanted her own identity, and certainly did not want to share with the other.

Chapter Six

THEY HAD EGGS FOR BREAKFAST NOW. GOOD
brown eggs with dark orange yolks and glossy whites
fried perfectly in hot lard and salted and peppered
to perfection. They should have been sold and the
money gone toward other household expenses, Annie
reasoned.

"Now why would we do that?" Dan asked, patting
her shoulder affectionately.

"Eggs are a good profit," she answered.

"You can't eat profit," he laughed. "I love a good
fried egg in the spring, and why should I eat eggs and
the children go without? I say we should eat them as
long as the hens are laying."

Enos and Ephraim nodded, their eyes never leaving their stepfather's face. All of Annie's children
lived with Dan, looked to him as a hero of deliver-
ance. There were eggs for breakfast, more meat, even
if it was merely slivers of beef in white milk gravy.
There were pies, and occasionally cookies made with

molasses, white flour, and sugar. Instead of bread with lard they had soft white bread and butter, sometimes with pear or apple butter.

But Dan's children looked on the eight Miller children as usurpers, upending their own stable relationship with their remaining parent, and used every available opportunity to remind them of this.

Walking home from school was the worst time, when they were safely out of earshot of both parents. "Emma, get off the road. There's a car coming," Amos shouted.

Emma One, his biological sister, called back, "Which Emma?" Although both Emmas stepped closer to the ditch, out of the way of the oncoming vehicle.

"You! There is no other Emma who is my sister."

Wide-eyed, seven-year-old Emma's feelings were extremely hurt. Tears formed as she hastily stuck her thumb in her mouth.

"She is too your sister," Ephraim shouted.

"No, she's not."

"Is too."

"Huh-uh."

Lunch boxes were thrown in the ditch, fists balled, and heads lowered as they met head on by the side of the road, hitting and pounding.

"Get offa me!" Amos yelled.

"Say she's your sister and I will," Ephraim grunted, pounding away while he straddled his back.

With both hands over his ears, Amos kept shouting. "She's not my real sister!"

Enos entered into the fray, always the peacemaker, trying to pull Ephraim off by his suspenders. Ida, always the tomboy, egged Ephraim on, saying, "Get him! Make him say 'Uncle!'"

Bloodied and mud-stained, the two boys crept up the back stairway, changed clothes, and wiped their faces as best they could, but neither one could hide the black eye or the raw scratches and bruises.

They sat on the bench to change socks, as guilty as thieves. Annie turned, already aware of unusual goings on, the way those two had crept up the back stairs. She laid down the towel she was folding and walked over to where they were seated.

Why was it so much easier to reprimand Ephraim than Amos? She so desperately wanted to feel the same about both boys, and yet there was a difference. She felt afraid, intimidated by Amos.

Ephraim had been hers since the day he was born. She had fed and diapered him, watched him take his first step, and he was a part of her life, a part of her being. Amos was acquired at the age of thirteen, and had not been hers at all one moment before then. She had to remind herself repeatedly that he was indeed hers, that he became hers the day she married Dan.

"What happened?" she began.

"Ephraim beat me up," Amos offered, sullenly, without remorse.

"What do you have to say for yourself?" she asked quietly.

"Mam, he said our Emma was not his sister, and she is, too."

"So that gave you enough reason to beat him?" Annie asked.

"He made her cry."

Why was it so hard to tear her eyes away from Ephraim's face and into Amos's? She felt so badly for both boys, but knew she needed to be courageous, to face this situation squarely.

Taking a deep breath, she plunged in.

"Alright, both of you."

She met the glowering eyes of her stepson.

"The day we were married, we became a family, alright? In God's eyes, we have fourteen children, so it's up to you to accept this. Emma is your sister, Amos. Yes, she is. She was not born your sister, but through marriage, she is. So we will hear no more of this about who is whose sister or brother."

Both boys were shame-faced now, felt their mistake by the spare words of a strong mother. And yet they felt her caring heart, too, even if they wouldn't have admitted it in that moment.

"We are all family. We aren't perfect, but no family is. Amos, you had no right to say Emma was not your sister. We won't say things like that again, OK?"

He nodded, his eyes downcast.

"Ephraim, apologize for beating him. Amos, apologize for saying that."

Ephraim spoke up.

"He shouldn't apologize to me. He should tell Emma he's sorry. I was sticking up for her."

"That can come later. Right now this is about you two."

They offered halfhearted apologies, but there was no real feeling. Annie decided it was enough that they had obeyed and left it at that, ushering them out to do chores.

When suppertime came, she had all the wash folded, and with Suvilla's help, it was all put back in drawers and closets, except for a stack of ironing in the clothesbasket. She was stirring the thick bean soup, her back turned to the kitchen, when she felt two strong hands grasp her waist, followed by Dan's face close to hers and a soft kiss placed on her cheek.

"My *glaeyne frau*," he murmured.

She smiled, leaned back against his chest for a moment. He smelled of wet earth and strong breezes, of cows and hay and, yes, manure. The smell she had been used to all her life. The smell of a farmer.

She turned to meet his eyes, the tender look she found there as sure as the rising sun. His temperament never changed. He was like a rock, a pillar of good humor and gentleness that supported the foundation of her being. When she was with him, nothing seemed impossible.

"I love you," she whispered, a hand going to his face. He smiled into her eyes, and they both turned to find many pairs of eyes watching them.

Dan smiled, stepped back, clapped his hand and said, "*Komm*, Rebecca." He beckoned her two-year-old. *Our two-year-old*, she reminded herself. *Not just mine.*

"*Komm*," he coaxed again. Rebecca watched him warily, then sidled shyly along the sofa until she reached him. He bent to pick her up, cradled her in his lap while she put her thumb in her mouth and closed her eyes.

They all laughed.

Rebecca was so shy, and her thumb was her refuge from every scary thing in her life. Closing her eyes was her way of shutting out whatever her thumb did not console.

"Funny girl, Rebecca," Dan laughed, holding her closer.

As Annie dished up the fragrant bean soup, a stab of guilt went through her, took away the comfort of

Dan's attentiveness. It all seemed so easy for him, so seamless. There was no effort in his reaching for her child; the attempts to win her over were completely genuine. Already the younger girls adored him, especially Lydia and Emma. For this, Annie was thankful, but it highlighted her own shortcomings.

The dinner table held two loaves of bread, three large dishes of apple butter, three plates of butter, and the steaming bowls of bean soup. There were fourteen hungry children lined on either side of the lengthy table. Dan sat at the end of the table, with Annie to his left, Rebecca on her other side.

The chattering and scraping of chairs stopped the minute Dan lifted a hand. *"Patties noona."* It was the signal to bow heads in unison, hands in laps, as silent prayers were whispered or thought, depending on the person's method of thanking the Lord for the food before them. Some children were conscientious, lowering their heads so their foreheads almost touched the tabletop, while others bowed their heads only slightly, their eyes sliding sideways while their elbows poked into ribs, snickers or whispers escaping them.

Ephraim didn't bow his head at all, resulting in a stern look from Dan.

Ephraim said he didn't know how Dan could see what he was doing if he kept his own head bowed the way he was supposed to. Amos countered that every parent was expected to watch his children's behavior; it didn't matter when. Enos rolled his eyes, knowing Amos would side with Dan (he could not bring himself to call him "Dat"), regardless of his actions.

They did get visitors. They descended on the Dan Beiler farm like a swarm of flies, trickling in one at a time, till there were as many as six or seven buggies parked along the front of the barn, or tied to the hitching rack, on any given Sunday.

They came to welcome Annie and her children. They wrung her hand, clasped it in both of their own, looking deep into her eyes with much love and understanding. They brought doughnuts and apple dumplings, sacks of licorice and pans of scrapple.

Ezra Lapp sie Anna handed her a bag of fresh lettuce and new red radishes, perfect red globes tied in a neat bundle with a rubber band secured around the green tops.

"Already?" Annie gasped, throwing her hands in the air.

"My now, Annie. Don't you have a hot bed?"

Annie shook her head no.

"*Mold oh*. We need to talk to Dan. Can hardly believe he didn't build a hot bed for Sarah. Any worthy frau needs a hot bed to sow lettuce and radish seeds in February or early March." With that, she took herself into the living room to shake Dan's hand and accost his unworthiness by not having a hot bed.

Dan looked into her face as she talked, nodded his head up and down in affirmation, said ya, ya, he would have to see to it. Then he did the unthinkable and told her he already had a warm bed with his new wife and that was *far* more important, which caused her to blush and snort and pshaw her way back to the kitchen as fast as possible.

Ezra Lapp was not a farmer. He started a welding shop in the twenties, called K and L Welding, and made a fairly good living for the first five years, till the Depression took away most of his trade. A quiet, unassuming man, he was married to an out-spoken robust woman four years his senior, who seemed to control him much the same way a puppet is controlled, by deft manipulation. Everyone knew when shy Ezra asked for her hand in marriage she told him she would marry him on one condition, and that was that he not milk cows or farm the land, that she was not going to smell cow manure and sour milk her whole life long. Some said he should have been warned by that; others said he wasn't dumb, he enjoyed his garrulous, decisive wife.

They said she was the one who had the funds to start up K and L Welding, that the K stood for her maiden name, Kauffman. He seemed perfectly happy to be put in the back seat and let his outspoken wife do most of the talking. He listened to her spit-flinging tirades with acceptance and interest, for he loved his round wife and admired her mind immensely. But when Dan told her about his warm bed, he threw back his head and howled with glee. He had never seen his Anna quite as flummoxed as he had then, and was delighted.

Back in the kitchen with Annie, Davey Zook sie Katie said a good way to stretch meat was to put it in *roasht*, that any meat was good that way, even ground beef or sausage. In fact, her favorite was *doggie fils*, which was *roasht* made with sliced hot dogs. She looked hopefully in Annie's direction, wondering if she would be the kind of wife to welcome others to her table. She was not disappointed when Annie said, "We could have it for supper. Will you all be staying?"

"Yes. Oh, indeed. Sure. But don't go to any bother, please."

The women rose as one to help peel potatoes and cut bread into cubes. There was no celery in spring, so they used onion and dried parsley, plenty of lard, and cut up canned hot dogs, and mixed everything in an enormous bowl with beaten eggs and chicken broth. Then they dumped it into a large roaster and popped it in the wood-fired oven.

Potatoes were put on the range to boil, milk gravy made with browned butter and flour, canned beans seasoned with salt, pepper, molasses, and a bit of pork fat. The meal was rounded out with bowls of applesauce, small dishes of sweet pickles, and pickled red beets.

The men and children ate first, which allowed the women to serve them, the traditional way of hosting a Sunday table for visitors. There were twenty-three present at the extended table, and all ate with a hearty appetite, even the smallest boy or girl.

Katie watched the men taking second helpings of the *doggie fils* onto their plates. She so loved it, and hadn't made it in a while, so her mouth watered all through. "The men always take so long," she told the other women in the kitchen.

"Oh, but they're hungry," Annie answered from her point at the stove, dishing up the fragrant beans.

"Well, we are, too. *Ach*. Annie, you're too sweet for your own good. *Hesslich*, everyone is going to walk all over you."

"Oh no," Annie laughed. "I can speak my mind. But after you have been a widow for a while, things look so much different. Appreciation comes more easily."

They saw the tears in her eyes, and everyone was touched. Here was a woman who had suffered bravely, who had carried on in these hard times, and didn't seem to hold the slightest bitterness in her heart.

Annie served bread and butter, along with strawberry preserves. Dessert was her high, quivering custard pie, a real treat for those who seldom had extra
eggs or milk. There were clear glass bowls of canned
peaches and a dense spice cake thick with raisins,
nutmeg, and cinnamon.

Oh, it was a wondrous meal, especially for
Depression times.

Dan himself had no idea the custard pies had been
made on Saturday morning, along with the twice
weekly ten loaves of bread. The spice cake smell had
lingered in the kitchen at lunchtime, but he'd figured
it was a bread pudding for supper.

The women all asked for the custard pie recipe,
and the men thought Dan a very fortunate man, even
before the appearance of spice cake and peaches.

"You have a good cook, Dan," Henry Beiler said,
leaning back in his chair and patting his full stomach
with appreciation.

Annie's face was flushed, moving from table to
stove, filling bowls and water glasses, replenishing the
bread plate.

Eventually, Dan looked around the table to be certain he was not hurrying a slow eater, before he spoke. "Did you get enough?"

Murmurs of appreciation and assent followed.

Dan smiled, cleared his throat, and ducked his head to thank the Lord for what they had just eaten in the second silent prayer.

Whooping with glee, the children and their friends slid off benches and made a mad dash for the door to continue their game of kickball. The men chewed on toothpicks or smoked their pipes or cigars in the living room. The women hurriedly cleared the table, emptied serving bowls into heavy kettles, and reheated, stirred, and reset the table, talking, laughing, enjoying the camaraderie. Sunday company was the high point of many hardworking women's social lives.

The table was almost filled the second time, and there was enough for everyone. Not everyone got a slice of the spice cake, but there was plenty of pie and peaches. The women all said they didn't know when they ever had better *doggie fils*. Annie demurred, saying it wasn't better than anyone else's, although she did add more chicken broth and eggs than her mother used to.

The house was messy, the floors tracked with muddy foot prints, and all the work she had put into the preparing of pies and cakes had disappeared in one Sunday evening. But the time of making new friends, the enjoyment of hospitality and fellowship, far outweighed the work.

By the time all the kids were in bed or in their rooms and Annie and Dan finally got to turn in for the night, her body ached with weariness. But her heart was filled with gratitude. She kissed her new husband, lay her head on his strong arm, and thanked him for everything he did for her. They both fell asleep with a smile on their lips.

Chapter Seven

AS SPRING TURNED INTO SUMMER, ANNIE'S workload doubled, at least. The sun's rays increased, drawing the many seeds into sprouts, the sprouts into beanstalks, potato plants, pea vines, and more. She stood to survey the sheer size of her garden.

It was a dewy morning, after a few days of intermittent rain and drizzle, so the weeds had gathered in force, taking over the well-tilled and hoed soil until it looked like a sea of green. And it was wet. So wet. How would they ever restore the garden to its original manicured state? She would be ashamed to have the neighbors see this. But then she smiled to herself, remembering that everyone's garden had been rained on, not just hers.

And it was a lovely morning. The dew was like jewels scattered across the yard, the lush green plants beaded with them, dripping off the perfect green leaves. The sun was a fiery ball of orange, already pulsating with the heat that left men leaning against a fence post, their hats tilted back as they swiped at rivulets of perspiration.

This was the time of homemade root beer, mint tea, and ginger water taken to the hayfields where the men forked loads of loose hay onto a wooden wagon drawn by faithful mules or Belgians. This was when every single vegetable from the garden was eaten or canned to put down cellar for the coming winter. For the hundredth time, Annie was grateful to have a kind and gentle husband, and the anxiety of providing for her family alone taken from her shoulders. She loved his strength, his way with the children, his patience and gentleness. How could it be that God had blessed her when she most certainly did not deserve all this?

She turned and went back into the house, only to find Joel and John, five and four, who were Dan's youngest children, in a heated argument with five-year-old Lydia, who was her own.

Oh, she hated that she still thought of them as *her* children and *his* children, but how else was she to make sense of the constant bickering and rivalry? These children had gone through so much, losing their mother and father, struggling with grief and childish sorrow, before being thrown together to live in one house. Remembering this gave her the compassion she needed to deal with the daily struggle of peacekeeping and discipline.

Joel was nearly six now, dark haired and dark eyed, with a brilliant mind and the vocal cords of a little preacher. He ruled John, who was a gentle, passive child, happy to go along with whatever his older brother wanted. Five-year-old Lydia, on the other hand, had inherited all the spit and vigor of Annie's own mother, including the loud voice and quick temper.

Joel and Lydia had both woken up in a foul mood, the heat upstairs causing them to sleep fitfully. Thirsty, unable to find their mother, they sat on the old davenport like uncomfortable little birds, eyeing each other, with sweet-natured John between them.

"Where's Mam?" John asked, his strident voice like a razor to Lydia's ill temper.

"She's not your mother."

"Yes, she is. She's as much our mam as she is your mam," Joel answered.

"How do you figure that?" Lydia sat forward, slid her feet to the floor, and twisted her head toward him, suspicion and challenge in her eyes.

"Well, you know. Since the wedding. We're all your mam's kids, and my dat is your father, too."

"Don't say 'kids.' Only English people say 'kids.'"

"Kids, kids, *kids*!" Joel said loudly.

"Stop it. Stop it this minute."

"Kids."

With her hand on her hips, Lydia faced her opponent squarely. "You say that one more time, and I'm going to the barn and telling Dat."

"No! No!"

Now that Lydia had the upper hand, she wasted no time in using her power to its full advantage, taunting him with every misdeed of the day before, of which there were plenty.

They both began to yell, which was how Annie found them when she entered the kitchen.

Again, it was easiest to tackle her own Lydia, before turning to the irate Joel, and by now, the deeply troubled John.

"What happened? Stop this now, both of you."

Lydia was indignant, her face flushed with anger. "He said we were 'kids.' Only goats have kids, and we are not supposed to say that."

"No, we don't say that, Joel. You are '*kinna*.'" Annie answered calmly.

"He just kept saying it," Lydia pouted, crossing her arms around her waist.

"I did not!"

"Yes, you did. Mam, he's telling a *schnitza*. He always lies!"

"Lydia, you go sit on that chair." Annie pointed to a cane-bottomed chair in the corner. "Even if you're right, you're being prideful and unkind." She turned to Joel. "What started this?"

Sullen, he refused to meet her eyes. She waited.

Finally, he spoke. "She said you were not my mother, and I said you were. At the wedding, the preacher said we all became one."

Annie's stern face softened. She could see the hurt and confusion beneath his petulant scowl.

"Yes, Joel, we are. We are all one family. We all live together in this big stone house and we all have to try and get along. I am everyone's mother, and

Dat is everyone's father." She turned to Lydia. "So, Lydia, it wasn't right to say what you said. And Joel, never refer to any of your brothers or sisters as 'kids,' alright?"

He stared at his toes, would not give her the satisfaction of a decent answer. Annie sat beside him, slid an arm around the stone-faced boy, and pulled him close. "Promise me?"

She was shocked when he flung himself into her lap and cried as if his heart would break, which set John into little sputters and then full-fledged howling, too.

Annie's heart seemed to melt within her. She reached out to include John in the hug, squeezing them tight to her as tears sprang to her own eyes.

"It's alright," she murmured, over and over.

She beckoned to Lydia to join their huddle, but she shook her head stubbornly, folding her arms across her chest and watching the display with bitterness glistening in her eyes.

Was ever anything all right, she wondered. She had pronounced these words over and over since the day she married her beloved Dan, but most days there was much more wrong than right. No one could prepare another person for this. It was like walking blindly down a sunlit path, never imagining the obstacles you would meet. Most stepmothers had only a few children, and she'd heard it could be hard, but this?

She thought of her mother's warning against marrying a man who didn't feel for her children. But Dan was fine with the children—he always seemed to know just what to say or how to act around them. Annie, on the other hand, constantly doubted that she was saying or doing the right thing. And there was simply not enough of her to go around. Some days she thought the sting of grief and poverty was easier to handle than the feeling of constant failure and inadequacy.

Suddenly, she could hear her grandmother's voice in her mind. "Annie, can you get nothing right? Must you ruin everything you touch? *Ach*, your poor husband someday. What a mess, Annie. What a mess you are . . ."

Annie felt her stomach clench up, the way it always did when she remembered her grandmother.

She took a deep breath and brought herself back to the present, back to the two needy children beside her. She held the two boys, told them they were very special to her, and that she would always be their real mother.

When Joel sat up and dug out his small, wrinkled handkerchief and wiped his eyes and nose, a shudder passed through him.

He looked up at Annie.

"Do you really mean that? You will always be right here?"

"Oh, I will. I love it here. I love your father and I love you."

The two pairs of eyes turned to her were guileless, the innocent eyes of children who were hungry for love, hungry for assurance of a mother who would never leave them.

From the corner came Lydia's disgusted voice.

"Well, it's nice you like *some* of us, at least."

"Come, Lydia. You know I have always loved you." Then she smiled and said teasingly, "*And* I like you, even when you're kind of a bossy little tattle tale."

At that, Lydia couldn't help but giggle a little, which got the rest of them laughing until their sides hurt.

Breakfast was two loaves of bread sliced and spread with peanut butter, laid in a wide soup plate with sugared coffee that was thick with cream poured over it. They all ate heartily of the good coffee soup, a staple in warm weather when the kitchen range would have to be fired too high to fry all that cornmeal mush. Sometimes Annie made oatmeal and they ate it with apple butter and biscuits, or a huge cast iron pan of fried potatoes, but only on mornings that were cool.

The happy chatter and clatter of spoons on granite plates reminded Annie how easily children forgave each other and moved on with their lives as if nothing had occurred. Dan praised the coffee soup, said the peanut butter really got a fellow going on these hot days. She smiled into his eyes and was rewarded with the tenderest look from his gentle countenance. For the hundredth time, she thought nothing could be impossible with Dan by her side.

Ida and Hannah, both eleven years old, were chosen to do dishes, while Ephraim, Lavina, and Emma were told to help their mother in the garden. Amos and Enos were expected to drive the horses, one to cultivate the cornfield, one to drive the wagon while Dan forked hay.

Suvilla was expected to start the washing. The water was already steaming in the iron kettle. Ida said she didn't know why she couldn't drive the horses. Hannah agreed, saying girls should be allowed to drive. In fact, she'd seen Emery Glick's girls, Fronie and Sadie, drive the hay wagon just the day before. Amos narrowed his eyes and said girls washed dishes and boys drove wagons around. Ida's eyes flashed fire as she sized up her stepbrother, but she kept quiet. Annie breathed easier when Hannah did the same.

Dan listened, smiled, then said probably girls were every bit as good at driving horses as boys, so if they washed the dishes real good for breakfast and dinner, he'd let them try this afternoon, seeing how he needed Amos and Enos to help him fork hay.

The girls looked on their father with an expression close to worship. Annie thanked him with her sweet smile.

Everyone was expected to work hard, right down to the two little Emmas and Hannah. They worked together as a team as the sun rose high over the gardens. The children were all suntanned, their muscles well developed, toughened by physical labor as well as vigorous play. They all knew the work came first, which could last most of the day. The smallest ones carried wooden bushel baskets by the wire handles and gathered the piles of weeds as the older children dug them out with hoes. Sometimes they sang or whistled, calling back and forth across the rows.

It was Hannah who found the first potato bugs. She alerted Ida, who knew exactly what to do, but she figured she'd better talk to her mother first. Annie and Suvilla were in the cellar, sweeping cobwebs and washing shelves that looked quite empty now. They would scour every inch before mixing powdered lime with water, then brushing it over the stone walls of the house's foundation, creating a sparkling white disinfected area to store the summer's bounty.

"Mam!"

"Yes?"

"Potato bugs! Millions of potato bugs!"

"*Ach* my. Wait, I'll help you get kerosene."

She found an old tin can, put on the shelf in the woodshed for this purpose, and poured some of the smelly fuel into it, then selected a short stick and handed it to her.

"There you go, Ida. Be careful to check the undersides of the leaves."

Ida loved this chore, as did the other children.

"Potato bugs!"

"Let me! Let me!"

Everyone swarmed around Ida, eager for a turn at knocking the shiny purplish brown beetles into the kerosene can until they died, which was not long at all. But Ida pushed her way through to the potato plants and began to whack them quite efficiently into their oily demise, with many pairs of keen eyes observing every move she made.

"They're dying," Joel announced solemnly.

"They are supposed to do that," Lydia told him, her nose in the air, taut with her own superiority.

"I know," Joel said.

Lydia, never able to let something go without having the last word, announced triumphantly, "You didn't know till I told you."

"I did. Kerosene kills anything."

"Not everything."

"Almost."

John sat between two rows of beans, snapping a yellow wax bean before putting it in his mouth, his head turning first to Lydia, then to Joel as the exchange continued.

"It doesn't matter," he said loudly.

"What?"

"About kerosene."

"What about it?"

"I don't know."

"I don't either."

Solemnly, the children continued picking up weeds, dragging the heavy wooden bushel basket between them. They did their job well, never complaining, only occasionally stopping for a drink of water. Now and then a conversation broke out, but the work always progressed steadily throughout the forenoon.

At twelve o'clock, Annie washed her hands at the pump, laid out bread and butter and glasses of mint tea for a quick lunch. Dan had gone to help a neighbor with the birthing of a first-time heifer, so there was only a snack. The biggest meal of the day would be after the evening milking.

The afternoon wore on, with the children losing energy as the heat of the sun became almost unbearable. Ida had long ago found the last potato bug, so it was back to hoeing, which did not seem fair at all, the way the weeds were so thick it didn't matter how hard she brought the hoe down, there were more weeds. The hotter it became, the more her temper flared.

"Dat said we could fork hay or drive horses. Instead we're still stuck in this garden," she fumed.

Suvilla was thinning corn, her hair blowing out and away from the kerchief around her head, her face almost the same color as the early cherry tomatoes. She slanted the irritable Ida a look. "What did you expect? Fathers never keep their promises." She pushed her hair back, leaving streaks of sweat and dirt on her forehead. "I, for one, am never getting married."

Ida stopped hoeing and drew down her eyebrows as she mulled over her sister's words. Puzzled, she asked what she meant by that.

"Dat always promised me he'd take care of us, but he didn't," Suvilla said sullenly, just loud enough for Ida to hear.

"But he couldn't help it that he died. He was in an accident."

"He still died."

"So?"

"So I'll never get married."

Ida considered this. "It's not like most husbands die so early," she ventured softly.

"Some do."

"But we have a new Dat, Suvilla. This one is much nicer. We have more to eat, and a bigger, better house. This Dat doesn't raise his voice, or become angry or anything."

"Not yet. He might, though."

Ida leaned on her hoe, looking for all the world like a wise old woman with her head cocked to one side, nodding to herself.

"You know, it's probably a good idea for you to stay

single. If you did get married, your husband would have to live with you constantly worrying about him dying or getting mad. You'd both be miserable."

"What do you know about marriage, Ida?" Suvilla barked.

"Enough to know you better stop feeling sorry for yourself unless you really do want to be a lonely old maid."

There was a loud call from the barn.

"Suvilla, Ida, Hannah! *Kommet!*"

Ida took off in long-legged strides toward the barn, Hannah and the two Emmas toddling behind.

Suvilla's brows lowered, her mouth set in a grim line, and she turned away. Slowly she gathered up the hoes and the bushel baskets, stacked everything in the woodshed, threw the weeds across the fence to the horses, and went to find her mother, who was just finishing up the whitewashing.

Annie took one look at Suvilla's glowering face before setting down the galvanized bucket, placing one hand on a hip, and saying, "What?"

Suvilla brushed past and went into the house, slamming the screen door behind her.

Chapter Eight

THERE WERE TIMES THAT SUMMER THAT Annie was so weary, so bone tired, she felt as if every muscle was protesting against one more step. Yes, it was the physical labor, but more than that it was the constant bickering, the competition between the children for her attention and love, that wore her out. No matter how she tried, she couldn't convince them that there was enough love to go around. Sometimes she thought maybe there *wasn't* actually enough love in her heart. When she lost her patience and snapped at one of the children, or struggled to feel the same way about Dan's little ones as she did about hers, she shuddered to think maybe she was as coldhearted as her unfeeling grandmother.

Every night she set the large round tub on the back porch for the children to wash their feet before bed. Such a long row of sun-browned and calloused feet that had dashed across grass and stones and plowed soil. She helped the little ones scrub and tried to remember to give each child a word of attention, something to let them know she was here, she was their mother, and she loved them all the same.

She tried, but had to admit, there was a difference, in spite of her best efforts. Lavina and Hannah had taken to eyeing her with dark baleful glances, which she ignored at first, but then catalogued as another form of rebellion. She knew she was not enough. There simply was not time to draw out each child and give them the attention—that delicate balance of loving care and discipline—that they needed.

After all the children were upstairs in bed, Annie and Dan retreated to the swing on the front porch. They rocked gently and the swing creaked and groaned from the rusty hooks in the ceiling. Crickets chirped lazily from their hiding place beneath the boxwoods; a procrastinating robin chirped loudly to its mate from the maple branch above them. A cow lowed softly, the sound of her hooves in the barnyard like suction cups, the mud drawing down on each heavy split hoof.

"Barnyard still wet?" Annie asked softly.

"Yes. Guess I'll have to clean it up. We are just blessed with plenty of rain this summer."

Annie laid her head on Dan's solid shoulder and placed a hand on his knee, something she would never have done with her first husband. He had so often carried resentment like a prickly armor, a porcupine of separation. Dan was, well, he was welcoming. His wide chest and shoulders were a haven for her weariness and concerns at the end of the day.

Now, when his arms went around her, drawing her against him, he bent to place a kiss on the top of her head.

"My precious little wife," he said, chuckling in the depth of his chest.

Annie closed her eyes and rested in his love.

"Dan, I'm sorry to come to you every evening with my concerns, but do you think Lavina and Hannah have a . . . have a problem with me?"

For a long moment Dan was quiet, the rise and fall of his chest the only sound. He sighed, cleared his throat, then drew a hand from her waist to her shoulder, where he began a gentle massage.

"Annie my love, I would never hurt your feelings if I could help it, you know that. But I think those two girls were hit very hard by the death of their mother. It wasn't just her passing. They spent a lot of time with her when she was struggling. So to grow up with a . . . a loss of love and attention, then to have to see their mother's passing . . . I always imagine them like leaking little boats pushed out to sea. It's hard for them. And . . . ."

He paused, drew a deep breath.

"I think maybe Ida is causing some jealousy. What do you think?"

Annie held very still. Ida. The one whose boundless energy and high spirits had often carried her through her darkest hours. She was blessed with a sunny disposition and a never-ending flow of good humor, finding ways of fun and delight where many children would have overlooked it. She loved Ida fiercely. It came so naturally. She had always hoped never to favor one above the other, but no one would disagree that Ida was a special girl.

Now, she thought of all the times she and Ida laughed together, sharing a moment of levity amidst the chores, while Lavina and Hannah looked on from a distance. Of course they would want that same kind of connection with her.

Silently, she began to weep.

"I'm so dumb," she said softly.

His arms tightened. "No, no, dear heart. No, you are not. You have your hands full, and I could be a help to you by mentioning only what I have observed. You know we will both always be drawn to our own children, the ones we raised as babies. We saw them being born, we cherished their tiny faces, the way all parents do.

"But we have to keep trying to do the best we can. I noticed Suvilla is having problems, but to tell you the truth, Annie, I feel totally useless in helping her. She hardly says two words to me, and I can't think of anything to say to her. So now look who's dumb."

"Suvilla? I had no idea. Oh my word, Dan. It has nothing to do with you, at all. She's just at the age where she has no confidence, where everything looks scary and unsure. She'll be joining the *rumschpringa* in a few months, and that is a frightening time for many of us."

"But she doesn't like me."

"She will, once her life is more settled."

A comfortable silence fell between them, as they gently pushed back and forth on the old wooden swing. The crickets chirped continuously, the half-moon hung above them to the east, bathing the farm in its soft glow.

"Annie?"

"Yes."

"We'll work this all out in time, won't we?"

"Of course. I love how easily I can talk to you about anything. If we can continue to do that, I see no reason why things can't be normal soon enough. Christmas. I'll give it till Christmas," Annie laughed, trying to feel as confident and she made herself sound.

"Can you imagine all the gifts? And all the Christmas dinners we'll have to go to? This one at home, my family on both sides, and your family on both sides. That's five Christmas dinners, Annie."

"What fun!" she answered.

"Now you sound like Ida."

She laughed.

Dan shook his head, looking sober again.

"Lavina is so much like her mother, I'm afraid. Just full of . . . well, whatever it was that drove her to be so miserable at times."

"Oh, but I'm so glad you've made me aware of it."

Dan yawned, stretched. Annie gave an answering yawn, and together they made their way into the house, and to the bed that was a haven for their weary selves.

They did not kneel by the side of their bed to pray, having done that with the fourteen children around the kitchen table. Sixteen people, on their knees, heads bent in various degrees of holiness, the gas light hissing softly as Dan's voice rose and fell, reading from the German book the prayer that sustained his faith.

After breakfast the next morning, Dan announced he and Annie would be going to the small town of Intercourse, the name implying the hub of a wheel, where many roads met, and that Ida and Lavina could ride along. Ida raised both arms and cavorted around the kitchen shouting her glee, while Lavina, intimidated by this display of excitement, watched with hooded eyes.

They took the spring wagon, sitting in the open air, the sun already hot on their backs, the open view around them an endless source of entertainment for Ida, who gave a loud opinion on all her observations. They had gone less than half a mile before she said Henry Miller's heifers had parasites.

Dan burst into a loud guffaw of laughter, his head thrown back as he slapped his knee.

"Whatever do you mean?" Annie gasped, appalled.

"Their coats are shaggy and they have ribs that show."

Dan nodded, then slanted Annie a look.

"You're probably right, Ida," he said.

Then it was, "Why do we have to wear a bonnet? They're so hot and I can't see a thing."

Lavina listened, said nothing.

"You saw Henry Miller's heifers."

"Keep your bonnet on. We don't go anywhere without them, you know that."

"I would change that rule if I was the bishop. Why doesn't he change it? He doesn't have to wear a bonnet."

The thought of old Joas Stoltzfus wearing a bonnet, his white beard tucked beneath the strings, was more than Dan could picture in his mind without the benefit of a good laugh.

Annie smiled, but said sternly, "Ida, shame on you for talking that way."

When they reached the town of Intercourse, they turned off to the left and pulled up beside a few more teams tied to the hitching rack in the back of Zimmerman's Grocery and Hardware. Dan leaped off the wagon and tied the sorrel horse securely to the hitching post before turning to extend a hand to Annie. The girls clambered down by themselves, then stood brushing the fronts of their dresses and aprons for any stray horse hairs before following their parents into the store.

The floorboards creaked as they walked along the aisles, looking at various objects they might need. Ida and Lavina walked behind their parents, careful not to touch the stacks of rope or leather halters, cakes of soap, bags of cornmeal, new buckets and brooms, colorful bolts of fabric.

The proprietor of the store was small and wiry, with a shining bald head that appeared to be varnished like a good hardwood floor. He smiled at Dan and Annie, greeted them with a "Hello, folks," then turned to Ida and Lavina.

"And how are the girls?"

Ida replied for both of them. "We're fine, thank you."

They bought fifty pounds of flour, five pounds of white sugar, coffee, tea, baking powder and soda, a small measure of raisins, and a bag of licorice sticks for the children. Dan talked with the store clerk for a long time after paying for his purchases, discussing the president, the Depression, the state of the political party they agreed with, and what would become of the United States if Mr. Roosevelt didn't do something.

Annie took the girls out to the spring wagon where they sat waiting obediently, the sun climbing higher with increasing heat.

"Well, if I have a husband, he's not going to stand around talking to bald-headed English men while I sit in the sun," Ida announced.

Lavina surprised Annie when she said, "You might never have a husband."

Even Ida was speechless. Annie turned to find the

two black bonnets turned toward each other, with no sound coming from either one.

Finally, Ida lifted a shoulder.

"Well," she said. "You might not either."

"Oh. I plan on it, though."

Annie smiled to herself. It was a very small beginning, but it was one. Lavina was speaking her own mind.

When Dan appeared, he was sober, his expression troubled.

Annie turned to him with questioning eyes, but he shook his head.

"You need rolled oats, right?" he asked.

"I do."

"Then it's off to Rohrer's," he said, untying the horse, climbing up into the spring wagon, drawing back steadily on the reins till the horse backed against the britchment strap, pushing the spring wagon backwards.

"*Komm na,*" he called softly, and the horse trotted off easily.

After that ride in the spring wagon, a new friendship began to develop between Ida and Lavina. By the time school started the first week in September, Lavina was like an unplugged drain, or an opened faucet, words that had been buried under sorrow and confusion now flowing freely.

The leaves turned various shades of yellow, orange, and red. It was the time of year when frost lay heavily in the hollows, withering the marigolds and petunias. Every tree was dressed in brilliant finery until a cold, slanting rain sent most of the leaves to the lawn below. The wind blew, wailing in from the north, and sent most of the leaves spinning off and away, so that there weren't too many to rake and burn at the end of the day.

Eleven children walked to school. Eleven lunchboxes were packed away every morning. Enos and Amos were in eighth grade, so this would be their last year, Annie thought, as she spread butter on eleven slices of bread, folded them, and wrapped them in waxed paper. Eleven sugar cookies and eleven apples. She had taken to baking the sugar cookies to a larger size, as the growing boys were all ravenous by the time they got home.

Every child went to school in bare feet, saving their shoes for the coming cold weather. With the frost on the ground, the calloused soles of their feet were cold, but not uncomfortably so, seeing how the sun warmed the earth before the first recess bell.

Joel and Lydia were in first grade, so that left only three-year-old Rebecca at home with Suvilla and Annie. The house was empty, the footsteps and footprints gone quiet, the shout and murmurs, the banging of doors and clattering of spoons absent, so that Annie said to Suvilla it seemed as if she couldn't breathe in this quiet air.

"Well, Mam. I for one, am happy to have them out of the way," she answered.

"Yes, we will get more accomplished, for sure."

The time of fall housecleaning was upon them, and every good Amish housewife took it seriously. No window could go unwashed, no walls or ceiling, and certainly no floor, left unscrubbed.

They lugged heavy buckets of scalding hot water up the stairs, then the second flight to the attic. Crates and cardboard boxes were pulled out from under the eaves, organized and cleaned, the floor underneath swept and scrubbed with hot lye soap and water. Windows were washed until they seemed polished.

No matter that no one would even set foot in Annie's attic. The dirt and spiderwebs weighed heavily on her conscience. What if one of them were to pass away and the community would descend on them like so many worker bees, cleaning, moving furniture, preparing the house for a funeral? It was a morbid thought, but it had happened to her once and it could happen again. Of course, if one of them were to die suddenly, the cleanliness of their home would not be forefront in her mind. But still, she always felt better having a clean and tidy house and knowing she was prepared for anything—as much as one can be, anyway.

Bucket after bucket of water was carried up the stairs, until the water turned dark gray with the dust and grime that always clung to the hewn floorboards. They surveyed their accomplishment with satisfaction. Even the sullen Suvilla seemed to find a hint of pleasure in the clean smell of the attic.

"Suvilla, when you have your own house, always remember I taught you how to clean an attic well," Annie remarked.

"I'll never have my own house," she huffed, her face taking on a deep shade of red.

Annie shook her head. "Oh, sure you will."

That ended the conversation. Suvilla had just joined the group of *rumschpringa*, and Annie knew she felt self-conscious about it. She was becoming quite a beautiful young woman, but if Suvilla felt humble about her appearance, it was best. Annie did not want a *grosfeelich* daughter who thought well of her own looks. How was a young girl to be discreet, a keeper at home, loving her husband, if she was puffed up with her own sense of vain glory? If Suvilla despised the breakouts on her skin, so be it. If she had only one Sunday dress and her friends had two or three, it could not be helped. Dan was a wonderful provider, but Annie was not about to waste money on fabric for dresses that the girls didn't really need.

How well she remembered her own time of *rumschpringa*, when she felt unworthy of any attention from young men. She was so deeply honored to have Eli Miller take notice of her and found it astounding that he should ask to come visit her that first Sunday evening.

Her wedding day had been every young girl's dream, and if Eli was less than perfect with the ambition that drove him, the quick temper and frequent needs, well, she wasn't perfect, either. She just had no idea back then, that any man could be what Dan was. Indeed, her year of grief, the crying for a night, had turned to the joy that came in the morning, just as the Bible promised. God had blessed her through her sorrow, the loss of the barn, so that He could lift her up to the height and strength of Dan's gentle love.

Even now, as she prepared a hasty lunch of buttered bread and bean soup, she waited eagerly for his step on the porch. He always met her eyes, that slow smile spreading across his kind face, as he asked how her work was coming along. She could trust him, trust that things would never change. His love was a beautiful thing.

She wished the same for Suvilla. She prayed that God would change her sullen nature. Yes, her father had passed away when she was a tender age, but many others went through the dark valley of sorrow. It was up to Suvilla to give herself up to whatever God chose to place before her, and the sooner she started to realize this, the better.

Chapter Nine

THE COLD WAS BECOMING MORE PRO-
nounced, so that shoes were brought out, handed
down, or new ones bought. After Thanksgiving,
there were coats to sew, mittens to crochet, scarves to
knit, so Annie was kept busy simply providing for the
children's needs. But the house cleaning was accomplished now, the yard raked and manure put on the
flower beds. The garden lay dormant under a cover
crop of fall oats, and the harvest was all down cellar
except for the cabbage and carrots.

No one went hungry, with plenty of milk from
the cows, cup cheese and cottage cheese, butter and
cold buttermilk. There were only enough eggs to sell
in the fall of the year, selling for a dollar a dozen,
which was phenomenal, according to Dan.

"You keep the egg money for Christmas gifts," he
told Annie.

"Oh, it's too much," she said, wide-eyed.

"No, I want you to get each child a nice present. Something special."

"*Ach*, well," was all she could think to say.

"They have all come a long way. None of this was easy for any of them. . . ."

"Except Ida," Annie reminded him.

"Except Ida," Dan laughed, shaking his head.

The egg money was put in a small dish on a shelf in the kitchen. All week she felt guilty as she returned from their trips to neighboring homes, pulling the old express wagon with egg boxes placed carefully in a cardboard box. She delivered eggs to the homes of several local English families, knocking on their doors, taking their money in exchange for the fresh eggs.

A dollar a dozen is not right, Annie thought for the hundredth time. The English families were hit by the Depression just as hard, if not harder, than the Amish community. The Amish families knew, at least, that they could turn to each other or to the church if they became desperate. Many of the English families did not have that kind of tight-knit community to support them.

"They don't have to buy these eggs," Dan assured her. "They want them, so if they pay a dollar, that's up to them. We're only making them available."

"But I feel as if I'm taking the money they should have to buy Christmas gifts."

"*Ach* Annie, now don't worry. If they want to buy eggs from someone else for less money, they can."

She had so many dollar bills, she decided to buy the candied fruit, nuts, raisins, and a brandy to make fruit cakes for Christmas. If she could sell a few cakes, it would make her feel better, as if she had at least earned the money that kept piling up in the dish.

The first snow arrived on the tenth of December, whirling hard little bits of ice on an Arctic wind that took her breath away that morning on her way to the barn for a jug of milk. She drew her scarf across her face, shivered, and slammed the milk house door. She stopped and held very still. From the cow stable came the sound of many voices, rising and falling, punctuated by ripples of laughter, a few lines of a silly song, carried along by the moist, acrid air that hung over a cow stable on a winter morning. She felt the rise of emotion in her throat. She walked toward the stable, a quick wave of gratitude formed the beginning of tears. *Thank you, Father.*

Here were her children and his children—Suvilla, Ephraim, Enos and Ida, Amos and Lavina—milking cows, forking hay, working together and seemingly having the time of their life.

"Hey, get over there, you dumb cow!"

"Watch it!"

She heard a clunking sound and knew a cow had placed a well-aimed kick and sent the bucket flying. Annie poked her head around the door to see a disgruntled Ephraim sprawled on his backside, with Ida standing in the aisle bent double slapping her knees with pure glee.

"There's manure on your pants!" she shrieked.

Suvilla poked her head out from between two cows, ready to restore order, then spied Ephraim and burst out laughing.

Annie backed away without having been noticed and made her way to the house through the whirling white snow.

Christmas was in the air with that first snowfall, so fruitcake making began in earnest. She had learned the art from her sister, the mixing, baking with a pan of water in the oven, the finished product wrapped and set in the pantry until the spices blended perfectly with the fruit and nuts. The children cracked walnuts and hickory nuts in the evening, and Annie stored them in glass jars. They would be used for cookies and cake throughout the year. Everything that grew on trees or in the garden was stored away. Chestnuts were roasted and eaten around the kitchen stove in the evening, although the children weren't allowed to eat all they wanted. Chestnuts could produce a stomachache.

There were two turkeys left in the barnyard, strutting around with their heads tucked in, their long beards wobbling across their puffed out chests. Joel and the two Emmas teased them with broomsticks, then ran howling in fear when one of them charged, the tail spread like a huge white fan, the pink eyes baleful.

Ida said if they didn't quit that they weren't going to be allowed to have *roasht* at the Christmas

dinner, but they didn't care. That is, until one afternoon a disgruntled goose chose to protect his barnyard friends and hissed in the farthest corner of the
fence, while the broomstick was making its rounds.
The children took no notice, until the wings were
spread, the long neck was lowered to a few inches
above the ground, the wide yellow feet propelled the
powerful body, and Joel was attacked with all the
force of a twenty-pound, very aggravated goose. The
strong yellow beak latched onto two of his fingers,
the young bones snapping like twigs, producing a yell
of mammoth proportion.

"Ow! Ow!" he screamed, clutching the injured
hand with the other. The two Emmas took one look
and ran on their skinny legs until they reached the
fence, scrambled up and over, falling down the other
side, to turn and peer between the boards with horrified eyes.

"Is he dead?" Emma Two whispered.

"Not yet," Emma One hissed back.

His yells of pain and outrage brought Dan to the
cow stable door, then running to his son who was
clearly in mortal pain. Joel was taken to Doctor Hess in

New Holland, sniffling beside his father on the buggy seat, every bump in the road causing more discomfort. The doctor set the two fingers, taped them to a wooden splint, and told him to stay away from the geese in the barnyard. He charged Dan nothing, saying he'd pick up a bag of potatoes when he was in the area. Dan was grateful, thanked the kind doctor with a handshake, and led his chastened son back to the buggy.

As the horse clopped along through the wintry landscape, Dan looked down at Joel and asked if he thought they should put the two geese into *roasht* for Christmas dinner instead of the turkeys. Joel nodded solemnly.

They dressed in their best everyday clothes, Dan wearing his black Sunday hat. Annie had her heavy shawl pinned over a winter coat, and she wore two pairs of stockings and her rubber boots pulled on over her sturdy black shoes. The day was cold and bright, the sun's rays turning the snowy landscape into a blinding white world capped by a dome of blue. The horse trotted eagerly, the harness stirring up little puffs of dust as it jiggled on the horse's winter coat, thick and coarse.

Annie sat contentedly, leaning against her husband's solid strength, tucked into the buggy with a heavy lap robe, watching the winter scenery through the glass window. She had money to buy Christmas gifts, and found it almost unbelievable. Dan assured her that the children deserved this, every one, and it was not wrong in God's eyes to give gifts that brought joy to a child's face.

Annie nodded, but couldn't seem to silence her mother's disapproving voice in her head. But Dan was her husband, and he was the one she would honor and obey. Obeying him was the easiest task ever, the way he was so gentle and easygoing, so thoughtful of her. And so she tried her best to enjoy the day, to stop the feelings of guilt, that voice in her head that swam around like a repetitive goldfish, gurgling *No, no, no, you shouldn't, you can't, no, no no, it isn't right, it isn't right.*

She chuckled to herself, hadn't realized she made a sound till her husband smiled, looked down at her.

"What?" he asked, his eyes already crinkling in the corners.

"Nothing."

"It was something."

"Just thinking what my mother would say about this Christmas shopping."

"Didn't she buy Christmas gifts?"

"No."

"Not at all?"

"Oh no. Gifts are not necessary except giving up our own will to the Christ child."

His eyebrows went up, then lowered.

"Well, I suppose everyone is entitled to their own opinion. But for me, Christmas is a special time, especially for the children. And this year . . ."

Annie looked at him with a question in her eyes, amazed to find his mouth working to keep his emotion in check. For a long moment, silence filled the buggy.

Then he spoke. "Annie, you and the children are my Christmas gift this year. I am blessed far beyond anything I have ever imagined. You are so good, so beautiful, so . . . well, friendly and sweet. I have the best wife in the whole of Lancaster County."

She raised her eyes to his, her heart and soul drinking in every word.

"Thank you," she whispered brokenly.

How often she was weary, discouraged. How many nights did she fight the feeling of unworthiness before an uneasy slumber overtook her, only to awaken to the beating of her own heart, a staccato sound of primal fear of failure. But if this was how her husband felt, then this was what she would use to keep those moments at bay. His love was priceless, pillars that would support her forever.

They bought a new scarf and gloves for Sammy, both made of gray wool that would look sharp with his black coat and hat as he drove his spirited horse in the courting buggy. Dan said he often wished he could have known her when she was young, courted her the way Sammy would court a young lady soon.

For Suvilla there were four yards of red fabric to turn into a new Sunday dress and a handkerchief to match. "It's too much," Annie breathed, but Dan assured her that it would be good for Suvilla to having something new to wear, that a boost of confidence might draw her out of her dark mood.

Enos, Amos, and Ephraim would each receive a slingshot made from sturdy wood and rubber, along with a pair of wool socks to keep their feet warm when they skated on the pond. Dan said he'd probably regret buying those slingshots, but he knew they would be pleased.

Lavina, Hannah, Ida, and the two Emmas would all receive a tiny china tea set, each one in a different pattern, to set on their dressers in the bedrooms they shared, to hold and to admire.

They would all receive a handkerchief with a red poinsettia design, their very own Christmas handkerchief to take to the Christmas dinners, the envy of all the cousins.

Lydia and Rebecca would each be receiving a new doll with such a pretty face it almost looked real little girl. Annie had never seen such a doll, and had certainly never considered purchasing one. She looked up at Dan.

"Are you sure these are not *app schtellt*?"

"What? A doll? Now why would they be forbidden? And I don't much care if they are. The little girls need a nice doll."

Annie knew Dan was a bit liberal, but not quite to this extent. But it wouldn't be right for her to question him again, so she smiled and nodded.

All her life, she had never owned a doll, not even a homemade rag doll. Her mother said they were idols, likeness made by man, teaching little girls to worship a manmade object. So she had poked holes in the largest corn cob she could find—two eyes, a nose, and a mouth—put her handkerchief on the head and another wrapped around the body, named her Veronica, and loved her with all her heart.

But this? This was too much. Yet she harbored a secret joy to think of Christmas morning.

Joel and John were not on the list, as Dan was carving and painting wooden horses and a wagon for them. He worked on the project for an hour or so every evening, sitting by the kitchen stove with a cardboard box on the floor to catch the shavings, his shoulders hunched in concentration.

It was those times when she wanted to tell him over and over how much she loved him, his solid, stable ways, his constant good humor. Would she never hear him kick his boots in a corner, slam a drawer, tug the roller towel that certain way that told her he was in a black mood? With Eli, she was often left wondering if she'd done—or not done—something to cause him to become so upset. And yet she had loved him wholeheartedly, never regretting their union.

Perhaps Dan and Annie had both been through the fire, had been shaped and molded and polished by their Creator, who worked in everyone's life until they shone in His image.

Whatever the reason, she walked up to Dan every evening, put her arms around his solid strength, and quietly laid her head on his back as he bent over the carving. There were no words, and none were necessary.

On the way home, the parcel containing Christmas gifts stowed under the back seat, Dan asked if she would like to stop for a visit to her grandmother, old Lizzie King. Annie could feel the hesitation before she quickly agreed. No need to let Dan in on all that.

"Yes, yes, of course."

She felt as if she was too loud and too eager, but was relieved when Dan merely smiled, her inner thoughts gone undetected.

Water under the bridge, she assured herself. All is gone and forgotten. She could not have prepared herself for the clenching in her chest as Dan guided the horse into the long lane that led to her grandparent's home.

Her mother's mother, her own blood relative, living out her years alone at the age of ninety-six.

Annie felt her heart quicken as they passed the old woodshed. No matter how desperately she had tried to do everything right, how many times had she been led to the woodshed strewn with shavings and slivers of bark, the smell of split wood, kerosene, and sawdust stinging her nose. It was there that her grandmother whipped her, the slice of the thin iron rod like a knife against her bare legs. It was only when she finally cried out, begged her to stop, that the rod was stilled, set in the corner to mock her own weakness, while her grandmother told her if she ever told her mother, there would be another whipping twice as bad.

Annie had never breathed a word of it.

These things must be forgotten, forgiven, buried forever in the haunted archives of human nature. Perhaps this was what she herself had experienced at the hand of her own grandmother, or mother, perhaps her own father. Who knew? Better to leave it buried, stomped beneath the fertile soil of forgiveness, the soil that God would nurture, heal with the growth of beautiful flowers and grasses, where butterflies and bees could drink their fill of sweet nectar.

To summon the courage to walk through the old door was a real test, to walk across the pine-boarded floor and shake the gnarled old hand, to allow the near blind eyes to search her face with recognition, a superhuman effort.

"Oh, Annie. It's you."

"Grandmother, this is Dan," she said, her voice weaker than she wanted it to be.

Slowly, the head turned; the rheumy old eyes watered to focus.

"Ya, ya. I heard you married again."

"Yes. I did."

"Fourteen children you have."

"Yes."

The old face crumpled; a claw-like hand searched in a dress pocket for a handkerchief as dry rasps of sound came from the ridged old throat.

"Be nice to them. Be nice to the children."

It was the last thing Annie expected to hear.

"Oh, we are. We try to be."

"Gute. Gute. Annie, I'm sorry . . . for, you know
. . ." She began to cry then, one slow tear down her
wrinkled cheek.

"*Ach*, Grandmother. Don't cry," Annie said, touched
and confused by the sudden display of emotion.

There was so much more to say, but somehow,
the words didn't really matter. Annie took her grandmother's hand and held it, and that was enough.

On the way home, Dan asked gently what that
had all been about. Annie found herself telling him
everything, the words opening a locked room in her
heart, tears flowing freely in the cold breeze. When
she was done, she felt like a weight had been lifted
from her chest.

Dan let her speak, listening in compassionate
silence, placing an arm around her shoulder and
drawing her close when she began to weep.

"There's one more thing," she said, looking down
at her lap.

"What's that?" he asked softly, almost a whisper.

"Sometimes . . ." She choked back a sob before
continuing. "Sometimes I lose my patience, or I feel

coldhearted toward our children, Dan. And I wonder if I am no better than my grandmother was to me. Dan, I'm afraid I don't deserve a kindhearted man like you."

He slowed the horses and turned his face toward her, looking very serious. They were on a quiet side road now, away from traffic and houses. "Annie, you cannot believe that," he said, with a voice that was deep, gentle, but firm. "You mustn't. You are exactly what our children need. You are kind and loving and wise. You are exactly what *I* need."

He pulled the horses to a stop. Annie turned her face toward his, searching his eyes and finding every evidence that he meant the words with his whole heart.

"Annie, no one is perfect—it is God who works through us to give us strength and goodness and love. But you, Annie . . . you are about as perfect as a woman can be. You are just right for our family, just right for me. I love you, Annie."

He leaned down and kissed her tears away, flooding her with a warmth and freedom she had never before known.

Chapter Ten

HOW COULD ANNIE FULLY DESCRIBE THE delight and anticipation with which she wrapped the gifts in newspaper and tied them with string?

She had never given Christmas gifts such as these, never spent money on a gift for her children. Sometimes, Eli had purchased a bag of oranges, or a small sack filled with hard candies, but never had she has much as imagined spending egg money for anything other than basic necessities, or handing it to Eli to help with the payment for the farm. She battled her guilt, from time to time, until she confided in Dan, and he again told her the Lord wanted to give his children happiness, things to enjoy, and gradually Annie allowed herself to accept his views. He even showed her the verse in the Bible that spoke of Jesus giving abundant life to His followers. "Of course you can live abundantly without possessions," he said, "but there is nothing wrong with enjoying God's physical blessings in our lives."

As if that extravagance wasn't enough, they made another trip to town to buy supplies for candy and cookies, pies and cakes. They met acquaintances, stopped to visit outside Zimmerman's grocery, shared news in the parking lot by the hitching rack in the cold gray air, the women clutching their black woolen shawls around their bodies, the men settling their black hats more firmly as the cold breeze toyed with the brims.

Becky Zook was a small, rotund woman with a face like a round, glistening plum. Her cheeks bobbed and wagged against the sides of her black bonnet as she spoke, her eyes darting from Dan's face to Annie's. "My oh, it's good to see you out and about together. I haven't been able to visit yet, which is no excuse. I'm sure you wondered where I was all this time."

Annie assured her it was quite all right. She didn't say out loud that her absence hadn't even crossed her mind. She hardly knew the woman.

"We live across the Pequea from you. Our land borders Elam and Rachel's farm. You know, Elam Beiler. They have that poor child."

"Oh, yes. We go to the same church. Yes, of course."

"See, they just divided our district a while back. Before you married Dan."

Here she stepped up and placed a gloved hand on Annie's forearm, her eyes filling with tears like two wet diamonds, the love and concern as priceless.

"I can't tell you how glad I am he has a wife. He did his best all those years, and presented a brave face to the rest of us, but I can't imagine what the poor man has seen in his life. You know his first wife was *opp im kopp*, don't you?"

Annie's eyes went to her husband uneasily. Here was a subject as prickly as a cactus. It felt far too much like gossip, and gossiping about her husband's late wife seemed especially wrong.

"But she was, you know. She was never quite right in the head."

She persisted until Annie said, quietly, "I am sure God had mercy and understanding for her condition."

Becky nodded, then tilted her head to one side, and pursed her lips. "The pneumonia was a mercy. I was always afraid she would . . ."

And here she stepped even closer, her breath a hot wave of half-digested food ". . . end it all by her own hand. And everyone knew those kinds of people are not buried in the cemetery, but outside the fence."

She stepped back, her eyes on Annie's face, watching her response.

"Well, God's ways are not our ways," was all Annie could think to say.

"*Ach*, yes, yes of course. Well, I do admire your attitude about it. Now tell me, how are the children doing? Do you find it hard to accept Dan's boys?"

"The children are doing well, really."

She ignored the second question, more anxious than ever to escape the conversation. She was relieved when Dan turned, asked if she was ready to go.

They bought white sugar and food coloring, boxes of confectionery sugar and chocolate, cocoa powder and coconut, all luxury items that were unnecessary, but Annie's protests did no good. Behind the cereal aisle, he told her if she didn't hush up, he would kiss her and he didn't care who saw them, either.

They were laughing together, Annie's face flushed with pleasure, when they ran into her mother, her face white and drawn, her lips pursed in distaste.

"Oh, Mam, how are you?" Annie asked breathlessly.

"Good. And you?"

"We are good," Dan answered.

"Well, I would imagine Annie can speak for herself," was her tart reply.

"I am well, Mam."

"Well, the children are adjusting, I presume."

"Yes, they are."

"I must be along. I am in town for chicken feed."

Mercifully, her black bonnet was drawn well over her face, like the blinders on a horse's bridle, and she could not see the bulging shopping bag in Dan's hand.

On the way home, a comfortable silence stretched between Dan and Annie, each lost in their own thoughts, not in a troubled fashion, but contemplating the great worth of community and friends. The ability to come and go as they pleased, the religious freedom the Amish enjoyed, and what the forefathers had done to establish this way of life.

The task of raising the fourteen children seemed daunting, but with God's help and guidance, it would be possible for all of them to keep the faith, to continue the plain way of life.

The cookie and candy making began in earnest in the week before Christmas. After the children went off to school (would she ever become used to packing eleven lunches?), she sat with Suvilla and went through all her recipes. Molasses cookies were Dan's favorites, and the ones with the least expensive ingredients. Sugar cookies would be replaced by sand tarts, which were thinner than sugar cookies but could still be cut into shapes with the aluminum cookie cutters, brushed with beaten egg, and dotted with raisins or colored sugar. There would be soft cookies with apples and nuts, glazed with a thin white frosting, also sprinkled with sugar. Oatmeal cookies would be next, and finally chocolate cookies with confectioner's sugar sprinkled across the tops.

They would make a cake roll, filled with strawberry jam. Then a huge three-layer nut cake made with the walnuts from the black walnut tree in the backyard, covered in brown sugar icing flavored with maple syrup. And for pies there would be mincemeat, pumpkin, and apple-raisin.

Suvilla's cheeks were flushed with anticipation, the sullen, rebellious look gone for now. The kitchen was awash in wintery sunlight and the promise of all the sweets they would soon be making. Suvilla loved to cook and bake, and she was good at it—she mixed bread dough with the best, and set cakes on the counter that always turned out light and airy.

"So, what do you suggest we start first?" Annie asked. Suvilla glanced at her mother, a challenge returning to her eyes.

"Why ask me? It's up to you."

"Not just me. We can decide together."

"If I was the boss—which I'm not, of course—I'd do everything but the sand tarts. You chill the dough outside, right?"

Annie nodded.

"Then maybe the little ones can help when they come home from school. What do you think?"

"An excellent idea, Suvilla. That is thoughtful of you, and I appreciate that so much."

Suvilla flushed, rose to her feet self-consciously, then bent to retrieve the large bowl she would be using to mix the molasses cookies. Annie watched her face, amazed to find her oldest daughter blinking away tears. She must remember to praise her more, she thought.

The house was filled with the smell of sugar and cinnamon, molasses and ginger. Sheets of cookies were emptied onto a clean white tablecloth, the kitchen range keeping a steady heat as they controlled the fire with just the right amount of wood, a skill perfected by years of experience. As the sun warmed the cold, snowy landscape, the temperature in the kitchen climbed steadily, until they admitted it was uncomfortable and opened a window to allow in a cooling draught.

When Dan came in for lunch, he was handed a cold ham sandwich with a cup of tea and told to taste test the cookies. He laughed and admitted to hoping they would give him that job. Annie marveled yet again at how easy it was to be with Dan. With Eli, he might have praised her for all her hard work, or he might have been in a dark mood and eaten lunch quickly before storming back outside to continue his work, leaving Annie to wonder if he disapproved of her baking.

It was only Suvilla being in the kitchen that kept Annie from putting her arms around Dan and telling him how much she appreciated his steady good nature. Annie had come to see that Suvilla had a problem with her adoration of her new husband. Perhaps Suvilla felt her mother was too happy, a bit loose with her show of love. Did she think Annie had moved on too quickly after Eli's death?

For the thousandth time, Annie whispered a prayer for the Lord to show her the way, to bless her navigation through the treacherous path of being a mother and stepmother. But this time, Dan's reassuring words echoed in her mind, reminding her that reaching for perfection would only lead to despair. She told God she would never be perfect, but that He had placed her here and so she trusted that He would help her through the tough times. She thanked Him for Dan's gentle love and asked Him to keep knitting their family together.

When the whole flock of children clattered into the washhouse after school, kicking boots into

corners, hanging coats, hats, and bonnets haphazardly across hooks, flinging scarves and mittens in the
general direction of the cardboard box meant to hold
them all, Annie found herself braced for the chaos
that would be sure to follow. She was grateful Suvilla
had had the foresight to pack most of the cookies
away in tins so they'd be out of sight, leaving only a
few plates of assorted cookies on the table.

"Cookies!" Ida yelled, her normal exuberance elevated to hysteria. Not to be outdone, the two Emmas
and Lydia ran in circles, lifted both arms in a hallelu-
jah dance of joy, while Joel and John promptly leaped
onto the table and gathered handfuls of molasses and
oatmeal.

"No, no, no, no," Suvilla said loudly above the
general hubbub. She grabbed them both by one arm
and hauled back. They howled in protest, which
brought Annie to the scene, telling them to replace
the cookies and wash their hands first.

Amos, Ephraim, and Enos remembered their
manners, and stood with hands in their pockets,
feigning disinterest, before asking in gruff voices how
many they were allowed to have.

Glasses of milk were poured, and Annie stood back, watching helplessly as the cookies disappeared before her eyes. It seemed like a matter of seconds before the tabletop was sadly depleted.

"Well, children," Annie said.

"What?"

"All of our cookies are gone!" she wailed in mock despair.

Faces were lifted with howls of glee, swift denials in the form of "I only had two!" followed by fair accusations of the truth. It was absolute bedlam. Finally Suvilla shouted over the din that she was going to get the washing off the line, that it was hopeless in here.

After the milk was drained from eleven tumblers, the last cookie crumb eaten, they were all dispatched to their various chores, leaving little Rebecca and Joel to amuse themselves with the wooden blocks till suppertime.

Annie made a big pot of beef stew, hastily cutting up potatoes, carrots, cabbage, and onion, with chunks of beef and the soup bone to flavor it all, then added the savory dumplings. This was served with applesauce and small green pickles, slabs of bread and molasses.

As she ladled the thick, rich stew on to the children's plates, she couldn't imagine how they could possibly be hungry after all those cookies, but they spooned up the thick stew, crunched the small pickles, and asked for seconds. The cold had turned their cheeks red, and now, by the warmth from the kitchen range, the faces turned even brighter, the many pairs of eyes glistening with the beginning of nightly fatigue.

Dishes were washed and the chilled sand tart dough brought in from the back porch, amid cries of appreciation and rolling pins held aloft like weapons. The older boys helped Dan with the milking, saying they wanted no part of cookie making, which was for girls and sissies, which brought Ida's hands to her narrow hips and a glare to her eyes that could have felled a cat.

Hannah told the boys they were just jealous, that they wished they were allowed to help with the baking. Annie watched the boys' eyes open wide in disbelief at this bit of truthful insight from the bashful Hannah, then clunk out to the washhouse where they pulled on their boots, asking each other what had come over Hannah to make her so bold all of a sudden.

Ida gave Hannah a gleeful smile, and Hannah batted her eyelashes and stepped up to the table, grabbed a rolling pin, and prepared to roll out the dough, which turned out to be trickier than it appeared. She leaned over the table with all her weight, flattening the cold dough as far as much as she could. When she had practically broken a sweat, Suvilla stepped in and rolled until the dough was thin enough for the cookie cutters to be put to use. The colored sugar was an endless source of wonder for the two Emmas, who did all the decorating, except for the raisin eyes and buttons on the gingerbread men. That job went to Lydia, while Ida took it on herself to supervise everyone . . . which did not go over well.

Suvilla told her mildly to go away and mind her own business, clearly exercising great restraint in her choice of words.

Ida puffed up her chest, drew down her eyebrows, and snorted.

"Ida," Annie warned, lifting a Christmas tree with a metal spatula.

"Mam, Suvilla isn't using enough flour. Her dough is sticking to the tabletop. Tell her."

"You know, Ida, your chance of becoming an old maid keeps getting better each year," Suvilla said forcefully.

"You have no idea. What if I choose to stay single? Huh? Then what? You don't have anything to say to that, now, do you?"

"I don't care if you marry someone or not."

For once, Ida didn't have a reply to that. And then, because it was Christmastime, and everyone felt the spirit of happiness and goodwill, the tiff blew over before it became serious, though Annie suspected Ida would pursue it again the minute she was safely out of her hearing.

Between the long hours on her feet, the mixing and rolling and feeding the fire, and the noise and commotion of all the children, Annie had developed a pounding headache above her right eye. She had just finished the dishes and swept the floor and was about to put away the last ingredients when Joel, trying to be helpful, dumped green sugar all over the floor, then turned and walked through it.

It was an accident, it was an accident, she thought, over and over. But she could not bring herself to smile at him or tell him it was all right. *He needs to learn to be more careful. And all that sugar wasted!*

When he sat on the couch with his thumb in his mouth, his bright eyes watching every move she made, she still didn't feel the need to comfort him. When Dan came in to wash up he asked her where there was another cake of soap. She was short with him, telling him to look for it in the washhouse somewhere, instead of offering to help.

No, she was not perfect. But she no longer spiraled into the depths of guilt and despair. Instead, she asked God for forgiveness for her shortcomings and went to bed.

In the morning, breakfast over and the eleven off to school, her strength and good humor returned. She'd had a good night of sleep and an extra cup of coffee laced with the cream that lay thick and rich on top of a gallon of milk.

Oh, she was spoiled. She was becoming used to coffee as a morning necessity instead of a luxury, but it was so good—the thick, rich smell that made her close her eyes as she breathed deeply. She hummed German Christmas carols under her breath as her sturdy arms plied the crumbs for another batch of pie dough.

Suvilla ran down cellar and brought the canned pumpkin for the filling, then separated eggs and beat the egg whites to a stiff peak.

Annie mixed the chopped beef, the broth, and many spices that would create the mincemeat pies. They mixed apples and brown sugar, butter and cinnamon for the apple-raisin pies, poured it all into prepared crust, and baked them to a golden-brown perfection.

Annie showed Suvilla how she could tell when the pumpkin pies were baked hard enough. "Just take them and give them a gentle shake," she said. "They should shiver a little bit in the middle, but not too much."

"That's not very specific," Suvilla muttered, but watched carefully as her mother closed the oven door to allow them to bake awhile longer. "Let's finish all the Christmas baking before they all get home from school."

"Why?" Annie laughed.

"You know why," Suvilla said dryly.

"Oh my, what a mess!" Annie laughed. "But it was worth it, every sticky surface and ruined cookie was worth every minute. The children seemed like brothers and sisters, every last one. Did you hear Emma One tell Emma Two how her gingerbread man looked like Elam sie Rachel, and Emma Two laughed so hard she bumped her heard on the corner of the table? He did look like her, the way the raisins were placed close together, low on the face."

"Those two Emmas are a team, aren't they?"

"Kindred spirits, indeed."

Annie straightened, telling Suvilla she would not trade place with anyone else on earth. "This is where God wants me to be, so I guess he'll supply strength for each new day and all the problems that come with it."

"Yes, Mam, but things aren't quite as hard as it was at first. We all seem to grow together somehow." Here her eyes narrowed, and her face took on an iron resolve. "But I'll tell you one thing. I can hardly wait for a home of my own, a tiny house with no one in it except my husband and me."

"Your husband being Henry King's Aquilla, perhaps?"

Suvilla's mouth opened, then closed, as her face became infused with color.

"Mam! I am shocked! You know nothing about Aquilla King."

Annie nodded, smiled, and would not meet her daughter's eyes.

Chapter Eleven

ON CHRISTMAS EVE, DAN GATHERED ALL THE children into the living room. In his gentle, deep voice, he read the Christmas story to them all, in English, since the little ones had not yet learned the German. They sat quietly, all fourteen of them, some cross-legged on the floor, some doubled up on a comfortable chair, and the smallest ones on the couch with him. As his voice rose and fell, they seemed spellbound, absorbing every word. Sammy was listening, his face softened by emotion. Suvilla sat with her face showing nothing, her eyes downcast, but the fact that she was there gave Annie a warm feeling.

When the story was finished, there was a collective sigh, a few swipes of hands across tired eyes, a yawn here and there. But all waited, knowing Christmas Eve would not be over till the evening prayer was read from the German prayer book. They watched as Dan reached to the bookshelf, then all of them turned as one, got on their knees as Dan did, and buried their faces in crooked arms or simply gazed through chair rungs. Their minds churned with everyday things, as happens when the prayer is long and the singsong monotone keeps rising and falling.

Then the children straggled off to bed, weary from an afternoon of play. The snow had accumulated to eight or ten inches, so the steep hill in the cow pasture sported an icy track made by hundreds of boot prints, a log, and the use of many sleds. Faces were wind-chapped, lips peeling and blistered from the combination of wind and sun, but a dollop of Vaseline helped them all to sleep without pain. None of them had any idea of the Christmas presents that would be waiting for them in the morning. She had wrapped each package in newspaper and would set them on clean plates at the breakfast table.

Annie had made fresh shoofly pie, and there would be the luxury of hot chocolate to go with it, all the eggs and home cured ham they could hold, stewed crackers and fresh pancakes with maple syrup.

She had a hard time falling asleep that night, thinking of the two dolls, more than anything else. She had never imagined one of her children owning a store-bought doll, an item she had longed for with secret intensity when she was a child. She hoped they were not damaging the little girls by spoiling them with such a large Christmas gift.

The alarm jangled at five o'clock on Christmas Day, the same time Dan and Annie arose every morning. There were chores to do, water pipes to thaw, fires to stoke with chunks of wood. Annie had to put the two geese in the oven that she would be using to make the *roasht*, and beat the cream with the egg beaters to mix with the cornstarch pudding.

She dressed eagerly, then called the oldest children to go get the milking started. Then she tiptoed to the bedroom closet and carefully brought out each package and laid them tenderly on every child's plate, then stood back and surveyed the wonder of it. What would they say?

She turned to find Sammy sitting on the couch, pulling on his cotton socks. Then Suvilla stumbled into the kitchen, stopped, and stared.

Her eyes went to Annie's beaming face.

"We have gifts?"

"We do!"

"What is it?"

"Well Suvilla, it's Christmas, so I guess you'll have to wait and see."

Suvilla raised her eyebrows, then smiled genuinely. "Huh," was all she said.

Sammy smiled at his mother, then followed Suvilla to the washhouse to dress in warm clothes.

Enos, Ephraim, and Amos clomped down the stairs, in various forms of wakening, wiping eyes, yawning, their hair in a mess of tangles.

"It's cold," Enos complained.

Annie smiled. "Good morning, boys."

Amos spied the wrapped gifts. His eyes shot open, wide, then wider, "Gifts!"

Ephraim and Enos snapped to attention.

"We have Christmas gifts!" they said, their voices barely above a shocked whisper.

"Can we open them?"

"Not till breakfast. Now hurry and get your chores done."

They fell over each other getting to the washhouse and out the door to the barn, pulling wool hats down over their ears as they ran. The dark and the cold was ablaze with excitement for all of them.

At six, Annie woke the rest of the children, helping them to dress and comb their hair. She brushed out snarls, wet the top of six little girls' heads, her fingers flying as she used a fine-toothed comb to flatten the hair before deftly rolling along the sides to two coils in the back. Those coils were then wound around and around to form a perfect circular bob, pinned tightly with steel hairpins. There were no barrettes or rubber ponytail holders, simply the coils of hair rolled and pinned into place by years of practice.

Once downstairs, Ida caught sight of the wrapped presents, and for once in her life she was speechless. Lavina stood beside her, gaping, followed by Hannah, Lydia, and the two Emmas.

Annie could not stop smiling.

She fried slices of ham, set the milk to heat, then mixed the batter for the pancakes with a song in her head. Today was the day of the Christ child's birth, so why wouldn't she rejoice with the heavenly host of angels, the very same ones who sang over the hills of Judea where the shepherd watched their flocks, or the ones who hovered over the stable in Bethlehem? Here was cause for a deep and abiding joy, a spiritual renewal for mankind.

Oh, that He had been born and died for her! The fact of it lent wings to her feet, sent the song to her lips.

She was singing "Hark! The Herald Angels Sing" softly when she heard Ida joining in, her sweet voice soon overtaking her own as the song grew louder and faster, until she was up off the couch, head bobbing, feet skipping, then arms out as she twirled around the living room.

"Now, Ida, we don't approve of dancing. Especially not to a Christmas hymn."

"Why not? It's the happiest day of my life!"

Annie laughed outright.

"Why of course it is."

Ida's brows compressed into a serious wrinkle.

"So far, at least."

She looked thoughtful for a few moments, before saying, "But I plan on having many more happy days, Mam."

"You will, Ida. You certainly will."

A clattering in the washhouse heralded the arrival of the herd of workers from the barn. After that, it was undisguised chaos, the children cheering when Dan caught Annie by the waist for a great Christmas bear hug. The din was irreparable, with Dan's wide smile, Annie's blushing face, especially when she announced it was time to fry the eggs and Dan would not let her go.

The gas lights hissed, casting a yellowish glow over the warm kitchen and the steaming platters and bowls of food. The coffeepot boiled, sending the rich aroma through the house, the salty odor of frying ham mingled with the browned butter in the cast iron pan, waiting for the dropped eggs.

On Christmas Eve, there had been the solemn story of Christ's birth, but today was the celebration. Each child could feel the joy of the Christmas spirit as they slid into their respective seats, each one touching the wrapped present with hands that hesitated, allowing only the tips of their fingers to come into contact with the layers of newspaper.

The food was brought to the table, presents set on the floor beside them, till the plates could be taken away.

Was ever a Christmas morning quite like this one?

The eggs slid from the plate, nestled beside a thick slice of ham, a serving of stewed crackers, rich and milky, dotted with browned butter. Spoons and forks clattered against plates till every morsel was scraped clean. It was almost unimaginable to have a pancake afterward, soaked in butter and drizzled with maple syrup, followed by all the shoofly pie they could hold. A steaming cup of hot chocolate brought more cheers, which Ida led, her voice rising above everyone else's.

Dan lifted a spoonful of shoofly pie, dipped it below the surface of the hot cocoa, put it in his mouth, and closed his eyes.

"Mmm . . . Mmm . . ."

Annie smiled. "You like my shoofly pie?"

"You know I do. They're the best. Along with the prettiest wife in Lancaster County, I get shoofly pies that are unbelievable."

"Hurry up, Dat," said Ida. "We're finished. Time for presents."

Dan looked up, his eyes softened, and for one moment Annie was afraid he would shed real tears.

"You called me Dat," he said.

Ida smiled at him, flashing her mischievous dimple to its full extent.

"You are my dat, the only one I have."

Was that a nodding from Sammy and Suvilla?

They allowed the youngest to open her package first, with Dan and Annie's help. As the face of the doll emerged, Rebecca's eyes became round with surprise, then her face crumpled and she began to cry.

"What? What is this?" Annie asked, quickly gathering her for a close embrace on her lap.

"Don't cry, Rebecca."

Little Rebecca had never seen a store-bought doll, and was frightened by the eyes that opened and closed. So they had Lydia open her gift, who was so thrilled she simply let out a high shriek of delight, then turned to say quite solemnly, "*Denke*, Mam und Dat."

Everyone was on their feet, crowding around, helping Rebecca unwrap the doll, smoothing the tiny gathers in the dress, opening and closing the doll's eyes, moving the arms and legs. The boys pulled on the thin socks, and when one fell on the floor, they were faced with Lavina's outrage, Ida's yanking on their shoulders, and a frown of disapproval from Suvilla.

Rebecca held the doll then, but carefully, afraid to touch the pretty face or the glistening fabric of the dress.

Dan got up from his chair, asked Joel and John if they had not noticed their plates were empty.

"Yes, we did. But you have something for us," they said, almost as one person. Annie was touched to see the faith they had, trusting Dan would bring them their gift.

The wooden wagon was painted green, with yellow wheels and fine black pinstriping for the spokes and the rim. The attached horse was painted brown with a black harness. Annie had made small cloth bags filled with rice, to load on the wagons—little bags of feed for the horse to take to town.

It was all bedlam after that. Even Sammy was on the floor, delighted with the ease of the wheels' motion.

Enos, Amos, and Ephraim thought they should be next, until the girls reminded them they were younger, and opened their package to find the most remarkable thing they had ever seen. Awed by the delicacy of this fine china, they carried it to the dressers in their room to be handled and admired every day. They were now the owners of genuine china dishes, and they carried themselves with a new lift of their shoulders.

When the boys opened their present to find a slingshot, Annie detected a note of envy in Ida's voice. Amid the howls of glee, Ida told them they'd never be able to hit the side of a barn with those things.

As Annie suspected, she had the slingshots in her hands almost as much as the boys, and became a dead shot with it before the winter was over.

The wool socks were drawn over their feet, proclaimed the warmest things they'd ever worn, followed by heartfelt, effusive "*Denke Denke.*"

Suvilla opened her gift, her face an incredulous mask.

Her mouth opened and closed. She stroked the wonderful fabric, smooth and soft, folded and unfolded the handkerchief, then lifted her face with eyes like the twinkling of stars.

"It's too much," she said finally.

Annie tried to smile, but found her mouth turning down of its own accord, a stinging in her nose the imposter that brought unwanted tears.

Her beautiful oldest daughter, so young and unspoiled, having gone through so much in her short life. Only God knew how much she had suffered, and how much love and nurturing she would need.

Dan saw Annie's face, reached for her hand and squeezed, a heartfelt signal of his support, the priceless gift of his love.

Sammy grinned, tried on the scarf and gloves, said it was exactly what he needed, then blushed to the roots of his hair, thinking about asking a certain young lady to the Christmas singing. Ida said it looked as if that scarf was really warm as red as his face became after a while.

They sang Christmas songs, one after another. They played games—tic-tac-toe, dice, ring toss. They popped popcorn, buttered and salted it, drank cider and all the coffee they wanted.

Annie took the two geese from the blue agate roaster, deboned them, mixed the meat with bread cubes, celery, onion, and eggs, popped it back into the oven, and set the potatoes to boil. She roasted squash, turnips, and sweet potatoes, and shredded cabbage for pepper slaw. Suvilla set the table with the best tablecloth, the good china, glass dishes of shivering strawberry jam, dark green pickles, and chow-chow. They shaped the warmed butter into Christmas bells, opened jars of applesauce and grape mush.

The dinner was eaten at three in the afternoon, before chores.

The children were hungry, raking huge amounts of *roasht* onto their plates, heaping spoonfuls of potatoes and gravy.

The black walnut cake was sliced and devoured with scoops of creamy cornstarch pudding and canned peaches. The mincemeat, cherry, and apple pies were brought from the pantry amid groans of protest.

Everything was just so plentiful, so rich and warm and cozy. The fire crackled in the range, savory odors wafted through the house, filling it with the sense of goodwill. The children sat together, playing games, admiring dolls, rattling horses and wagons across the floor, the security of having a mother and father watching over them.

The snow fell like a benediction that Christmas day, wrapped the house and barn in a soft, glistening blanket, covered the ground like a coating of grace, hiding the mud and weeds and sharp stones, the way Christ's gift covered the multitude of wrongdoings of men.

All this was not lost on Dan or Annie, as they got up to put another log on the fire, or to fill a glass with grape juice or a cup of coffee.

Bedtime was later; the children's begging produced results from contented parents who saw nothing wrong with an extension of this joyful day. When at last Annie spied John pushing his horse and wagon while lying prostrate on the floor, his heavy eyelids falling occasionally, she said it was time for the evening prayer, and then rose from her chair and shoed them all to bed, after the evening prayer.

Dan was sweeping the floor when she came back down the stairs, so she began picking up, sorting toys and gloves and socks. She washed dishes while he finished sweeping the kitchen, then grabbed a tea towel and started to dry them.

"Are you very tired?" he asked, in his soft voice.

"I shouldn't be. We sat around all afternoon," she said.

"Would you be interested in going for a walk with me?"

"A walk?"

"Yes, in the snow."

She didn't hesitate, thinking of the pure snow falling in a gray winter night when every sound was hushed, even footfalls whispered.

After bundling themselves in warm outerwear and heavy boots, they walked past the barn and outbuildings, down the field lane, until the whole world was a sea of white and gray, the snowflakes falling soundlessly as they fell to earth.

Dan stopped, took her shoulder, and turned her toward him, "Annie, I want to tell you now, on this blessed Christmas Day, that you are the best earthly gift I have ever received or even hope to receive in the future. You are an amazing woman."

She could think of no reply at all, so she said very soft and low, "Oh, Dan. *Ach.*"

He took her in his arms and kissed her gently, sealing his love for her now and forever.

The snow fell steadily on the farmhouse roof where fourteen children of various ages lay sleeping peacefully, content in the knowledge that they were family now, and would always be, as long as God allowed them to live on this good earth.

The End

Glossary

Ach—Oh (an expression of surprise)

Alaubt—allowed

App schtellt—forbidden

Ausbund—German hymnal

Boova—boys

Bowa feesich—bare feet

Chackets—jackets

Da mon—the man

Dat—dad

Denke—thanks

Die boova sinn do—The boys are here.

Da full dienscht—bishop

Die Englishy—the English (non-Amish people)

Die glany boovy—the little boys

Die gute schtup—the good room, i.e., the living room

Die schveshta—the sister

Diener zum buch—minister

Doggie fils—a casserole made with sliced hot dogs and cubed bread

Eisa kessle—iron kettle
Fer-fearish—misleading
Fliesichy boova—ambitious boys
Gebet buch—prayer book
Gebet büchly—small prayer book
Glaeyne frau—my little wife
Glauk—complaint
Gluck—sitting hen
Gook mol—look
Greishas—yelling
Grischtag essa—Christmas dinner
Grischt Kindly—Christ Child
Guta Marya, boova—Good morning, boys
Gute boova—good boys
Grosfeelich—haughty
Gute nacht, Kinna—Good night, children
Hausfrau—housewife
Haus schtire—wedding gift
Hesslich—seriously
Hesslich hinna-noch—behind schedule
Huddlich—messy; chaotic
Ich gleich net ihn—I don't like him
Kesslehaus—washhouse

Kinna—children

Knecht—hired hand

Komm na—come now

Komma—to come

Kommet—come here

Kopp-duch—head scarf

Maud—maid

Mit die fuhr—with the team, i.e., horse and buggy.

Mold oh—Look here

Müde binnich—a German evening or bedtime prayer for children

Opp im kopp—mentally ill; literally, off in the head

Ordnung—literally, "ordinary," or "discipline." The Amish community's agreed-upon rules for living, based upon their understanding of the Bible, particularly the New Testament. The *Ordnung* varies some from community to community, often reflecting the leaders' preferences and the local traditions and historical practices.

Patties noona—Hands down, an expression meaning to pray before a meal

Ponhaus—scrapple

Rishting—preparing

Roasht—roast chicken and filling

Rumschpringa—a time of courtship, in which Amish teenagers participate in organized social events

Schem dich—you should be ashamed

Schoene boova—nice boys

Schnitza—lie

Schpinna hoodla—spider webs

Schtruvvel—disheveled

Schtruvvlich—messed-up hair

Unbekimmat—uncaring

Ungehorsam—disobedient

Vassa droke—water trough

Vella essa—Let's eat

Vell. Voss hen ma gado?—Well, how did we do?

Youngie—the youth

Yung-Kyatte—newlywed

Ztzvilling—twins

About the Author

LINDA BYLER WAS RAISED IN AN AMISH FAMILY and is an active member of the Amish church today. Growing up, Linda loved to read and write. In fact, she still does. Linda is well known within the Amish community as a columnist for a weekly Amish newspaper. She writes all her novels by hand in notebooks.

Linda is the author of several series of novels, all set among the Amish communities of North America: Lizzie Searches for Love, Sadie's Montana, Lancaster Burning, Hester's Hunt for Home, The Dakota Series, and the Buggy Spoke Series for younger readers. She also wrote *The Healing* and *A Second Chance*, as well as several Christmas romances set among the Amish: *Mary's Christmas Goodbye*, *The Christmas Visitor*, *The Little Amish Matchmaker*, *Becky Meets Her Match*, *A Dog for Christmas*, and *A Horse for Elsie*. Linda has coauthored *Lizzie's Amish Cookbook: Favorite Recipes from Three Generations of Amish Cooks!*

OTHER BOOKS BY
LINDA BYLER

LIZZIE SEARCHES FOR LOVE SERIES

BOOK ONE   BOOK TWO   BOOK THREE

TRILOGY   COOKBOOK

SADIE'S MONTANA SERIES

BOOK ONE

BOOK TWO

BOOK THREE

TRILOGY

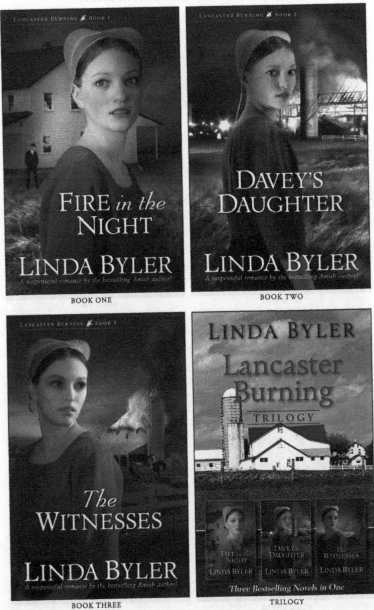

LANCASTER BURNING ✦ BOOK 1

FIRE *in the* NIGHT

LINDA BYLER

A suspenseful romance by the bestselling Amish author!

BOOK ONE

LANCASTER BURNING ✦ BOOK 2

DAVEY'S DAUGHTER

LINDA BYLER

A suspenseful romance by the bestselling Amish author!

BOOK TWO

LANCASTER BURNING ✦ BOOK 3

The WITNESSES

LINDA BYLER

A suspenseful romance by the bestselling Amish author!

BOOK THREE

LINDA BYLER
Lancaster Burning
TRILOGY

FIRE *in the* NIGHT LINDA BYLER

DAVEY'S DAUGHTER LINDA BYLER

The WITNESSES LINDA BYLER

Three Bestselling Novels in One

TRILOGY

THE DAKOTA SERIES

BOOK ONE

BOOK TWO

BOOK THREE

TRILOGY

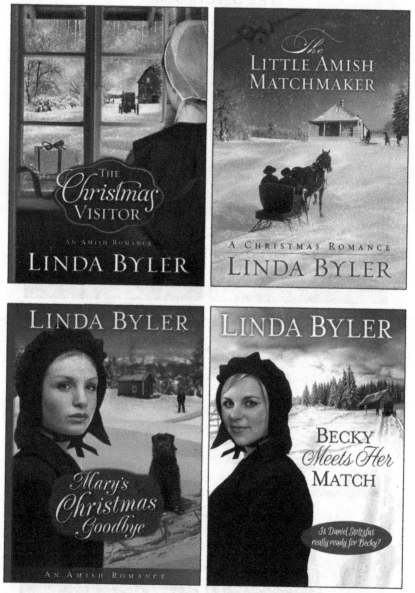

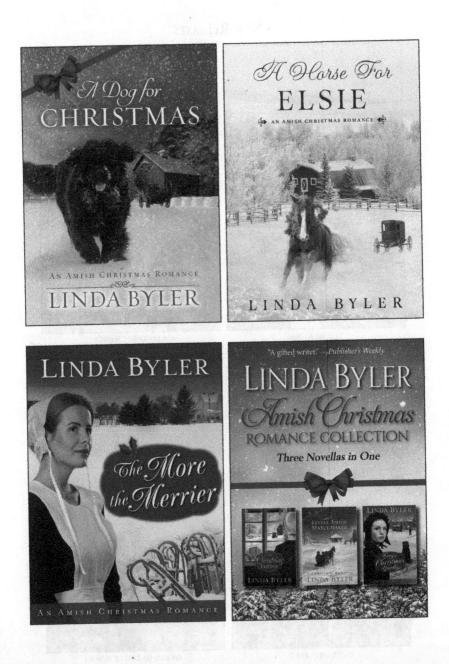

THE HEALING

A SECOND CHANCE

HOPE DEFERRED

LOVE IN UNLIKELY PLACES